Pokémon The Rise of Darkrai

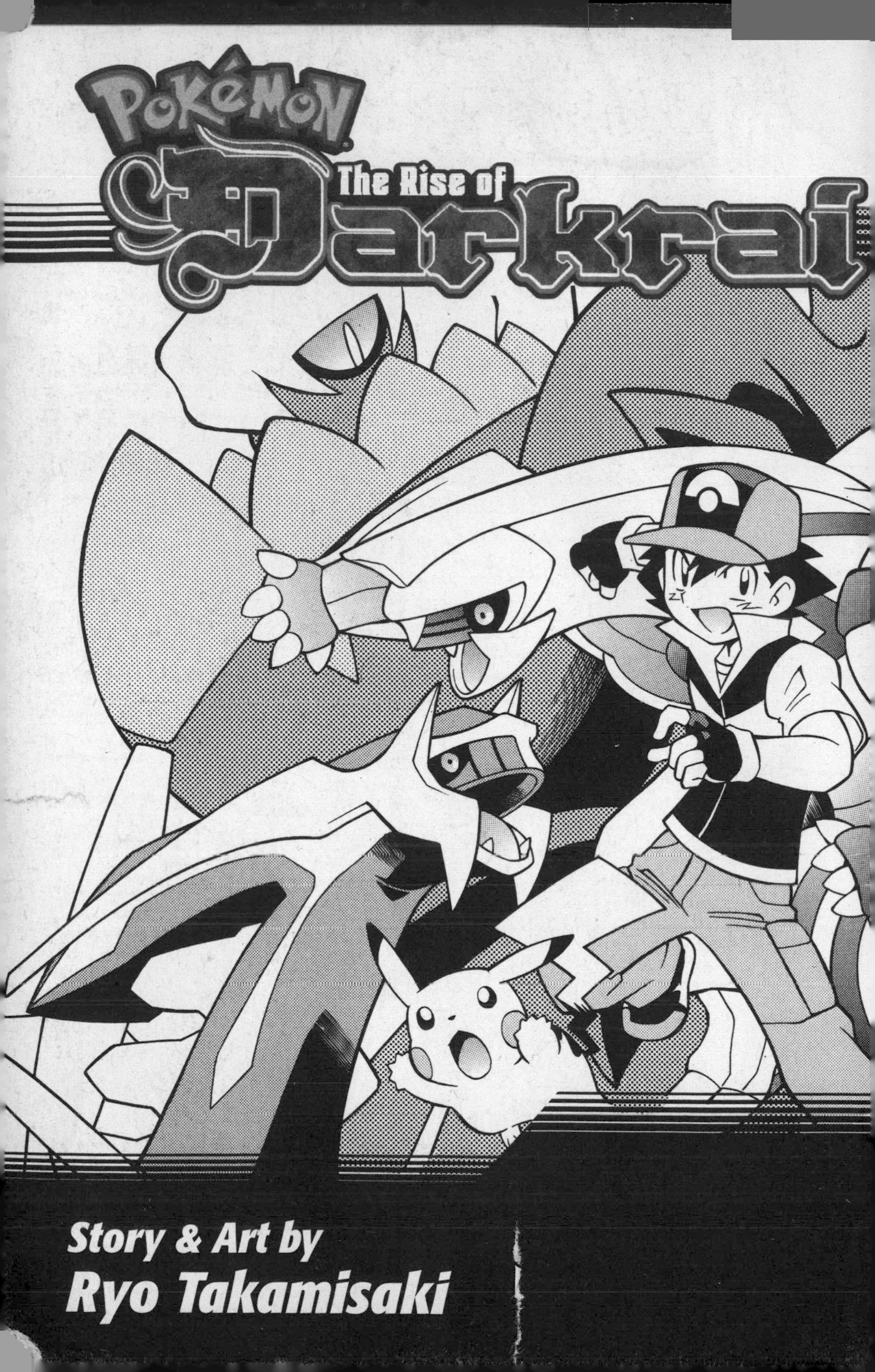

Story & Art by
Ryo Takamisaki

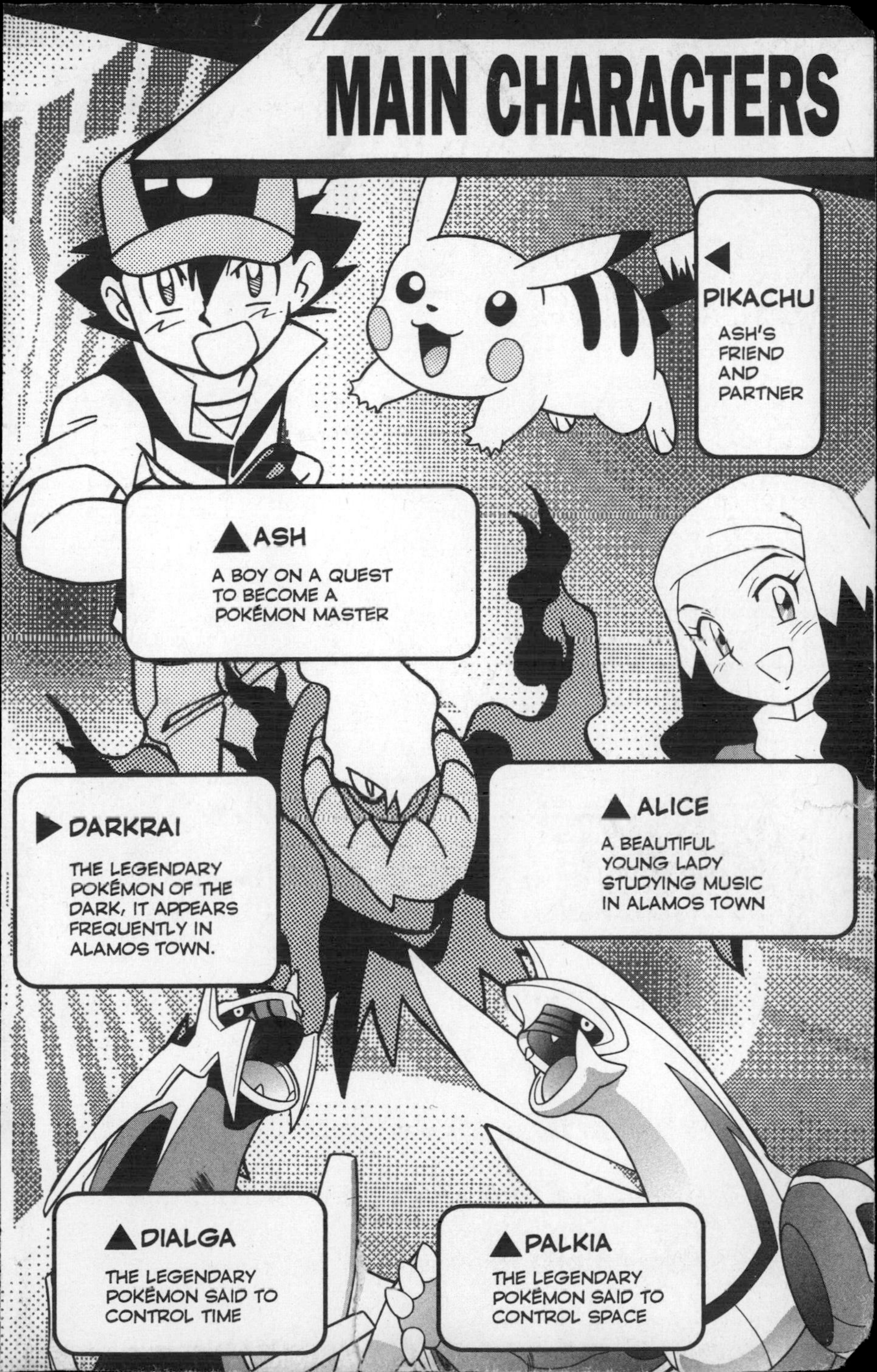
MAIN CHARACTERS
PIKACHU
ASH'S FRIEND AND PARTNER
ASH
A BOY ON A QUEST TO BECOME A POKÉMON MASTER
ALICE
A BEAUTIFUL YOUNG LADY STUDYING MUSIC IN ALAMOS TOWN
DARKRAI
THE LEGENDARY POKÉMON OF THE DARK, IT APPEARS FREQUENTLY IN ALAMOS TOWN.
PALKIA
THE LEGENDARY POKÉMON SAID TO CONTROL SPACE
DIALGA
THE LEGENDARY POKÉMON SAID TO CONTROL TIME

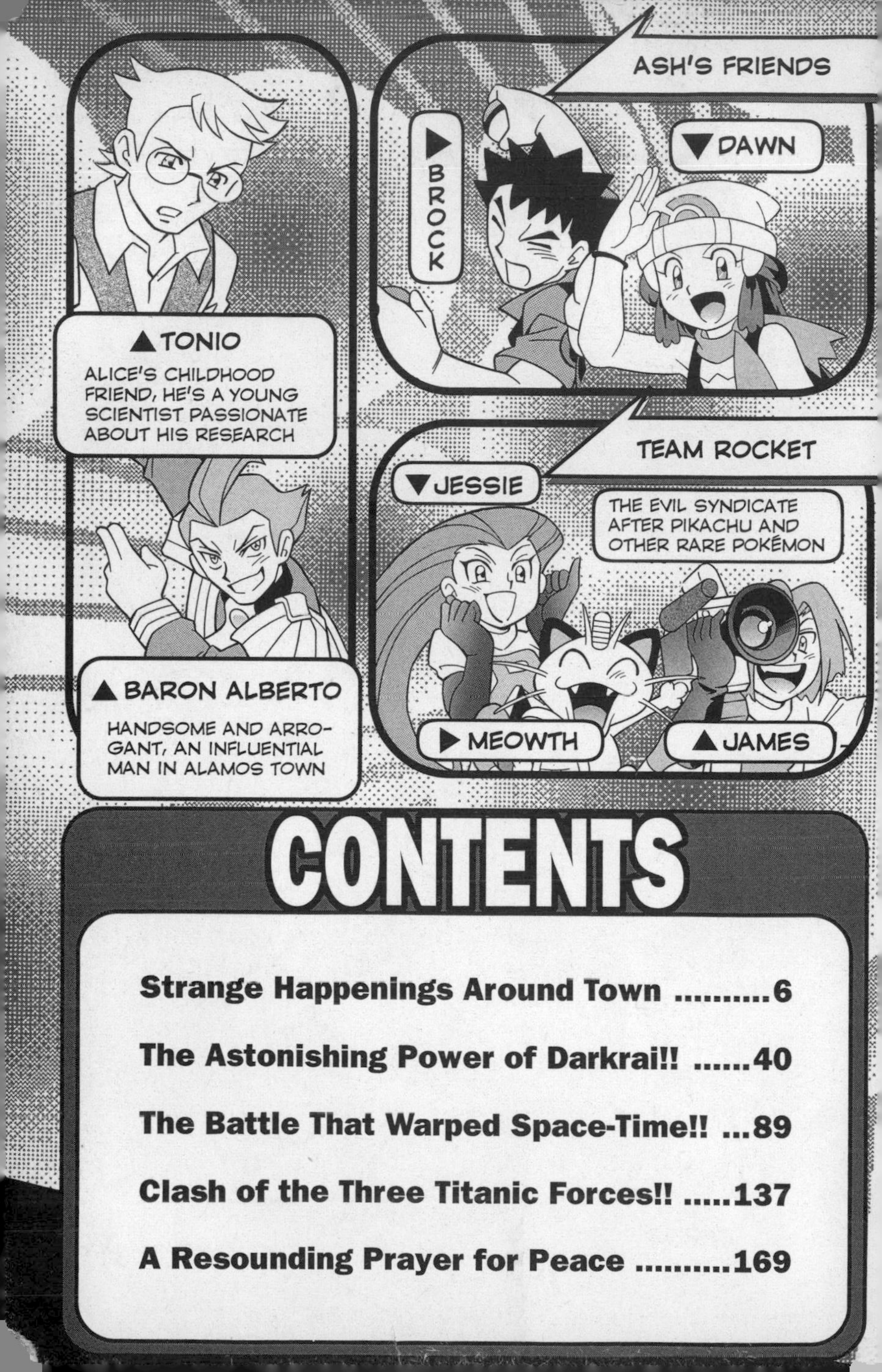
ASH'S FRIENDS
▼DAWN
▶BROCK
TEAM ROCKET
▼JESSIE
THE EVIL SYNDICATE AFTER PIKACHU AND OTHER RARE POKÉMON
▶MEOWTH
▲JAMES
▲TONIO
ALICE'S CHILDHOOD FRIEND, HE'S A YOUNG SCIENTIST PASSIONATE ABOUT HIS RESEARCH
▲BARON ALBERTO
HANDSOME AND ARRO-GANT, AN INFLUENTIAL MAN IN ALAMOS TOWN

CONTENTS

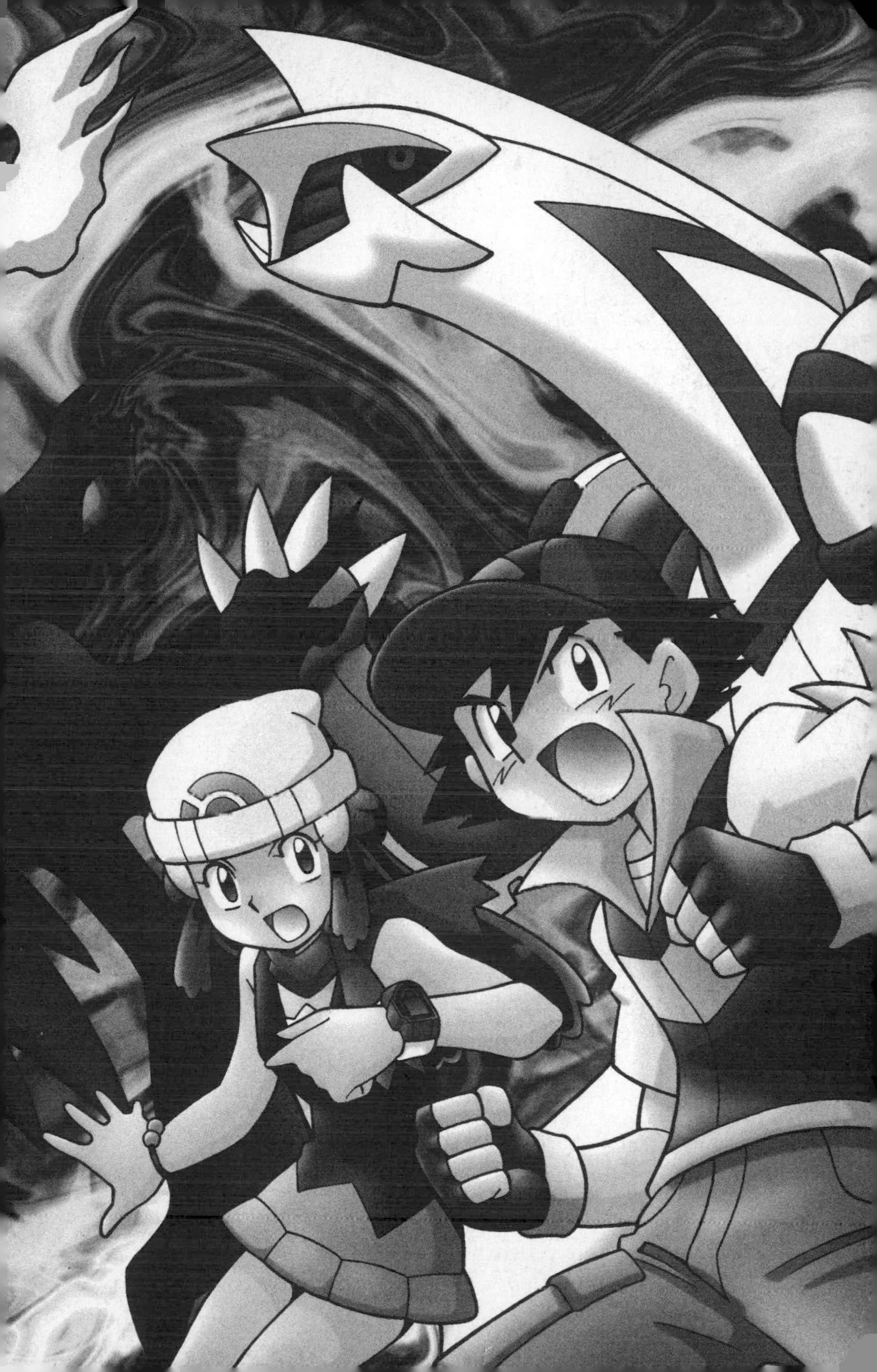

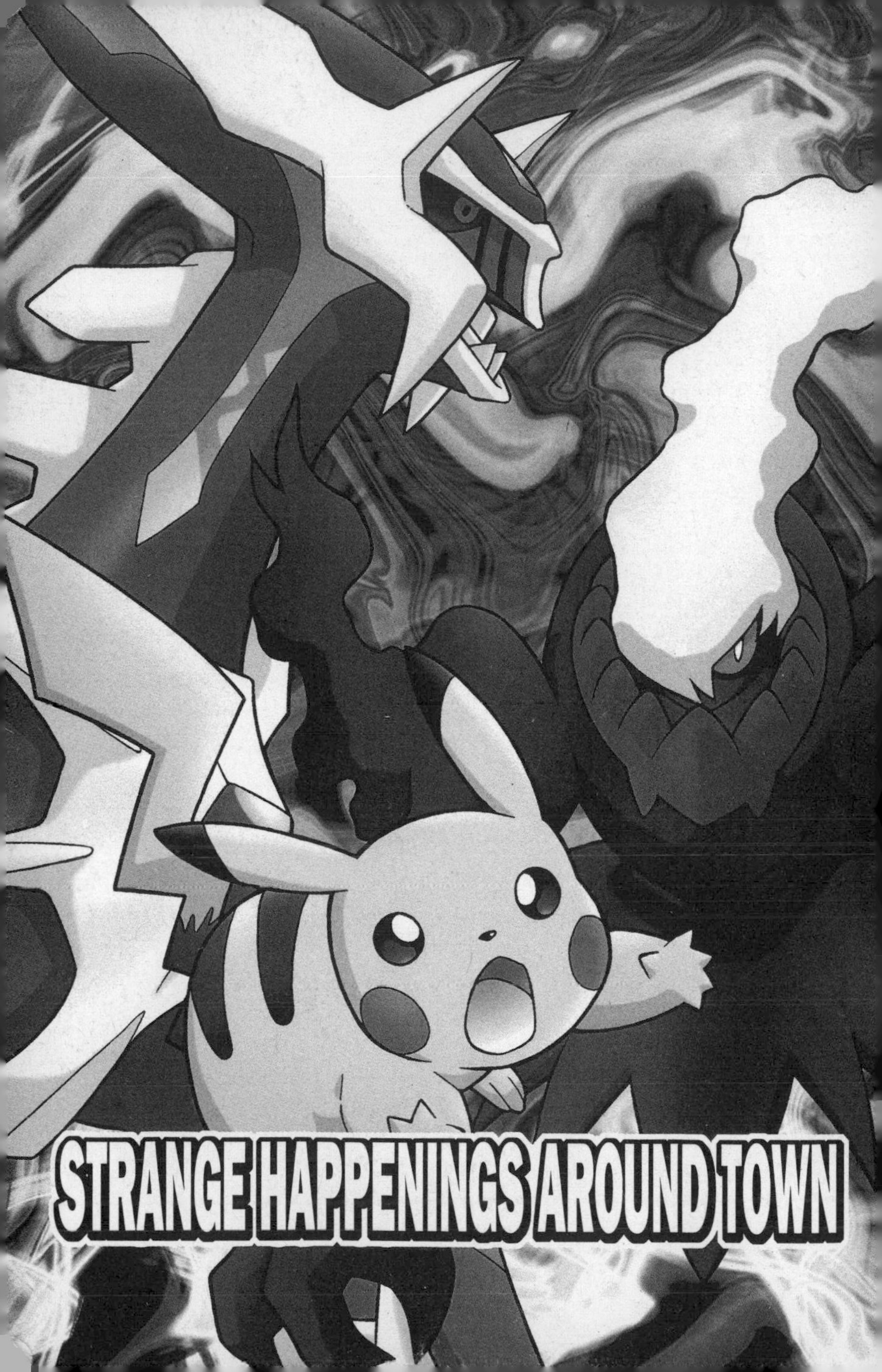
STRANGE HAPPENINGS AROUND TOWN

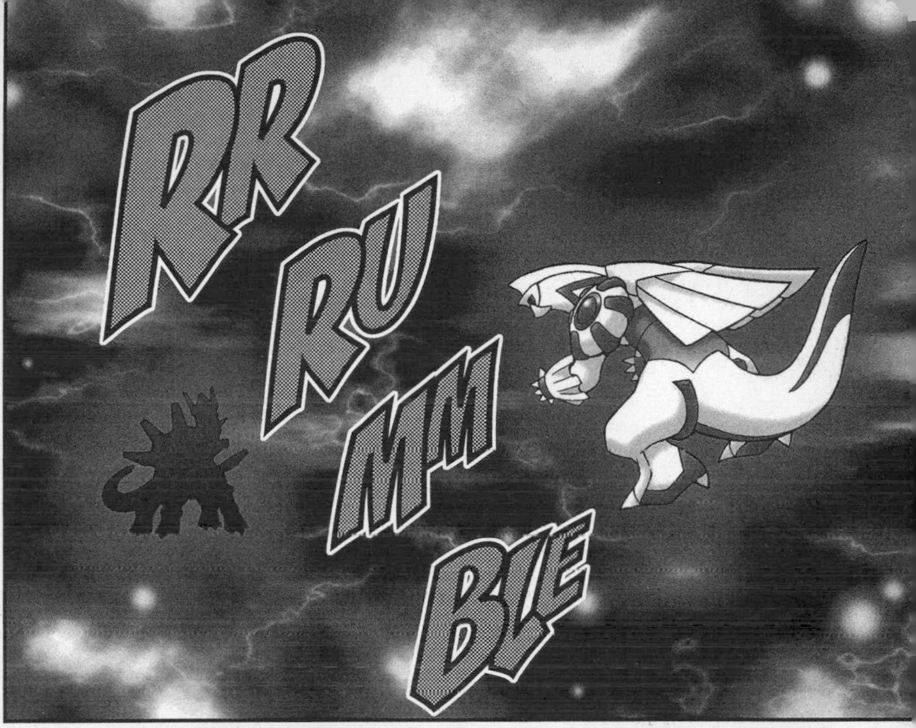
RRRUMMBLE

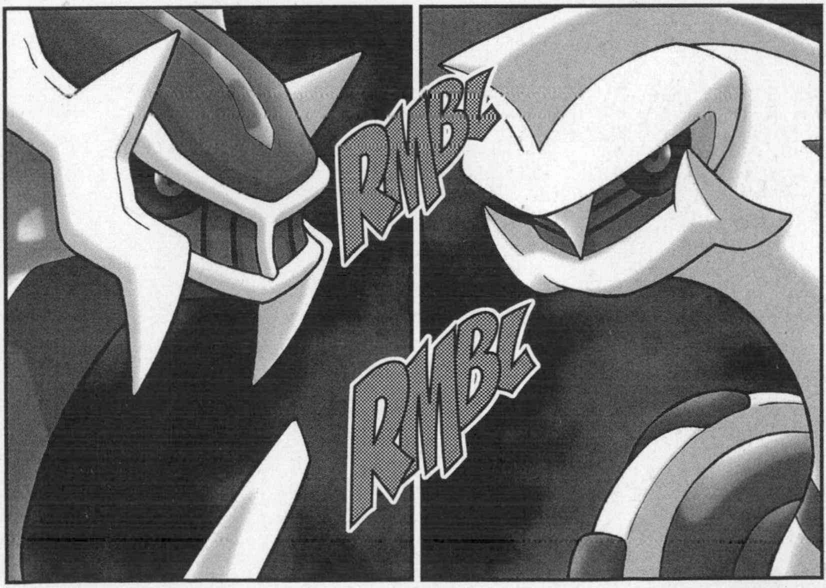
RMBL
RMBL

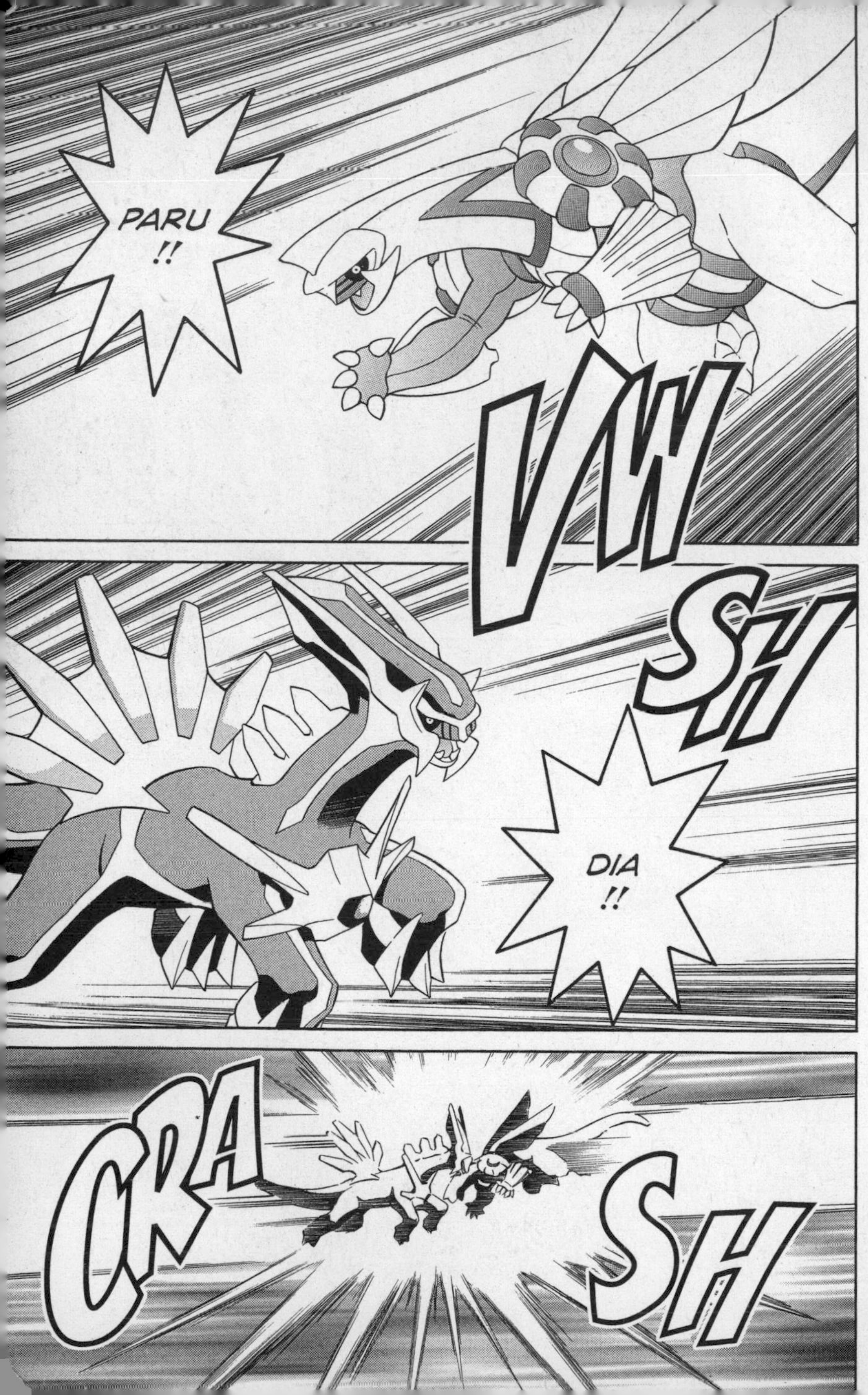
VWISH
PARU !!
DIA !!
CRASH

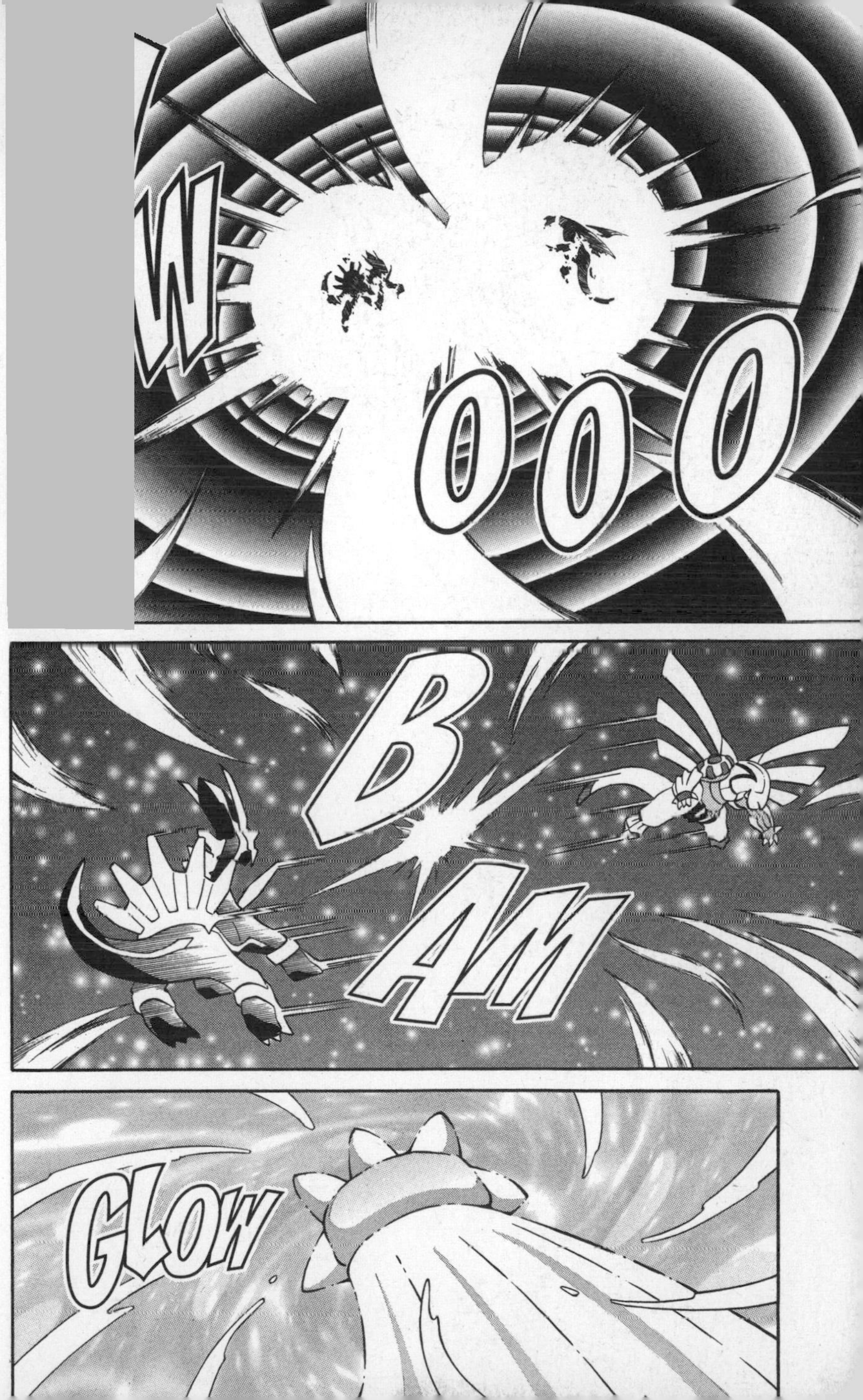
WOOO
BAM
GLOW

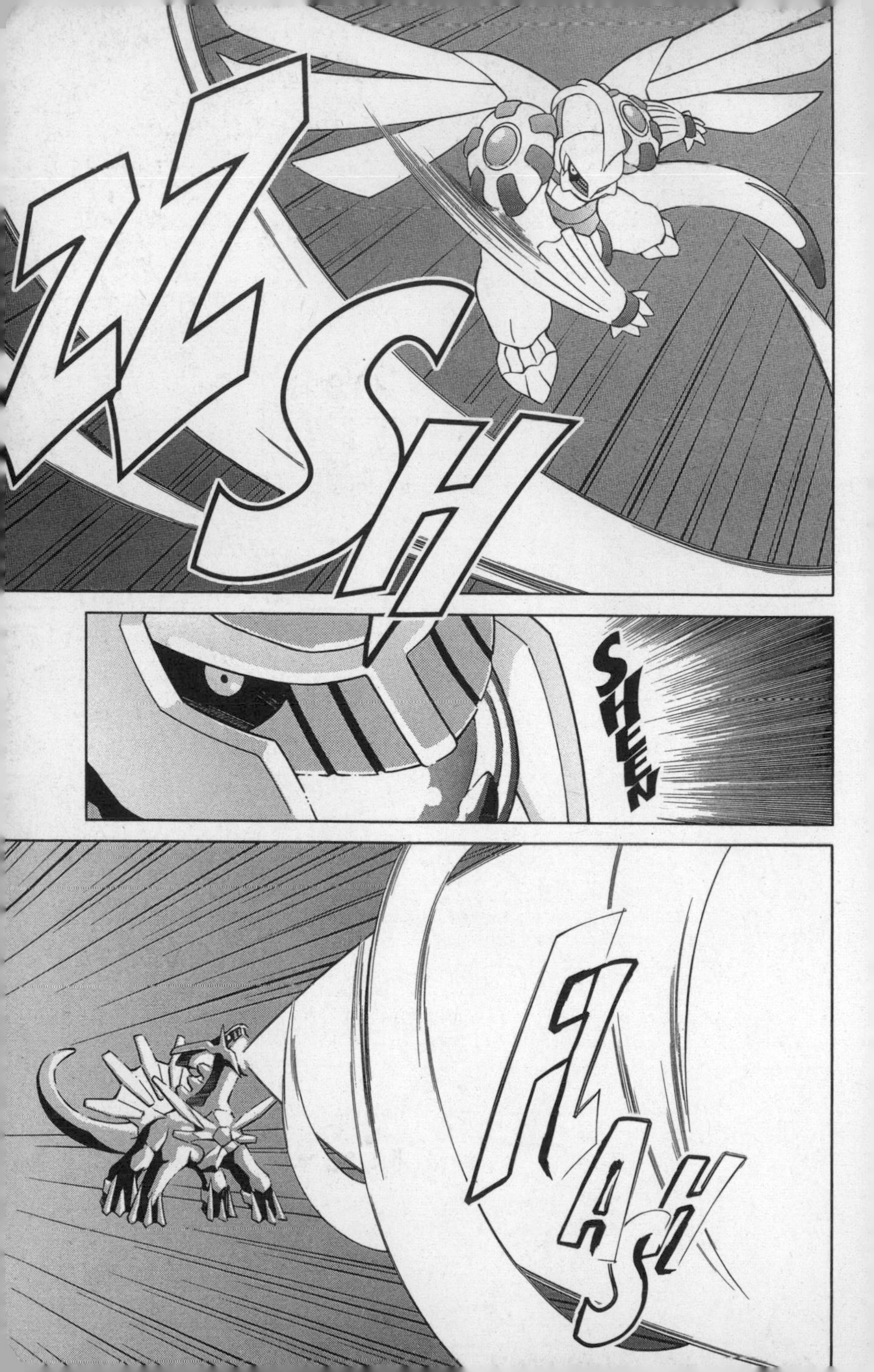

ZZSH
SHEEN
FLASH

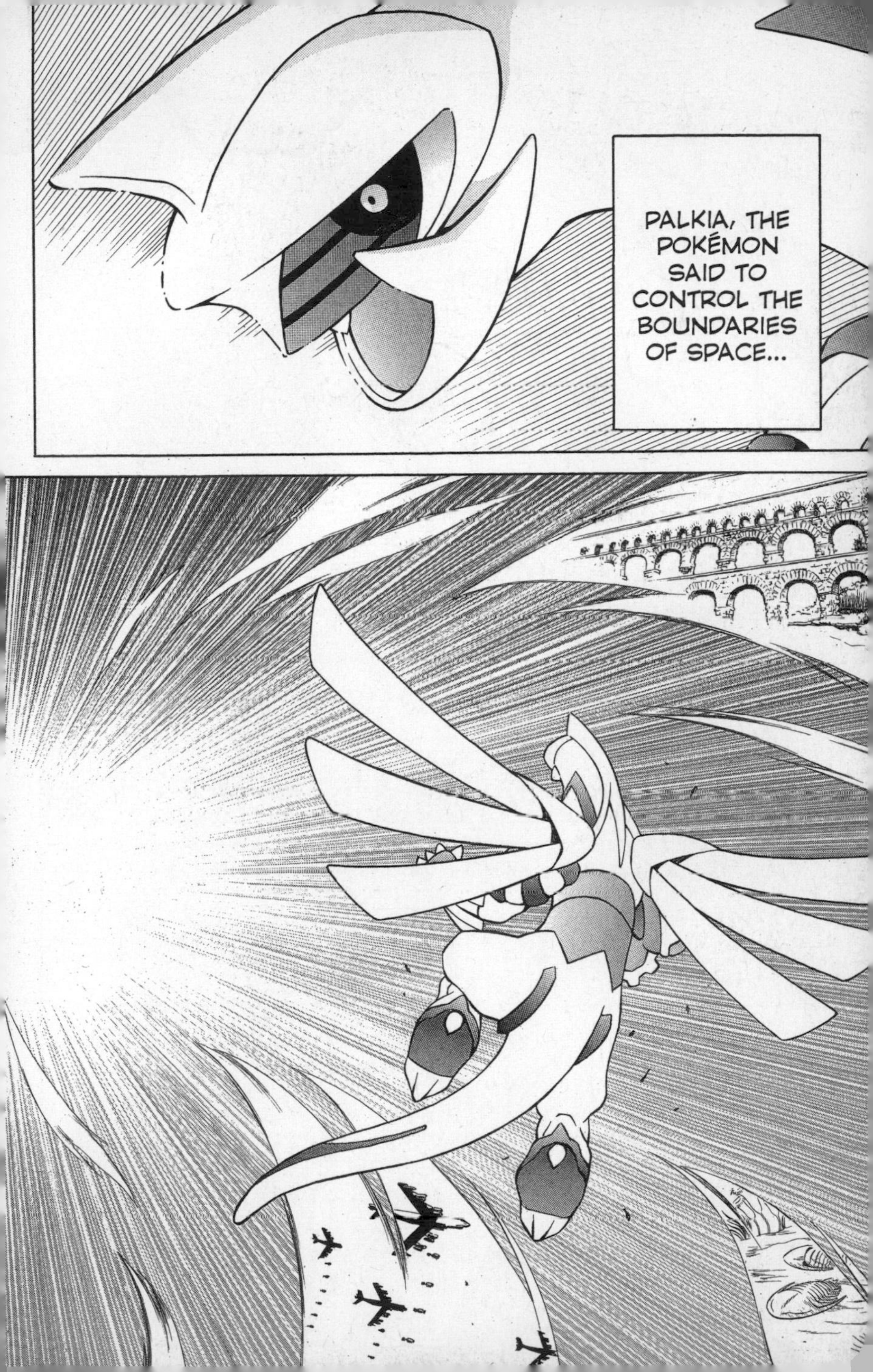
PALKIA, THE POKÉMON SAID TO CONTROL THE BOUNDARIES OF SPACE...

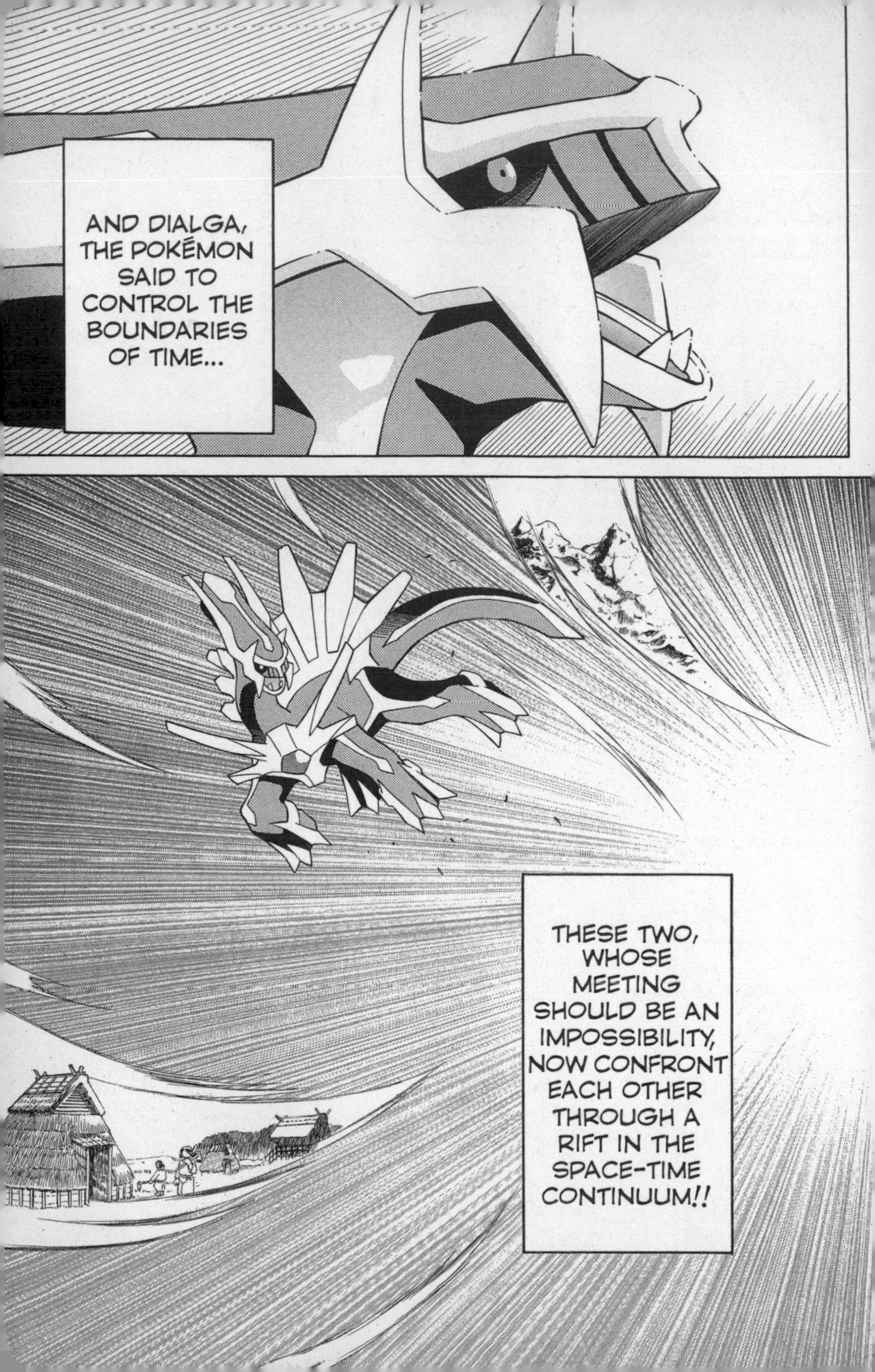
AND DIALGA, THE POKÉMON SAID TO CONTROL THE BOUNDARIES OF TIME...
THESE TWO, WHOSE MEETING SHOULD BE AN IMPOSSIBILITY, NOW CONFRONT EACH OTHER THROUGH A RIFT IN THE SPACE-TIME CONTINUUM!!

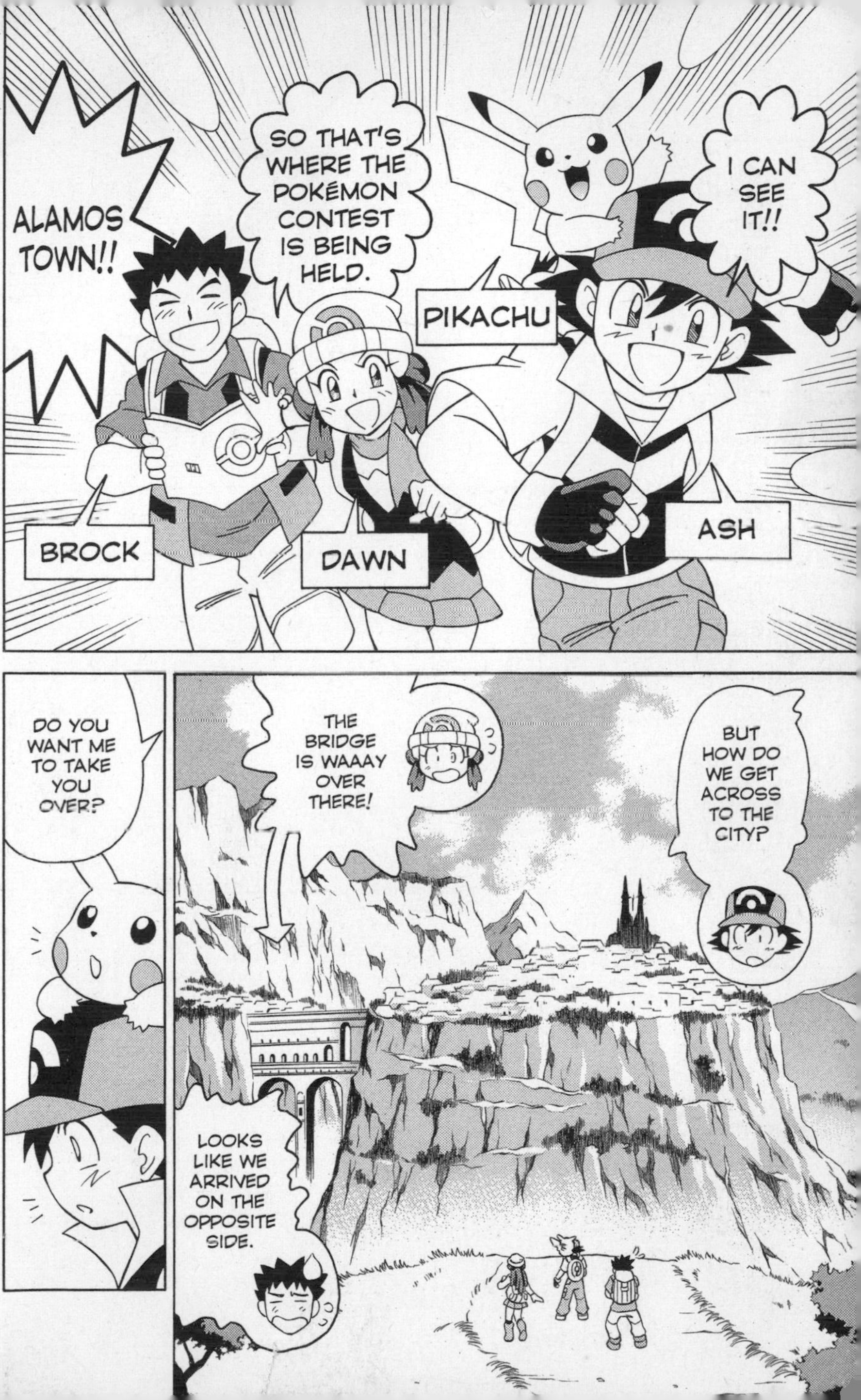
I CAN SEE IT!!
ASH
PIKACHU
SO THAT'S WHERE THE POKéMON CONTEST IS BEING HELD.
DAWN
ALAMOS TOWN!!
BROCK
BUT HOW DO WE GET ACROSS TO THE CITY?
THE BRIDGE IS WAAAY OVER THERE!
LOOKS LIKE WE ARRIVED ON THE OPPOSITE SIDE.
DO YOU WANT ME TO TAKE YOU OVER?

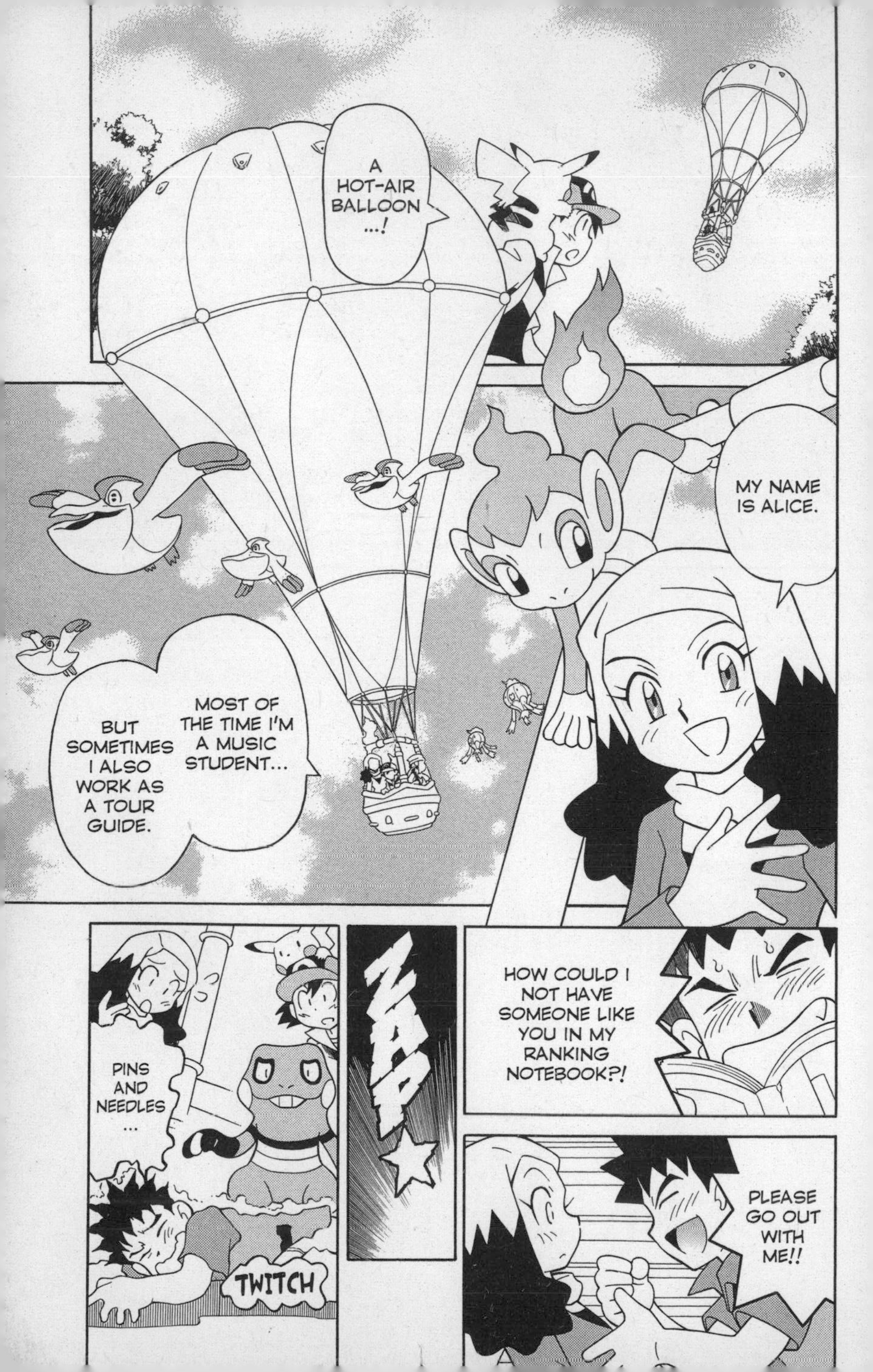
A HOT-AIR BALLOON ...!
MY NAME IS ALICE.
MOST OF THE TIME I'M A MUSIC STUDENT...
BUT SOMETIMES I ALSO WORK AS A TOUR GUIDE.
HOW COULD I NOT HAVE SOMEONE LIKE YOU IN MY RANKING NOTEBOOK?!
PLEASE GO OUT WITH ME!!
ZAP
PINS AND NEEDLES ...
TWITCH

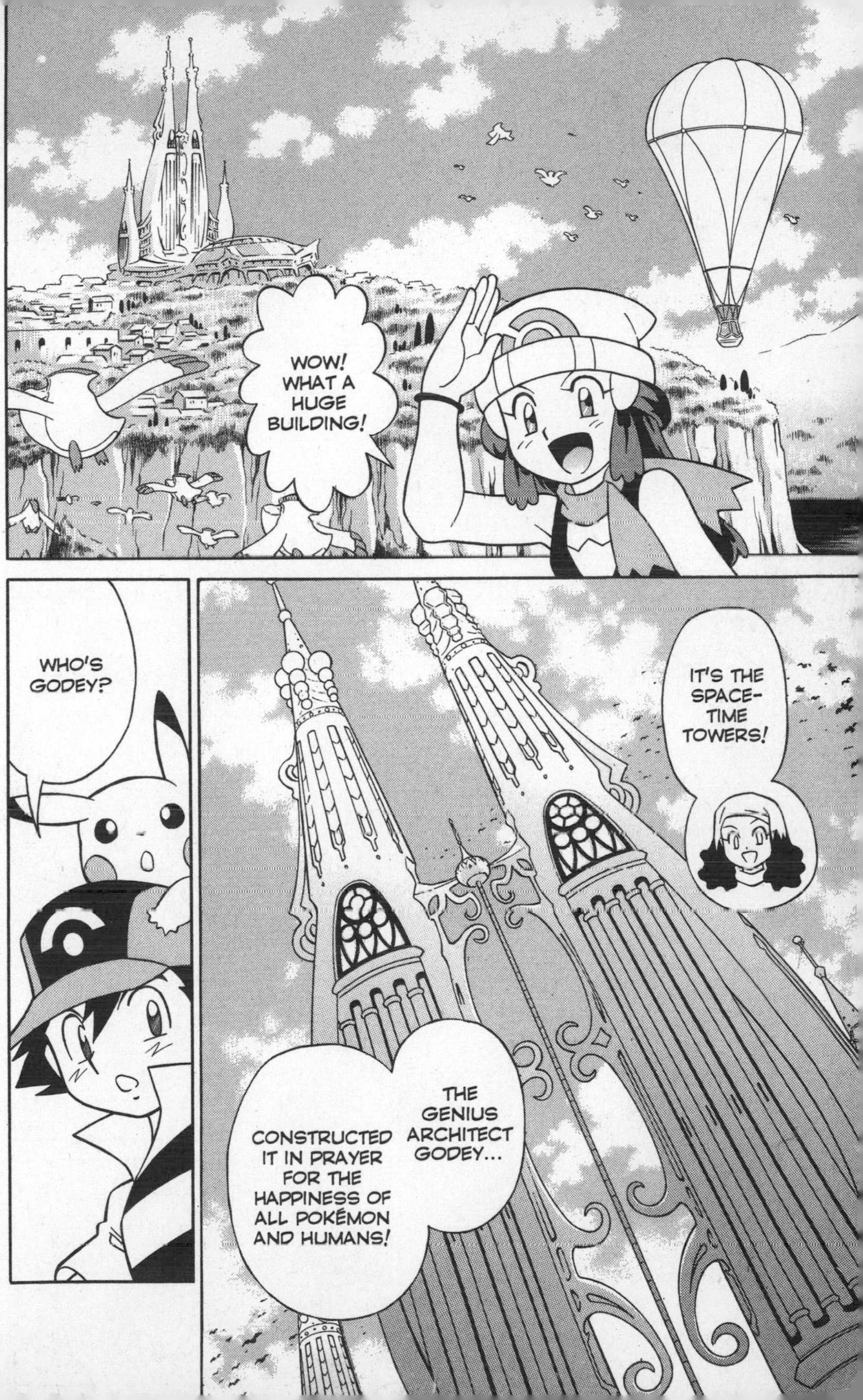
WOW! WHAT A HUGE BUILDING!
IT'S THE SPACE-TIME TOWERS!
THE GENIUS ARCHITECT GODEY...
CONSTRUCTED IT IN PRAYER FOR THE HAPPINESS OF ALL POKÉMON AND HUMANS!
WHO'S GODEY?

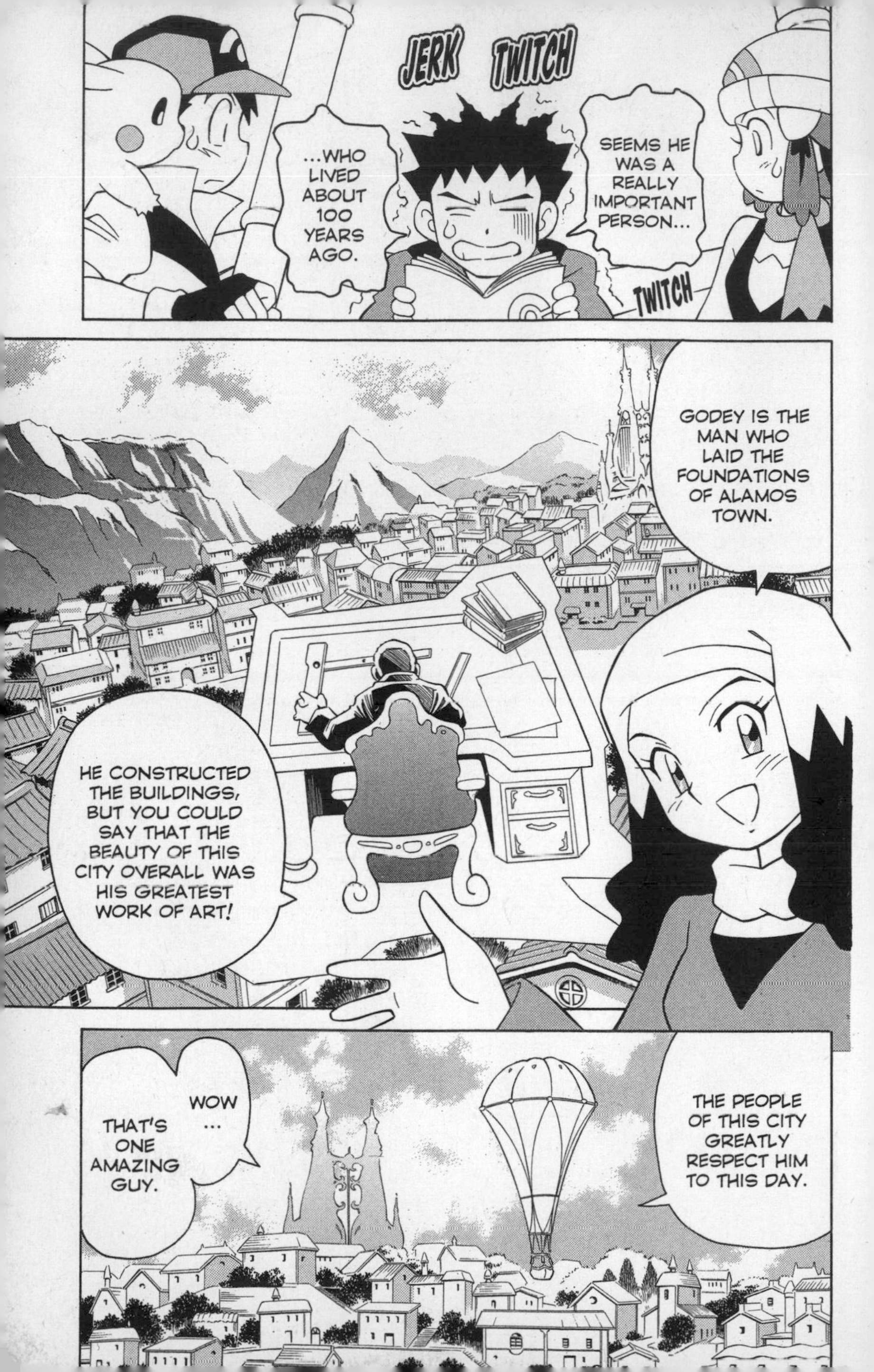
JERK TWITCH
SEEMS HE WAS A REALLY IMPORTANT PERSON...
...WHO LIVED ABOUT 100 YEARS AGO.
TWITCH
GODEY IS THE MAN WHO LAID THE FOUNDATIONS OF ALAMOS TOWN.
HE CONSTRUCTED THE BUILDINGS, BUT YOU COULD SAY THAT THE BEAUTY OF THIS CITY OVERALL WAS HIS GREATEST WORK OF ART!
THE PEOPLE OF THIS CITY GREATLY RESPECT HIM TO THIS DAY.
WOW...
THAT'S ONE AMAZING GUY.

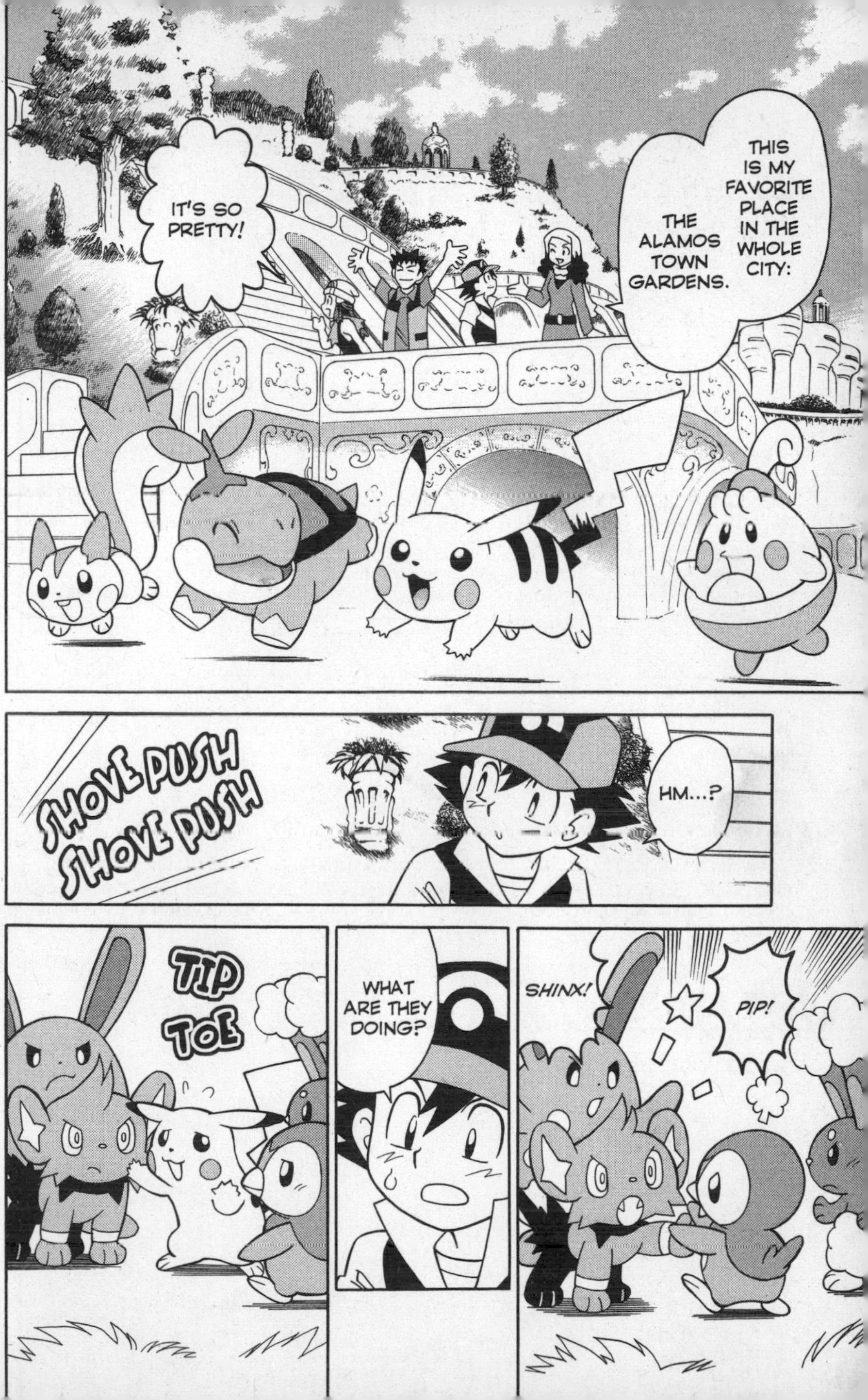
THIS IS MY FAVORITE PLACE IN THE WHOLE CITY:
THE ALAMOS TOWN GARDENS.
IT'S SO PRETTY!
HM...?
SHOVE PUSH SHOVE PUSH
PIP!
SHINX!
WHAT ARE THEY DOING?
TIP TOE

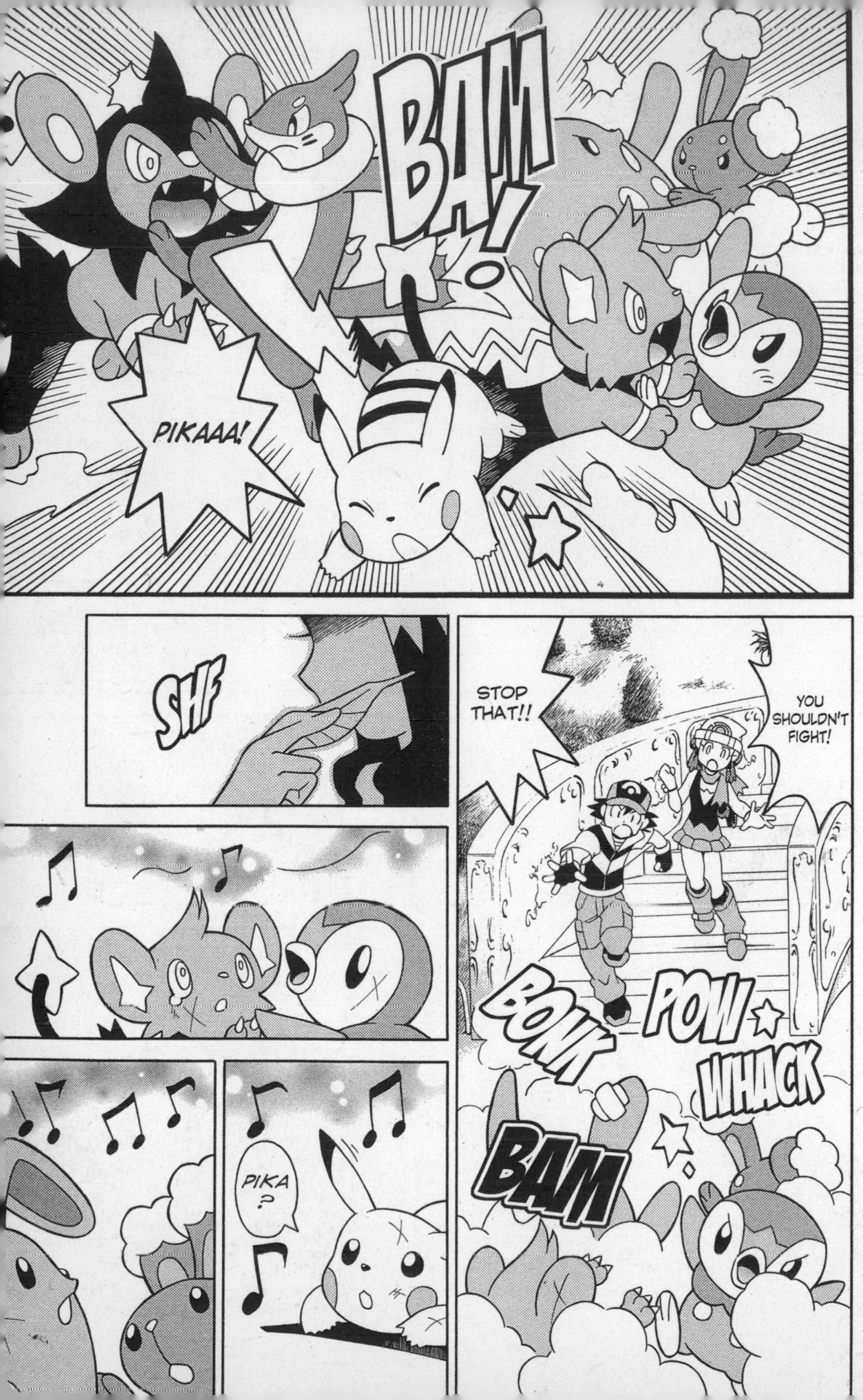
BAM!
PIKAAA!
YOU SHOULDN'T FIGHT!
STOP THAT!!
POW
BONK
WHACK
BAM
SHF
PIKA?

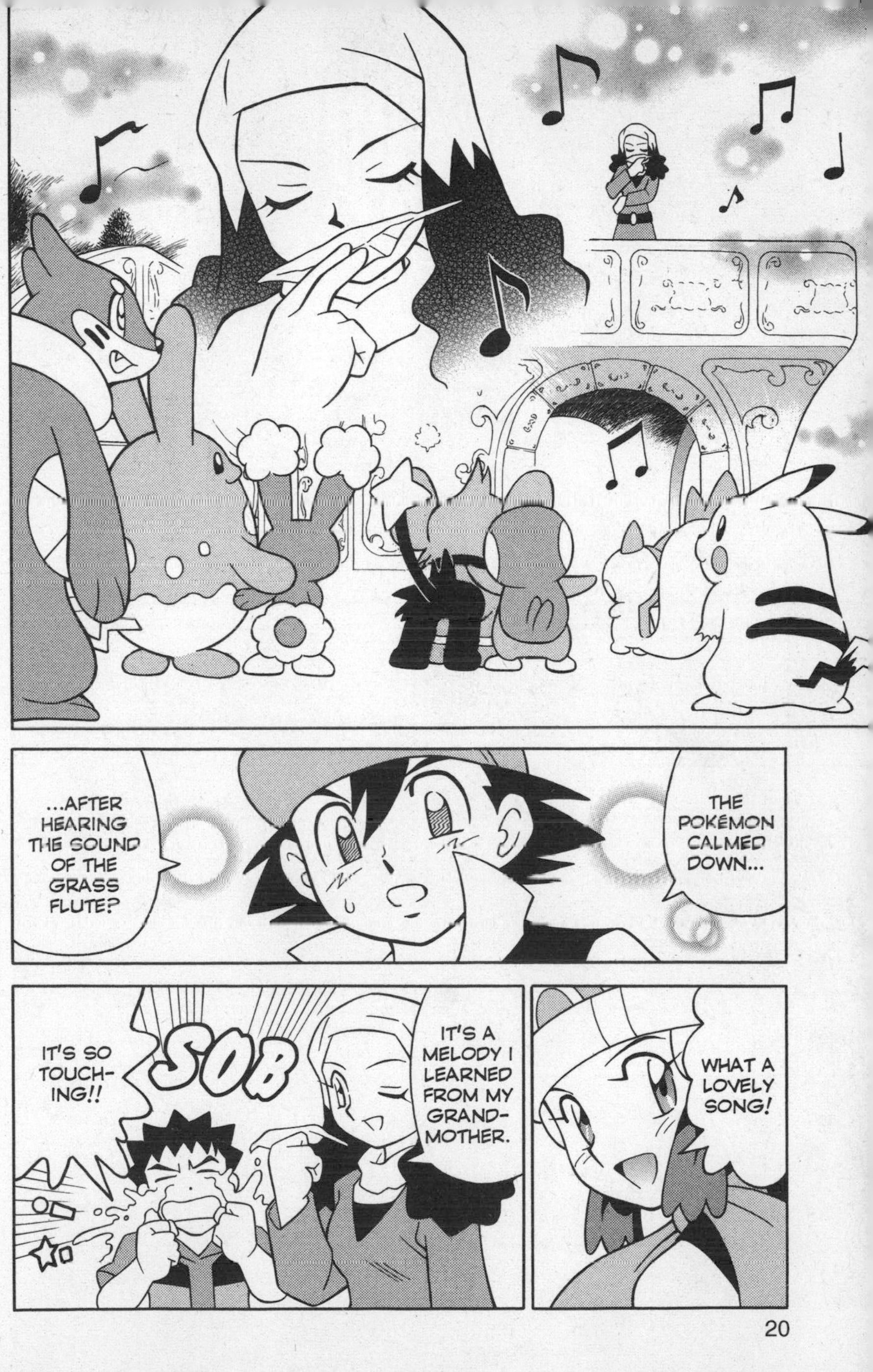
THE POKÉMON CALMED DOWN...
...AFTER HEARING THE SOUND OF THE GRASS FLUTE?
WHAT A LOVELY SONG!
IT'S A MELODY I LEARNED FROM MY GRAND-MOTHER.
SOB
IT'S SO TOUCH-ING!!

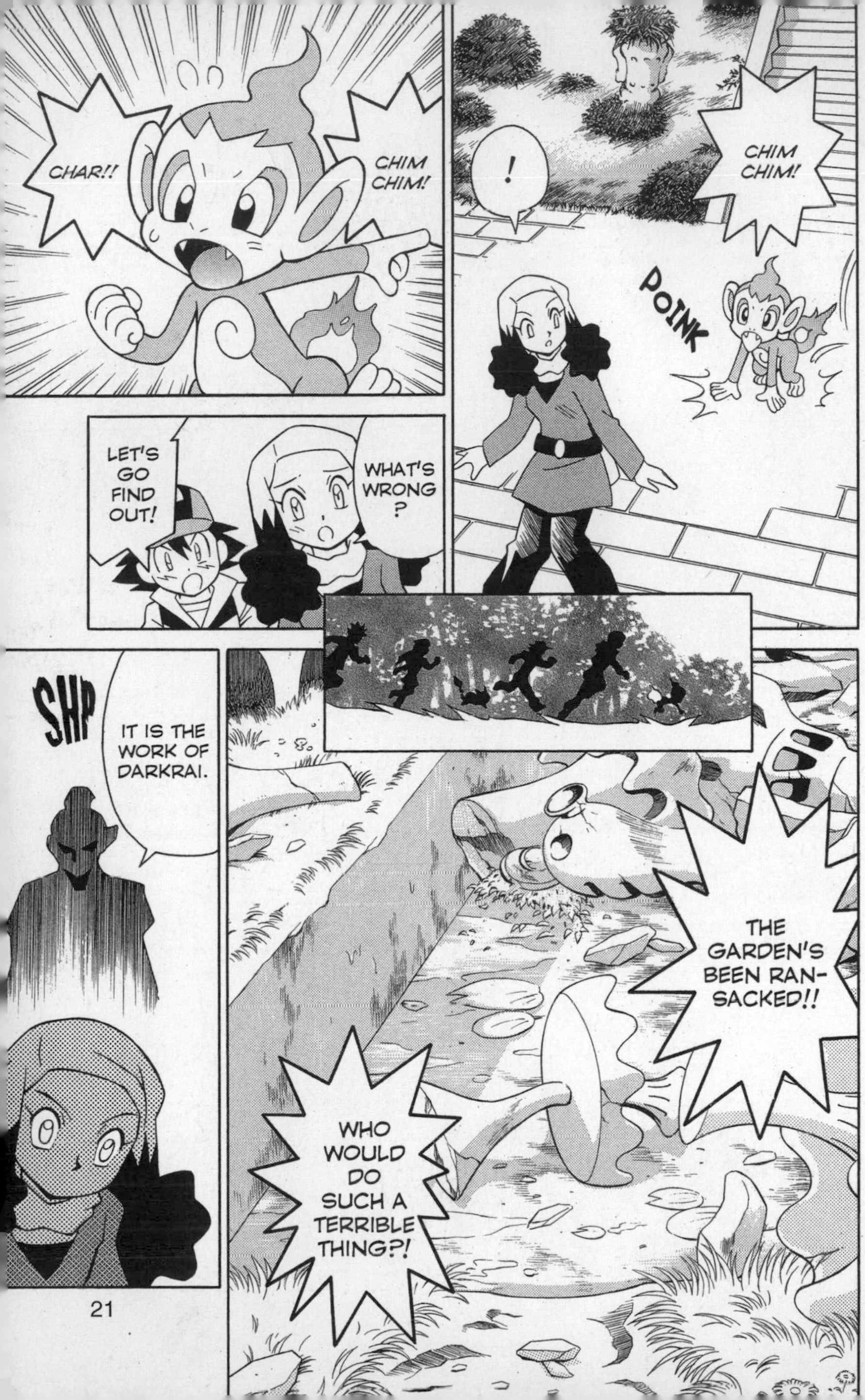

!
CHIM CHIM!
POINK
CHIM CHIM!
CHAR!!
WHAT'S WRONG?
LET'S GO FIND OUT!
THE GARDEN'S BEEN RAN-SACKED!!
WHO WOULD DO SUCH A TERRIBLE THING?!
SHP
IT IS THE WORK OF DARKRAI.

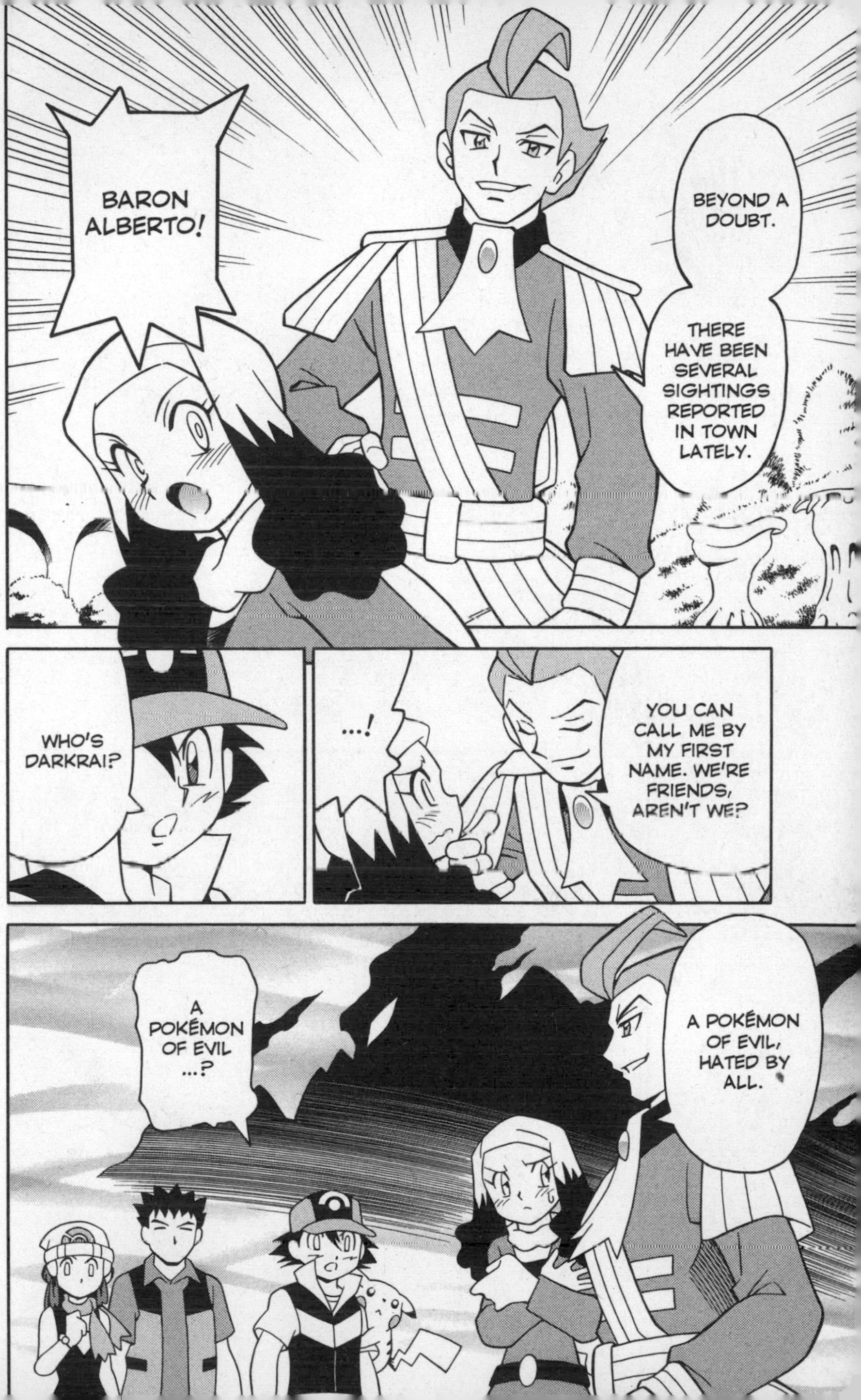
BEYOND A DOUBT.
THERE HAVE BEEN SEVERAL SIGHTINGS REPORTED IN TOWN LATELY.
BARON ALBERTO!
YOU CAN CALL ME BY MY FIRST NAME. WE'RE FRIENDS, AREN'T WE?
...!
WHO'S DARKRAI?
A POKÉMON OF EVIL, HATED BY ALL.
A POKÉMON OF EVIL ...?

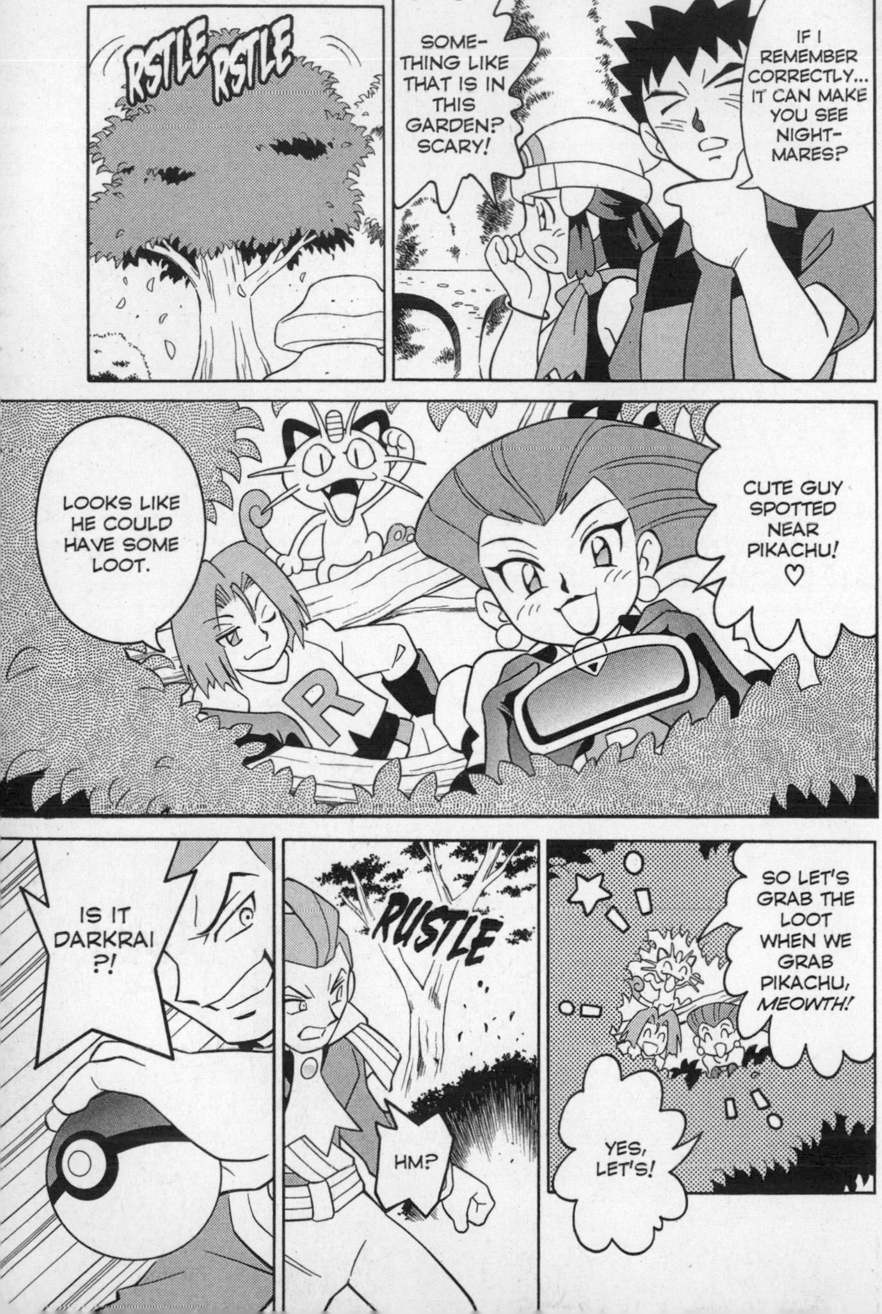
IF I REMEMBER CORRECTLY... IT CAN MAKE YOU SEE NIGHTMARES?
SOMETHING LIKE THAT IS IN THIS GARDEN? SCARY!
RSTLE RSTLE
CUTE GUY SPOTTED NEAR PIKACHU! ♡
LOOKS LIKE HE COULD HAVE SOME LOOT.
SO LET'S GRAB THE LOOT WHEN WE GRAB PIKACHU, *MEOWTH!*
YES, LET'S!
RUSTLE
HM?
IS IT DARKRAI?!

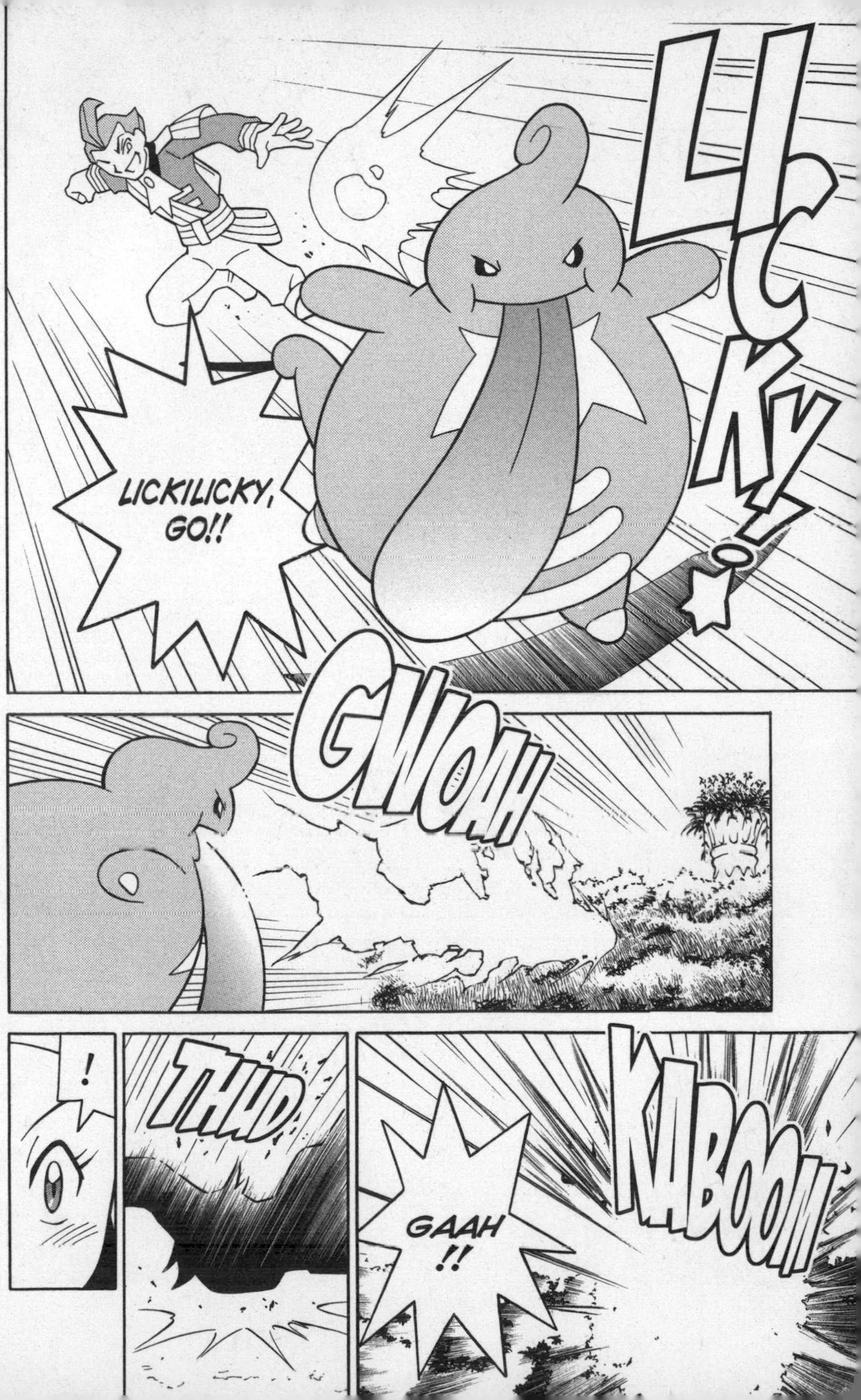
LICKY!
LICKILICKY, GO!!
GNOAH
KABOOM
GAAH!!
THUD
!

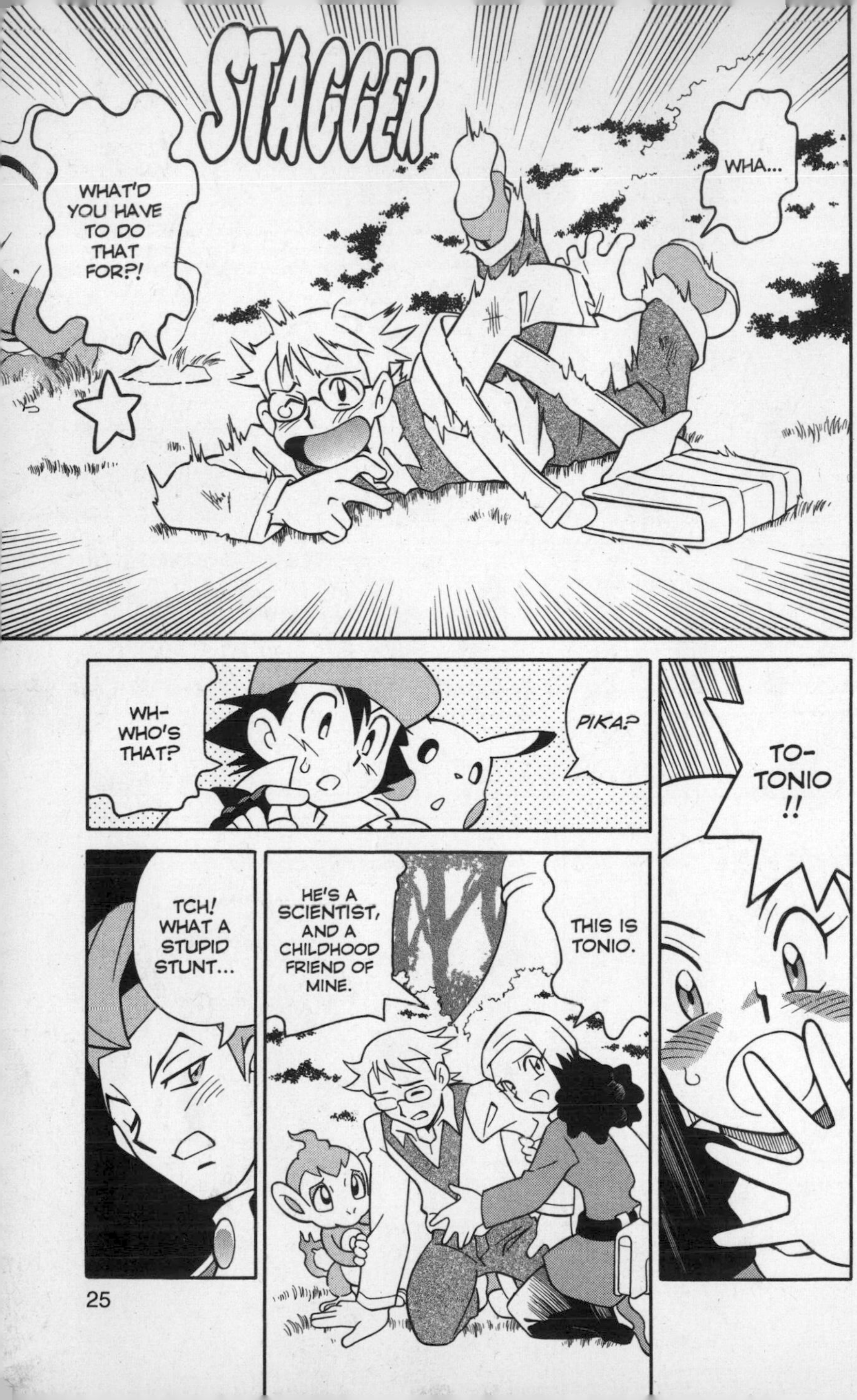
WHA...
STAGGER
WHAT'D YOU HAVE TO DO THAT FOR?!
TO-TONIO!!
PIKA?
WH-WHO'S THAT?
THIS IS TONIO.
HE'S A SCIENTIST, AND A CHILDHOOD FRIEND OF MINE.
TCH! WHAT A STUPID STUNT...

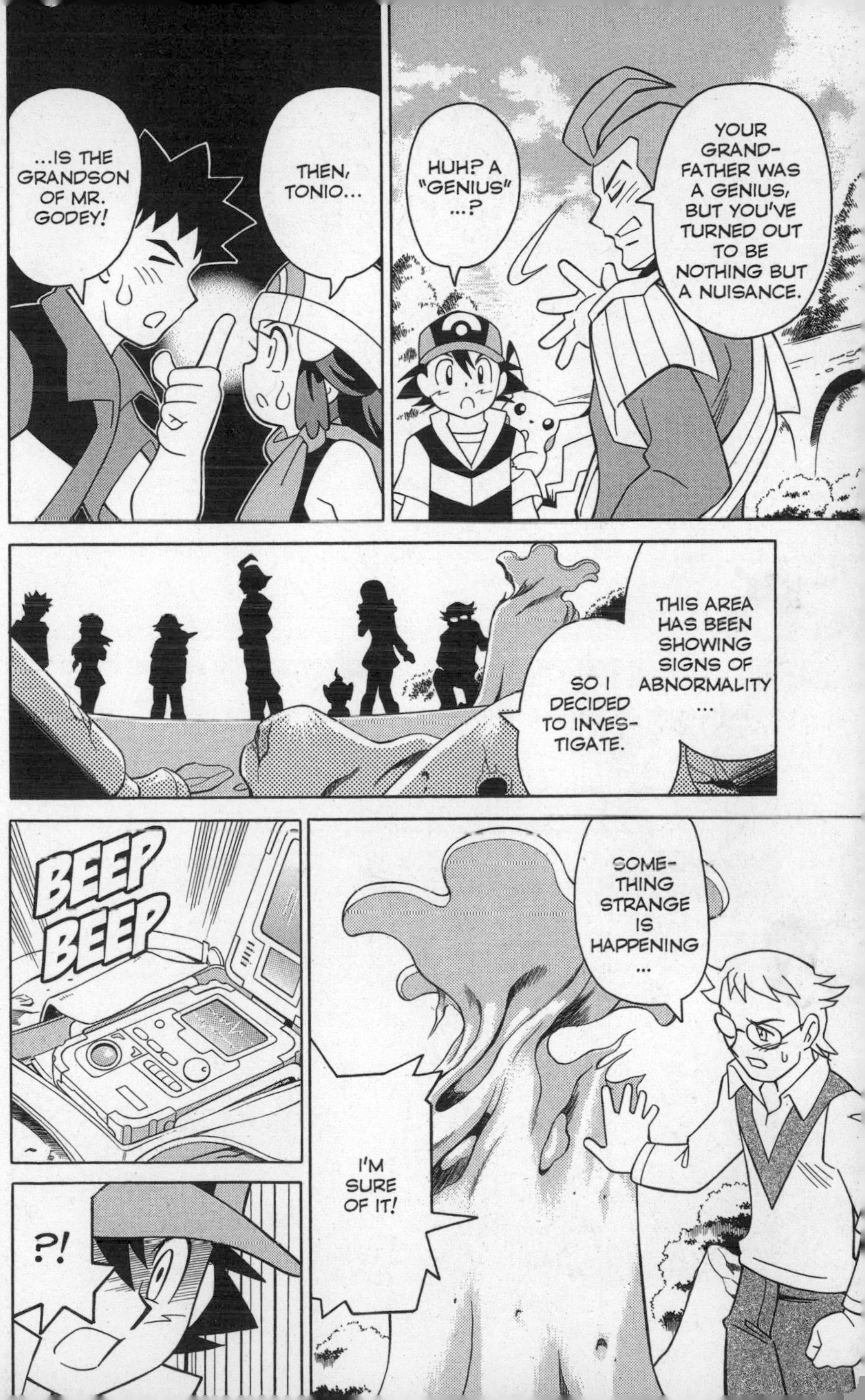
YOUR GRANDFATHER WAS A GENIUS, BUT YOU'VE TURNED OUT TO BE NOTHING BUT A NUISANCE.
HUH? A "GENIUS" ...?
THEN, TONIO...
...IS THE GRANDSON OF MR. GODEY!
THIS AREA HAS BEEN SHOWING SIGNS OF ABNORMALITY...
SO I DECIDED TO INVESTIGATE.
SOMETHING STRANGE IS HAPPENING...
I'M SURE OF IT!
BEEP BEEP
?!

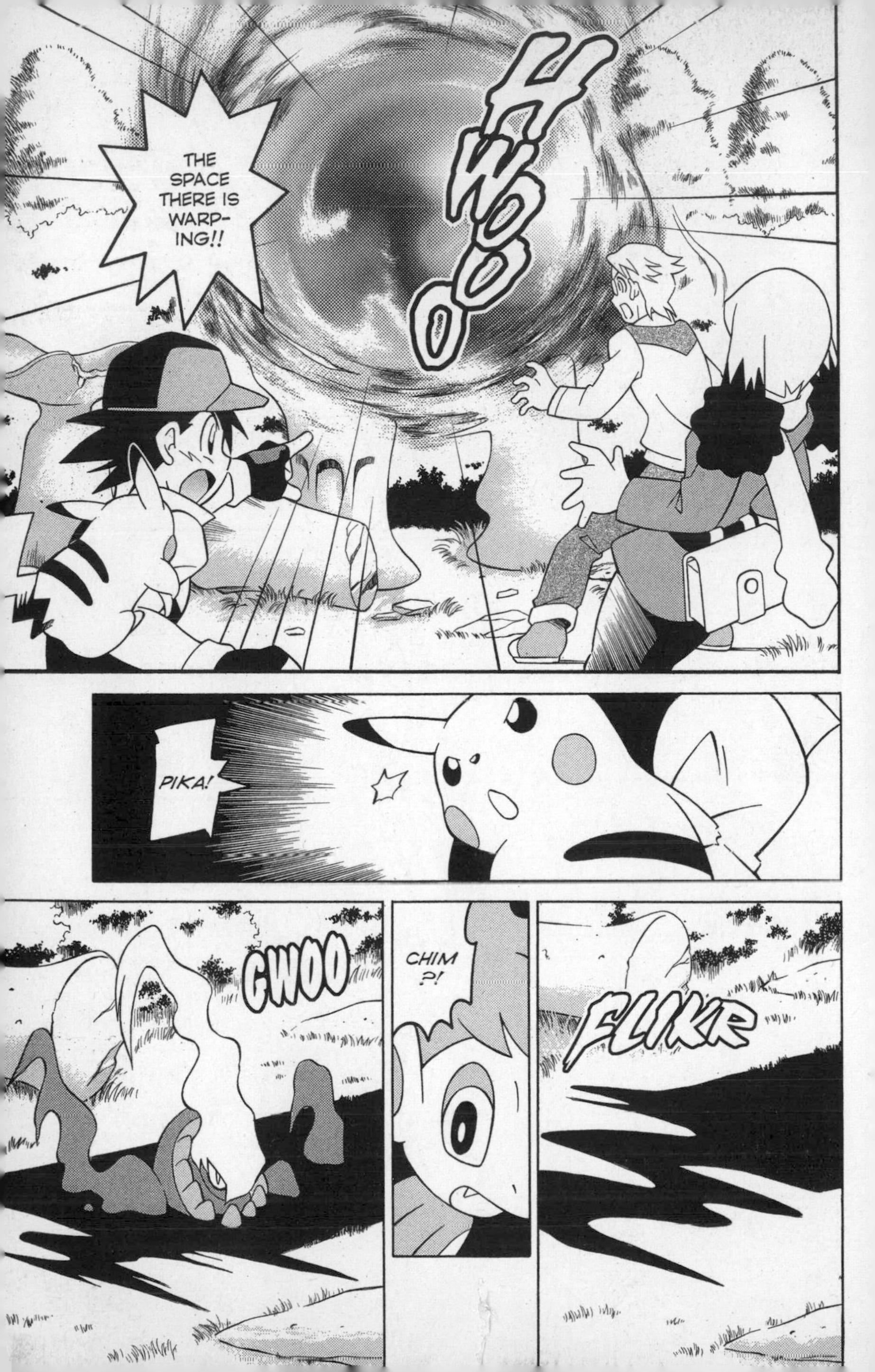
HWOOO
THE SPACE THERE IS WARP-ING!!
PIKA!
FLIKR
CHIM ?!
CWOO

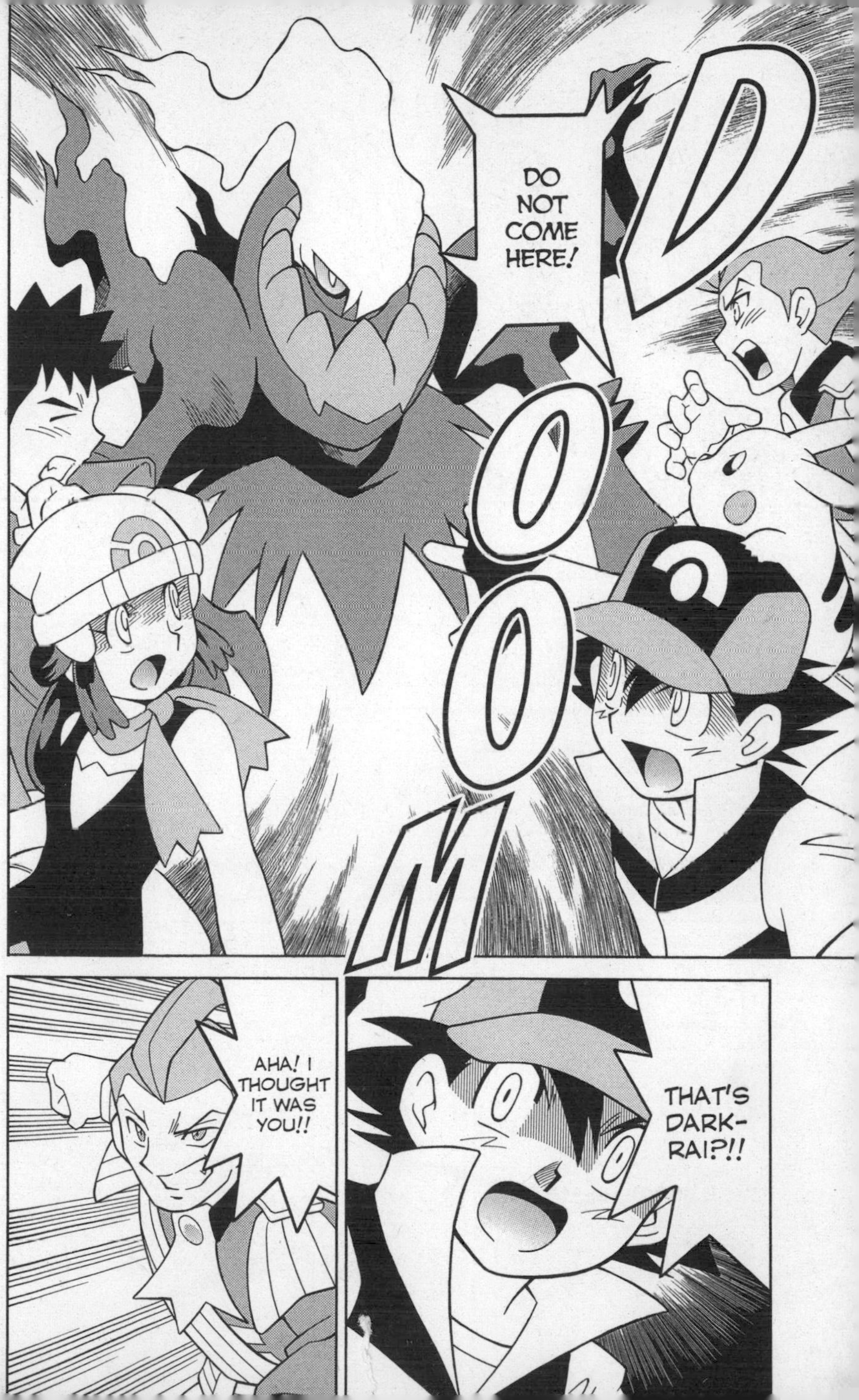
DO NOT COME HERE!
DOOOM
THAT'S DARK-RAI?!!
AHA! I THOUGHT IT WAS YOU!!

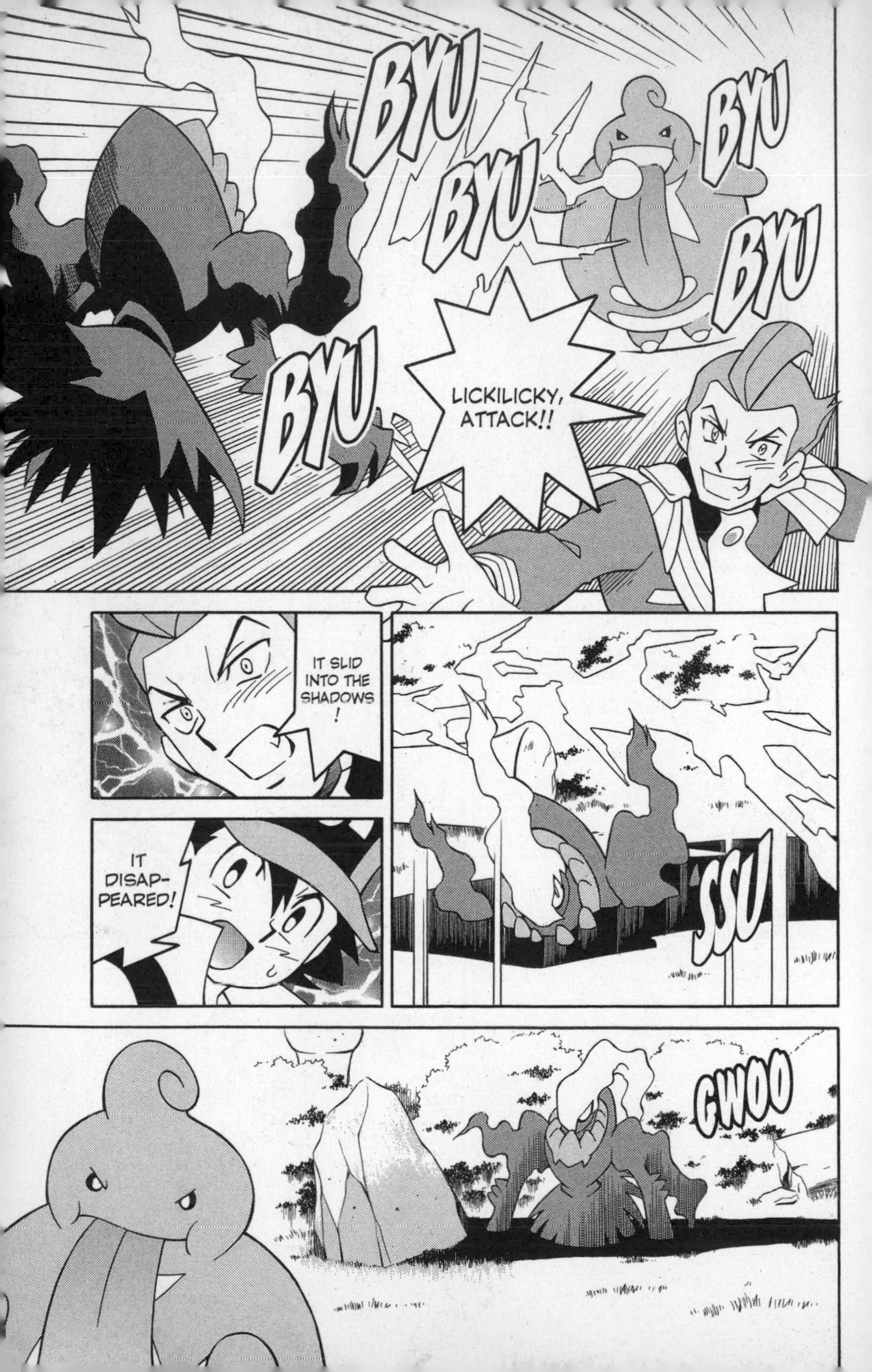
BYU
BYU
BYU
BYU
LICKILICKY, ATTACK!!
BYU
SSU
IT SLID INTO THE SHADOWS!
IT DISAP-PEARED!
CWOO

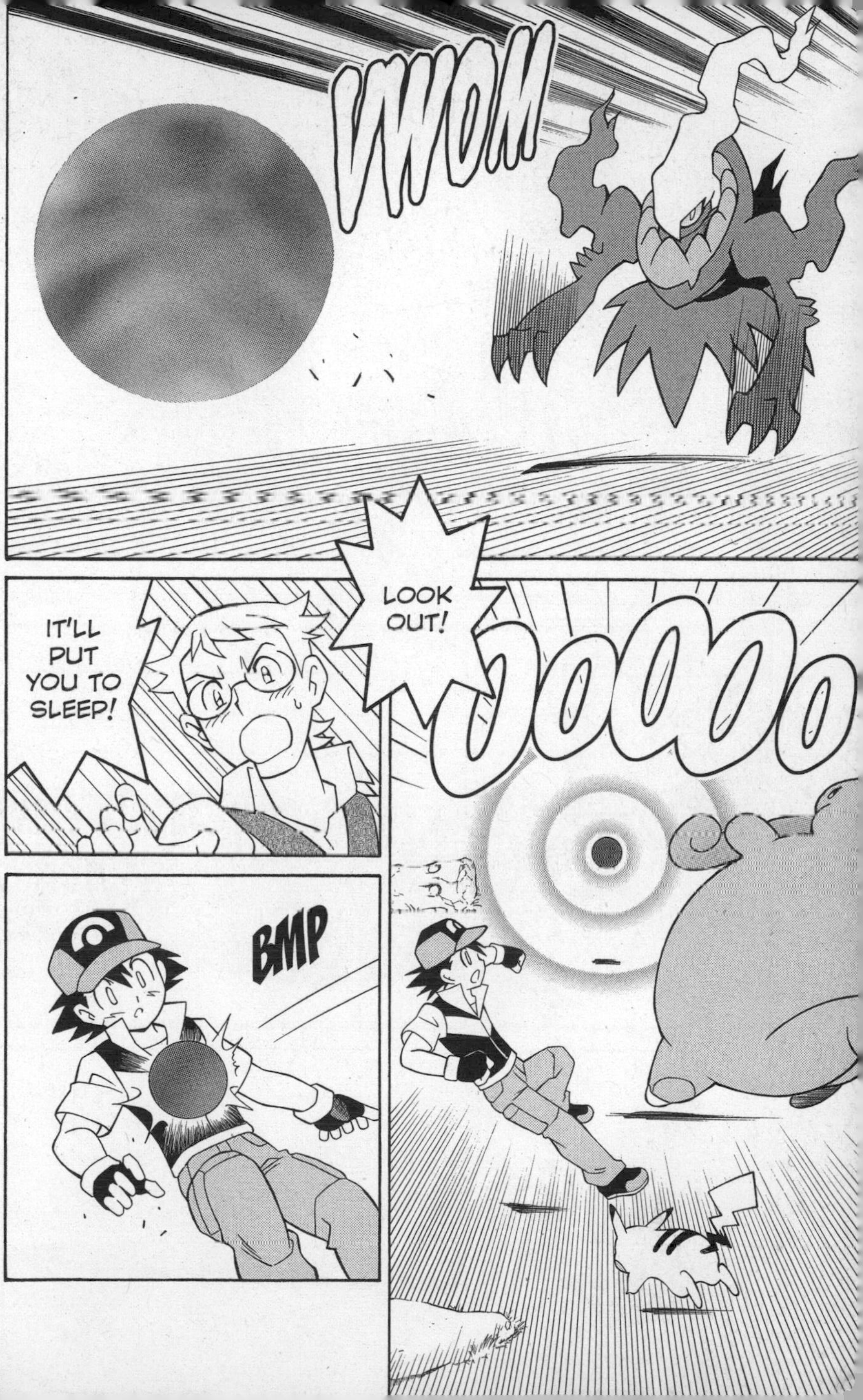
VWOM
LOOK OUT!
OOOOO
IT'LL PUT YOU TO SLEEP!
BMP

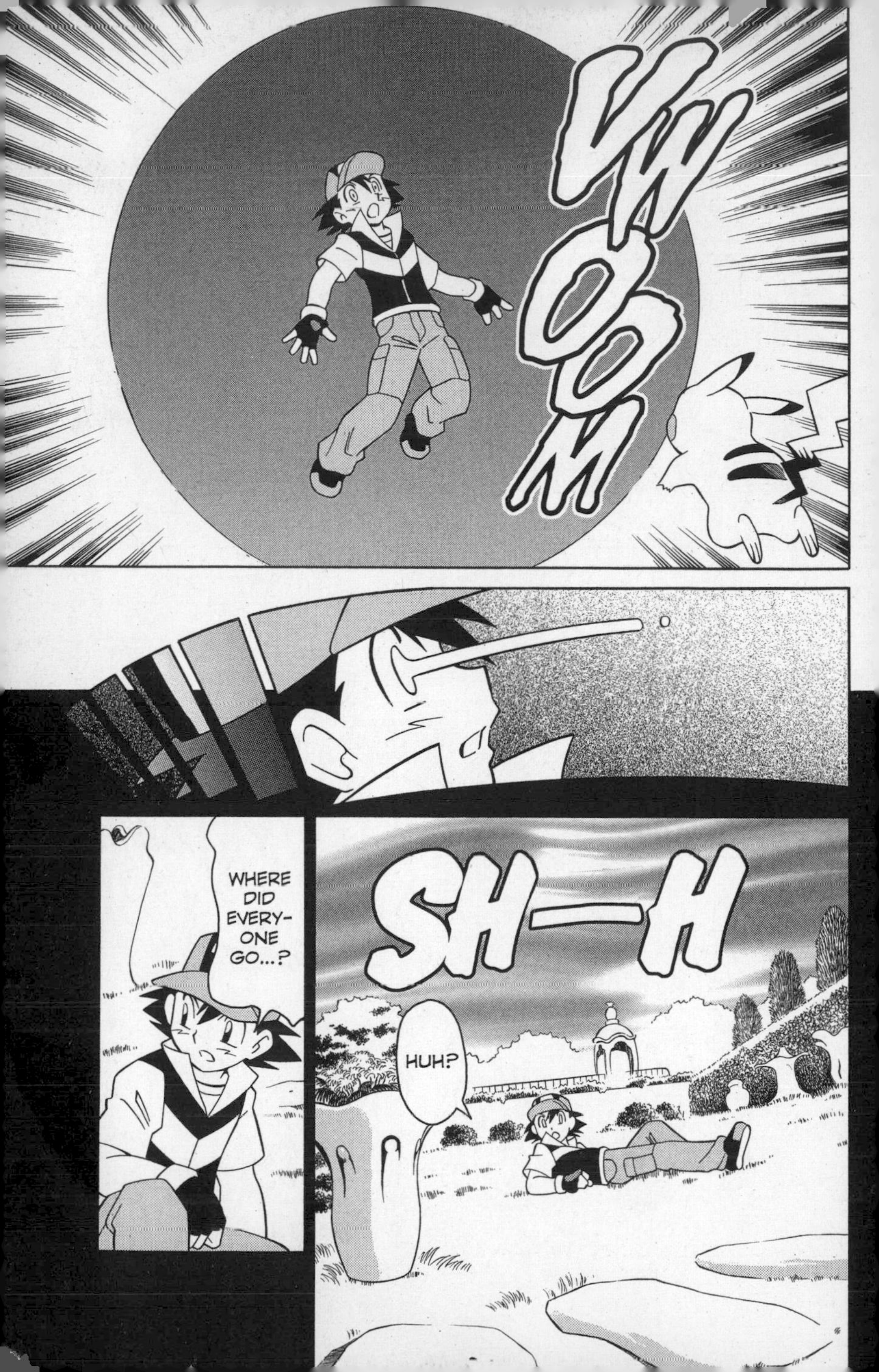
VWOOOM
SH—H
HUH?
WHERE DID EVERY-ONE GO...?

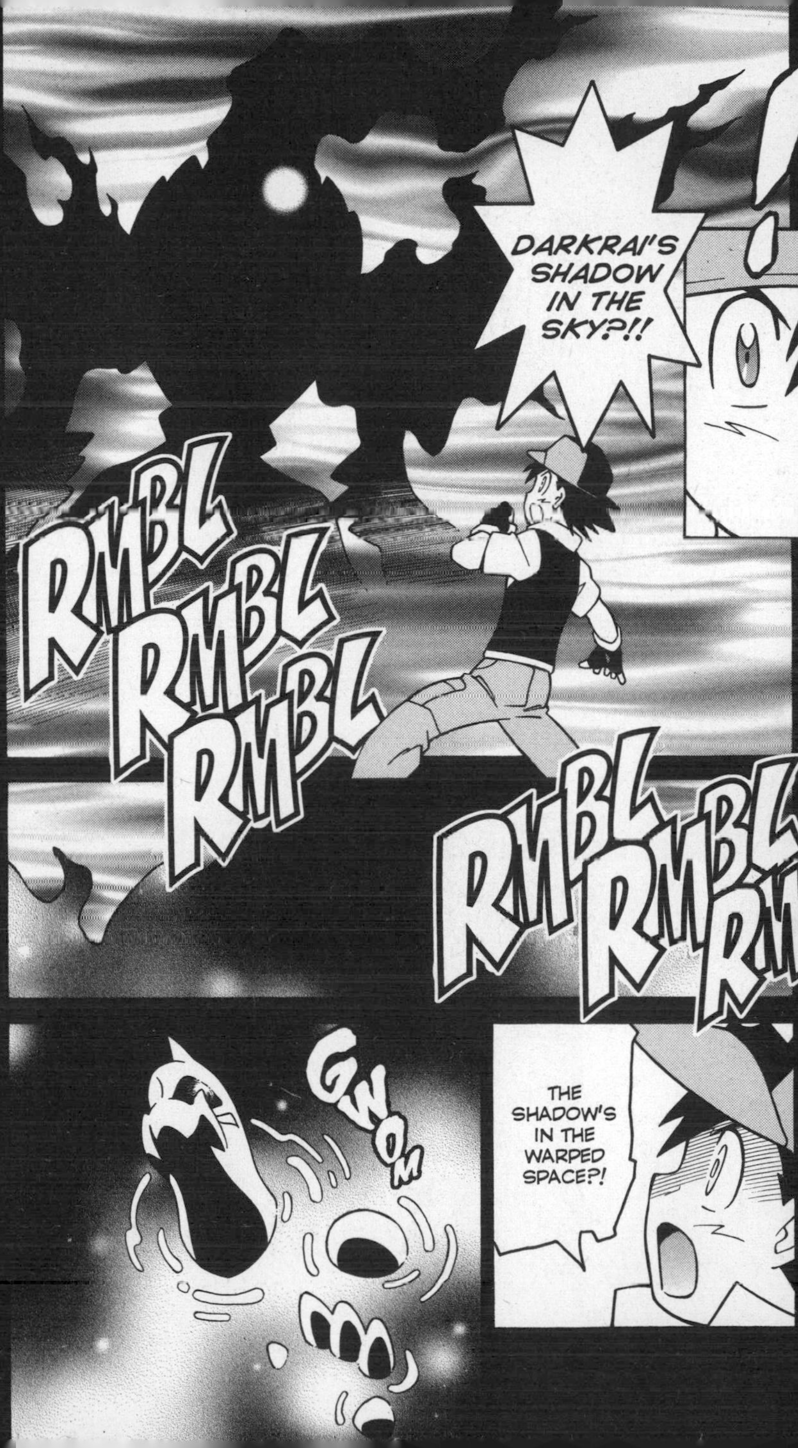
DARKRAI'S SHADOW IN THE SKY?!!
RMBL RMBL RMBL
RMBL RMBL RMBL
THE SHADOW'S IN THE WARPED SPACE?!
GNOM

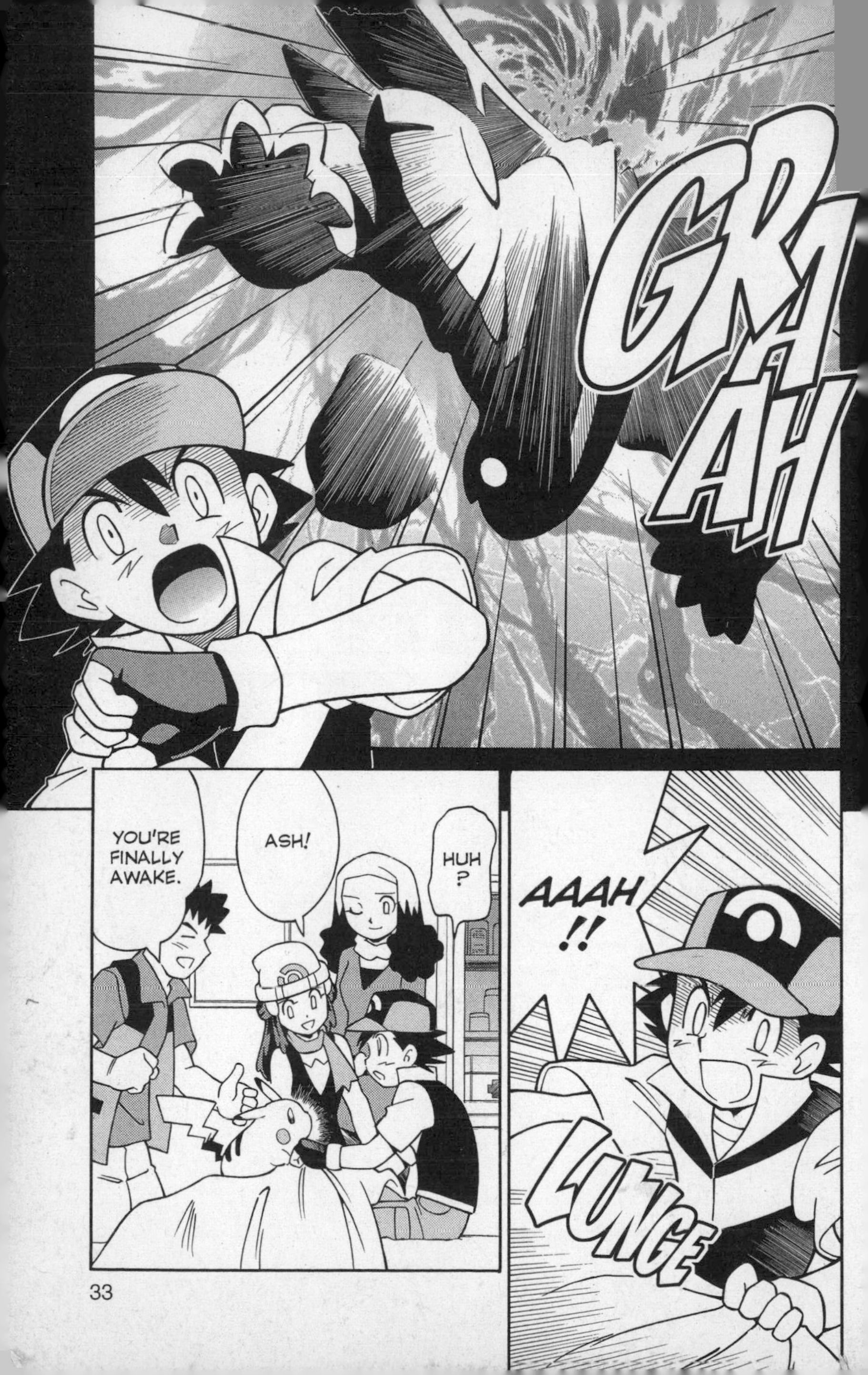
GRAAH
AAAH!!
LUNGE
HUH?
ASH!
YOU'RE FINALLY AWAKE.

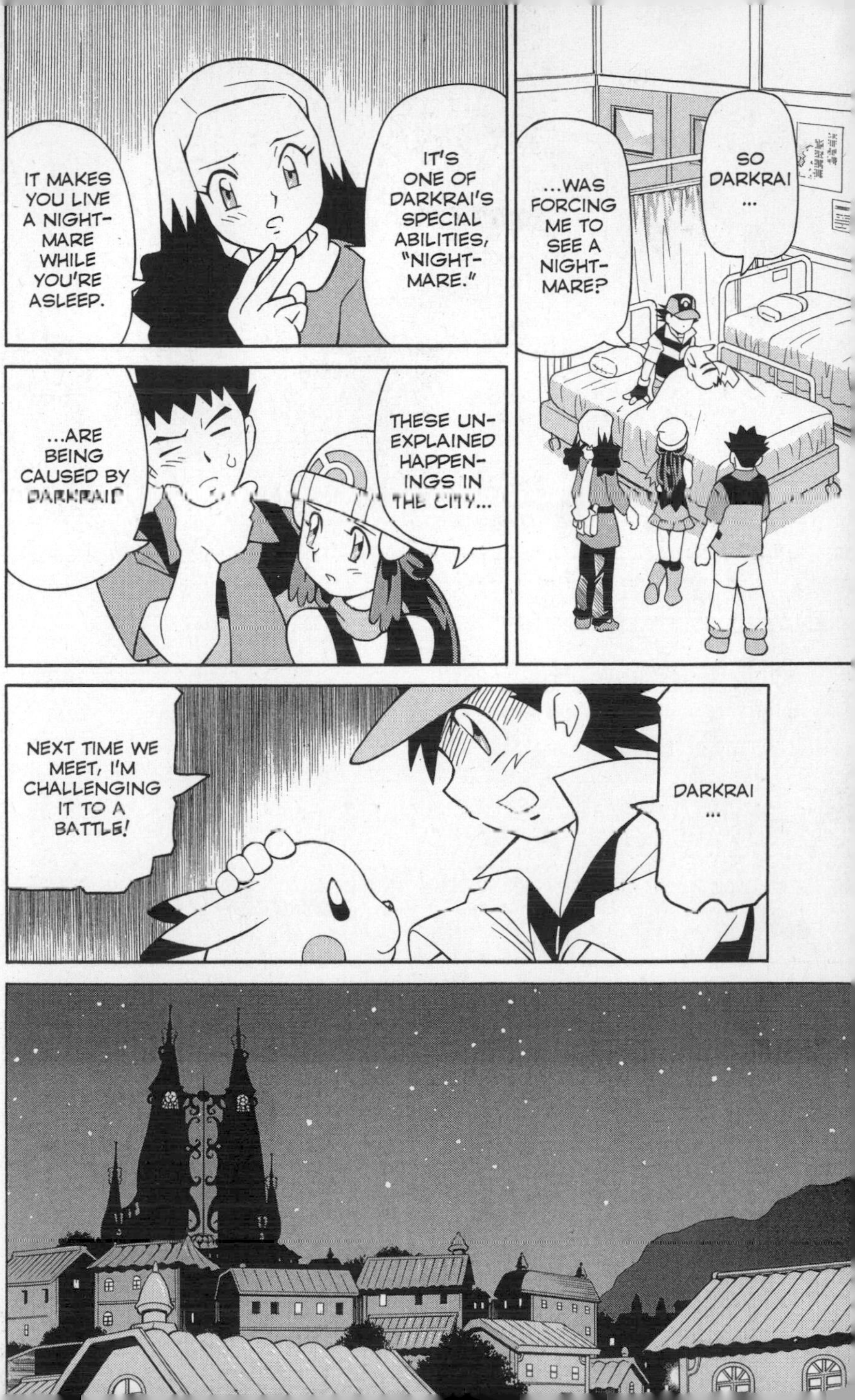
SO DARKRAI ...
...WAS FORCING ME TO SEE A NIGHT-MARE?
IT'S ONE OF DARKRAI'S SPECIAL ABILITIES, "NIGHT-MARE."
IT MAKES YOU LIVE A NIGHT-MARE WHILE YOU'RE ASLEEP.
THESE UN-EXPLAINED HAPPEN-INGS IN THE CITY...
...ARE BEING CAUSED BY DARKRAI!
DARKRAI ...
NEXT TIME WE MEET, I'M CHALLENGING IT TO A BATTLE!

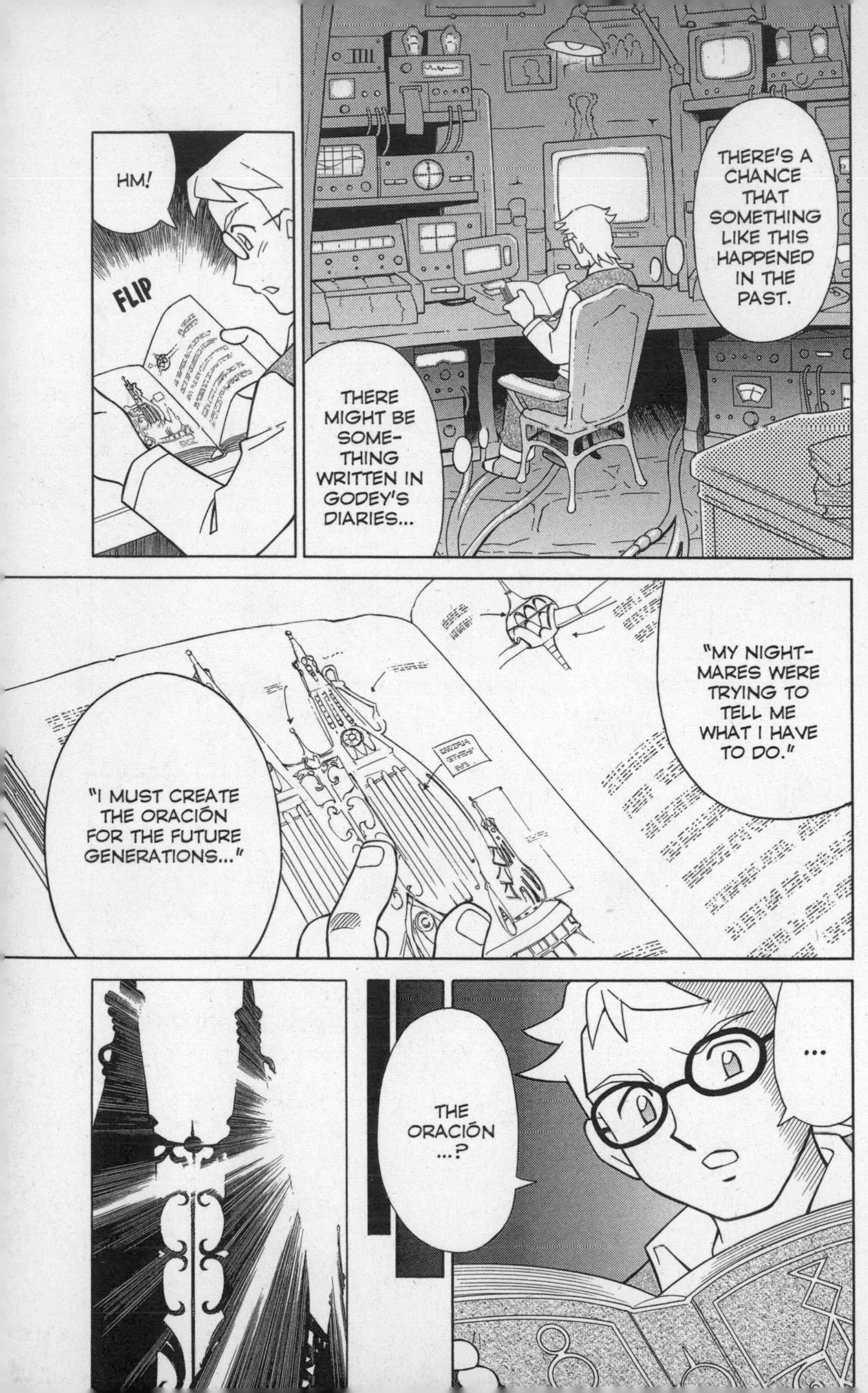
THERE'S A CHANCE THAT SOMETHING LIKE THIS HAPPENED IN THE PAST.
THERE MIGHT BE SOME-THING WRITTEN IN GODEY'S DIARIES...
HM!
FLIP
"MY NIGHT-MARES WERE TRYING TO TELL ME WHAT I HAVE TO DO."
"I MUST CREATE THE ORACIÓN FOR THE FUTURE GENERATIONS..."
...
THE ORACIÓN ...?

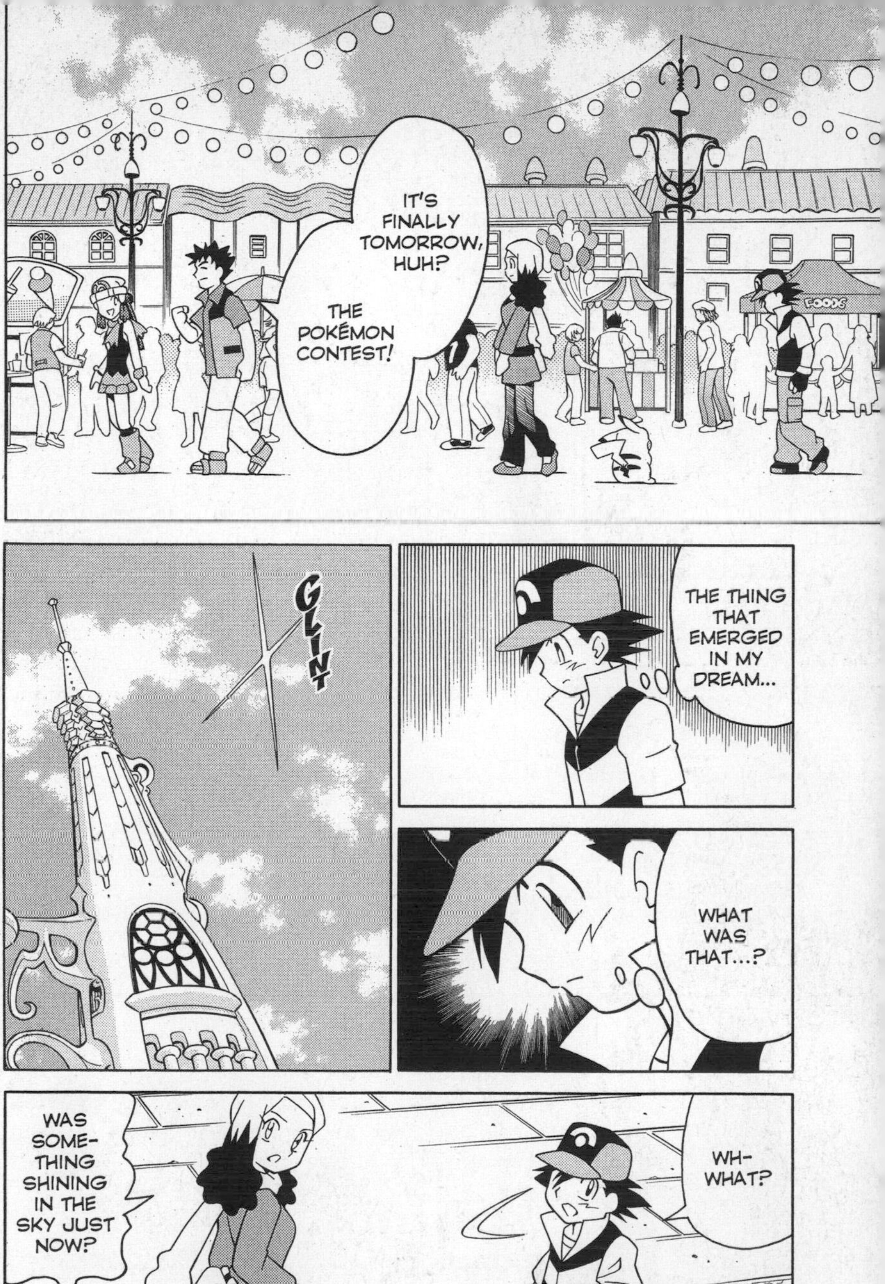
IT'S FINALLY TOMORROW, HUH?
THE POKÉMON CONTEST!
THE THING THAT EMERGED IN MY DREAM...
WHAT WAS THAT...?
GLINT
WH- WHAT?
WAS SOME- THING SHINING IN THE SKY JUST NOW?

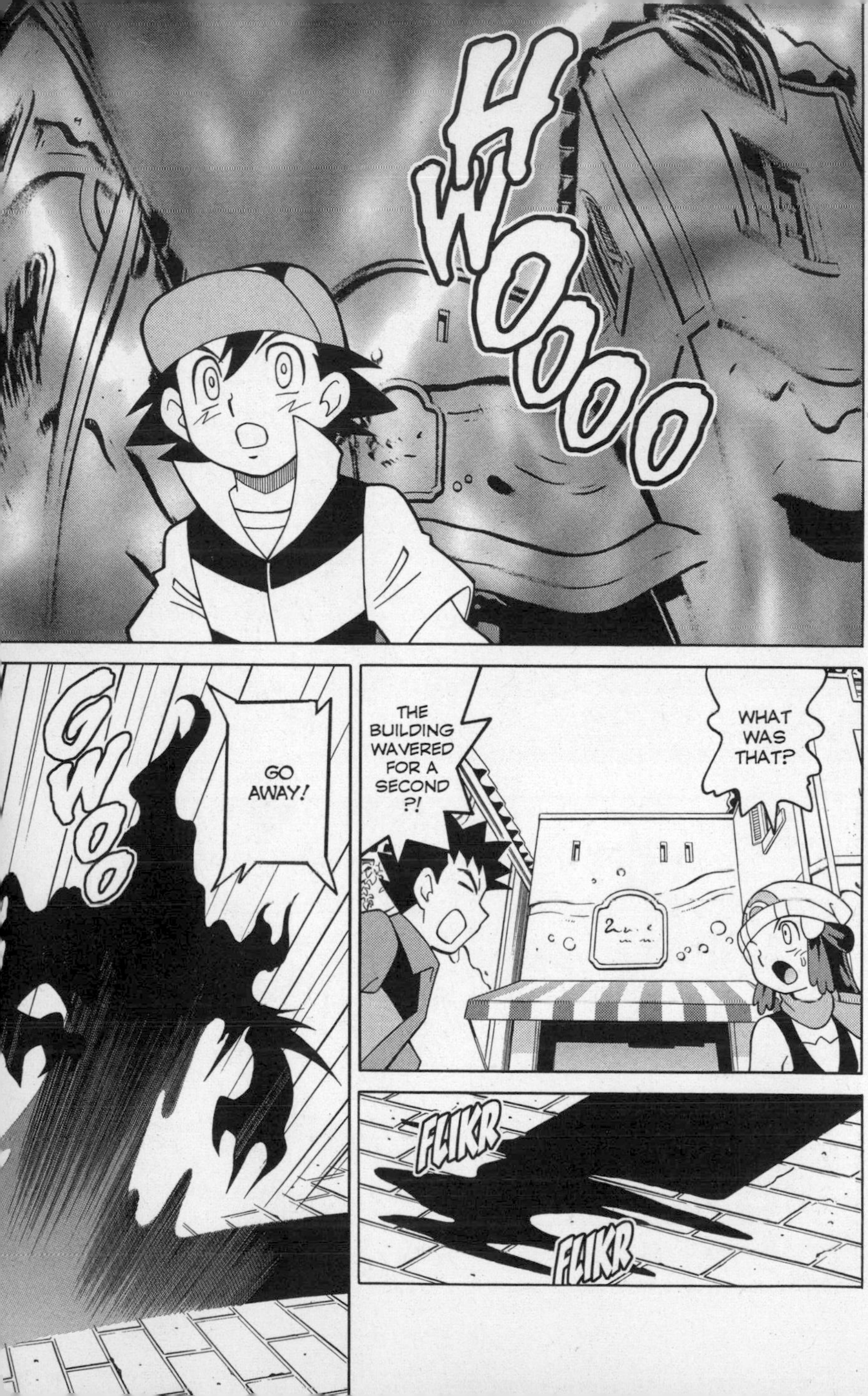
HWOOOOO
WHAT WAS THAT?
THE BUILDING WAVERED FOR A SECOND?!
FLIKR
FLIKR
GWOO
GO AWAY!

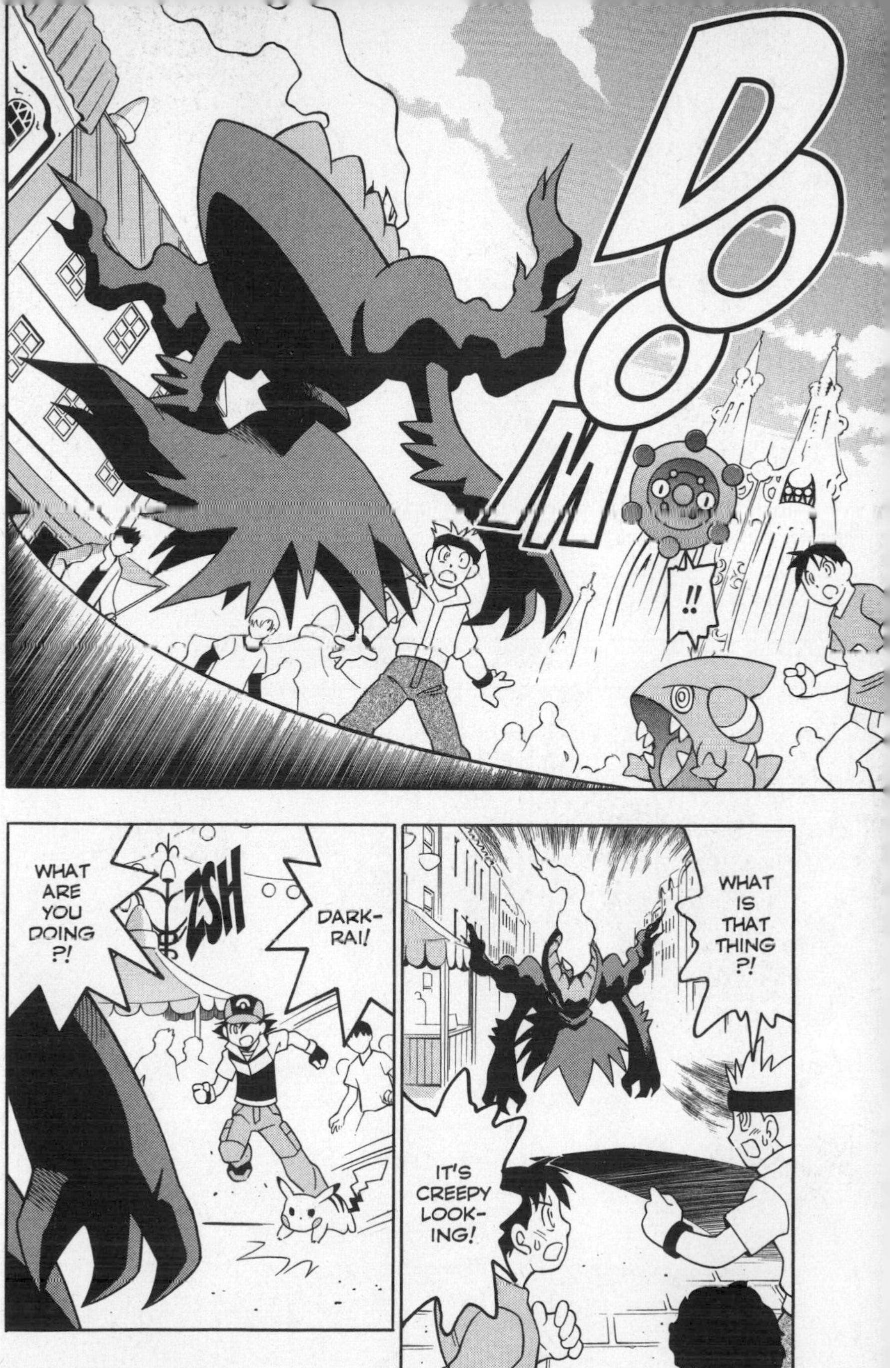
DOOM
!!
WHAT IS THAT THING?!
IT'S CREEPY LOOKING!
DARK-RAI!
ZSH
WHAT ARE YOU DOING?!

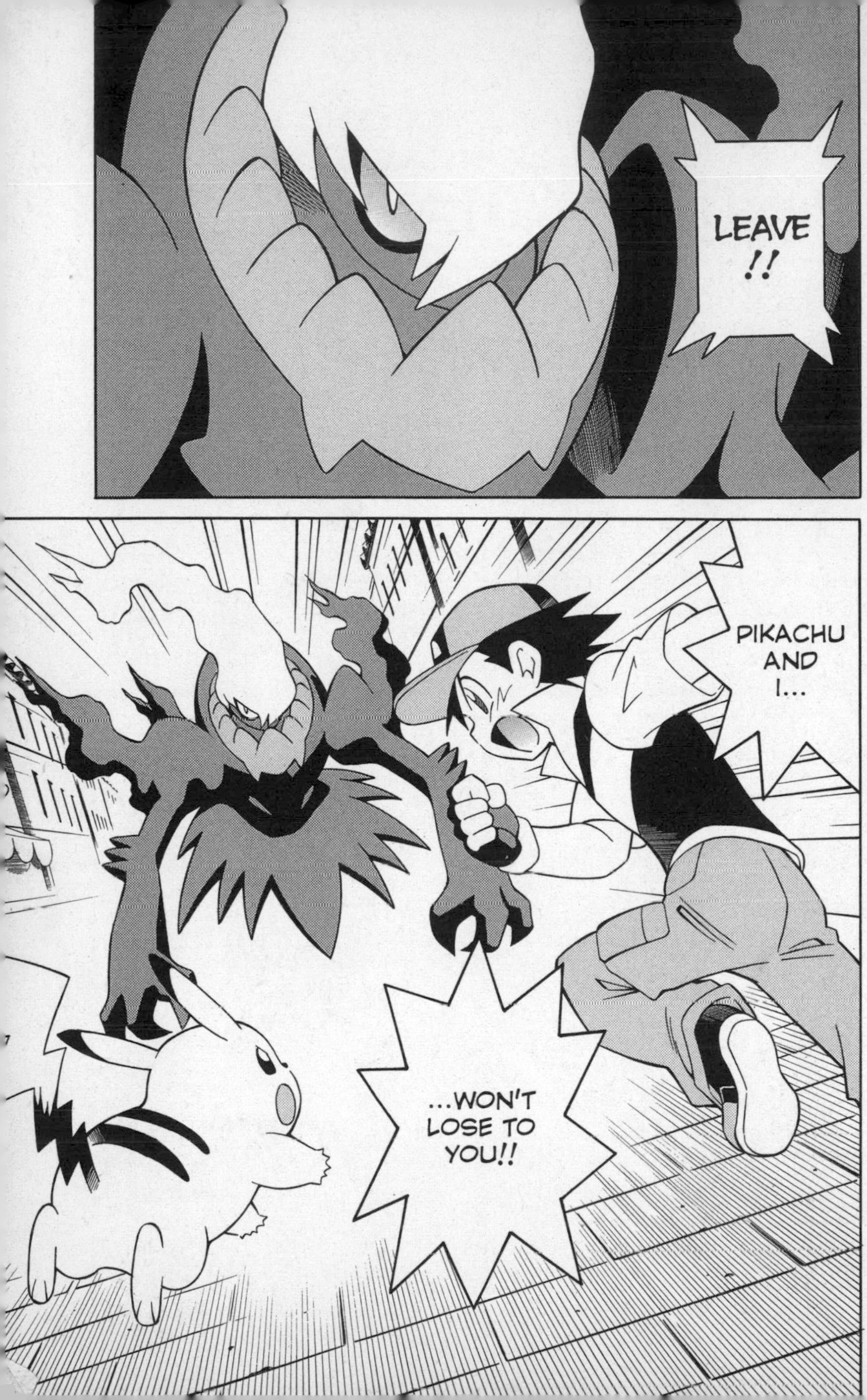
LEAVE !!
PIKACHU AND I...
...WON'T LOSE TO YOU!!

THE ASTONISHING POWER OF DARKRAI!!

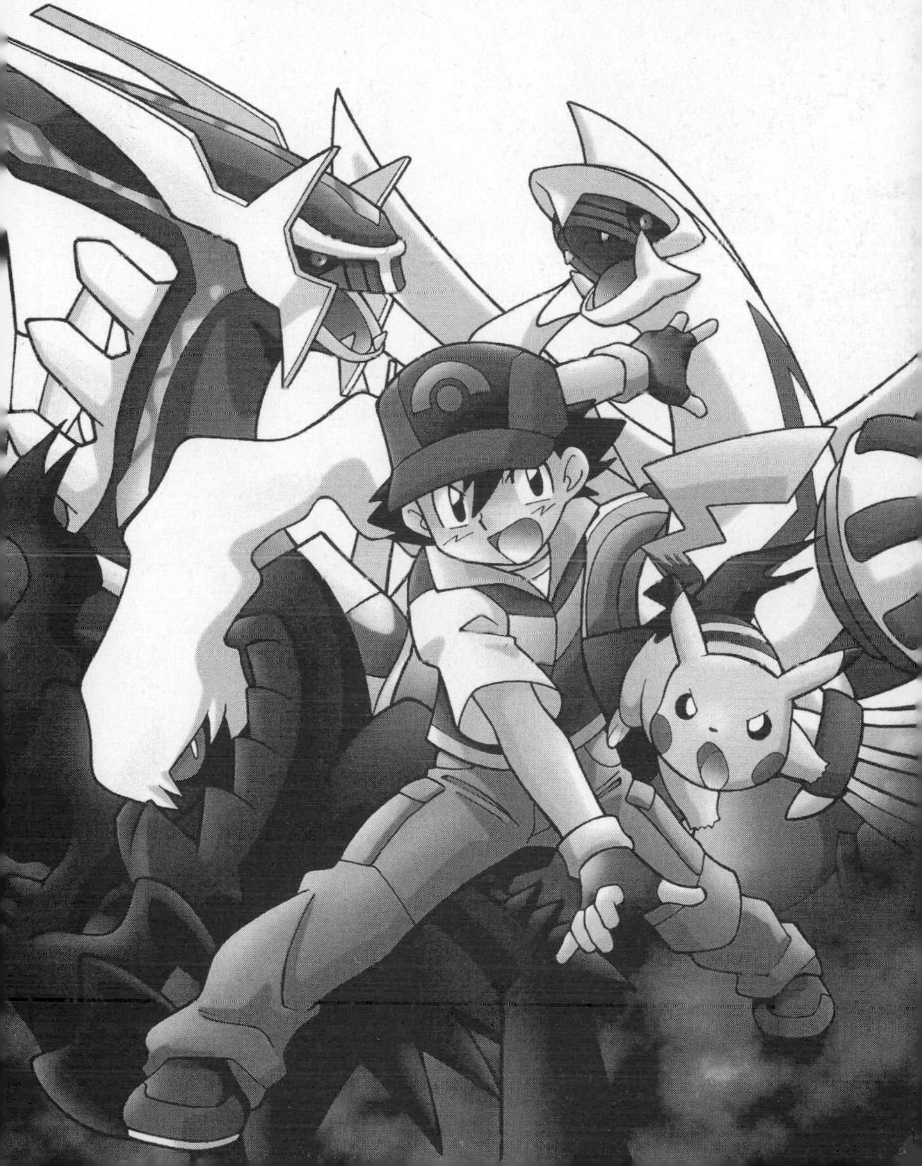

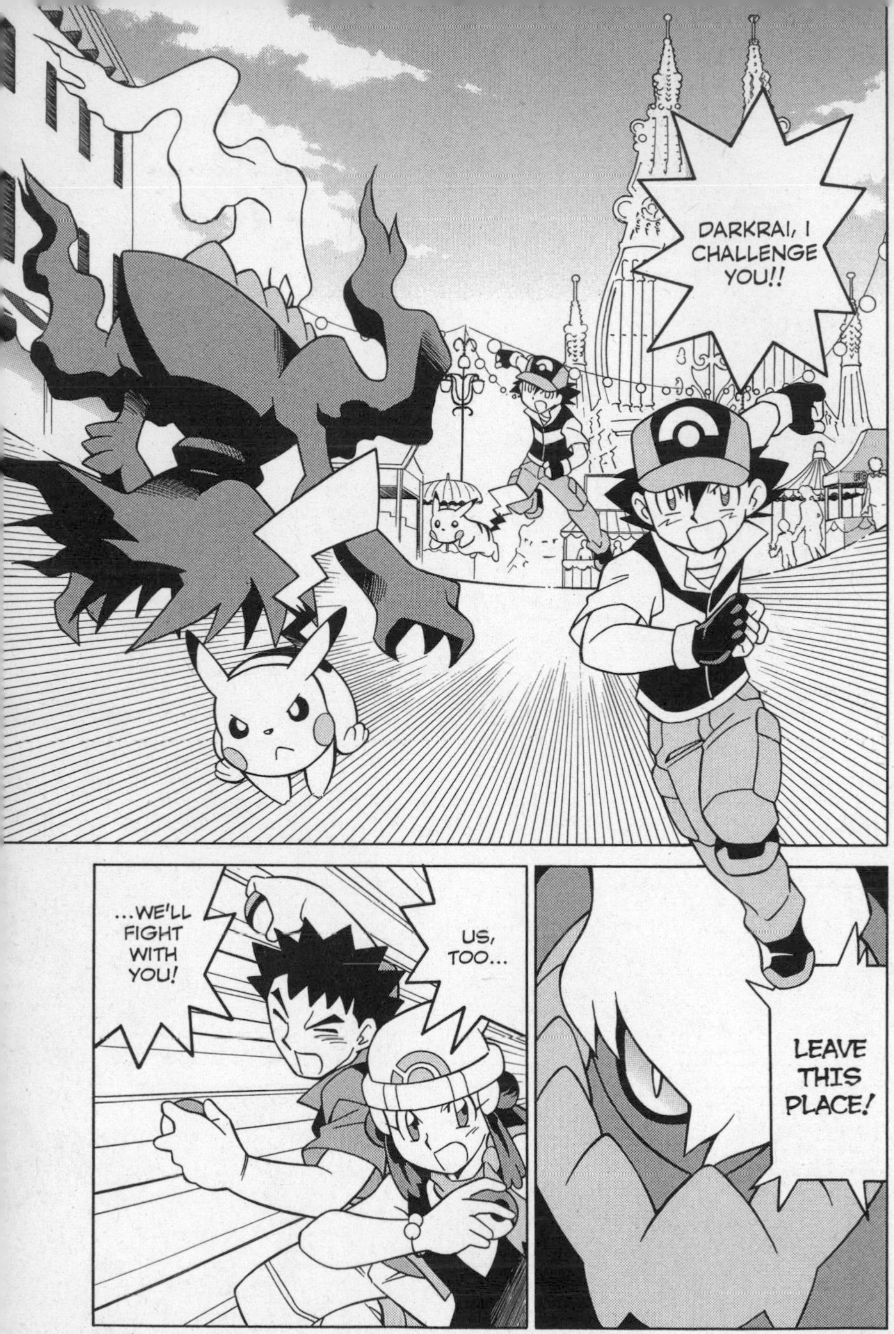
DARKRAI, I CHALLENGE YOU!!
LEAVE THIS PLACE!
US, TOO...
...WE'LL FIGHT WITH YOU!

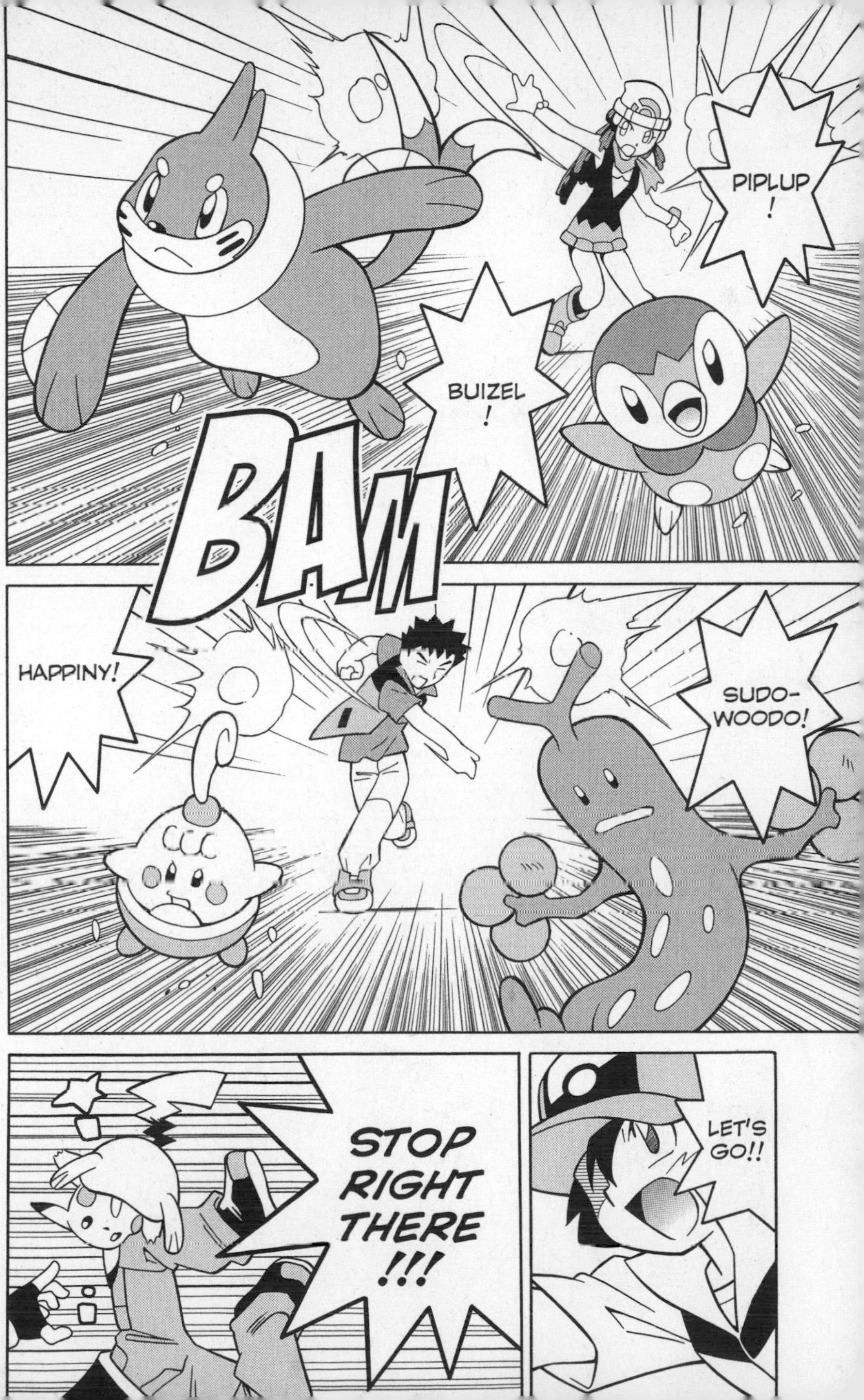
PIPLUP!
BUIZEL!
BAM
SUDO-WOODO!
HAPPINY!
LET'S GO!!
STOP RIGHT THERE!!!

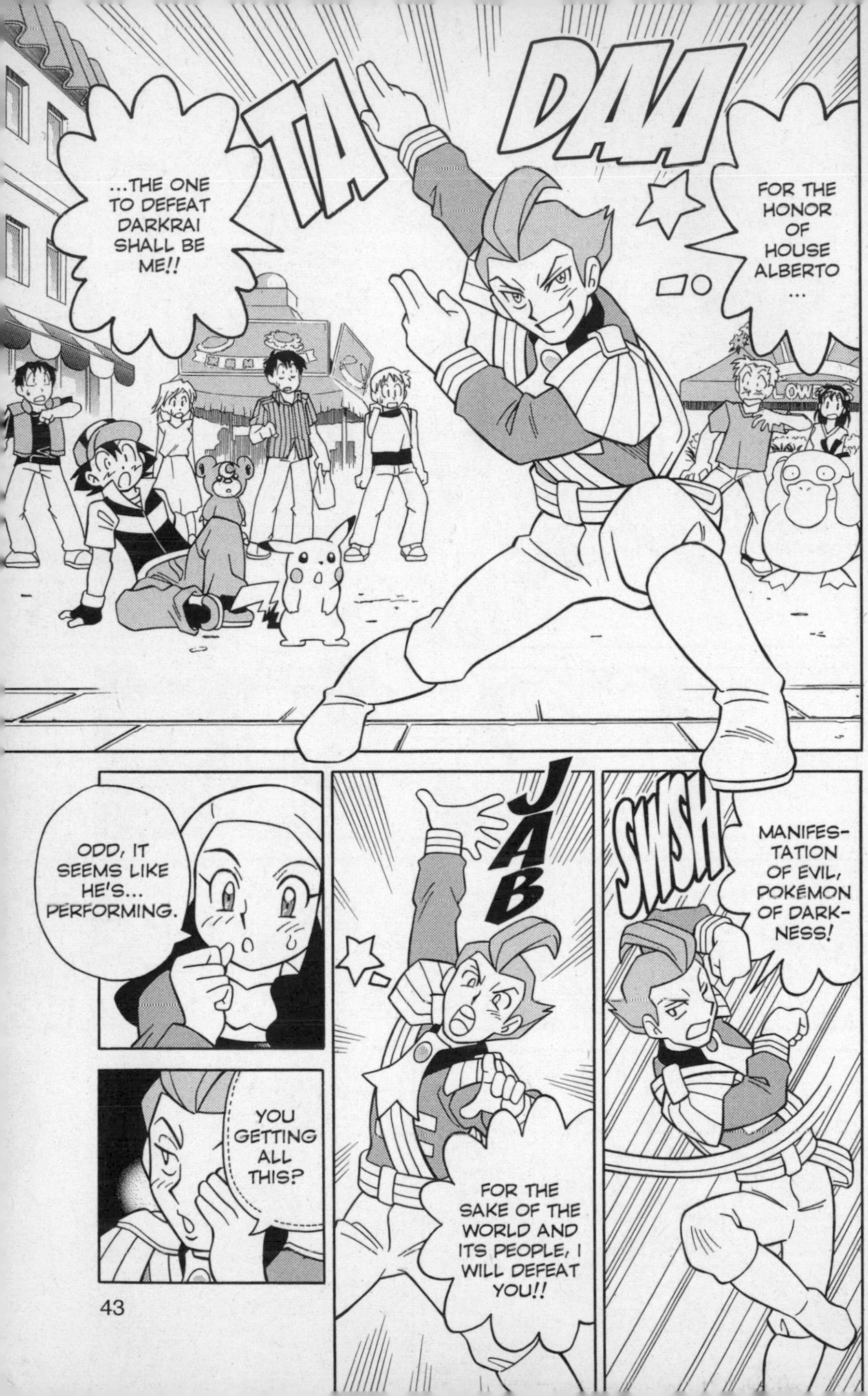
FOR THE HONOR OF HOUSE ALBERTO ...
TA DAA
...THE ONE TO DEFEAT DARKRAI SHALL BE ME!!
SWSH
MANIFES-TATION OF EVIL, POKÉMON OF DARK-NESS!
JAB
FOR THE SAKE OF THE WORLD AND ITS PEOPLE, I WILL DEFEAT YOU!!
ODD, IT SEEMS LIKE HE'S... PERFORMING.
YOU GETTING ALL THIS?

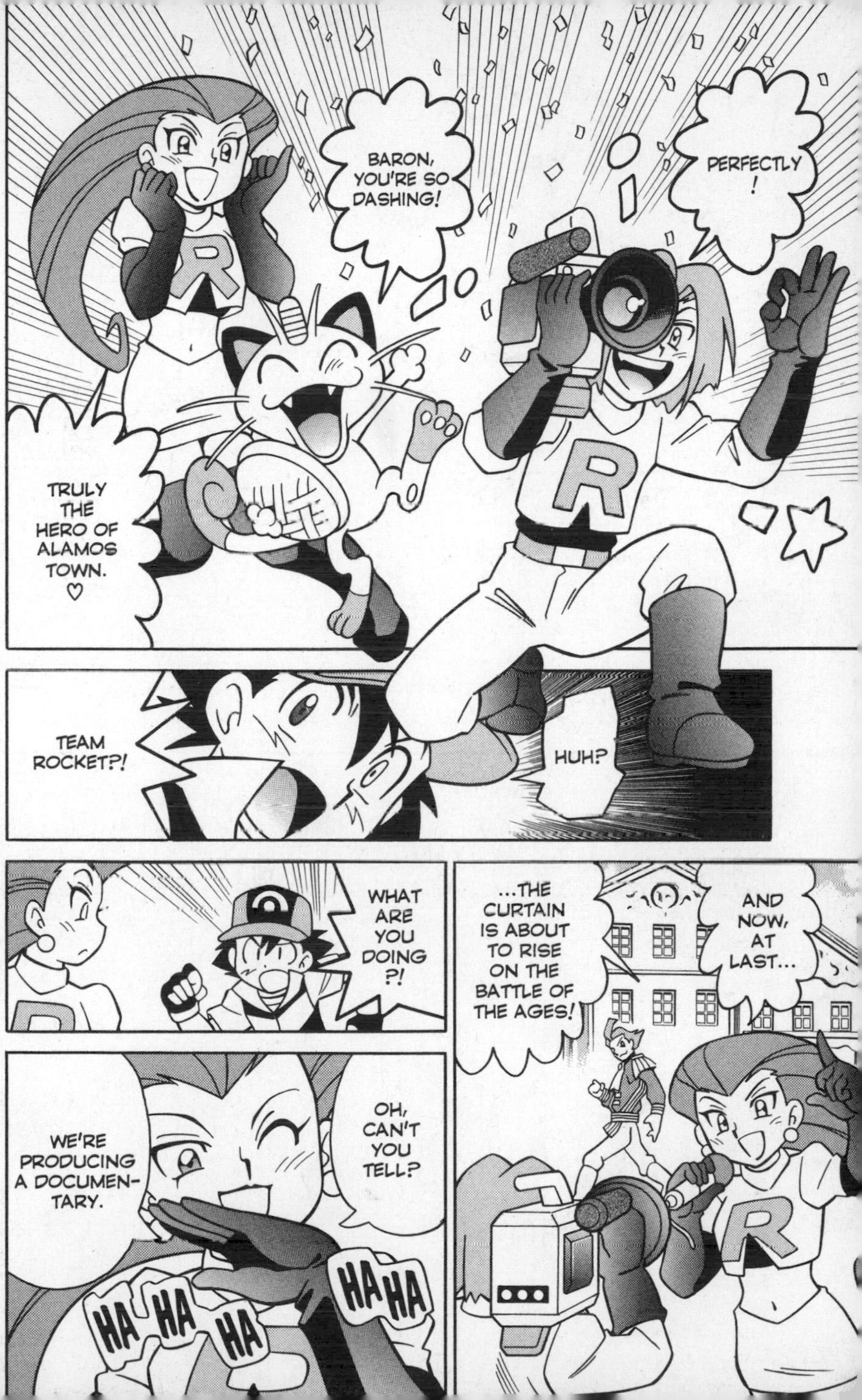
PERFECTLY!
BARON, YOU'RE SO DASHING!
TRULY THE HERO OF ALAMOS TOWN. ♡
HUH?
TEAM ROCKET?!
AND NOW, AT LAST...
...THE CURTAIN IS ABOUT TO RISE ON THE BATTLE OF THE AGES!
WHAT ARE YOU DOING?!
OH, CAN'T YOU TELL?
WE'RE PRODUCING A DOCUMENTARY.
HAHA
HA HA HA HA

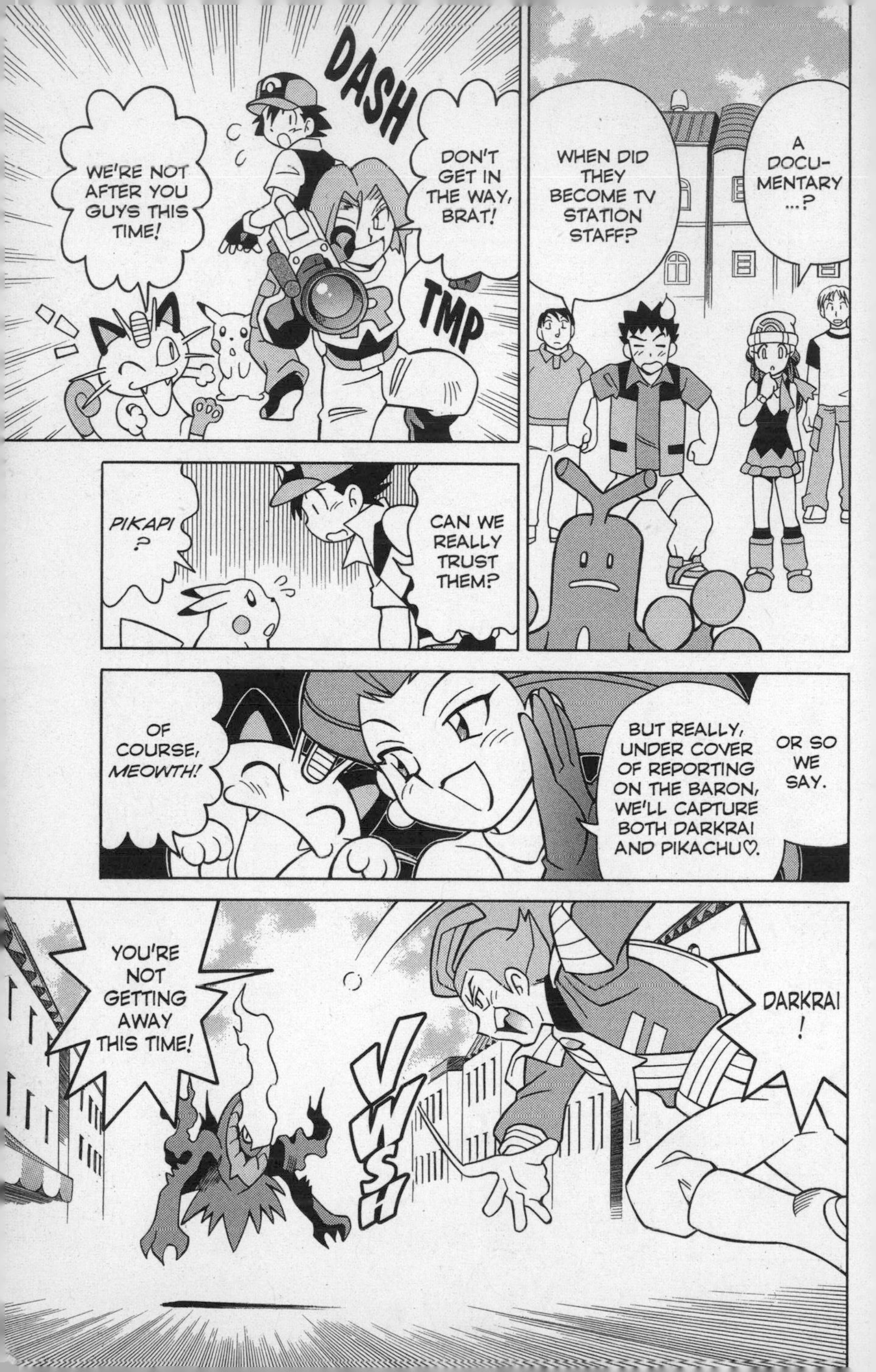
A DOCU-MENTARY ...?
WHEN DID THEY BECOME TV STATION STAFF?
DASH
DON'T GET IN THE WAY, BRAT!
TMP
WE'RE NOT AFTER YOU GUYS THIS TIME!
CAN WE REALLY TRUST THEM?
PIKAPI?
OR SO WE SAY.
BUT REALLY, UNDER COVER OF REPORTING ON THE BARON, WE'LL CAPTURE BOTH DARKRAI AND PIKACHU♡.
OF COURSE, MEOWTH!
DARKRAI!
VWSH
YOU'RE NOT GETTING AWAY THIS TIME!

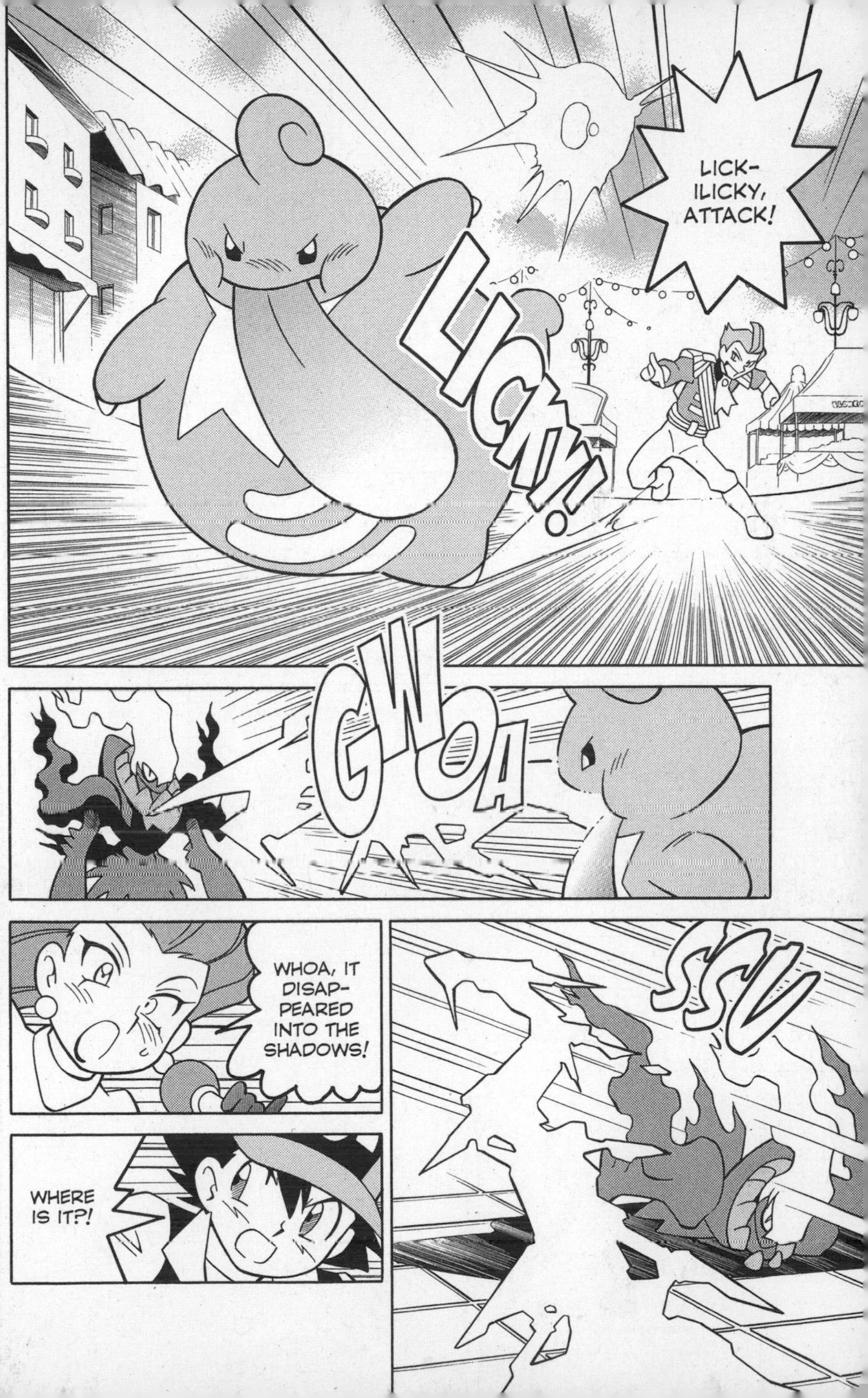
LICK-ILICKY, ATTACK!
LICKY!
GWOA
SSU
WHOA, IT DISAP-PEARED INTO THE SHADOWS!
WHERE IS IT?!

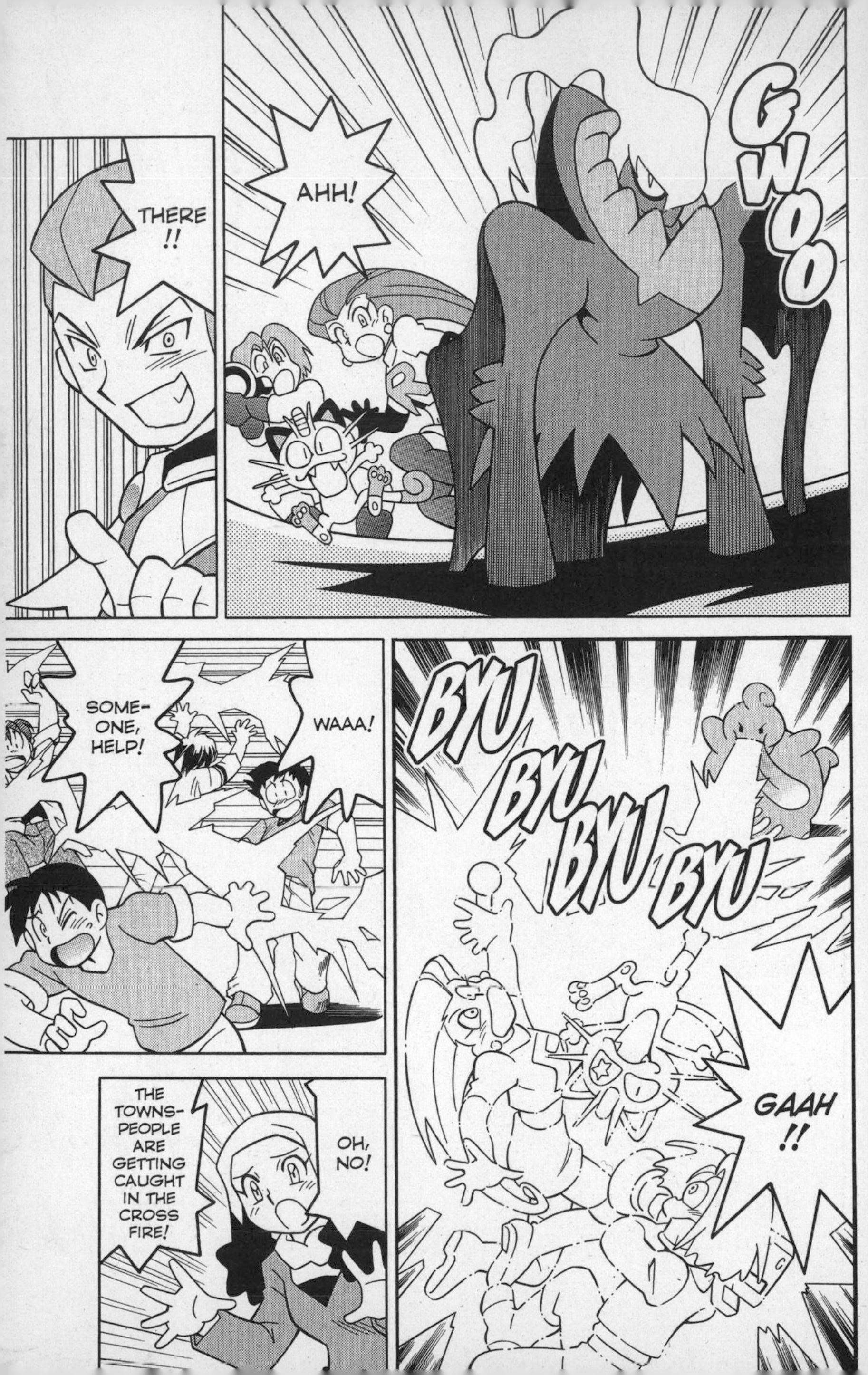
GWOO
AHH!
THERE !!
BYU BYU BYU BYU
GAAH !!
WAAA!
SOME-ONE, HELP!
OH, NO!
THE TOWNS-PEOPLE ARE GETTING CAUGHT IN THE CROSS FIRE!

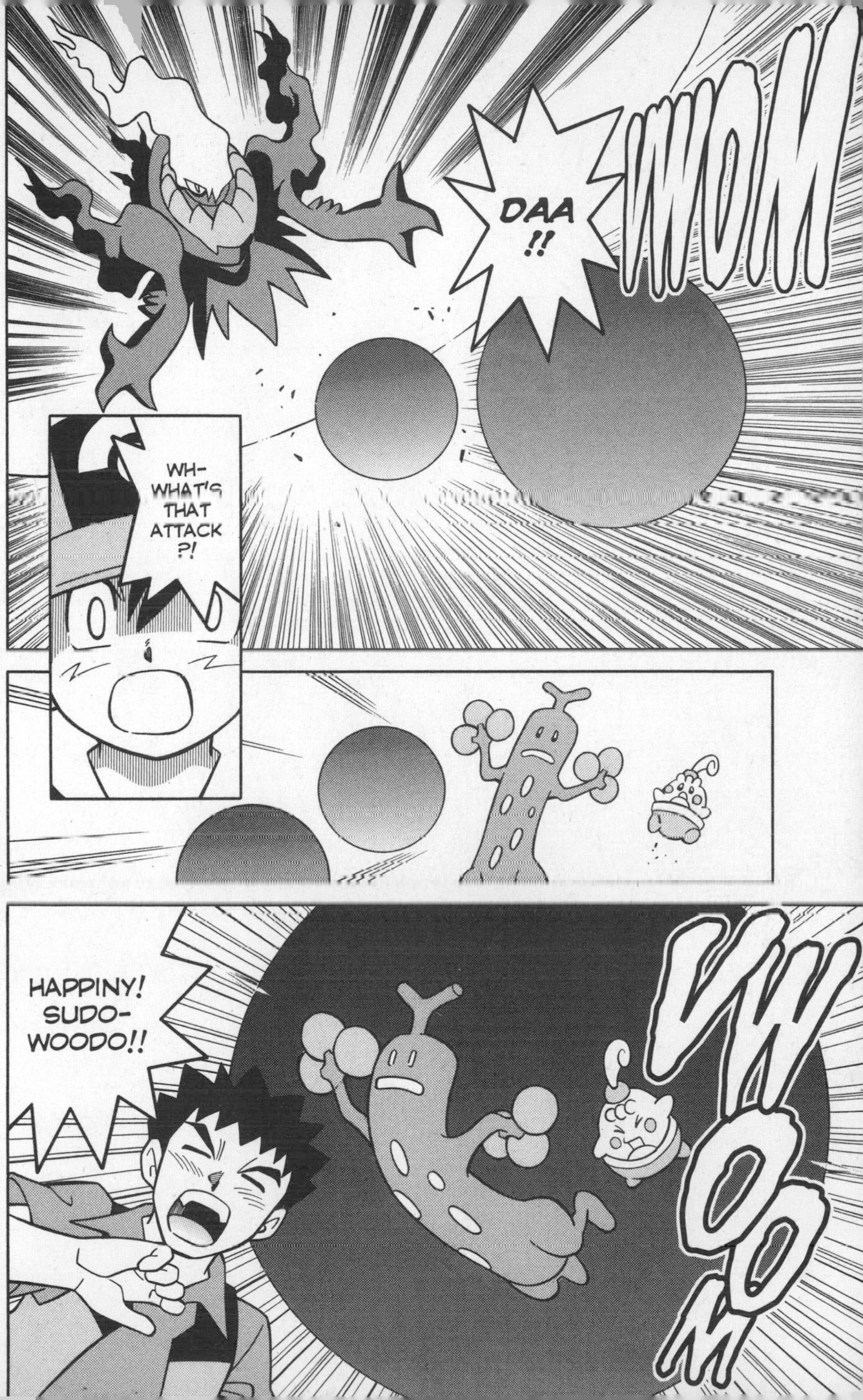
VWOM
DAA!!
WH-WHAT'S THAT ATTACK?!
VWOOM
HAPPINY! SUDOWOODO!!

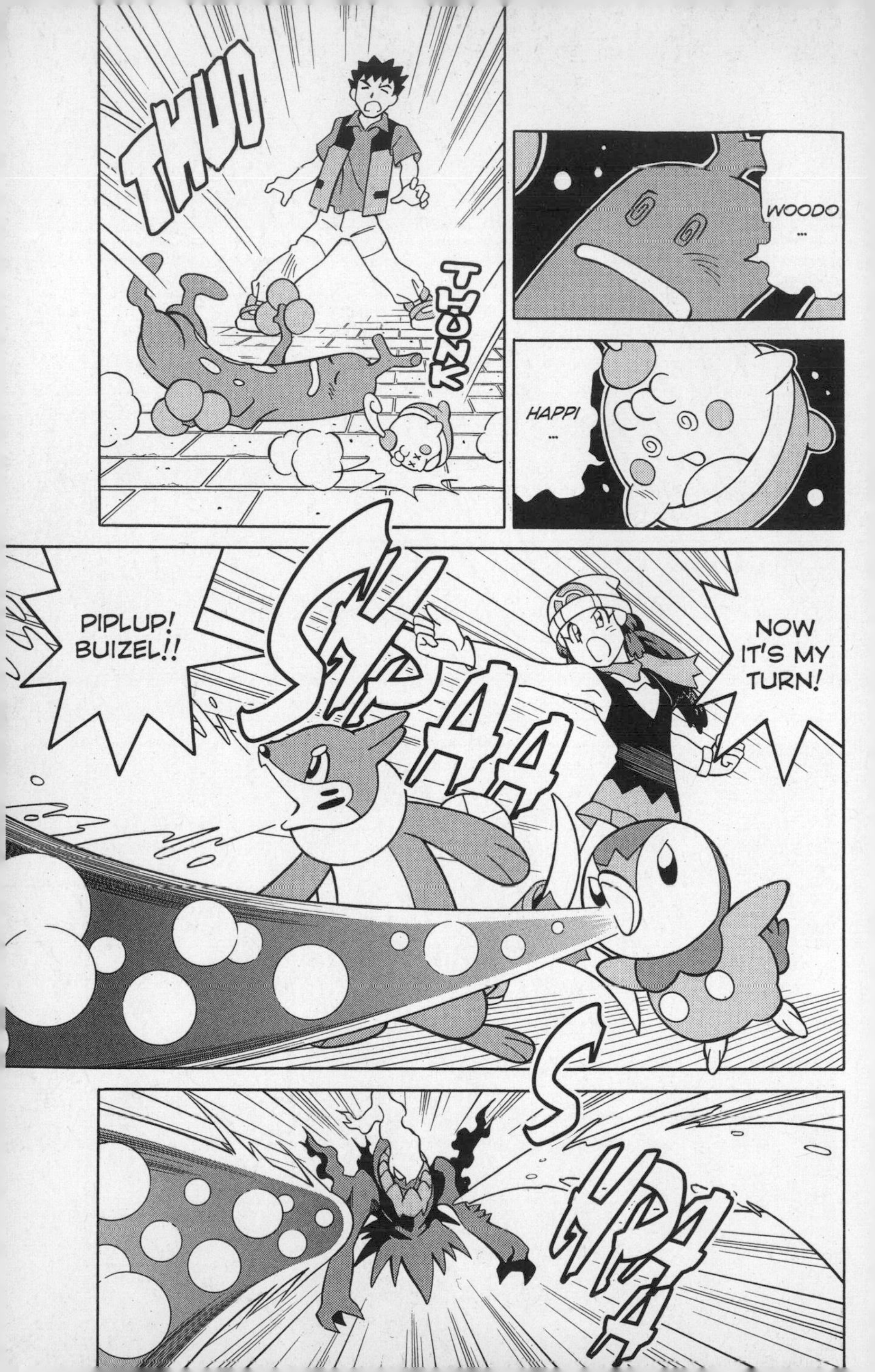

WOODO ...
HAPPI ...
THUD
THUNK
NOW IT'S MY TURN!
PIPLUP! BUIZEL!!

HOW CAN IT MOVE SO FAST?!

VWO VWO VWO

VWSH VWSH VWSH

50

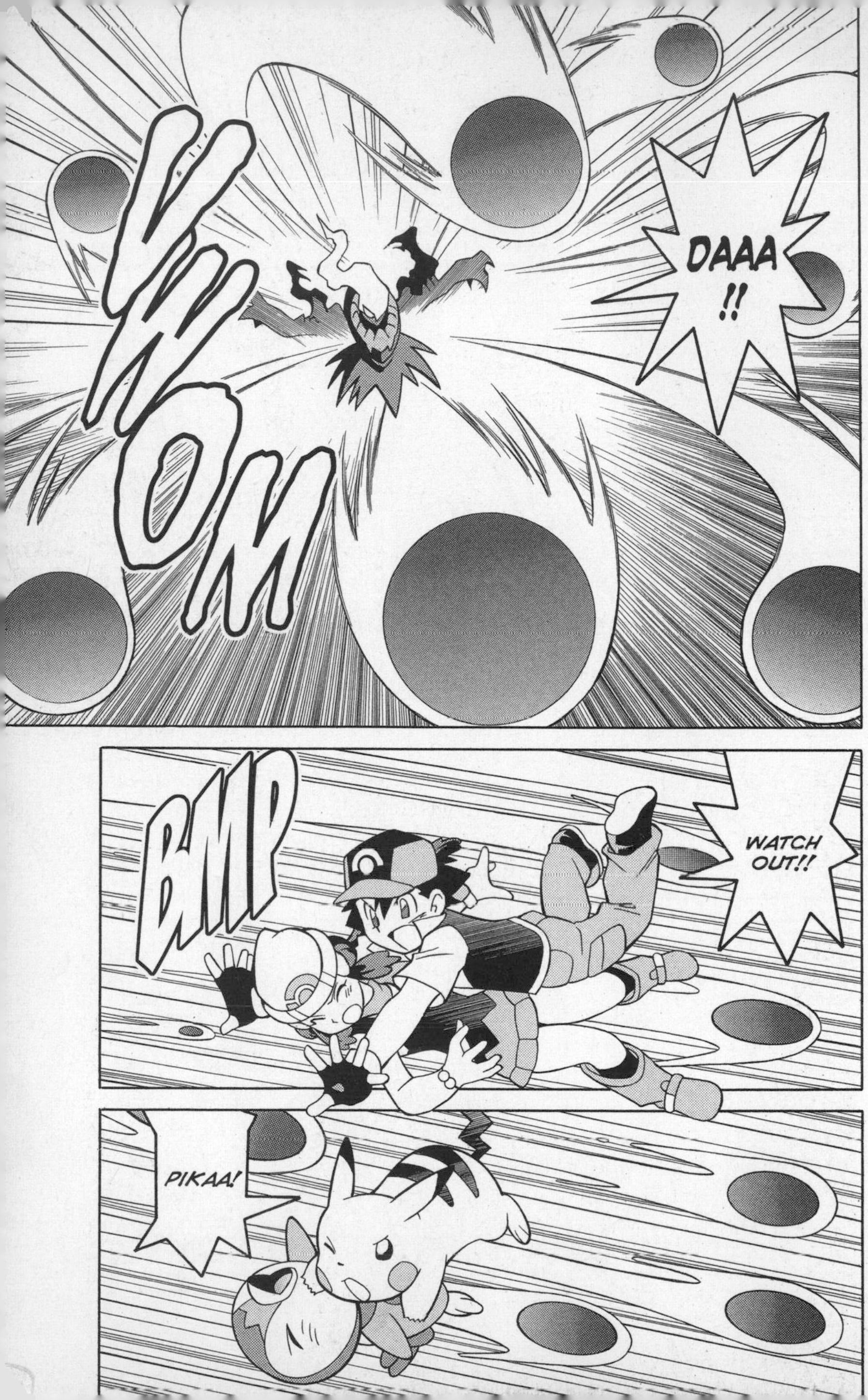
DAAA !!
VWOM
WATCH OUT!!
BMP
PIKAA!

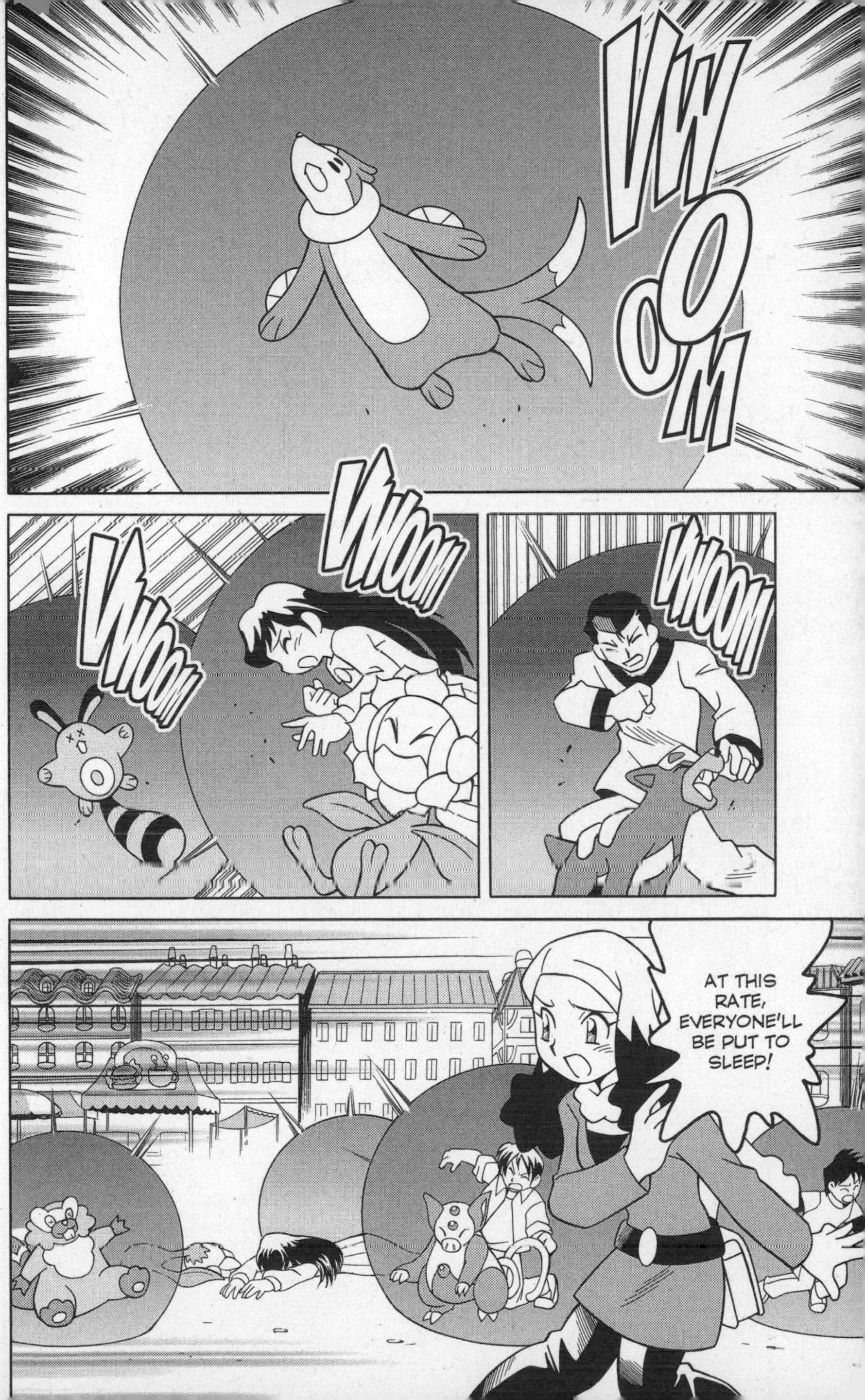
VVWOOM
VWOOM
VWOOM
VWOOM
AT THIS RATE, EVERYONE'LL BE PUT TO SLEEP!

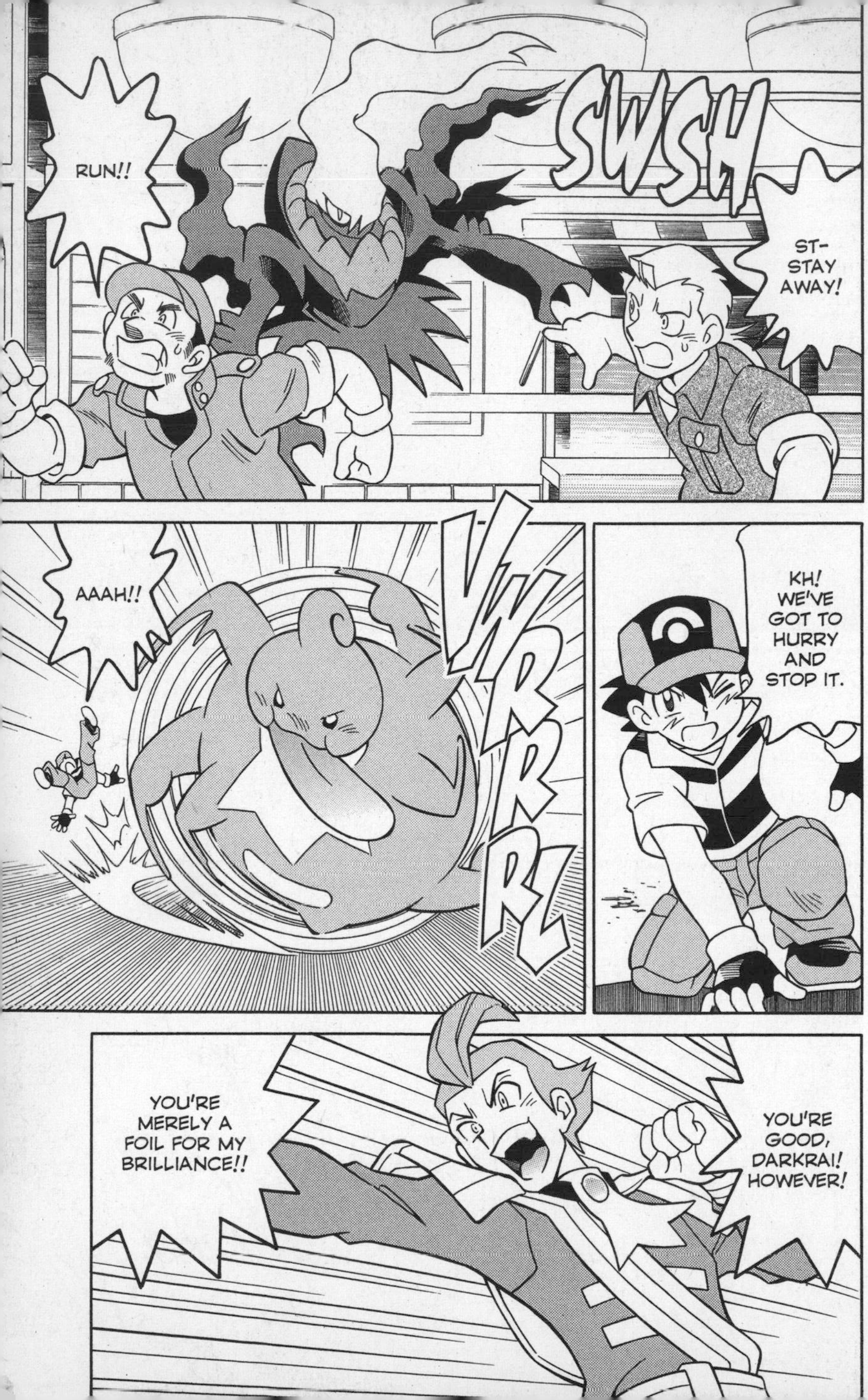
SWSH
ST-STAY AWAY!
RUN!!
KH! WE'VE GOT TO HURRY AND STOP IT.
VWRRRL
AAAH!!
YOU'RE GOOD, DARKRAI! HOWEVER!
YOU'RE MERELY A FOIL FOR MY BRILLIANCE!!

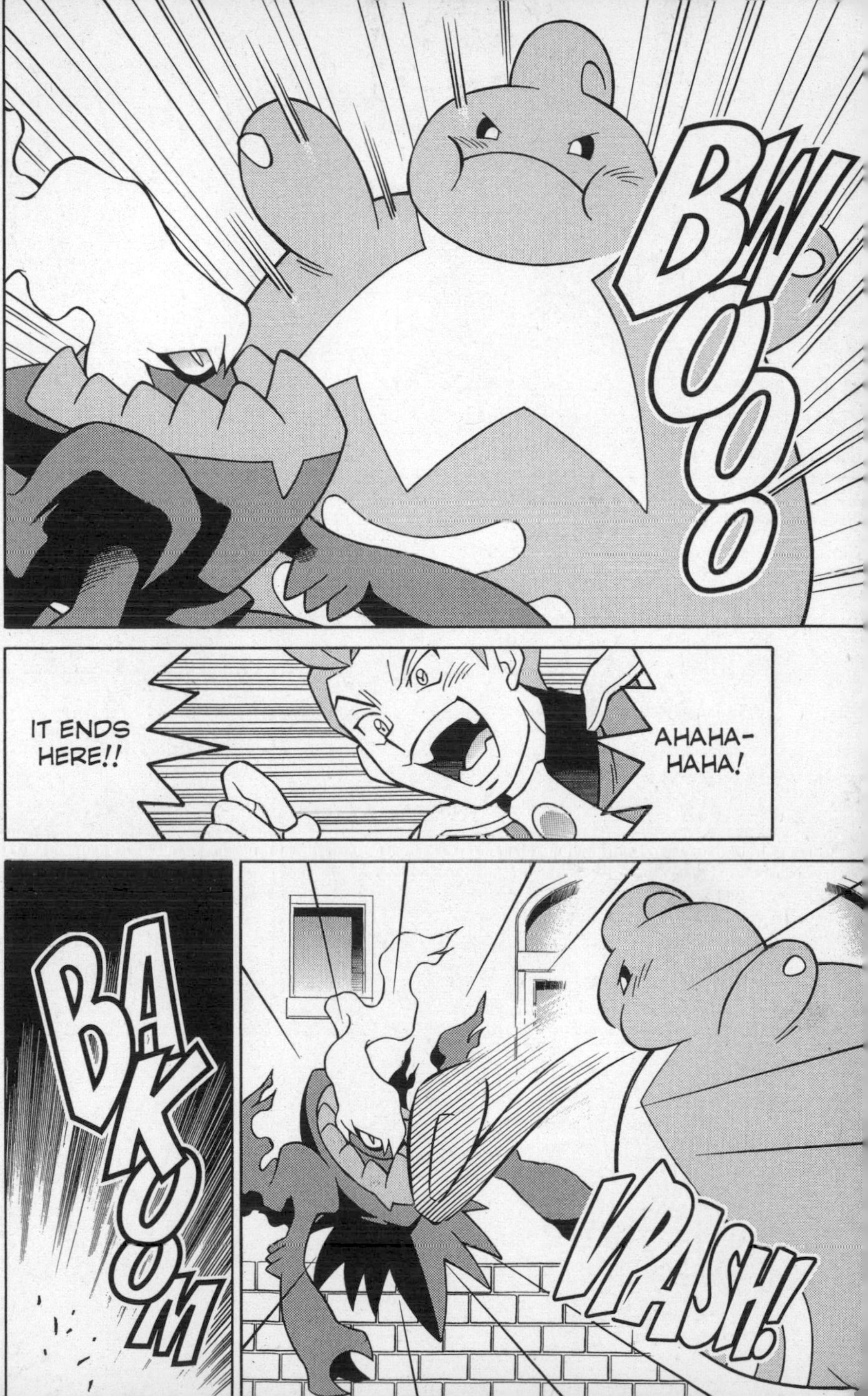
BWOOOO
AHAHA-HAHA!
IT ENDS HERE!!
VRASH!
BAKOOM

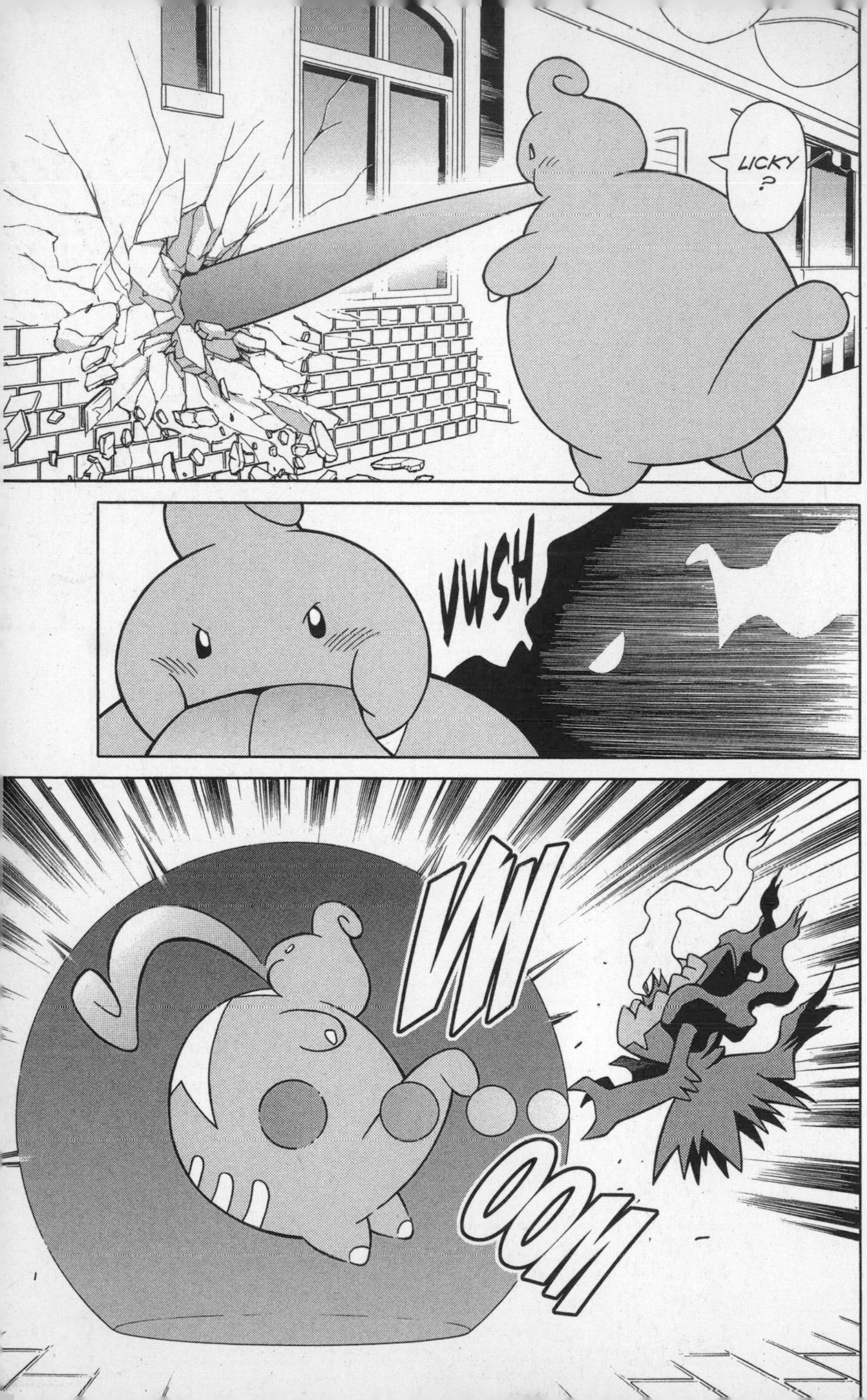
LICKY ?
VWSH
VWOOM

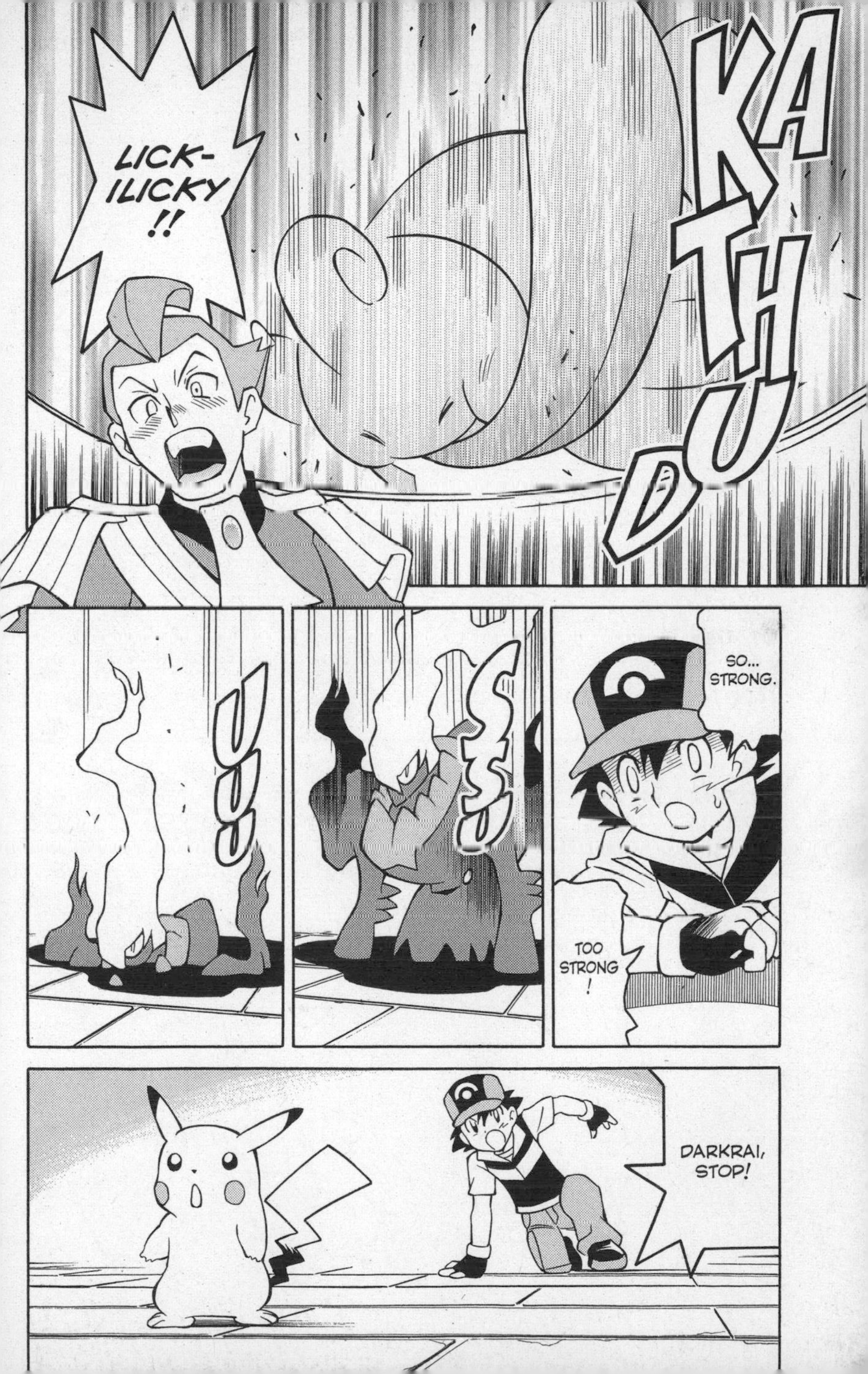
KATHUD
LICK-ILICKY!!
SO... STRONG.
TOO STRONG!
DARKRAI, STOP!

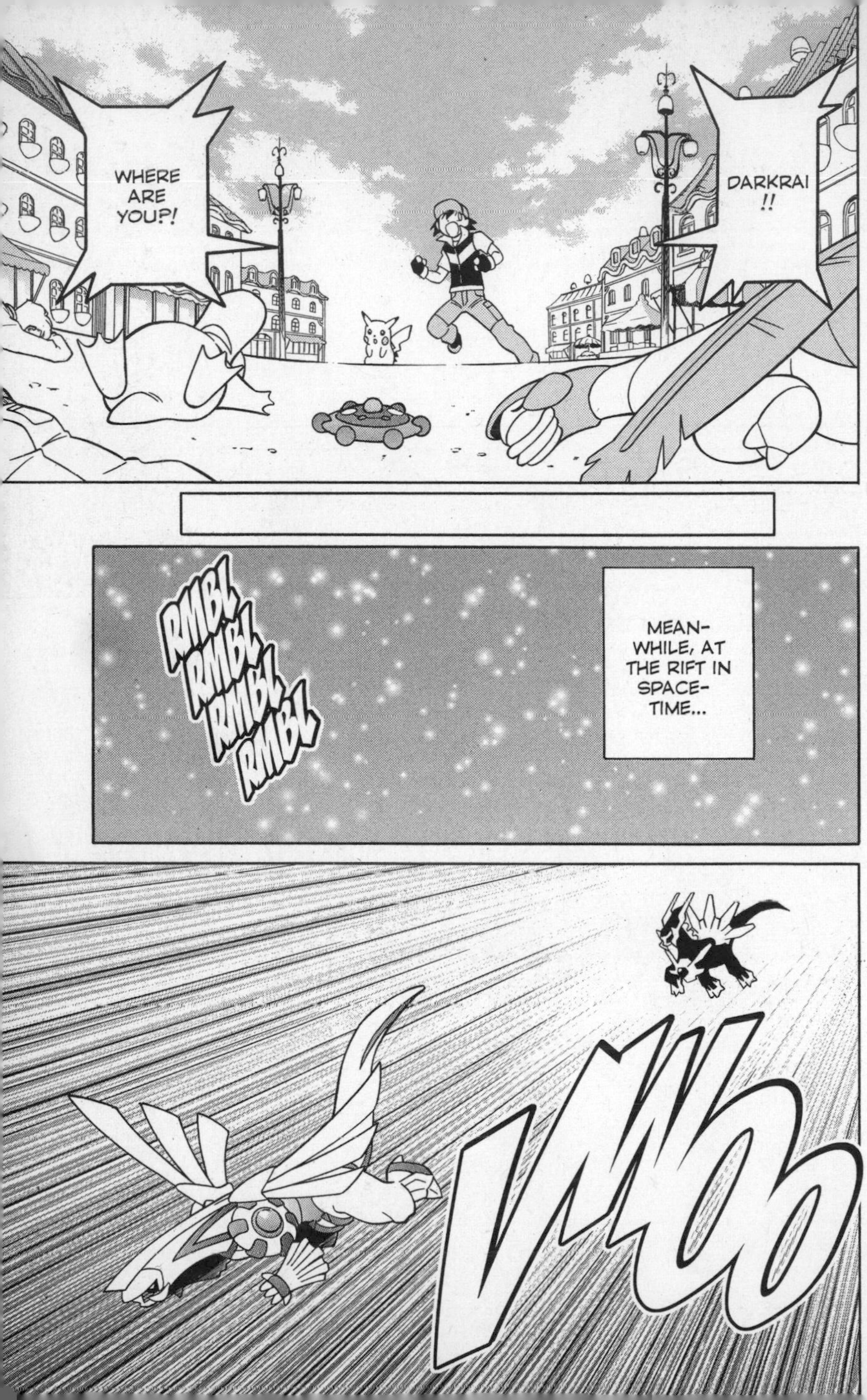
DARKRAI !!
WHERE ARE YOU?!
MEAN-WHILE, AT THE RIFT IN SPACE-TIME...
RMBL RMBL RMBL RMBL
VWOO

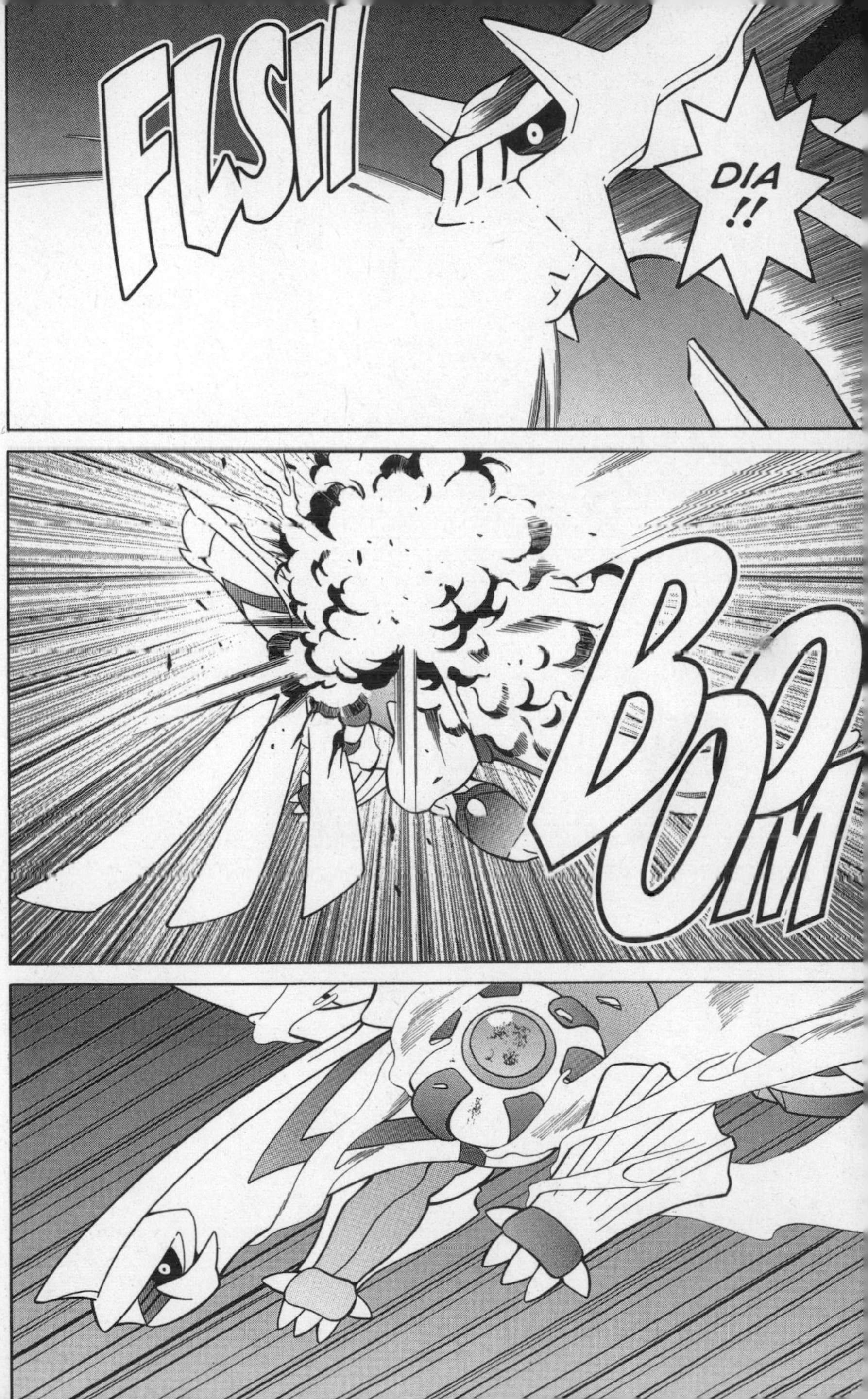
DIA !!
FLSH
BOOM

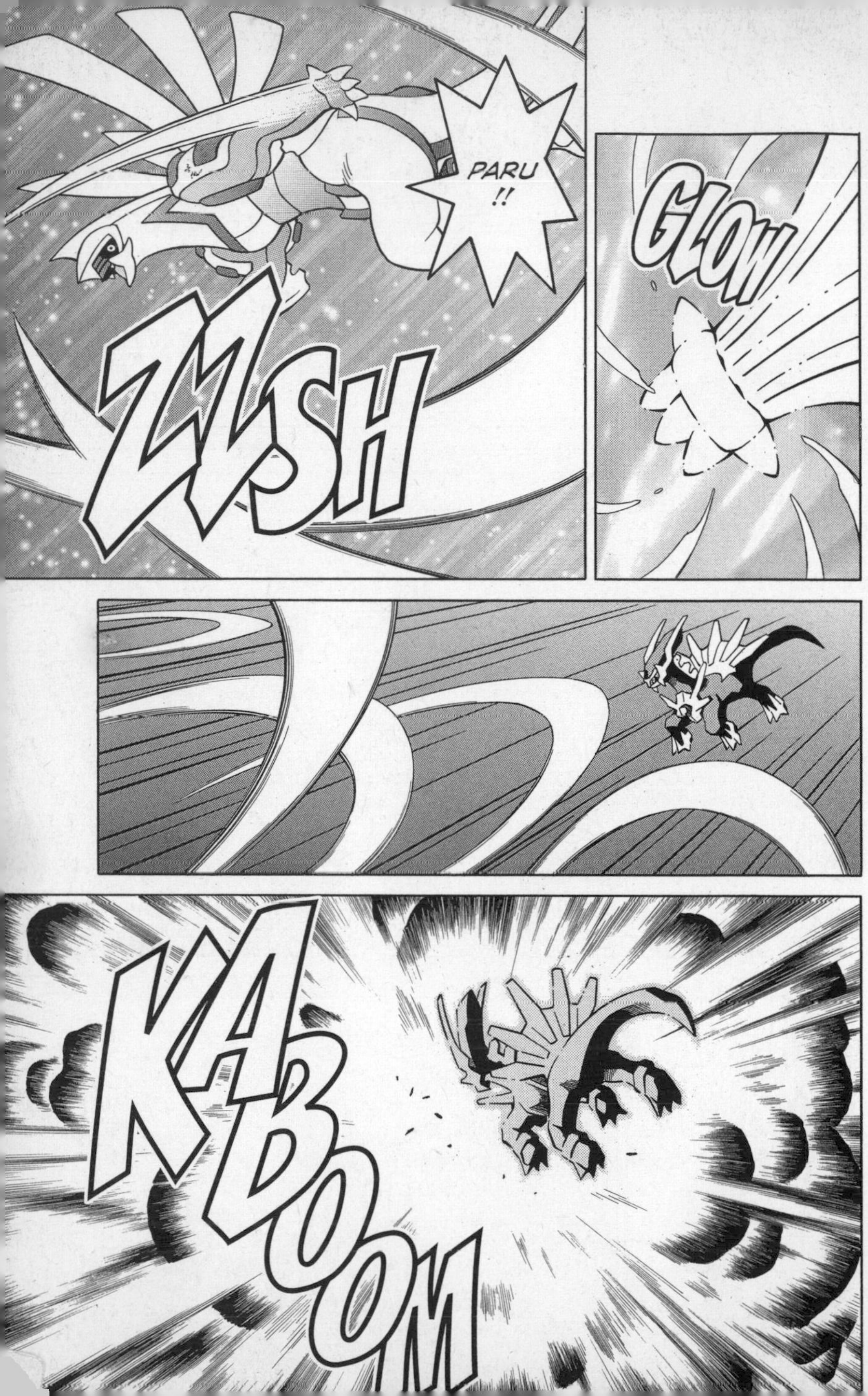
GLOW
PARU !!
ZZSH
KABOOM

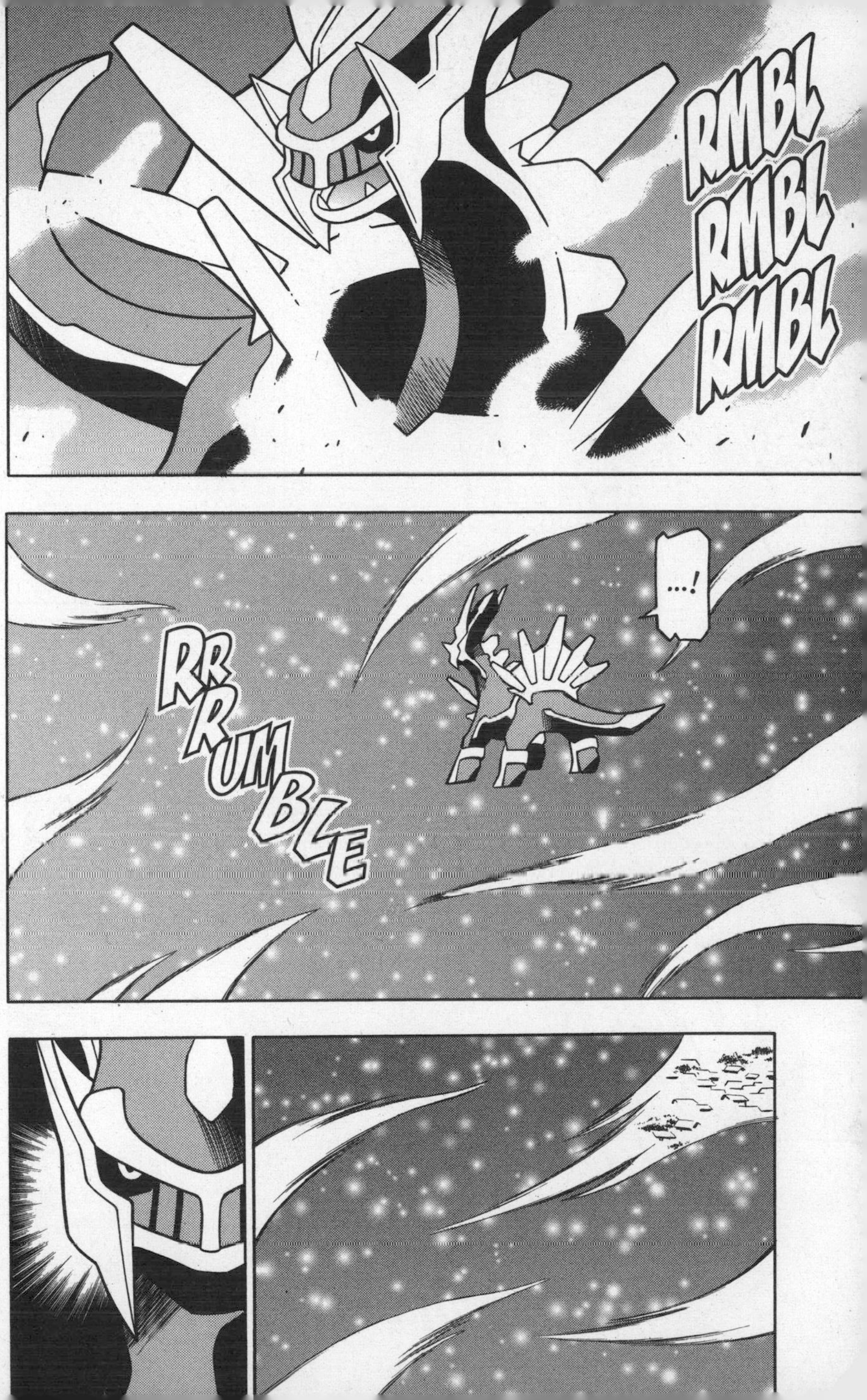
RMBL
RMBL
RMBL
...!
RRRUMBLE

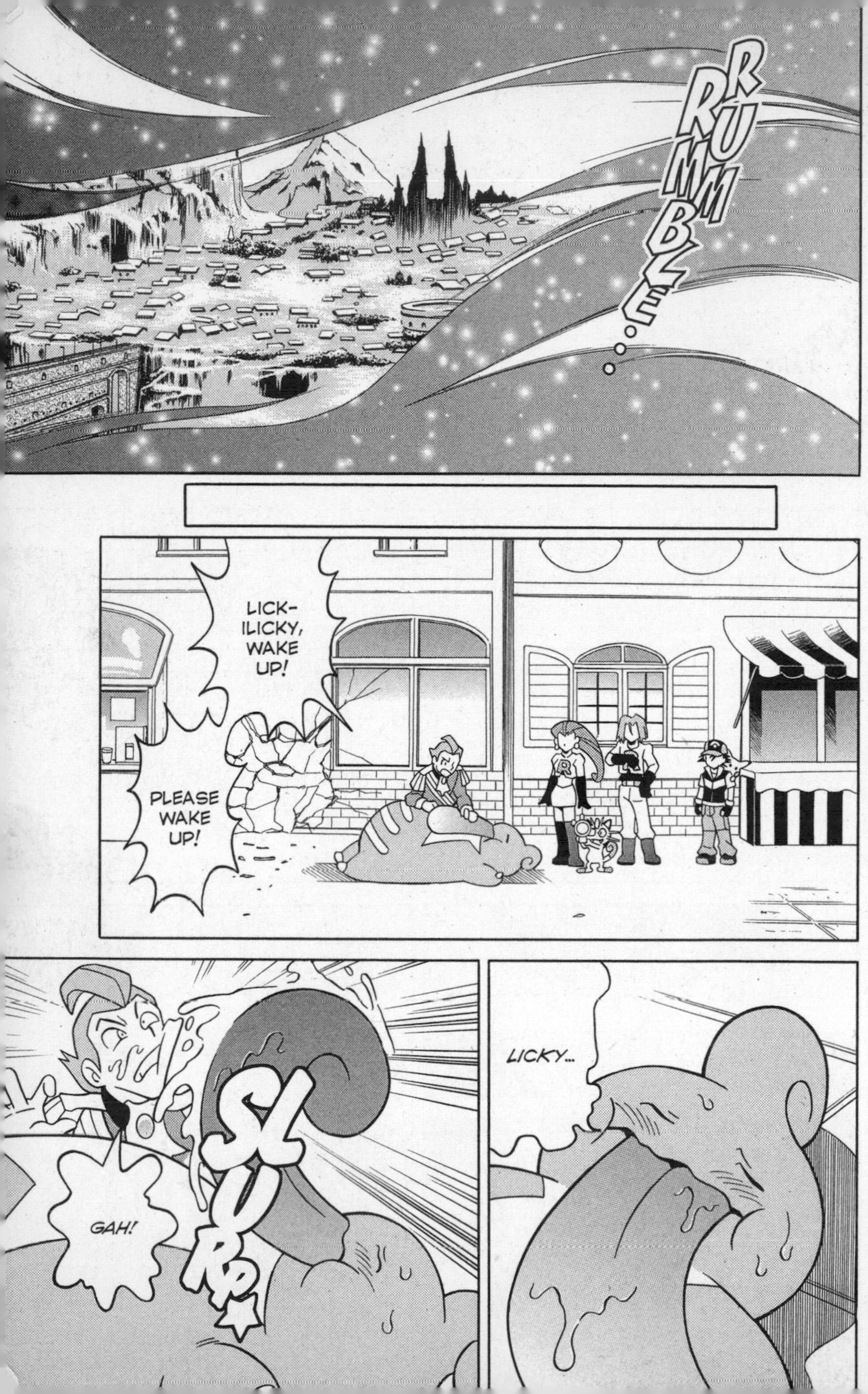
RRUMMBLE...
LICK-ILICKY, WAKE UP!
PLEASE WAKE UP!
LICKY...
SLURP
GAH!

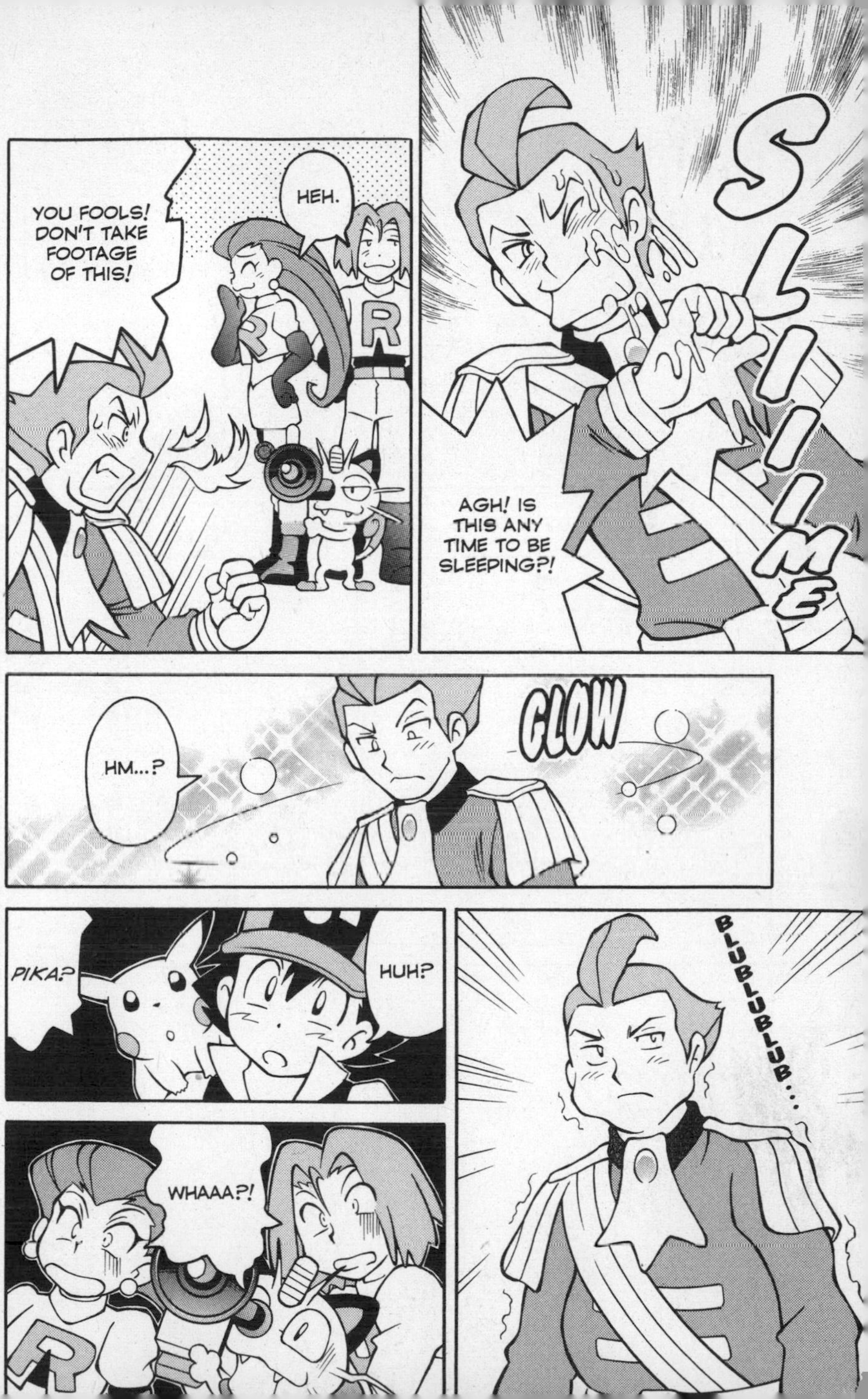
SLIIIME
AGH! IS THIS ANY TIME TO BE SLEEPING?!
HEH.
YOU FOOLS! DON'T TAKE FOOTAGE OF THIS!
GLOW
HM...?
BLUBLUBLUB...
HUH?
PIKA?
WHAAA?!

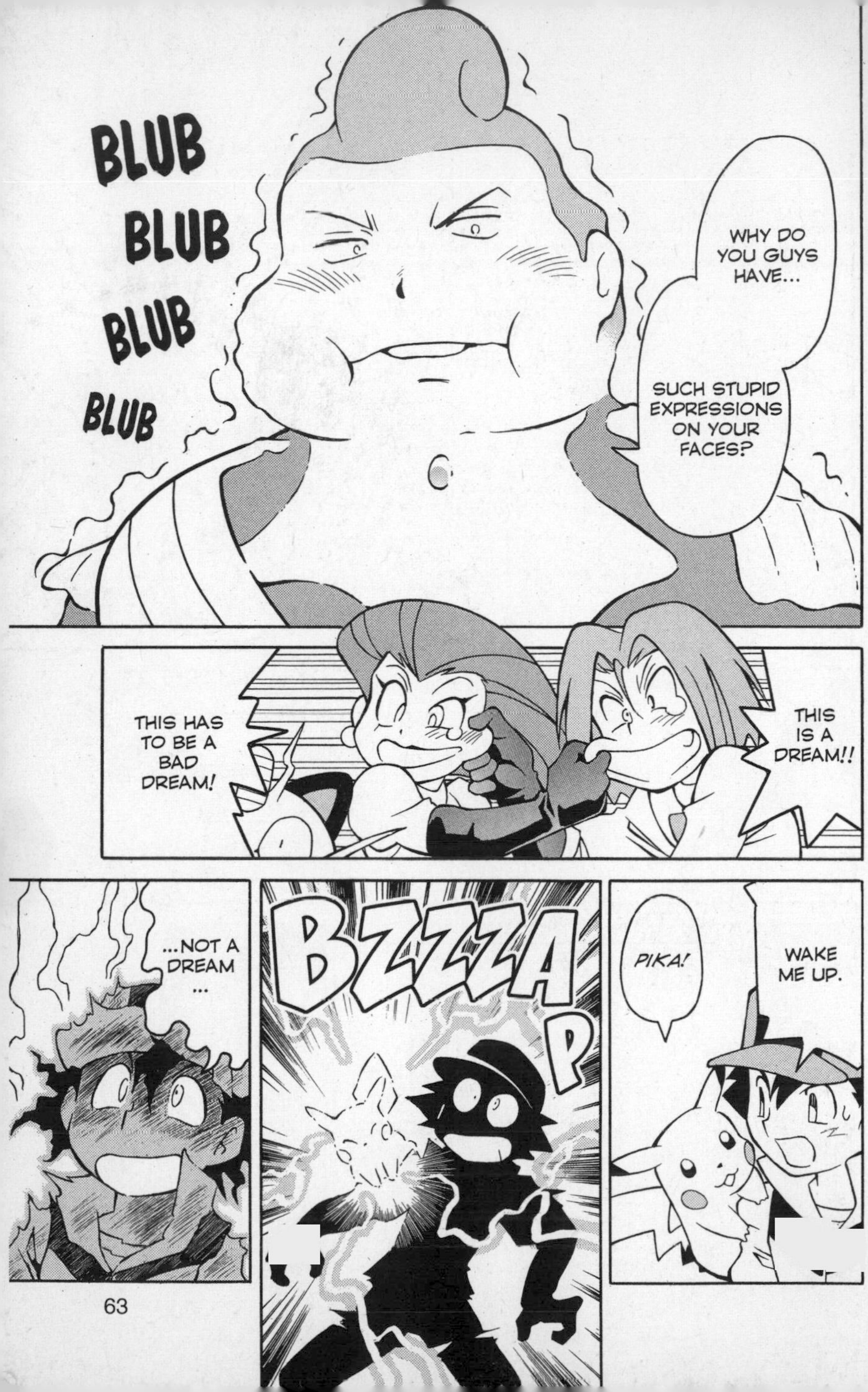
BLUB
BLUB
BLUB
BLUB
WHY DO YOU GUYS HAVE...
SUCH STUPID EXPRESSIONS ON YOUR FACES?
THIS IS A DREAM!!
THIS HAS TO BE A BAD DREAM!
WAKE ME UP.
PIKA!
BZZZAP
...NOT A DREAM ...

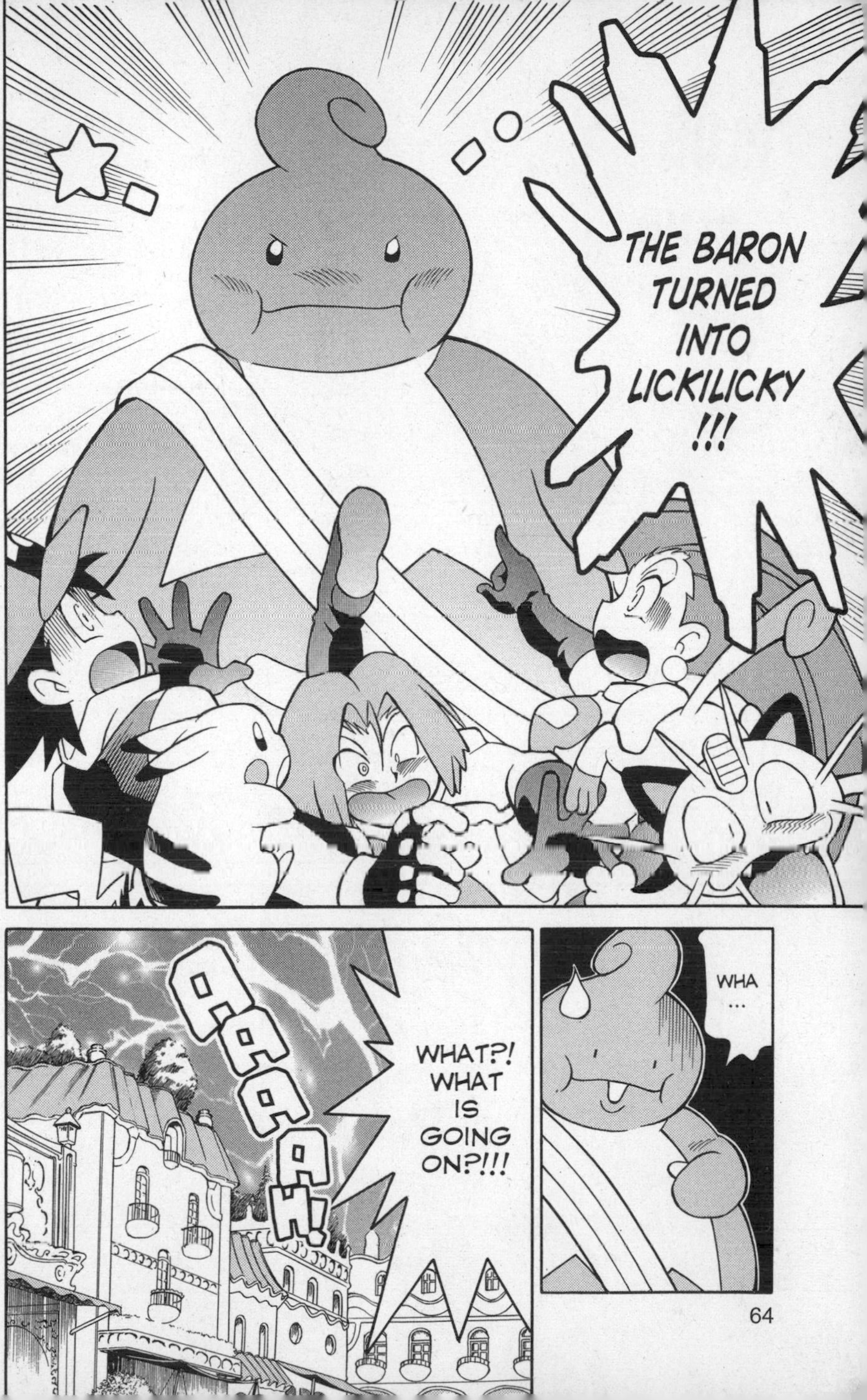
THE BARON TURNED INTO LICKILICKY !!!
WHA ...
WHAT?! WHAT IS GOING ON?!!!
AAAAAH!

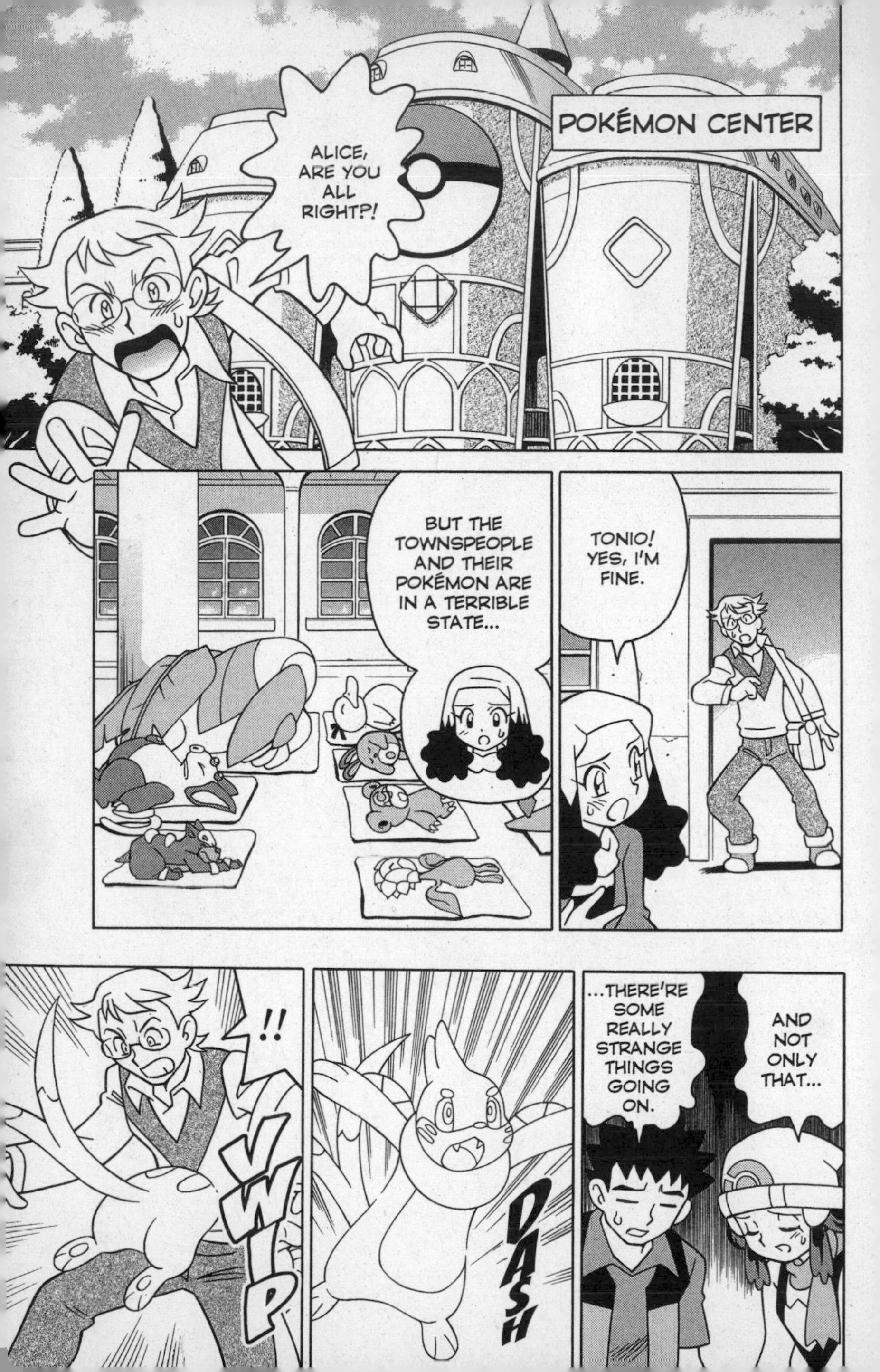
POKÉMON CENTER
ALICE, ARE YOU ALL RIGHT?!
TONIO! YES, I'M FINE.
BUT THE TOWNSPEOPLE AND THEIR POKÉMON ARE IN A TERRIBLE STATE...
AND NOT ONLY THAT...
...THERE'RE SOME REALLY STRANGE THINGS GOING ON.
DASH
!!
WHIP

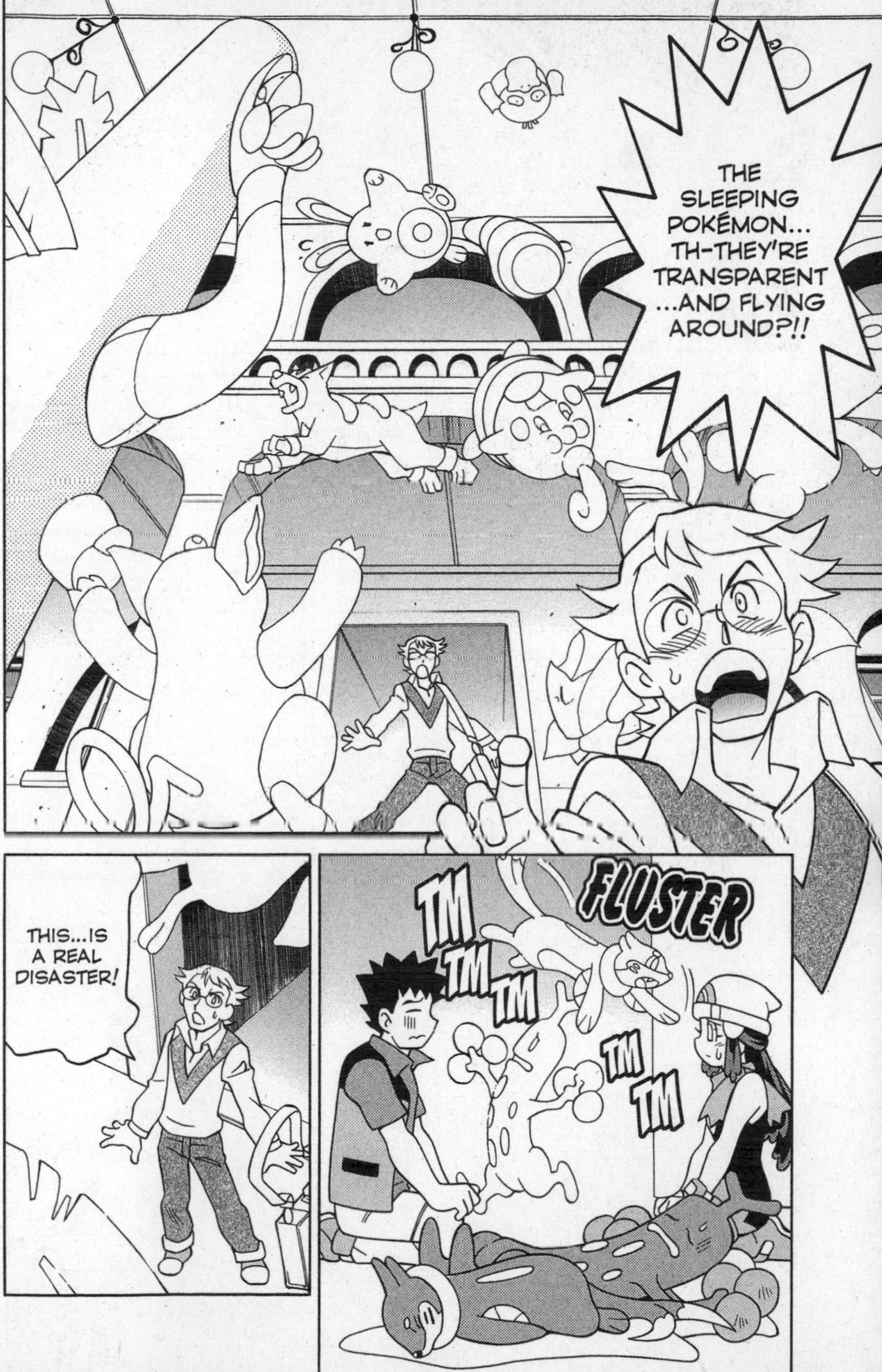
THE SLEEPING POKÉMON... TH-THEY'RE TRANSPARENT ...AND FLYING AROUND?!!
FLUSTER
TM
TM
TM
TM
TM
THIS...IS A REAL DISASTER!

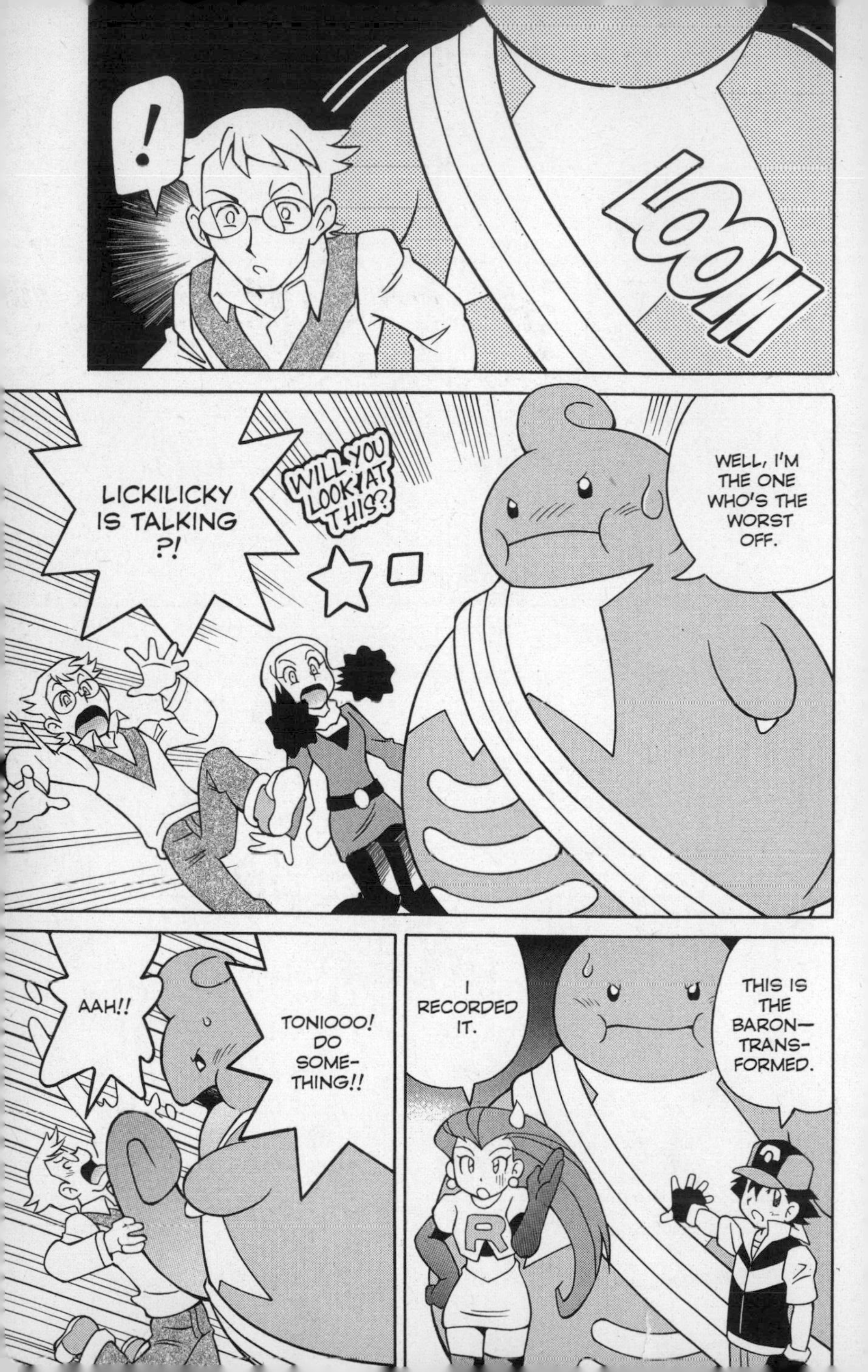
LOOM
!
WELL, I'M THE ONE WHO'S THE WORST OFF.
WILL YOU LOOK AT THIS?
LICKILICKY IS TALKING ?!
THIS IS THE BARON—TRANSFORMED.
I RECORDED IT.
TONIOOO! DO SOME-THING!!
AAH!!

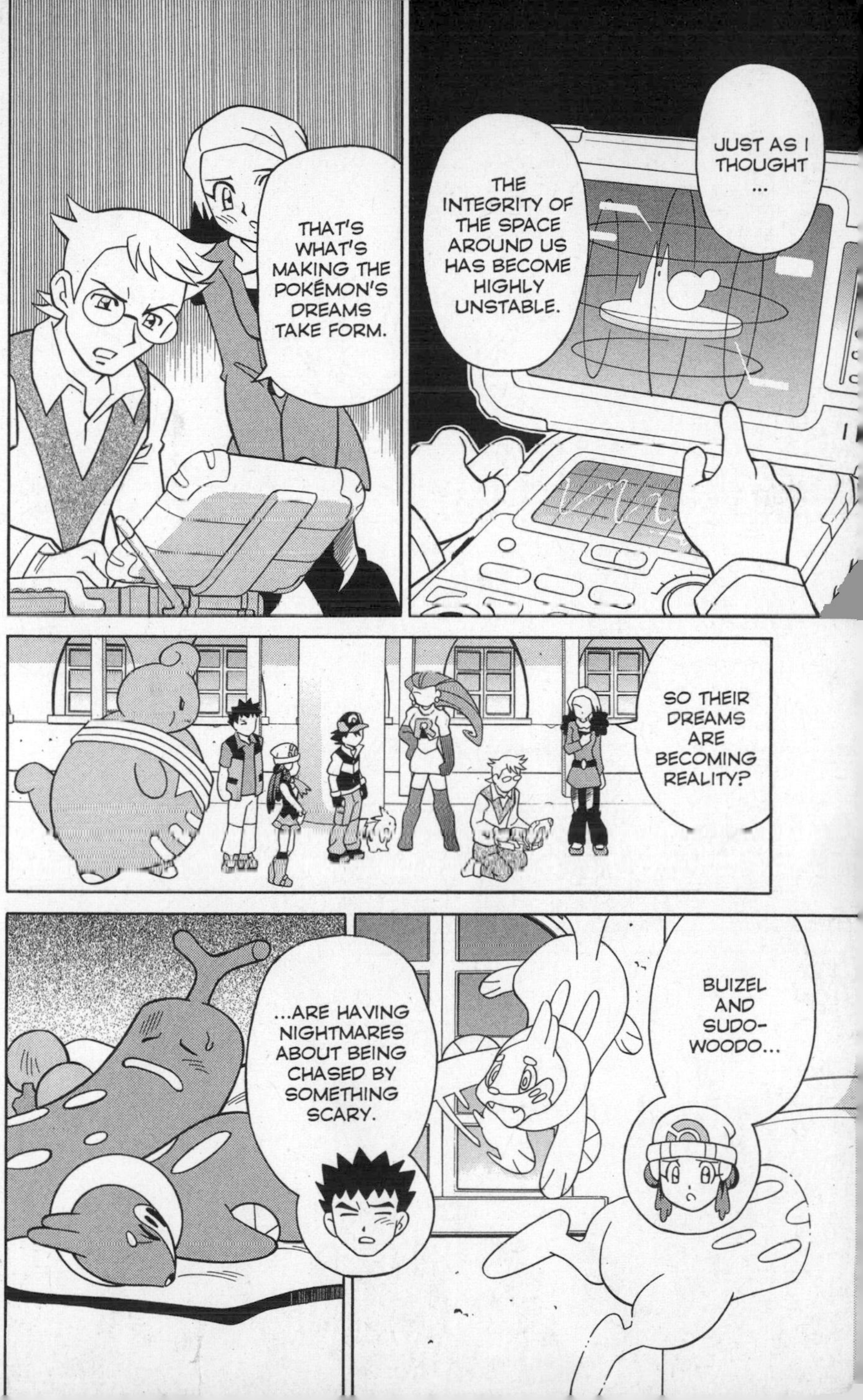
JUST AS I THOUGHT ...
THE INTEGRITY OF THE SPACE AROUND US HAS BECOME HIGHLY UNSTABLE.
THAT'S WHAT'S MAKING THE POKÉMON'S DREAMS TAKE FORM.
SO THEIR DREAMS ARE BECOMING REALITY?
BUIZEL AND SUDO-WOODO...
...ARE HAVING NIGHTMARES ABOUT BEING CHASED BY SOMETHING SCARY.

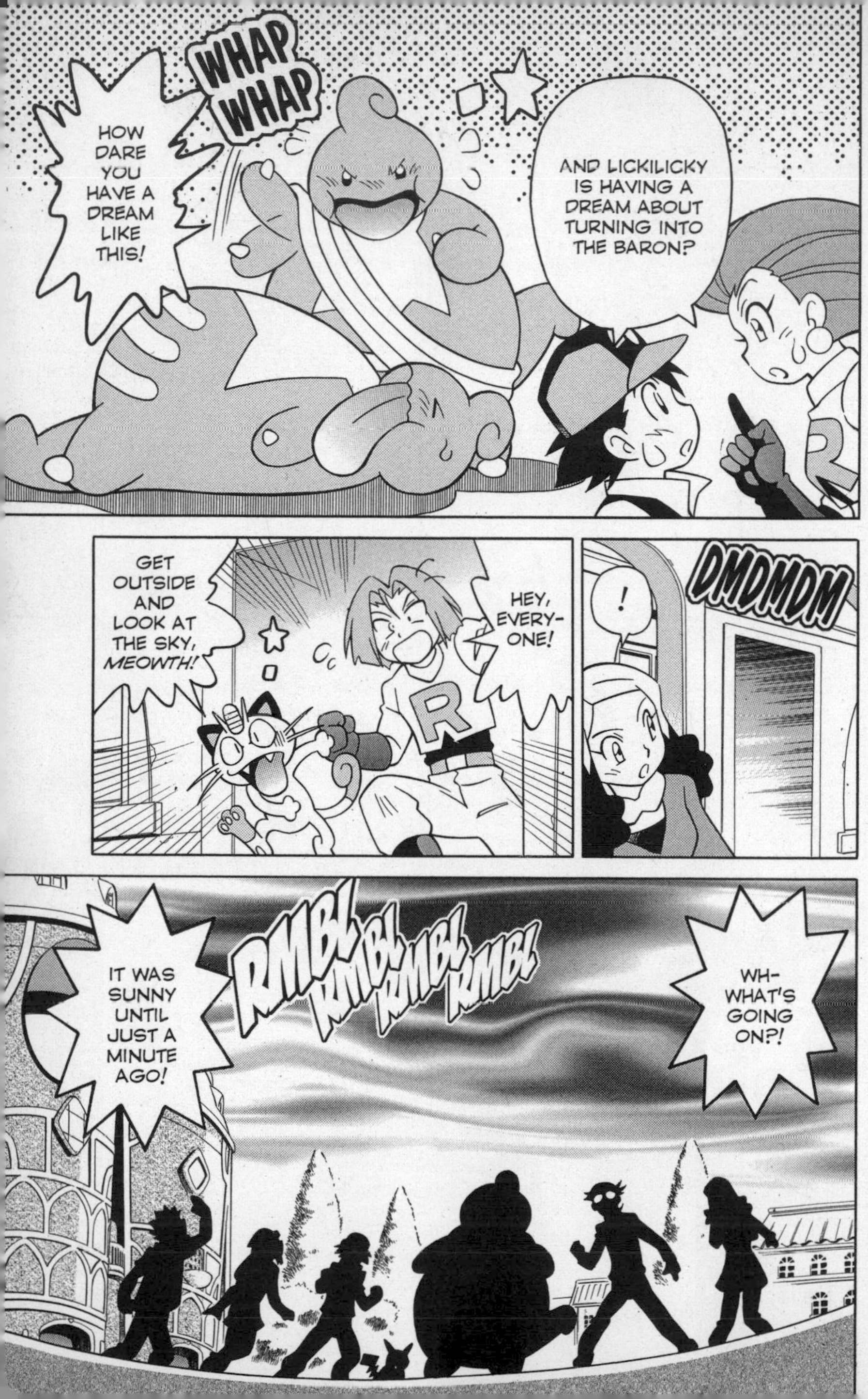
AND LICKILICKY IS HAVING A DREAM ABOUT TURNING INTO THE BARON?
WHAP WHAP
HOW DARE YOU HAVE A DREAM LIKE THIS!
DMDMDM
!
HEY, EVERYONE!
GET OUTSIDE AND LOOK AT THE SKY, *MEOWTH!*
WH-WHAT'S GOING ON?!
RMBL RMBL RMBL RMBL
IT WAS SUNNY UNTIL JUST A MINUTE AGO!

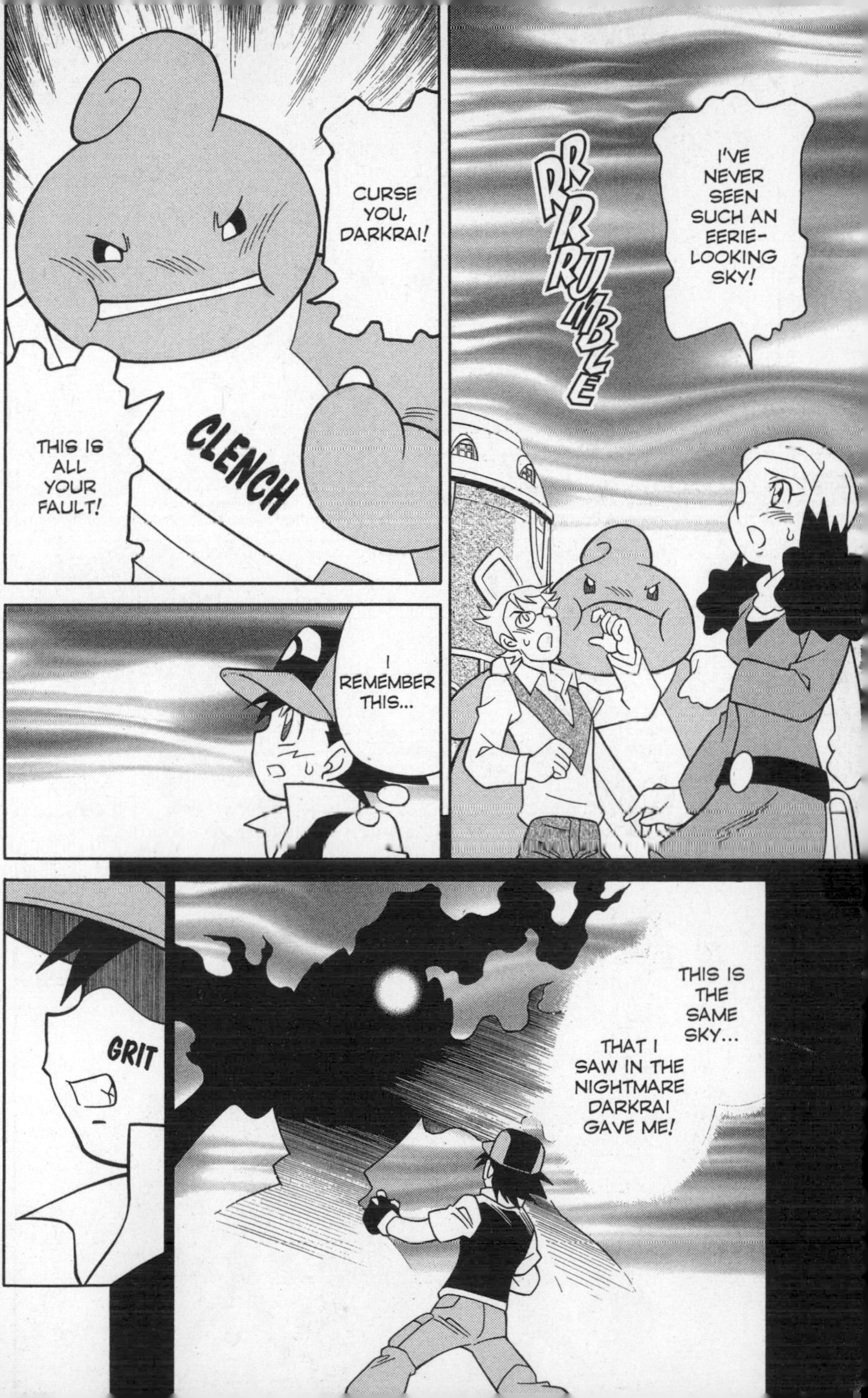
I'VE NEVER SEEN SUCH AN EERIE-LOOKING SKY!
RRRRUMBLE
CURSE YOU, DARKRAI!
THIS IS ALL YOUR FAULT!
CLENCH
I REMEMBER THIS...
THIS IS THE SAME SKY...
THAT I SAW IN THE NIGHTMARE DARKRAI GAVE ME!
GRIT

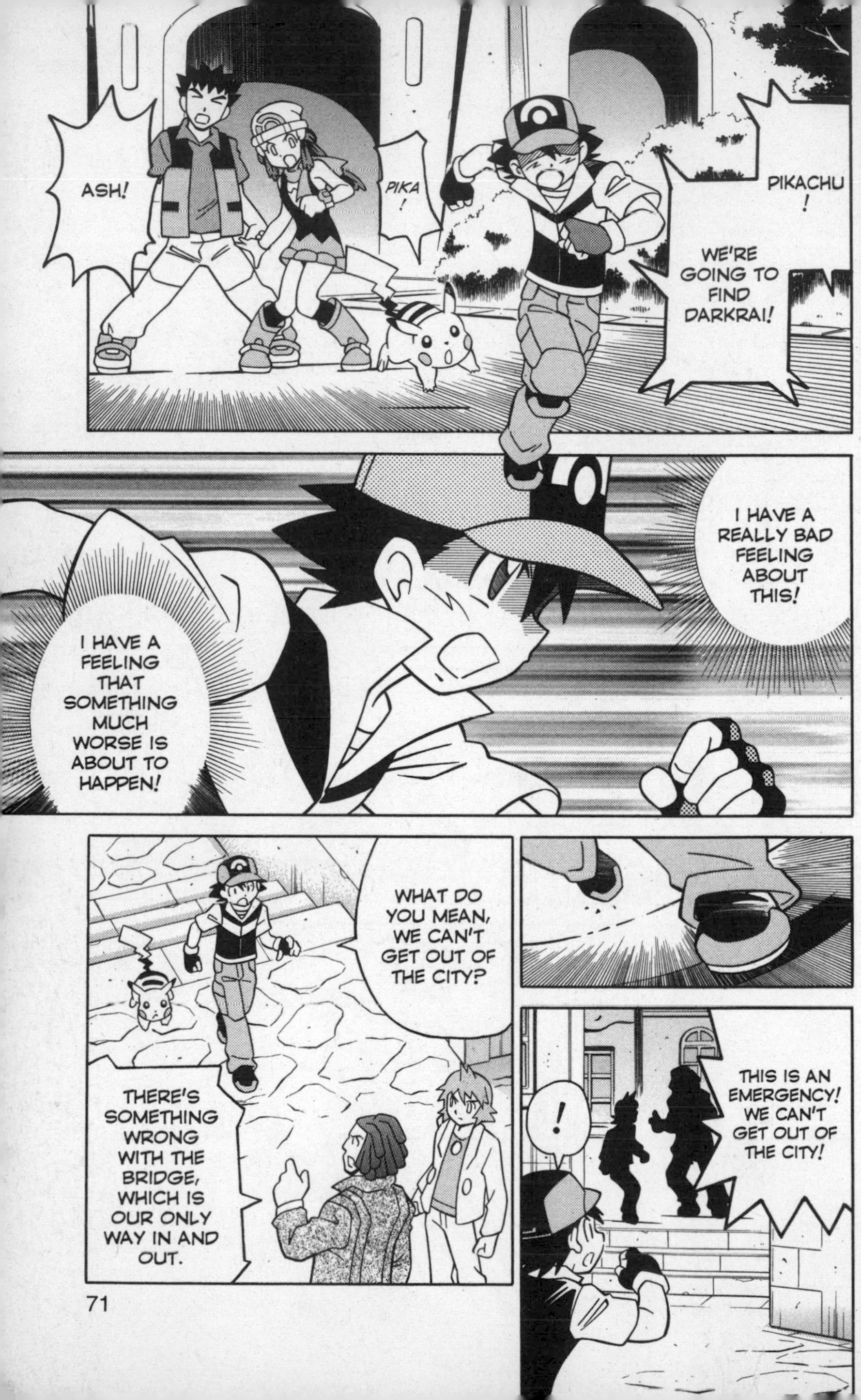
PIKACHU!
WE'RE GOING TO FIND DARKRAI!
PIKA!
ASH!
I HAVE A REALLY BAD FEELING ABOUT THIS!
I HAVE A FEELING THAT SOMETHING MUCH WORSE IS ABOUT TO HAPPEN!
THIS IS AN EMERGENCY! WE CAN'T GET OUT OF THE CITY!
!
WHAT DO YOU MEAN, WE CAN'T GET OUT OF THE CITY?
THERE'S SOMETHING WRONG WITH THE BRIDGE, WHICH IS OUR ONLY WAY IN AND OUT.

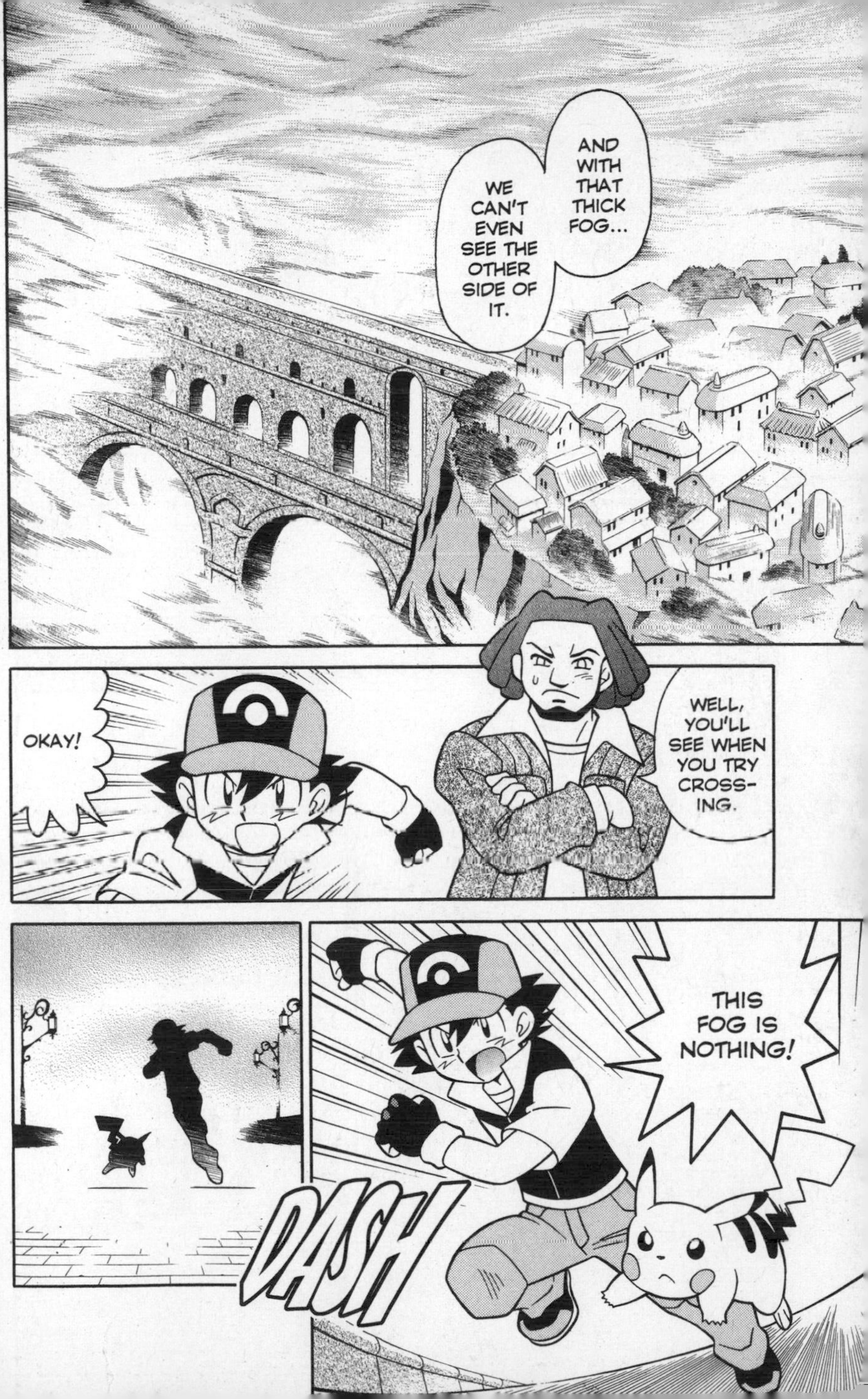
AND WITH THAT THICK FOG...
WE CAN'T EVEN SEE THE OTHER SIDE OF IT.
WELL, YOU'LL SEE WHEN YOU TRY CROSS-ING.
OKAY!
THIS FOG IS NOTHING!
DASH

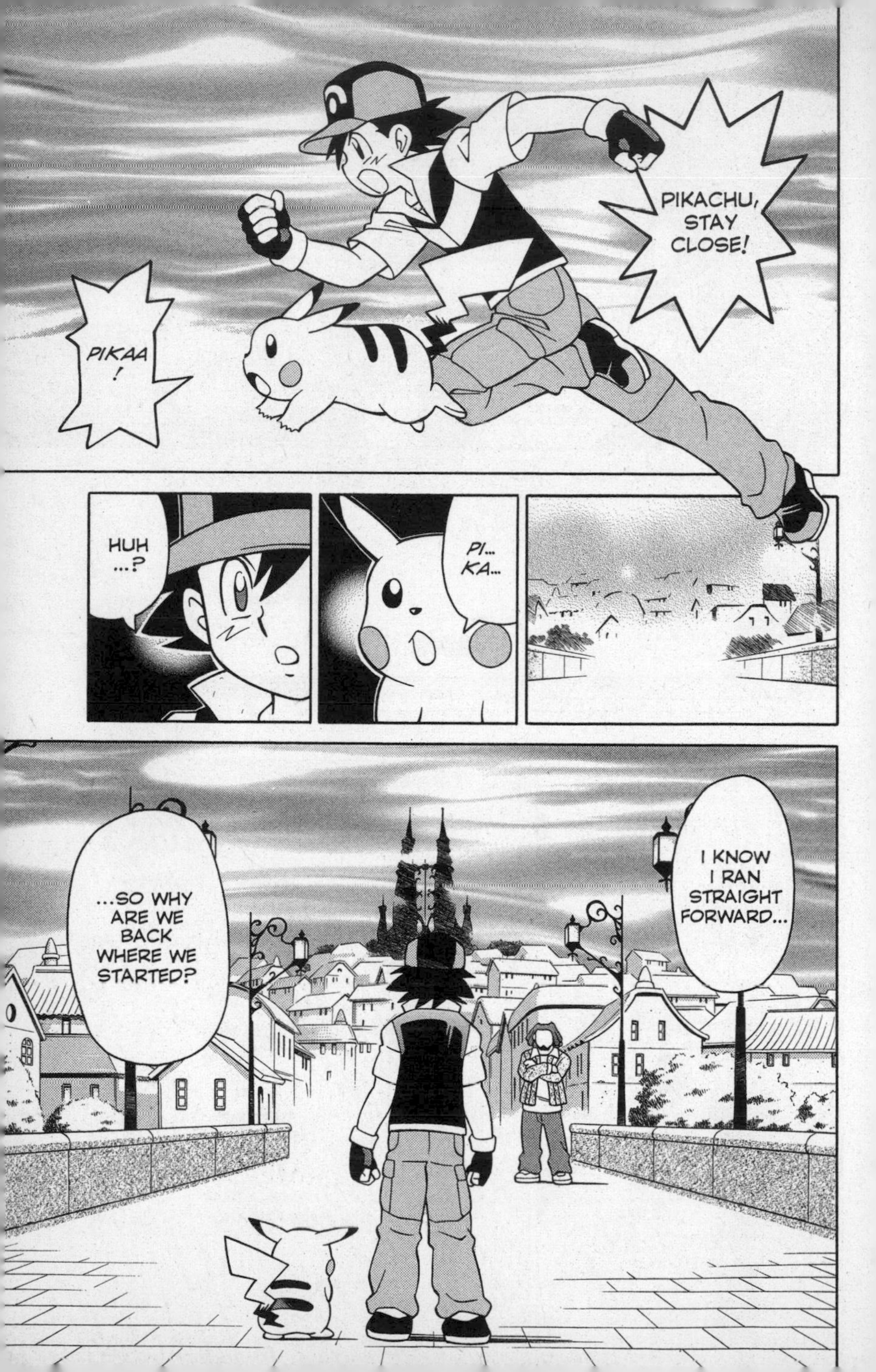
PIKACHU, STAY CLOSE!
PIKAA!
PI... KA...
HUH ...?
I KNOW I RAN STRAIGHT FORWARD...
...SO WHY ARE WE BACK WHERE WE STARTED?

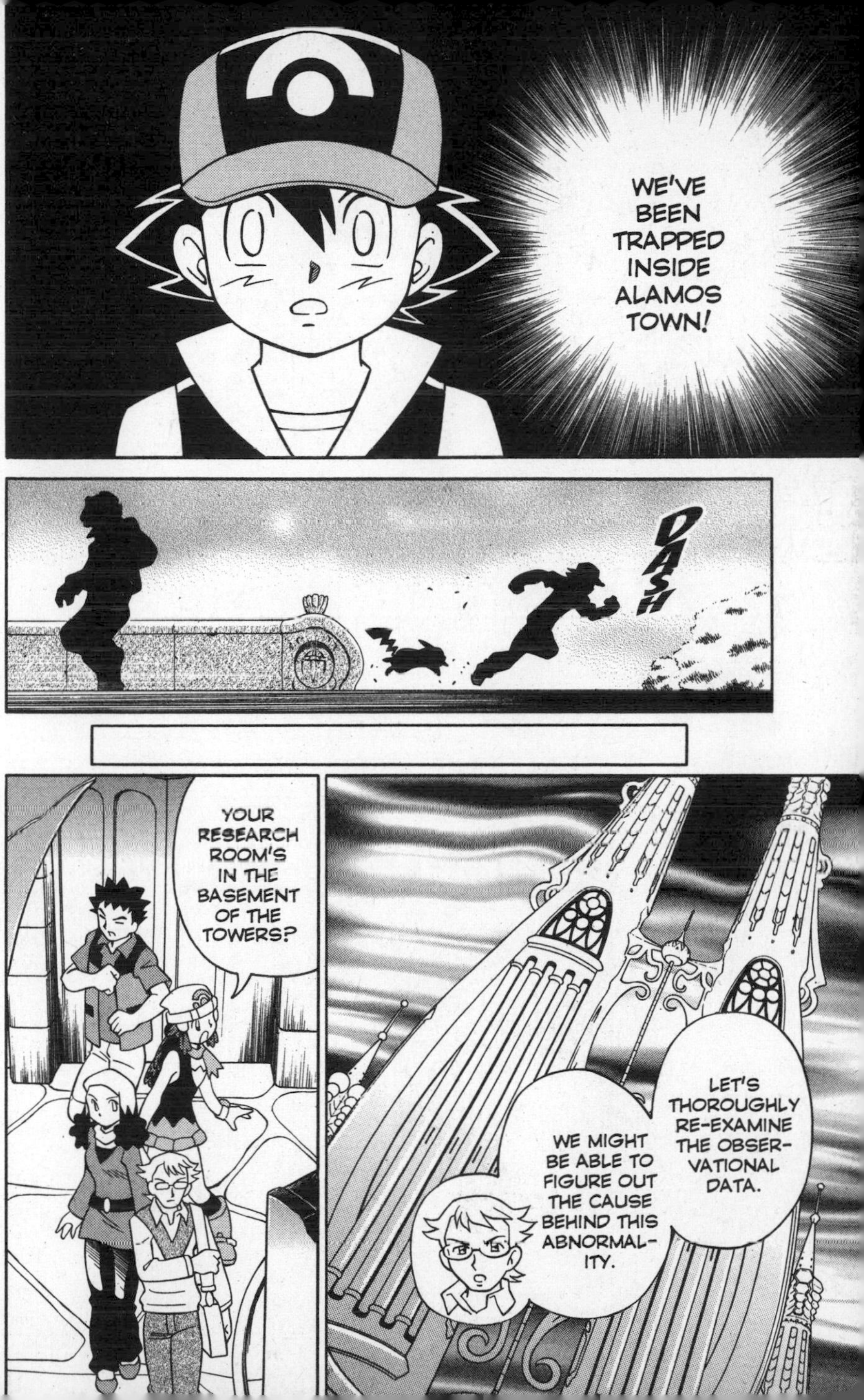
WE'VE BEEN TRAPPED INSIDE ALAMOS TOWN!
DASH
LET'S THOROUGHLY RE-EXAMINE THE OBSER-VATIONAL DATA.
WE MIGHT BE ABLE TO FIGURE OUT THE CAUSE BEHIND THIS ABNORMAL-ITY.
YOUR RESEARCH ROOM'S IN THE BASEMENT OF THE TOWERS?

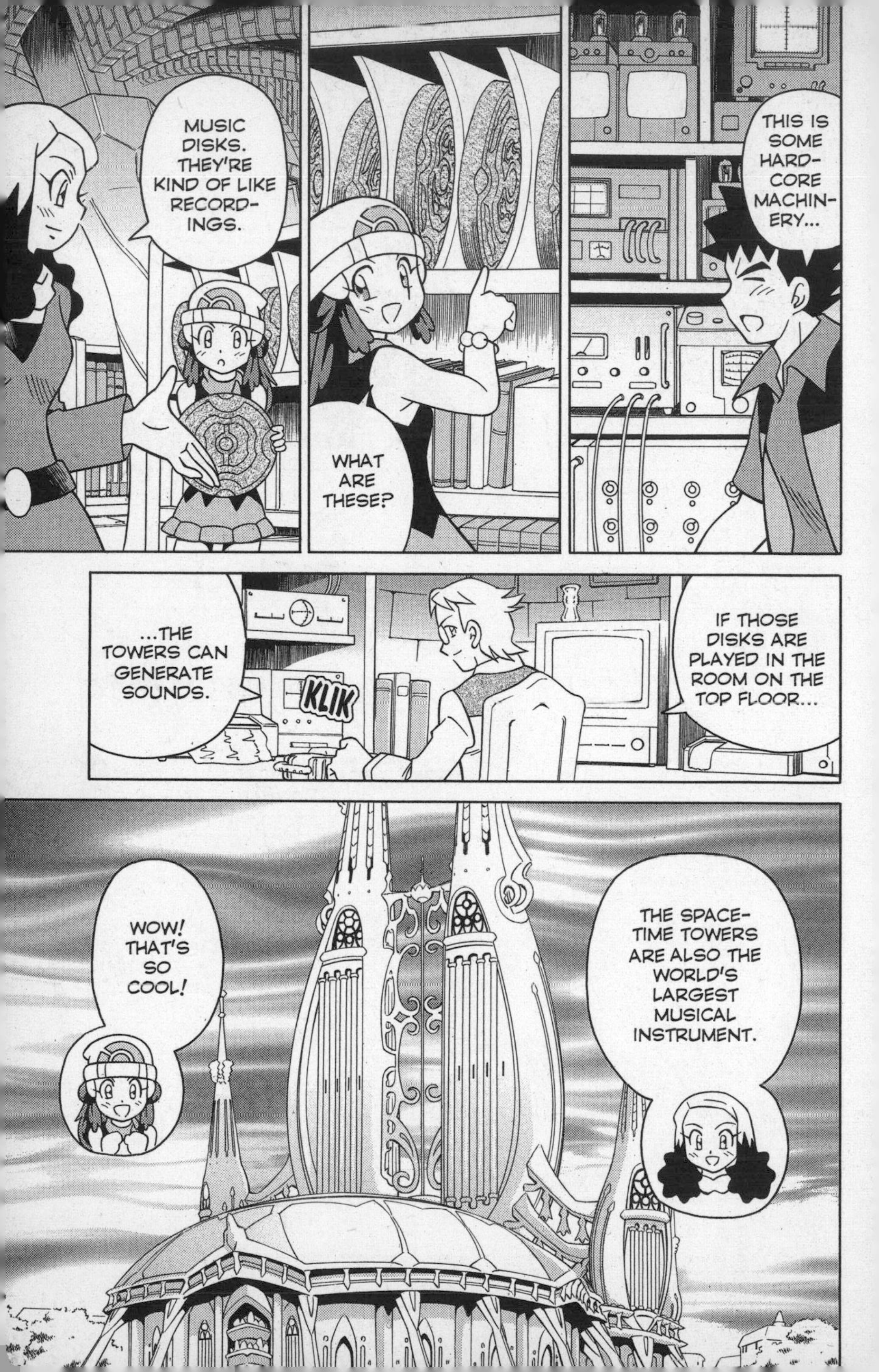
THIS IS SOME HARD-CORE MACHIN-ERY...
WHAT ARE THESE?
MUSIC DISKS. THEY'RE KIND OF LIKE RECORD-INGS.
IF THOSE DISKS ARE PLAYED IN THE ROOM ON THE TOP FLOOR...
KLIK
...THE TOWERS CAN GENERATE SOUNDS.
THE SPACE-TIME TOWERS ARE ALSO THE WORLD'S LARGEST MUSICAL INSTRUMENT.
WOW! THAT'S SO COOL!

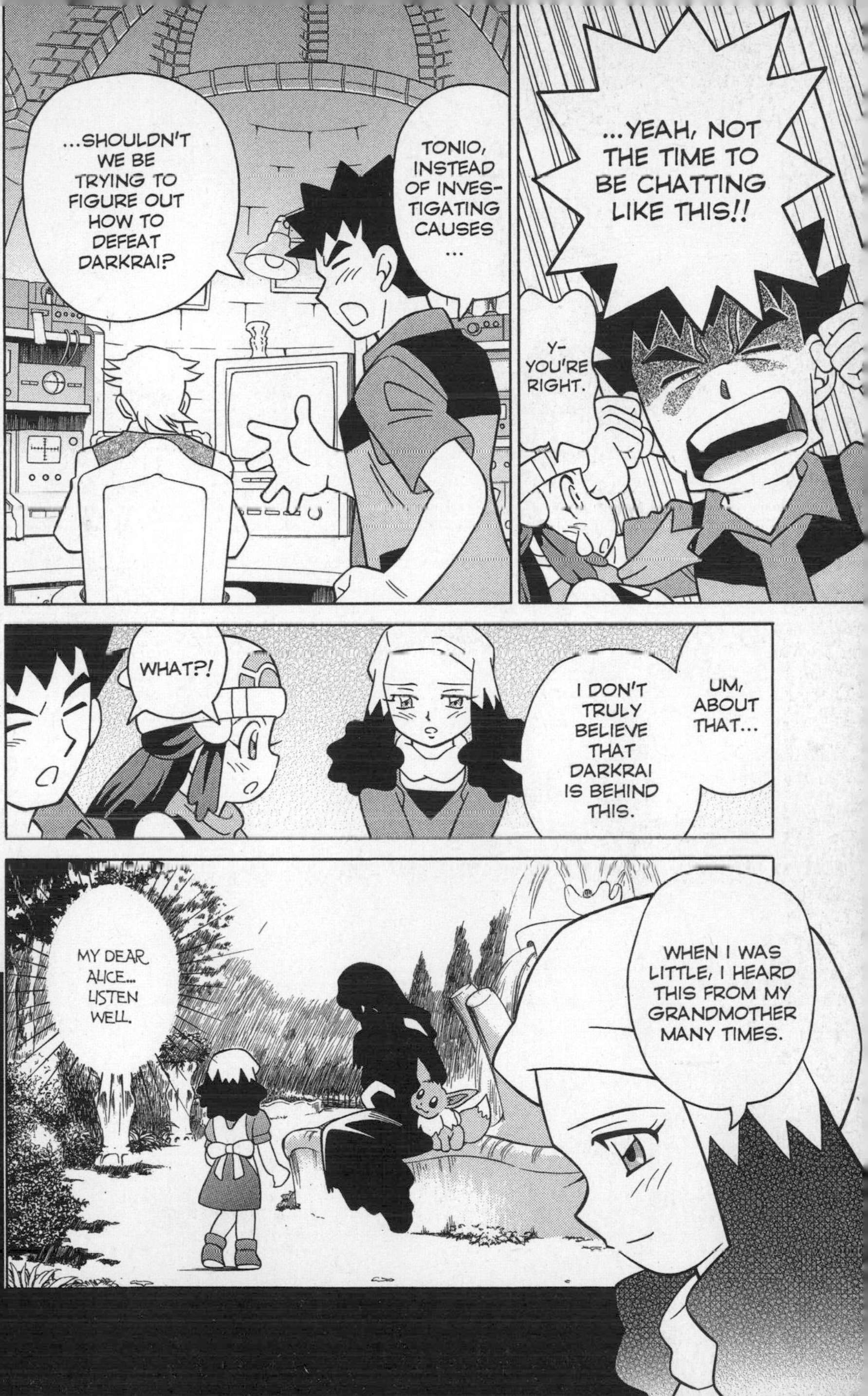
...YEAH, NOT THE TIME TO BE CHATTING LIKE THIS!!
Y-YOU'RE RIGHT.
TONIO, INSTEAD OF INVES-TIGATING CAUSES ...
...SHOULDN'T WE BE TRYING TO FIGURE OUT HOW TO DEFEAT DARKRAI?
UM, ABOUT THAT...
I DON'T TRULY BELIEVE THAT DARKRAI IS BEHIND THIS.
WHAT?!
WHEN I WAS LITTLE, I HEARD THIS FROM MY GRANDMOTHER MANY TIMES.
MY DEAR ALICE... LISTEN WELL.

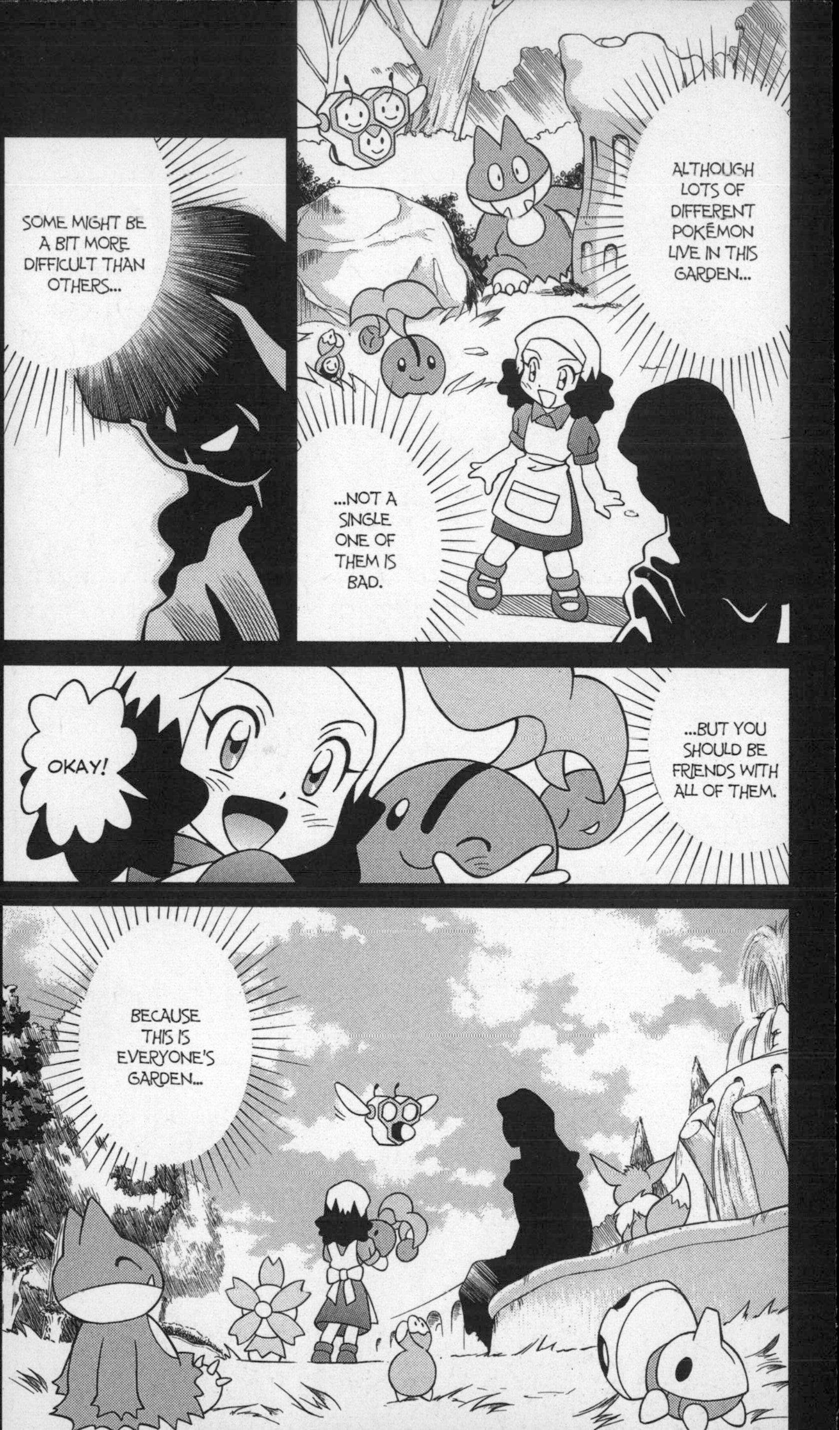
ALTHOUGH LOTS OF DIFFERENT POKÉMON LIVE IN THIS GARDEN...
...NOT A SINGLE ONE OF THEM IS BAD.
SOME MIGHT BE A BIT MORE DIFFICULT THAN OTHERS...
...BUT YOU SHOULD BE FRIENDS WITH ALL OF THEM.
OKAY!
BECAUSE THIS IS EVERYONE'S GARDEN...

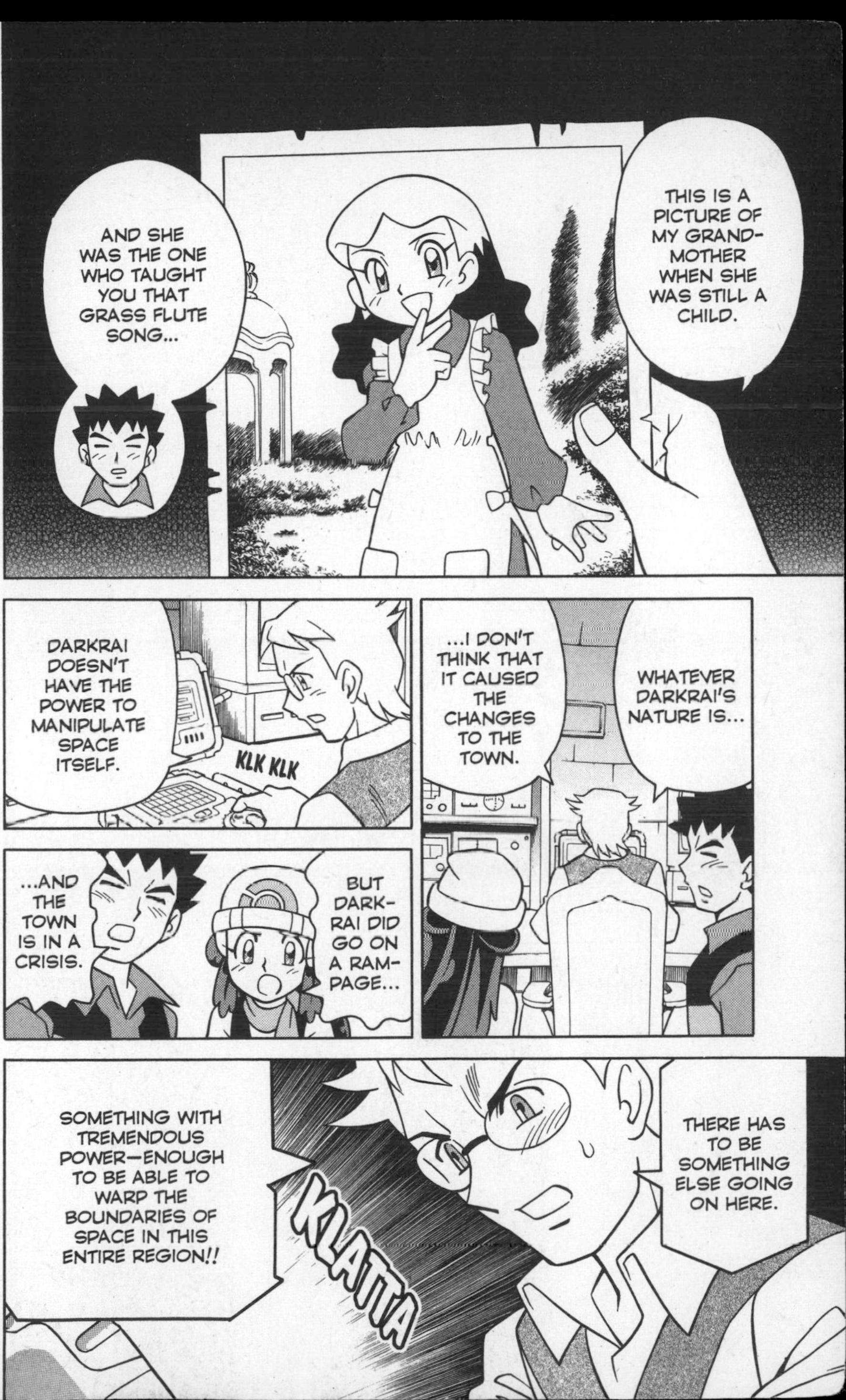
THIS IS A PICTURE OF MY GRAND-MOTHER WHEN SHE WAS STILL A CHILD.
AND SHE WAS THE ONE WHO TAUGHT YOU THAT GRASS FLUTE SONG...
WHATEVER DARKRAI'S NATURE IS...
...I DON'T THINK THAT IT CAUSED THE CHANGES TO THE TOWN.
DARKRAI DOESN'T HAVE THE POWER TO MANIPULATE SPACE ITSELF.
KLK KLK
BUT DARK-RAI DID GO ON A RAM-PAGE...
...AND THE TOWN IS IN A CRISIS.
THERE HAS TO BE SOMETHING ELSE GOING ON HERE.
SOMETHING WITH TREMENDOUS POWER—ENOUGH TO BE ABLE TO WARP THE BOUNDARIES OF SPACE IN THIS ENTIRE REGION!!
KLATTA

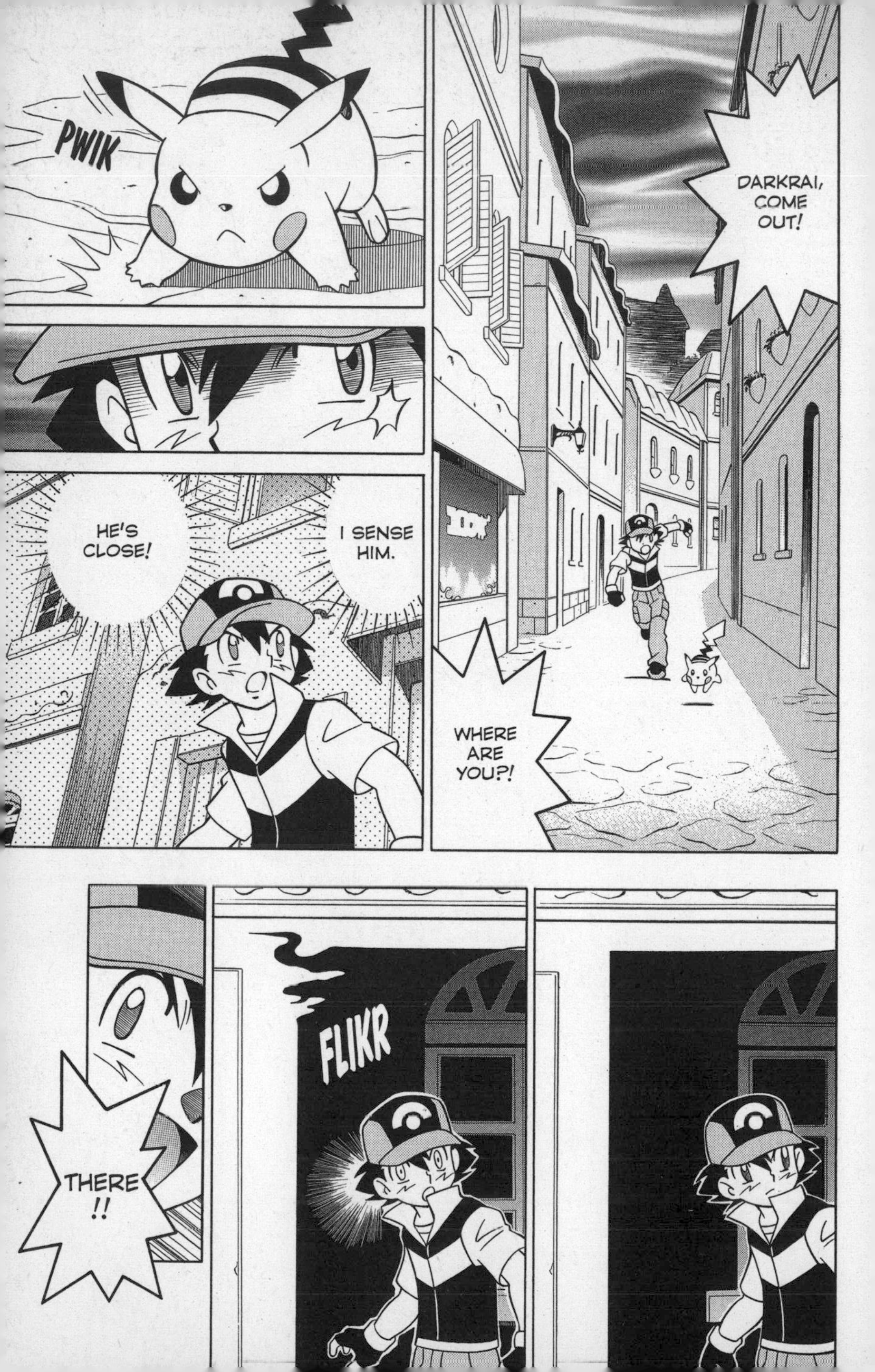
DARKRAI, COME OUT!
WHERE ARE YOU?!
PWIK
I SENSE HIM.
HE'S CLOSE!
FLIKR
THERE!!

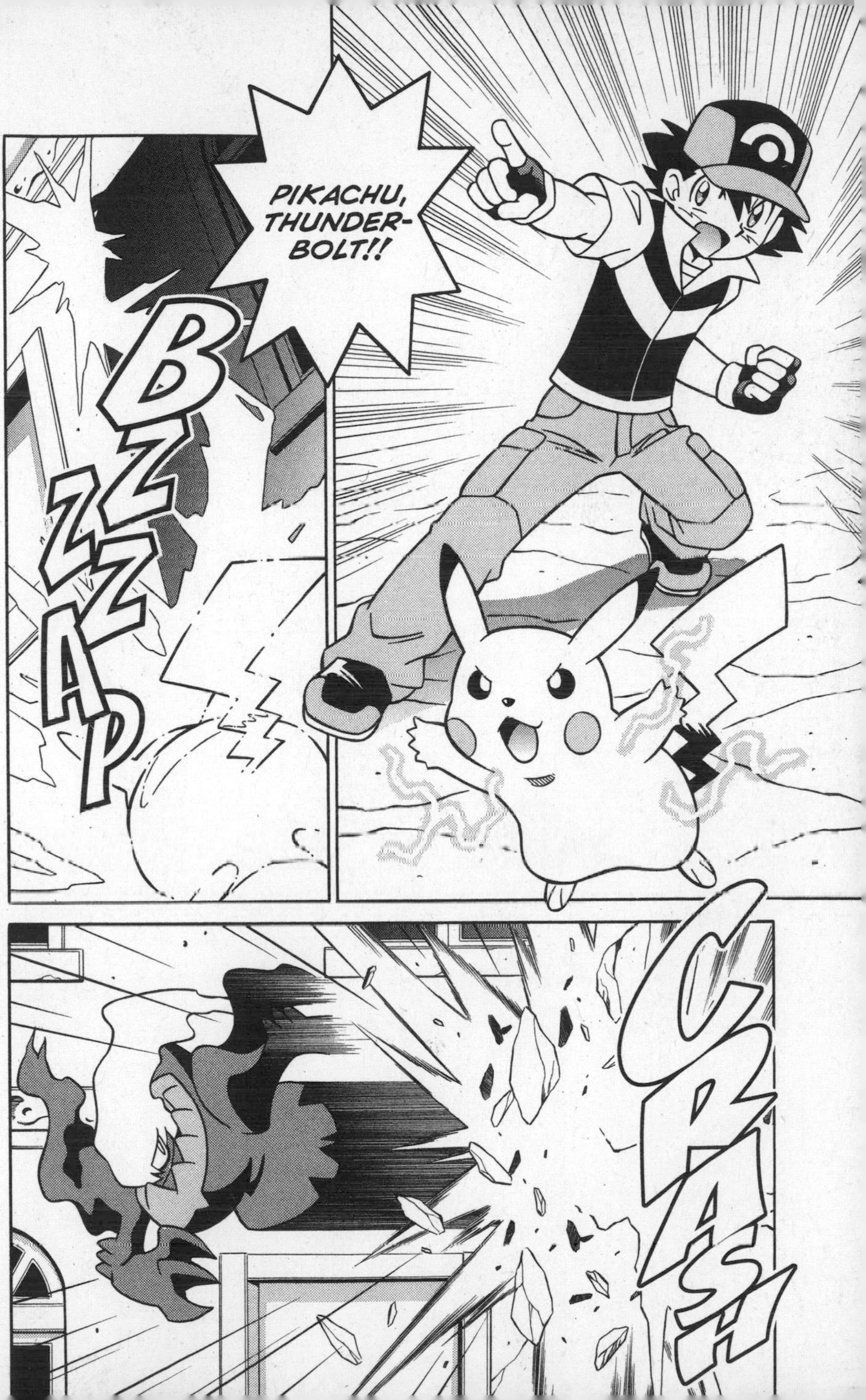
PIKACHU, THUNDER-BOLT!!
BZZZAP
CRASH

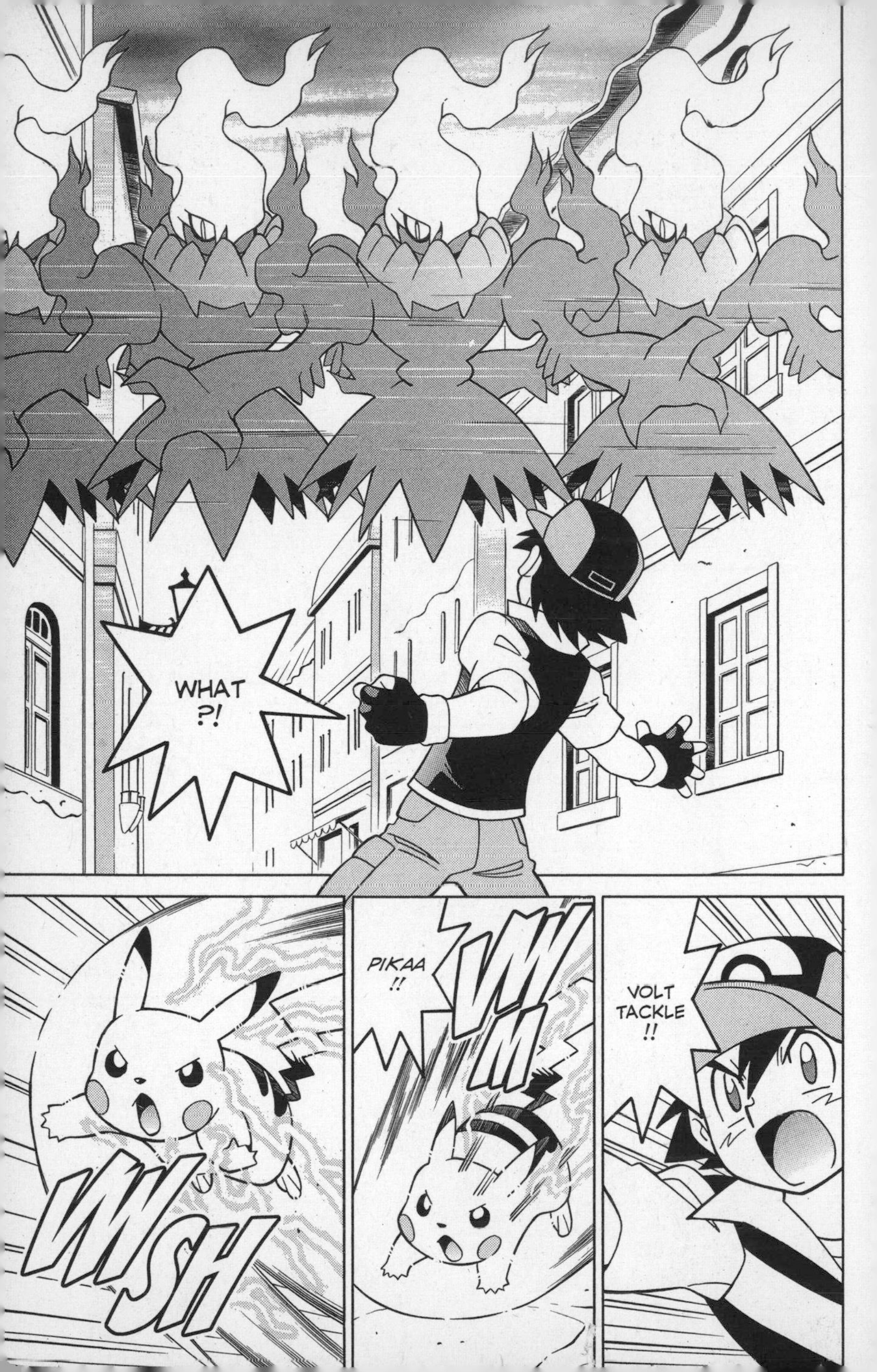
WHAT ?!
VOLT TACKLE !!
PIKAA !!
VWM
VWSH

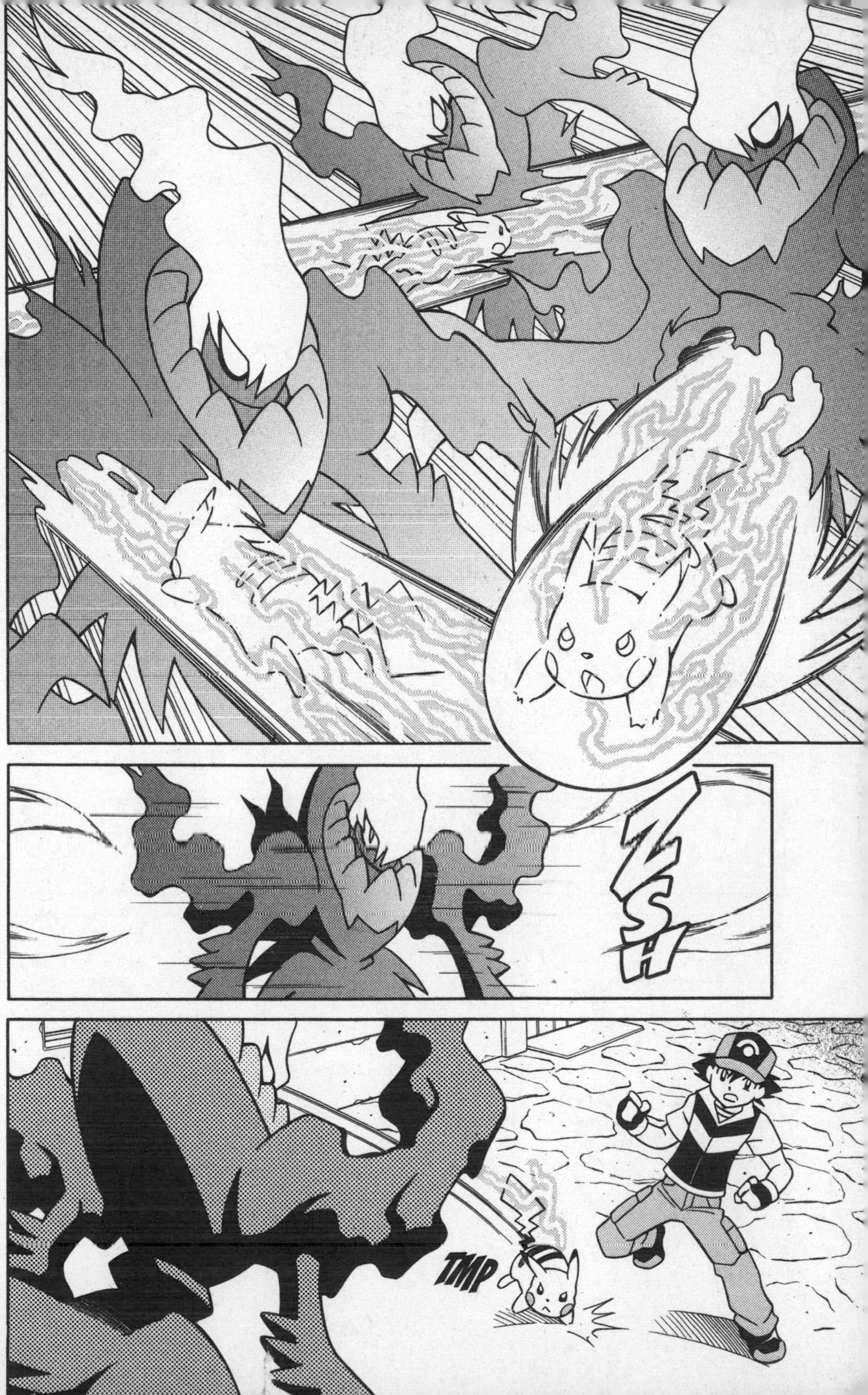
TMP

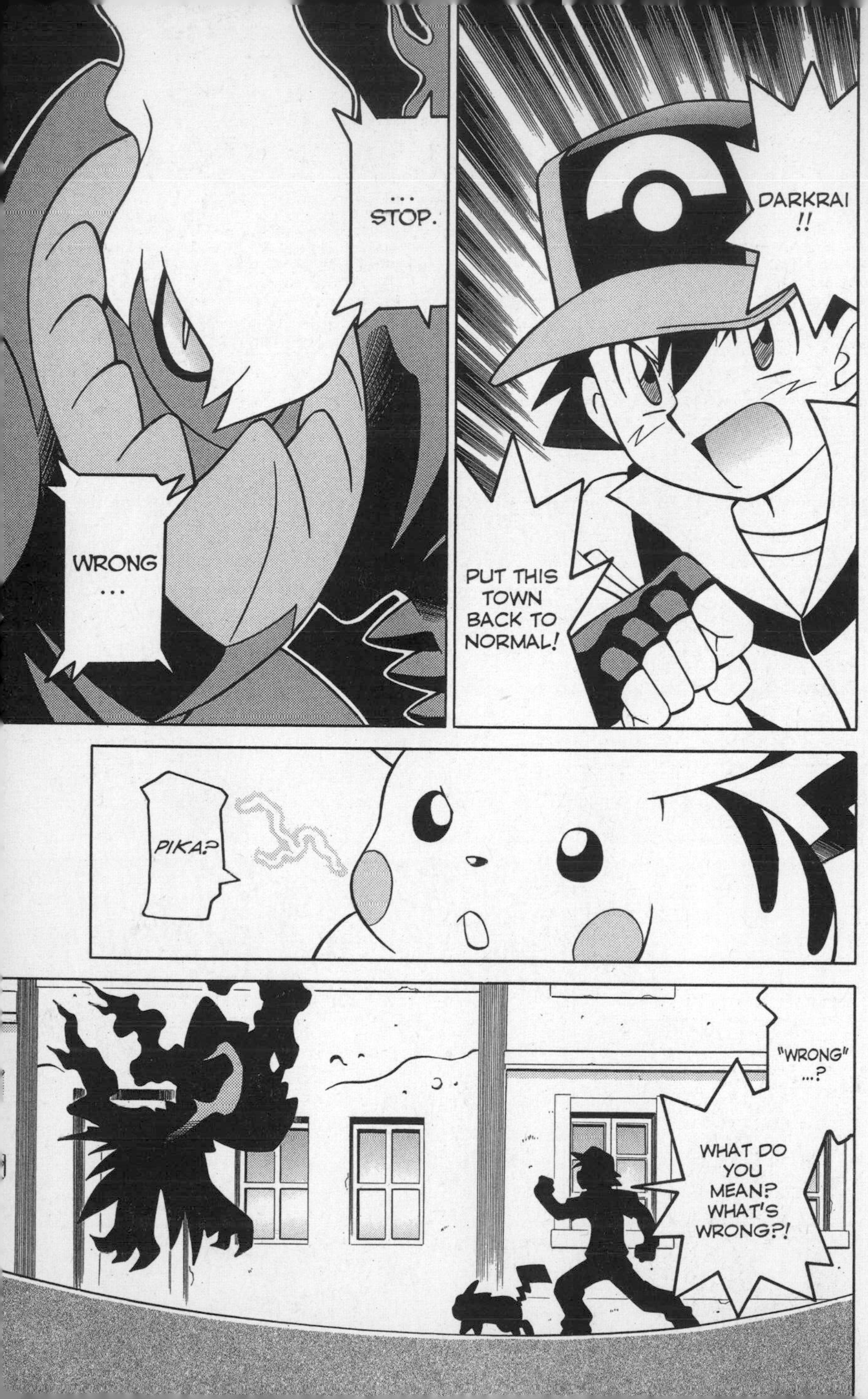
DARKRAI !!
PUT THIS TOWN BACK TO NORMAL!
... STOP.
WRONG ...
PIKA?
"WRONG" ...?
WHAT DO YOU MEAN? WHAT'S WRONG?!

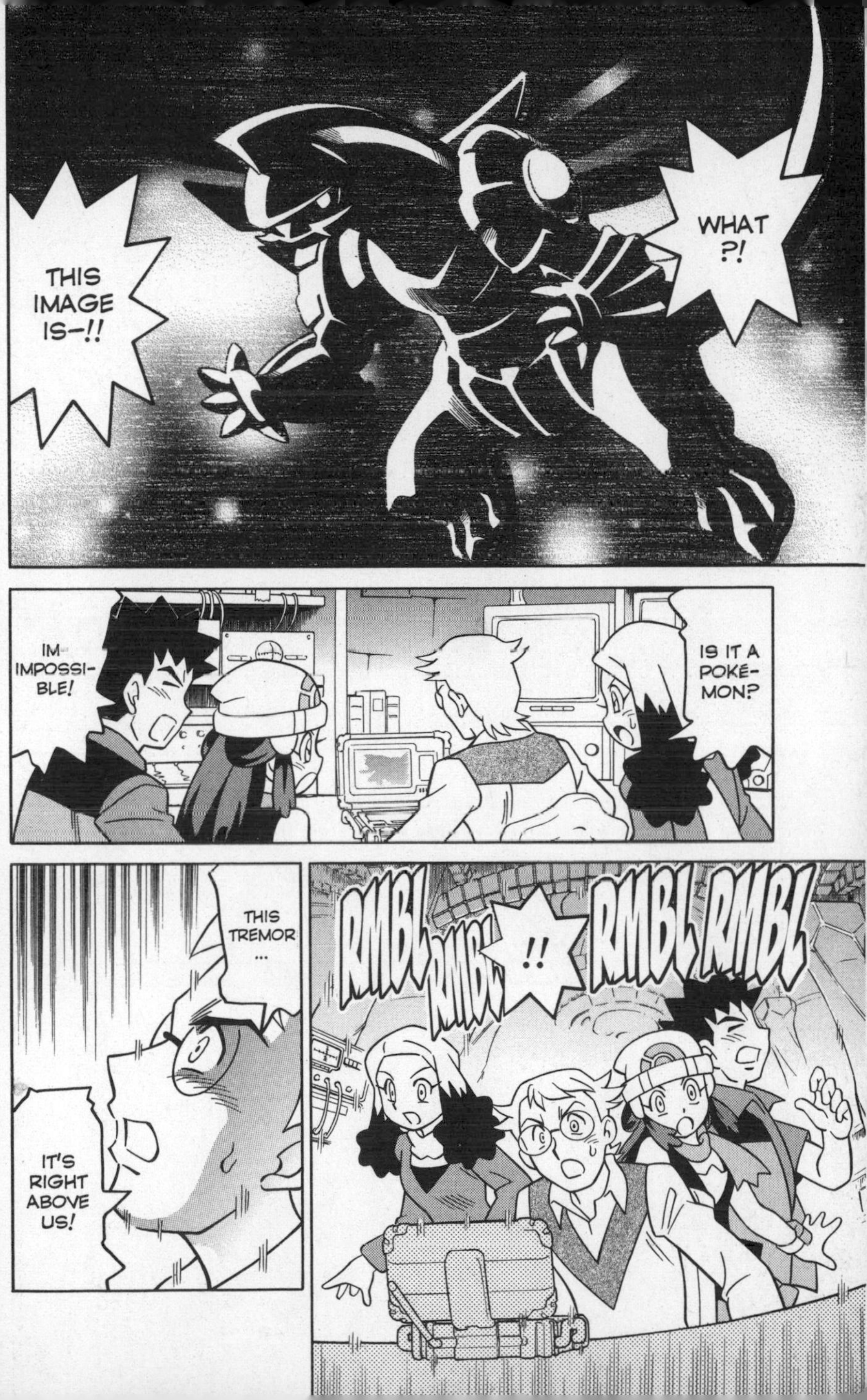
WHAT ?!
THIS IMAGE IS—!!
IS IT A POKÉ-MON?
IM IMPOSSI-BLE!
RMBL RMBL
!!
RMBL RMBL
THIS TREMOR ...
IT'S RIGHT ABOVE US!

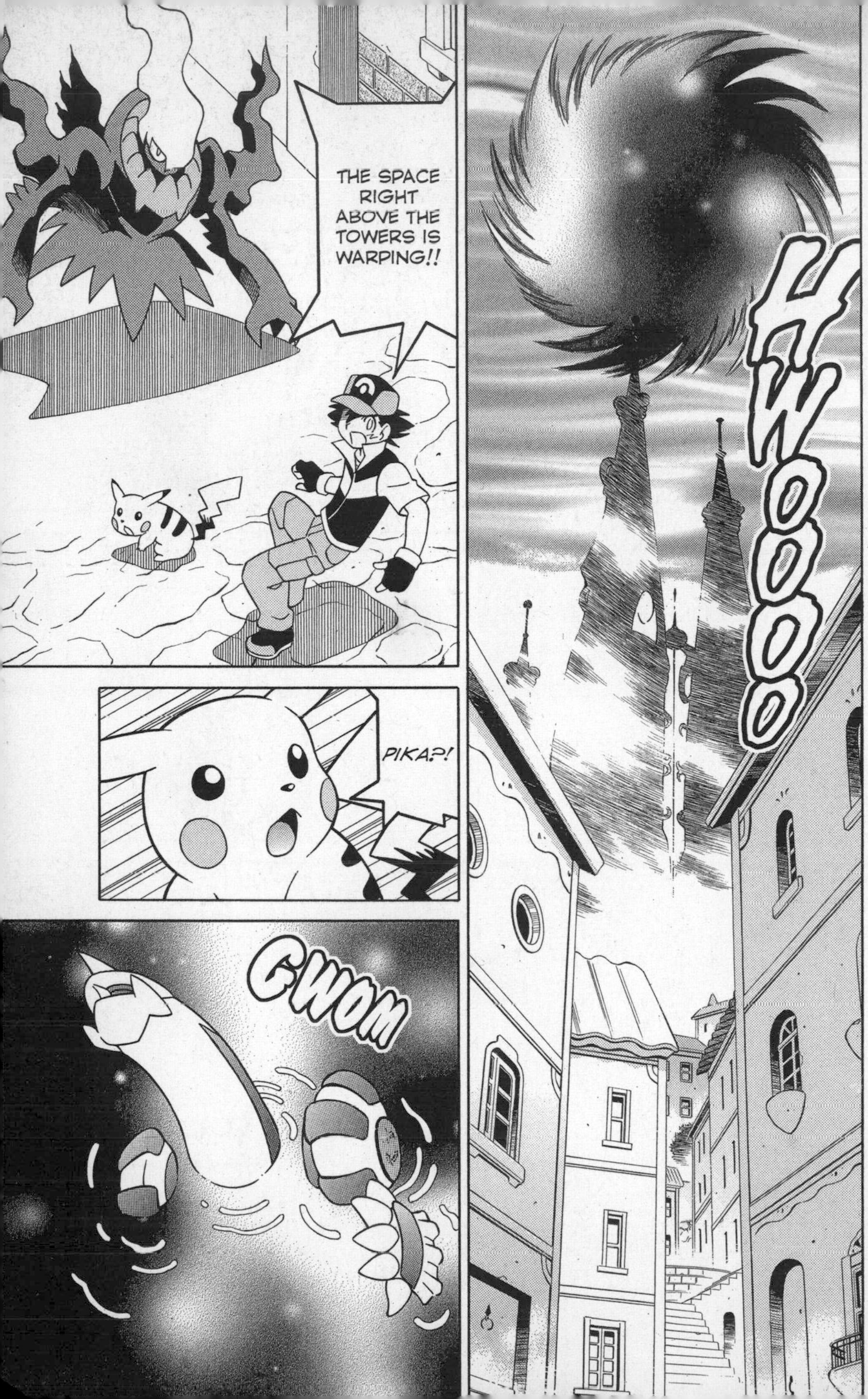
HWOOOO
THE SPACE RIGHT ABOVE THE TOWERS IS WARPING!!
PIKA?!
GWOM

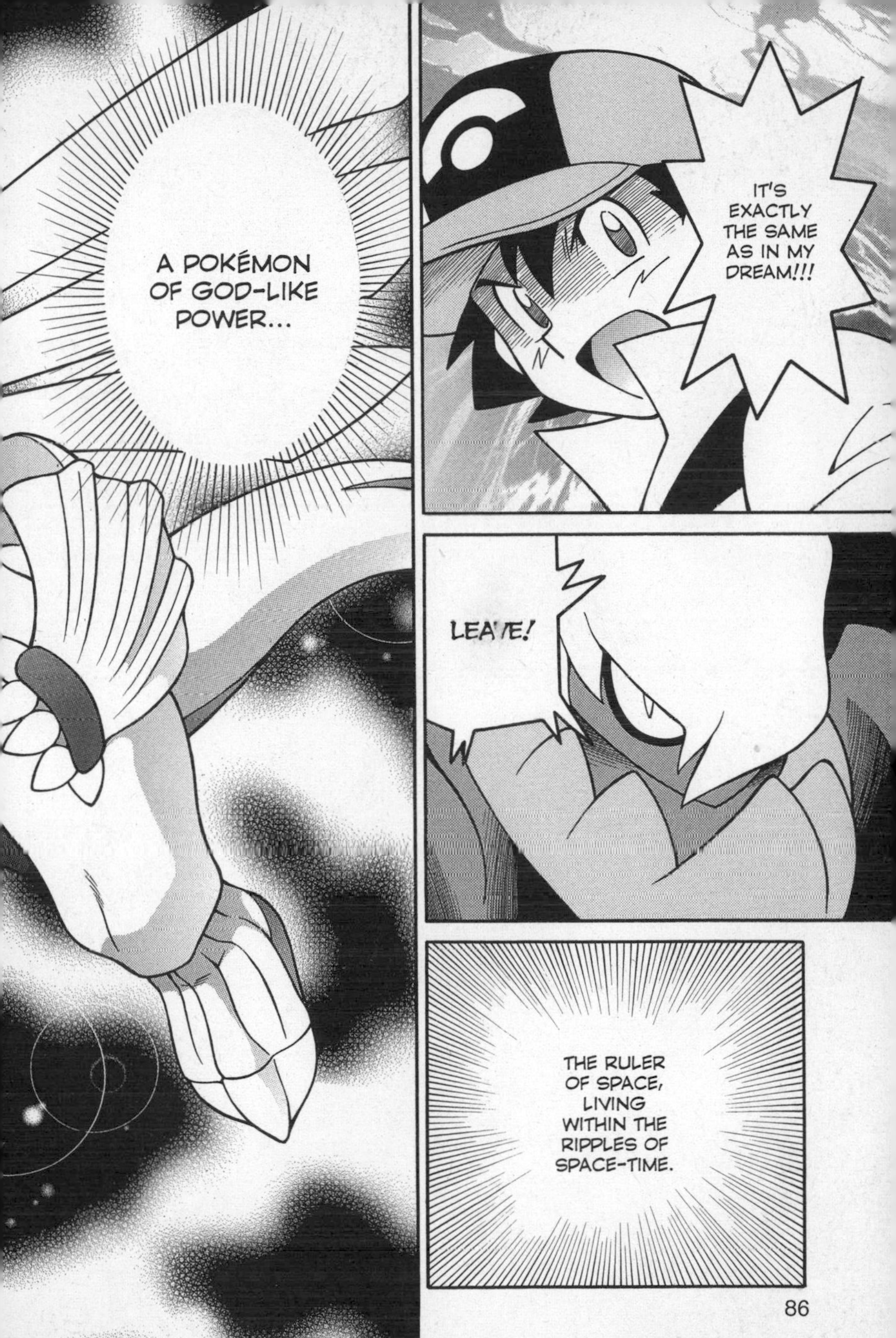
IT'S EXACTLY THE SAME AS IN MY DREAM!!!
LEAVE!
THE RULER OF SPACE, LIVING WITHIN THE RIPPLES OF SPACE-TIME.
A POKÉMON OF GOD-LIKE POWER...

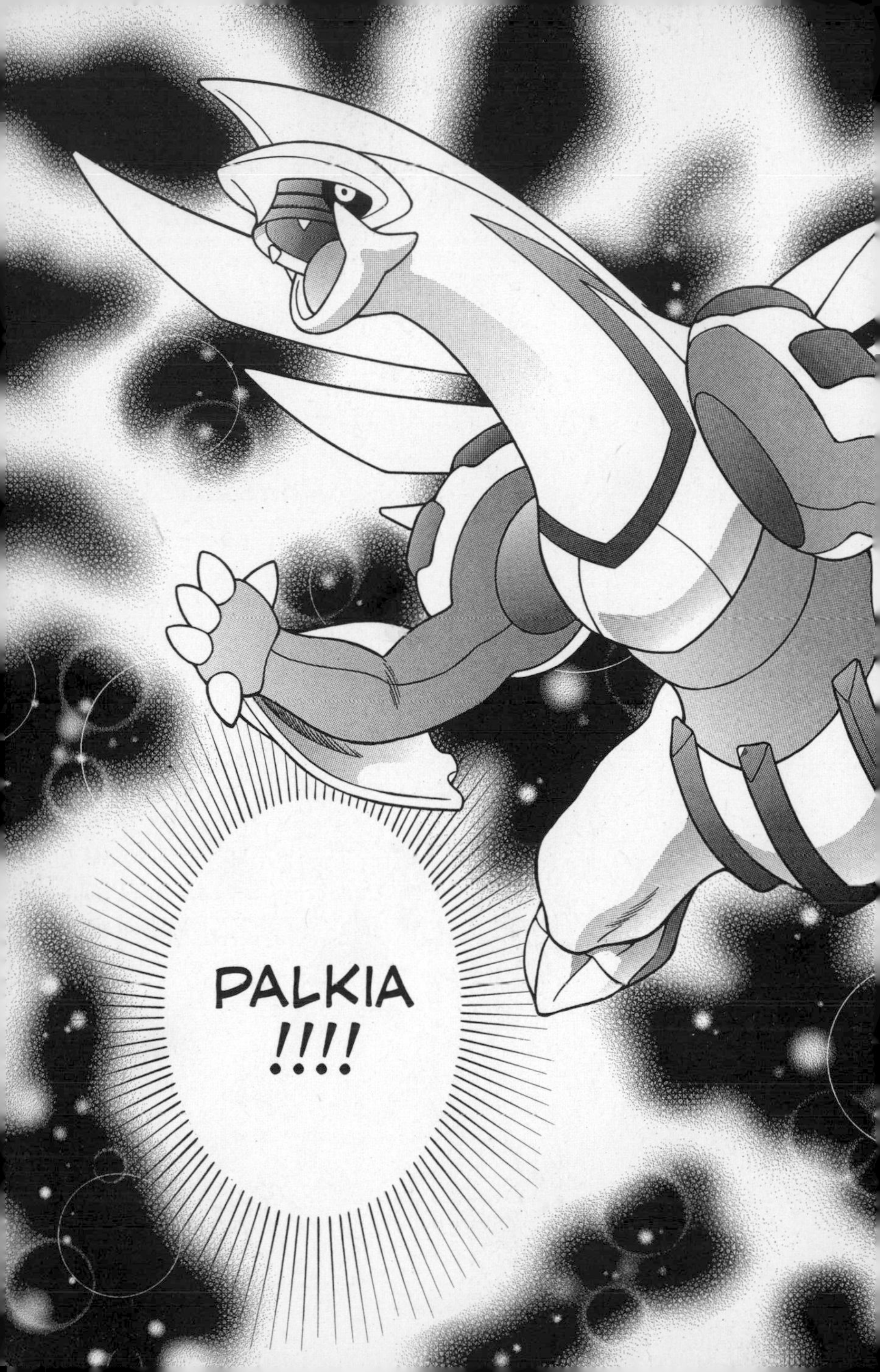
PALKIA
!!!!

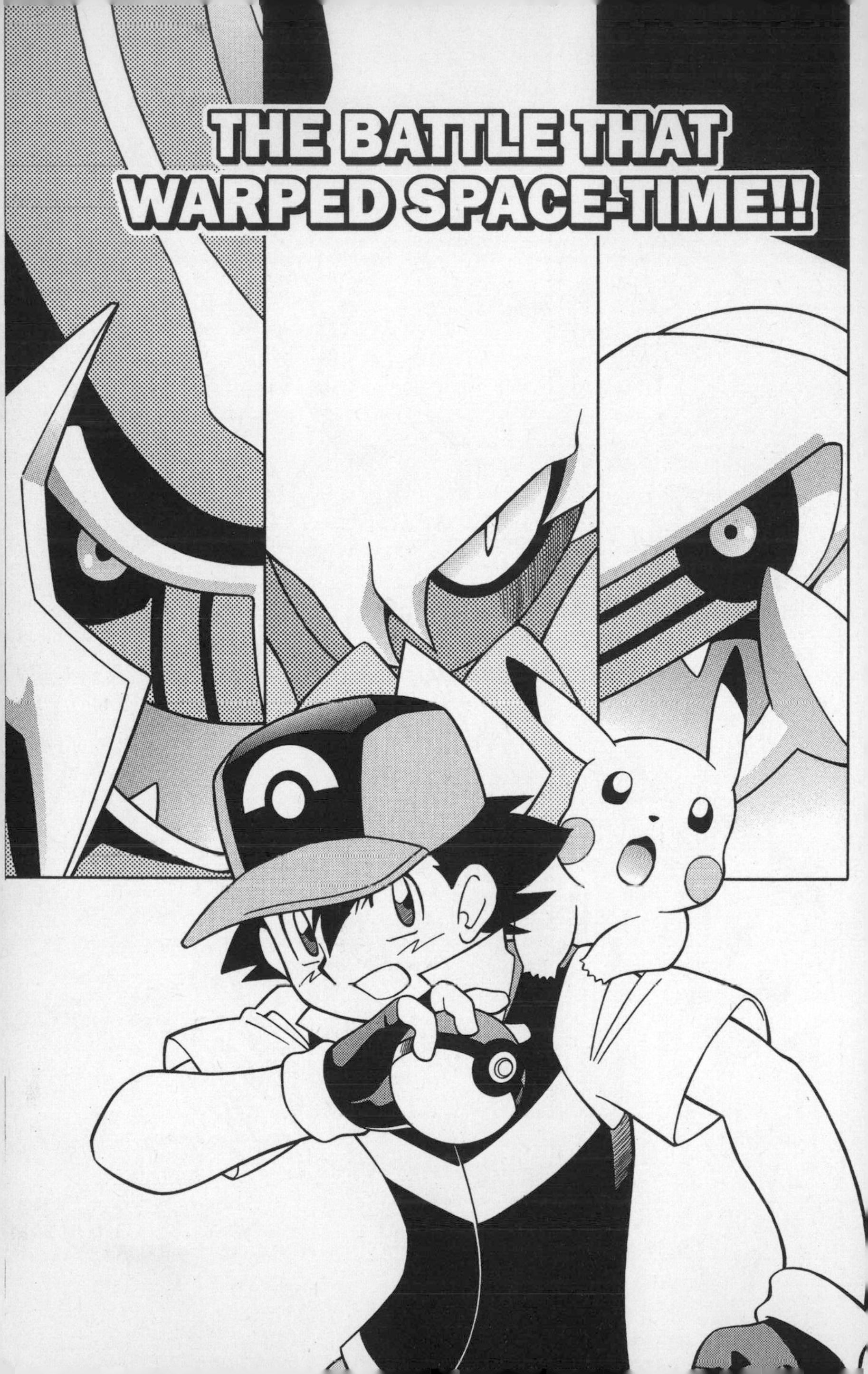
THE BATTLE THAT
WARPED SPACE-TIME!!

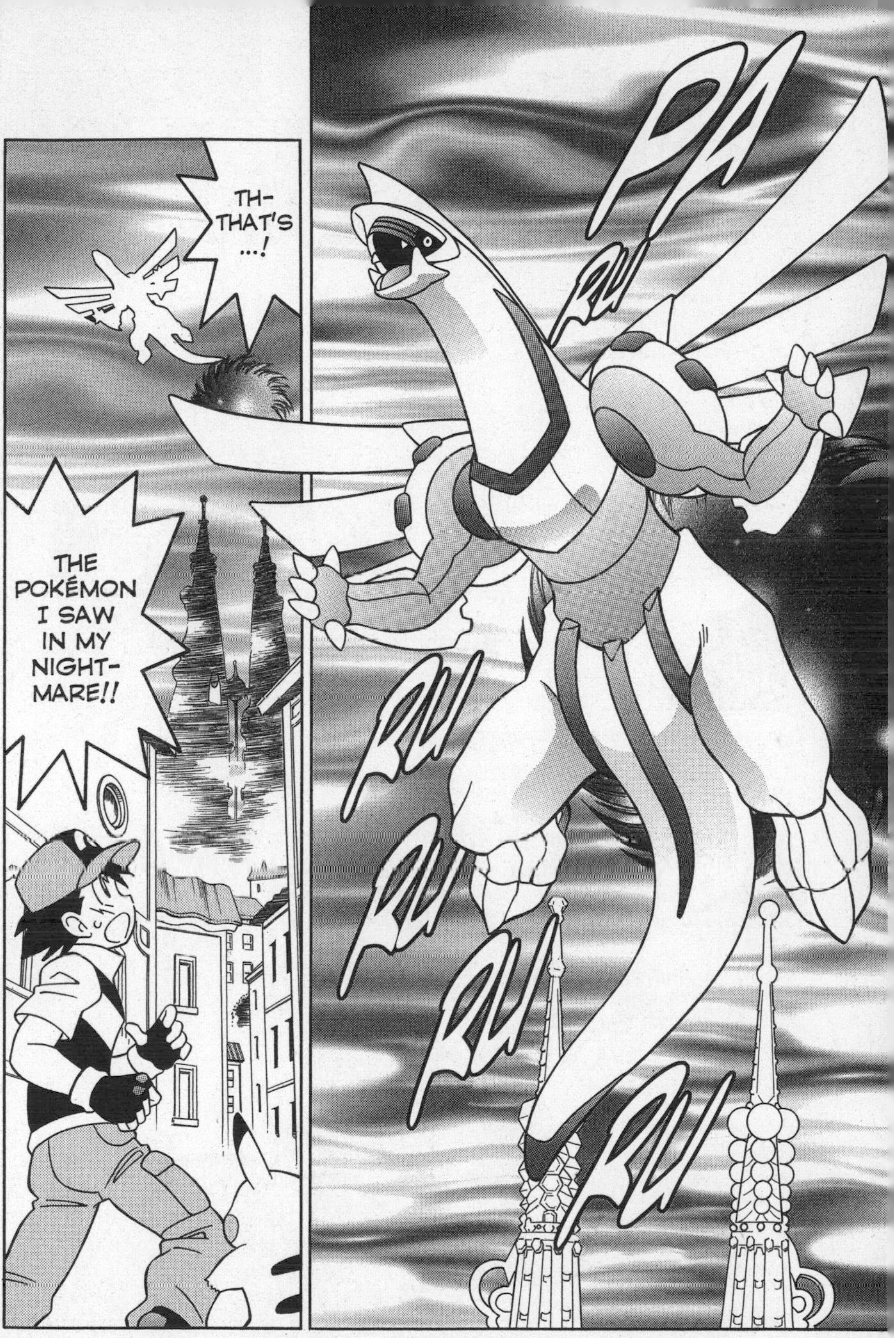
PA
RU
RU
RU
RU
RU
TH-THAT'S ...!
THE POKÉMON I SAW IN MY NIGHT-MARE!!

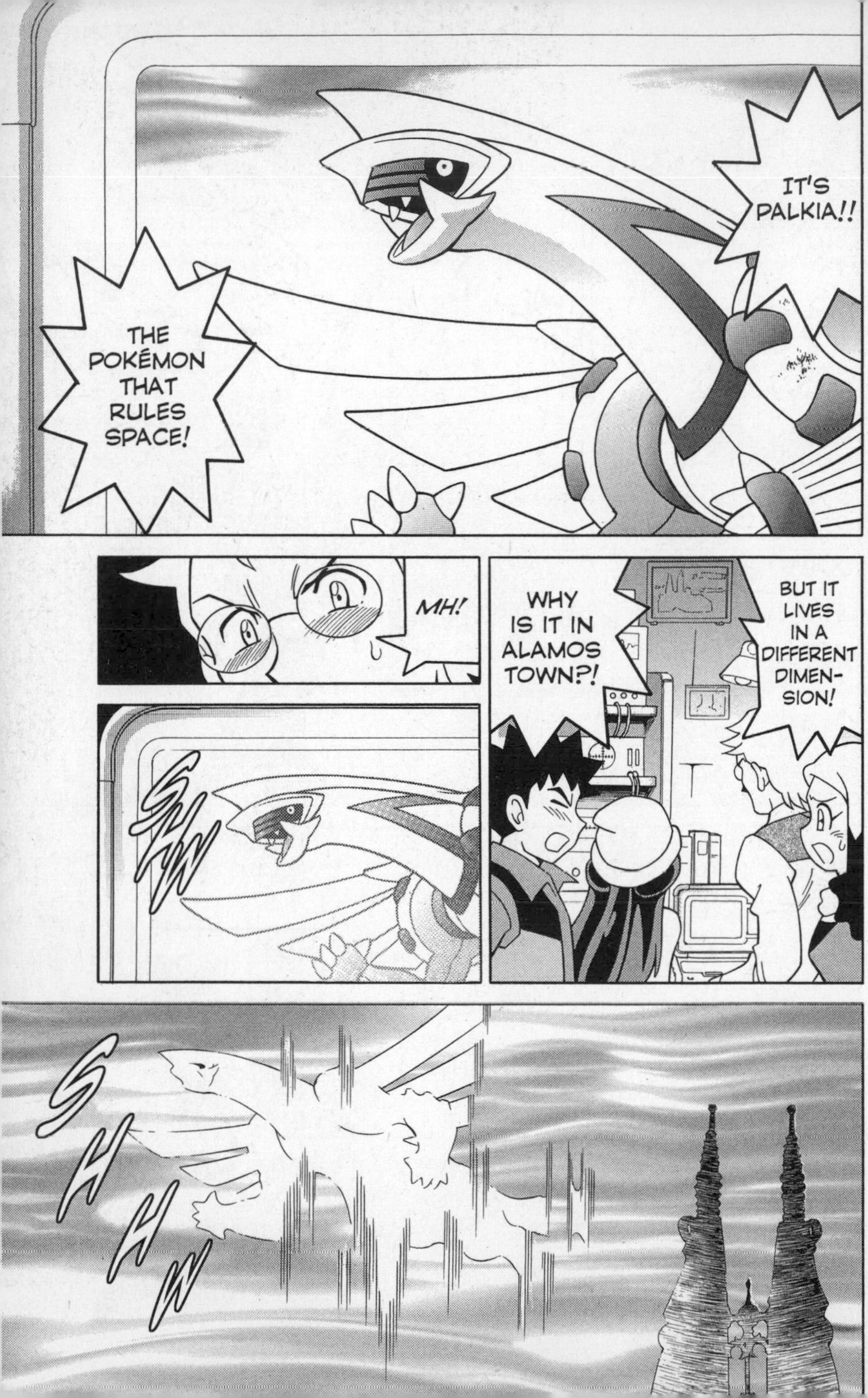
IT'S PALKIA!!
THE POKÉMON THAT RULES SPACE!
BUT IT LIVES IN A DIFFERENT DIMENSION!
WHY IS IT IN ALAMOS TOWN?!
MH!
SHW
SHHHW

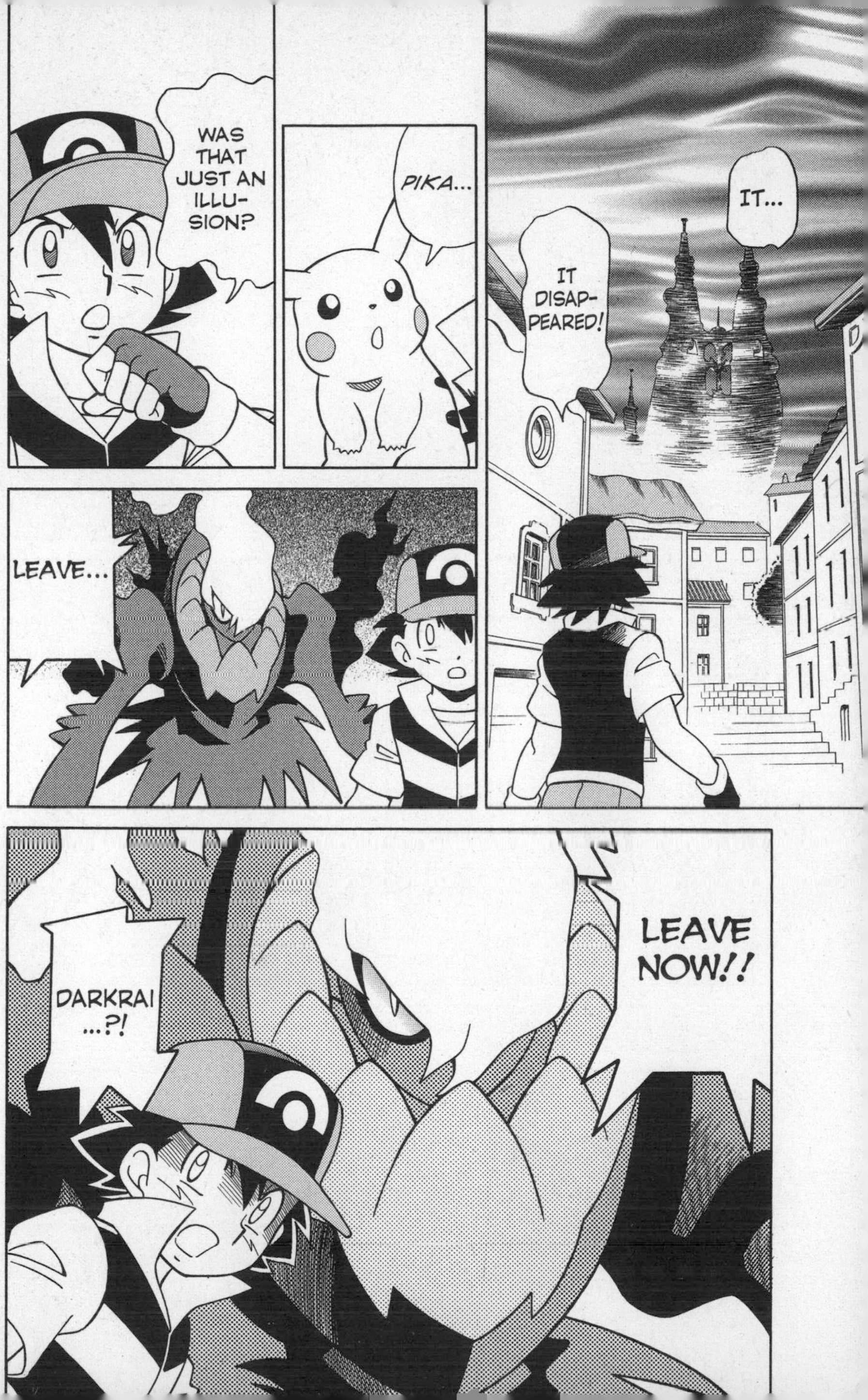
IT...
IT DISAPPEARED!
PIKA...
WAS THAT JUST AN ILLUSION?
LEAVE...
LEAVE NOW!!
DARKRAI ...?!

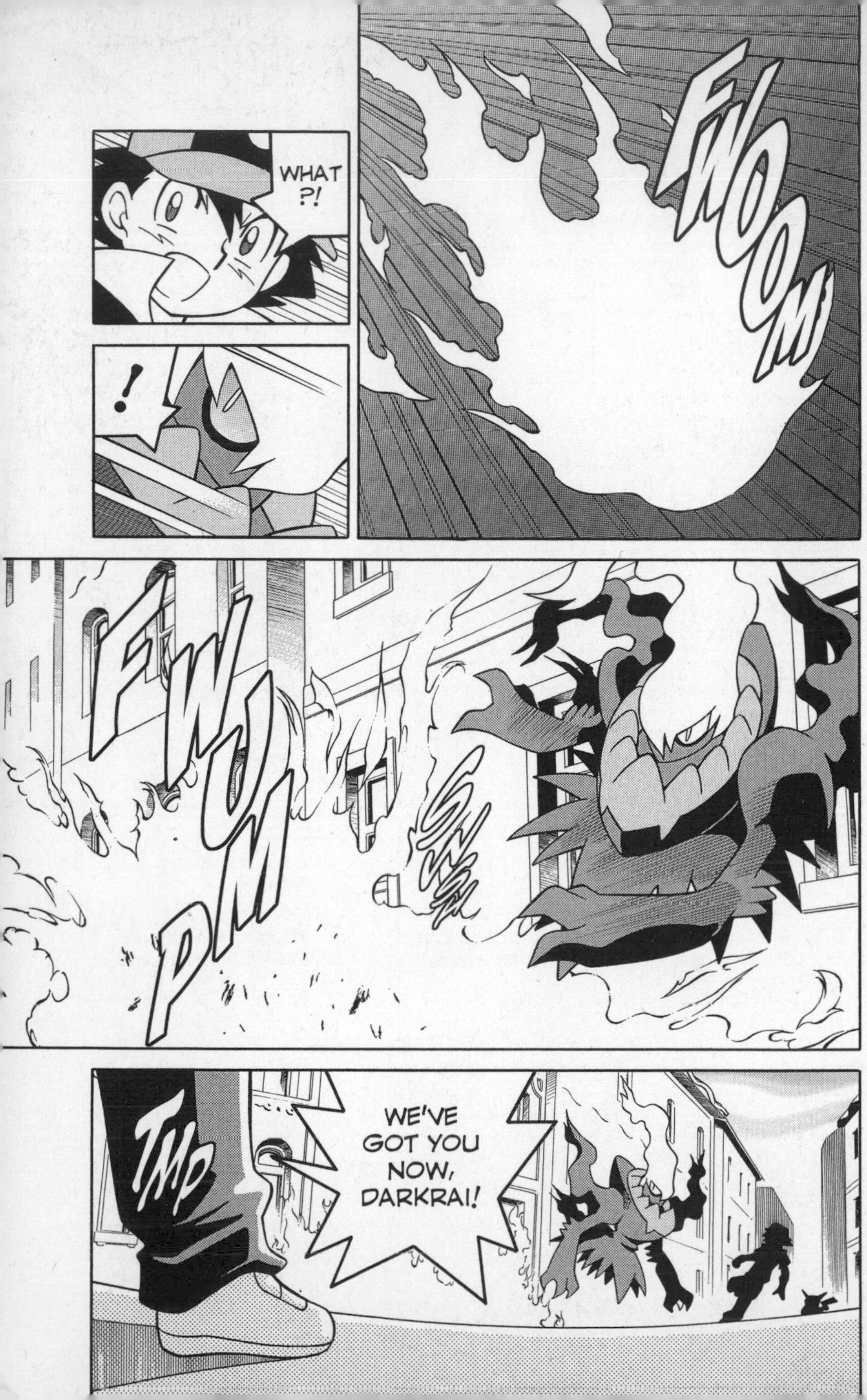
FWOOM
WHAT?!
!
FWUMP
TMP
WE'VE GOT YOU NOW, DARKRAI!

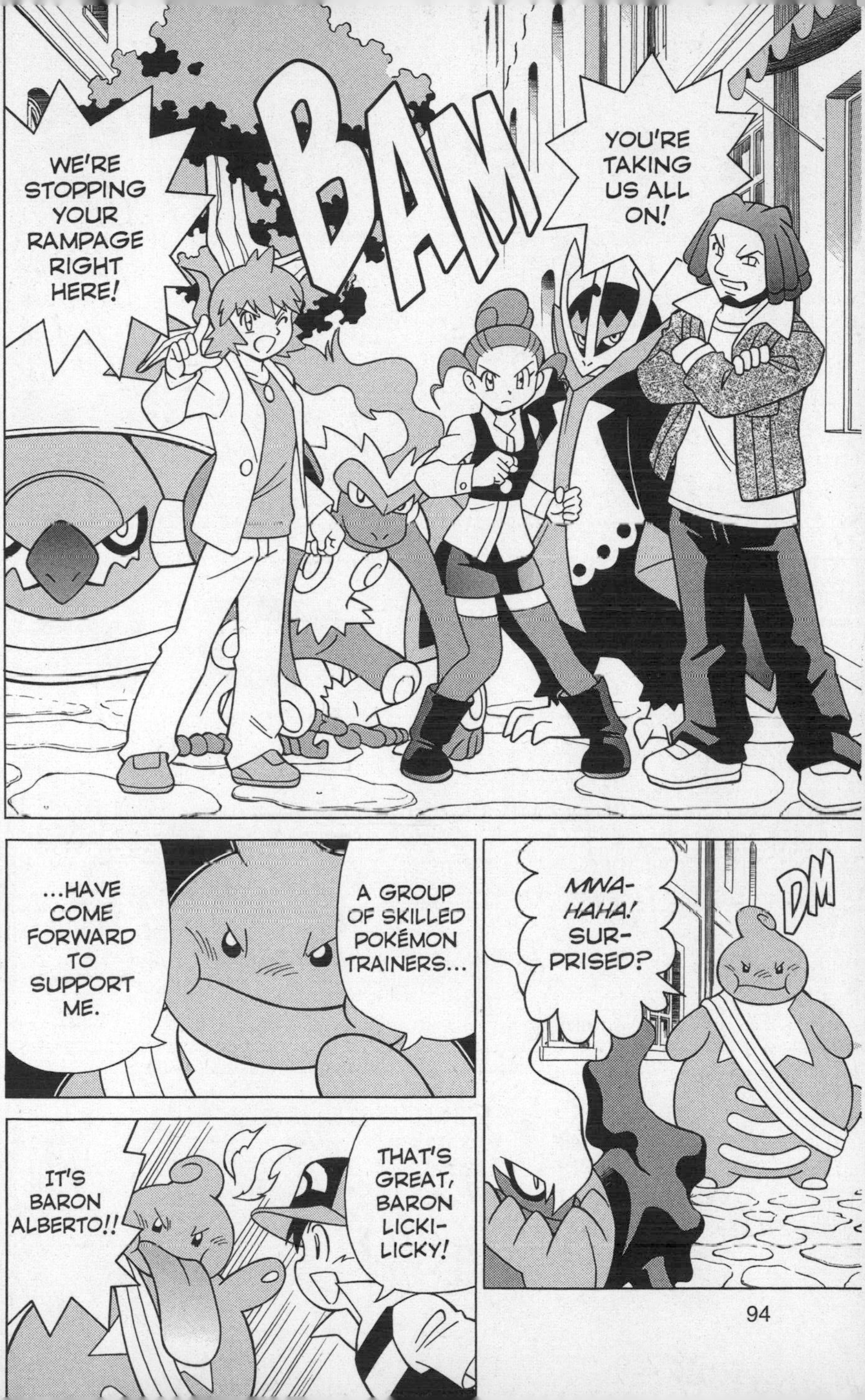
YOU'RE TAKING US ALL ON!
BAM
WE'RE STOPPING YOUR RAMPAGE RIGHT HERE!
MWA-HAHA! SUR-PRISED?
DM
A GROUP OF SKILLED POKÉMON TRAINERS...
...HAVE COME FORWARD TO SUPPORT ME.
THAT'S GREAT, BARON LICKI-LICKY!
IT'S BARON ALBERTO!!

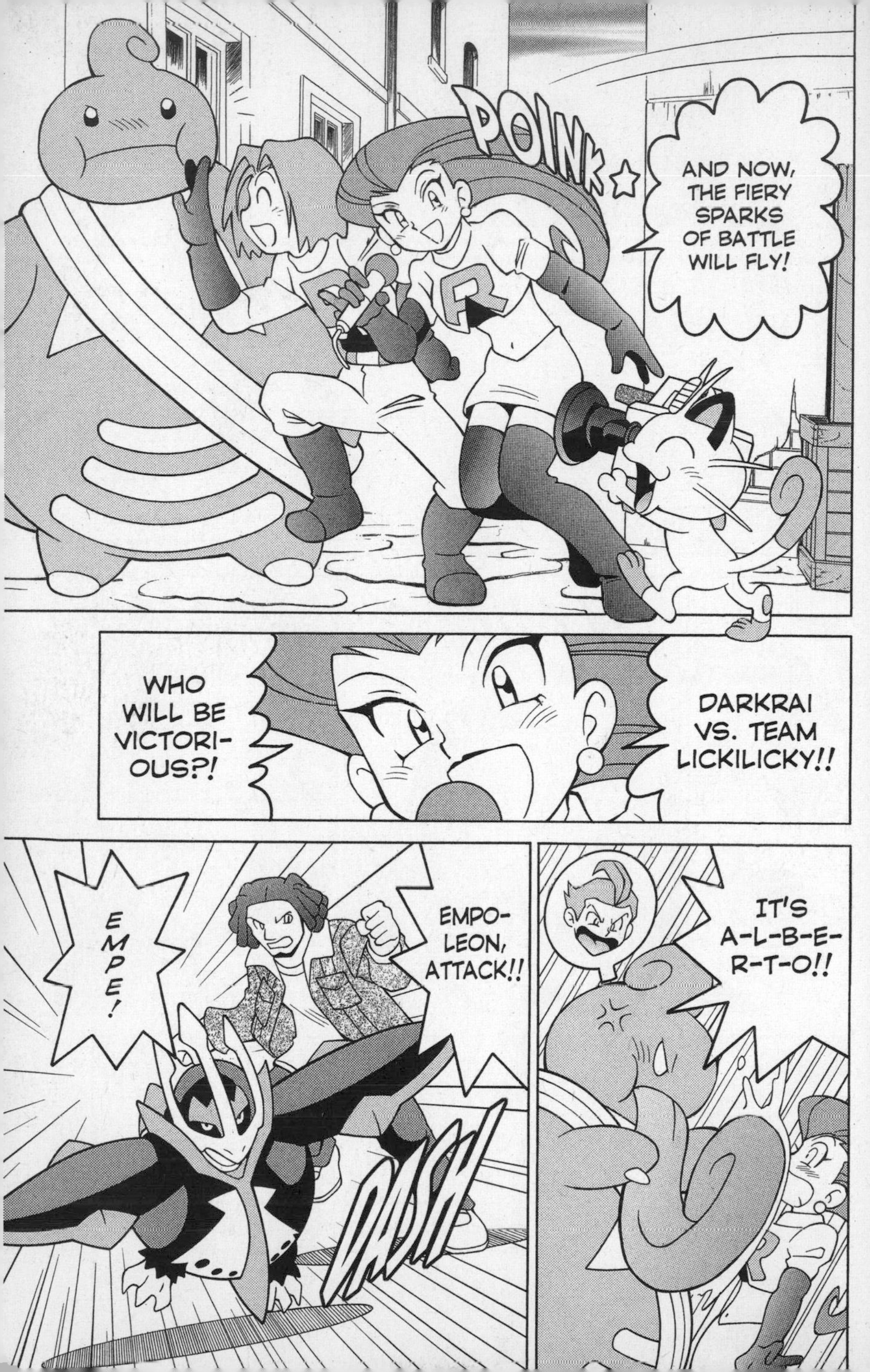
POINK
AND NOW, THE FIERY SPARKS OF BATTLE WILL FLY!
DARKRAI VS. TEAM LICKILICKY!!
WHO WILL BE VICTORI-OUS?!
IT'S A-L-B-E-R-T-O!!
EMPO-LEON, ATTACK!!
EMPE!
DASH

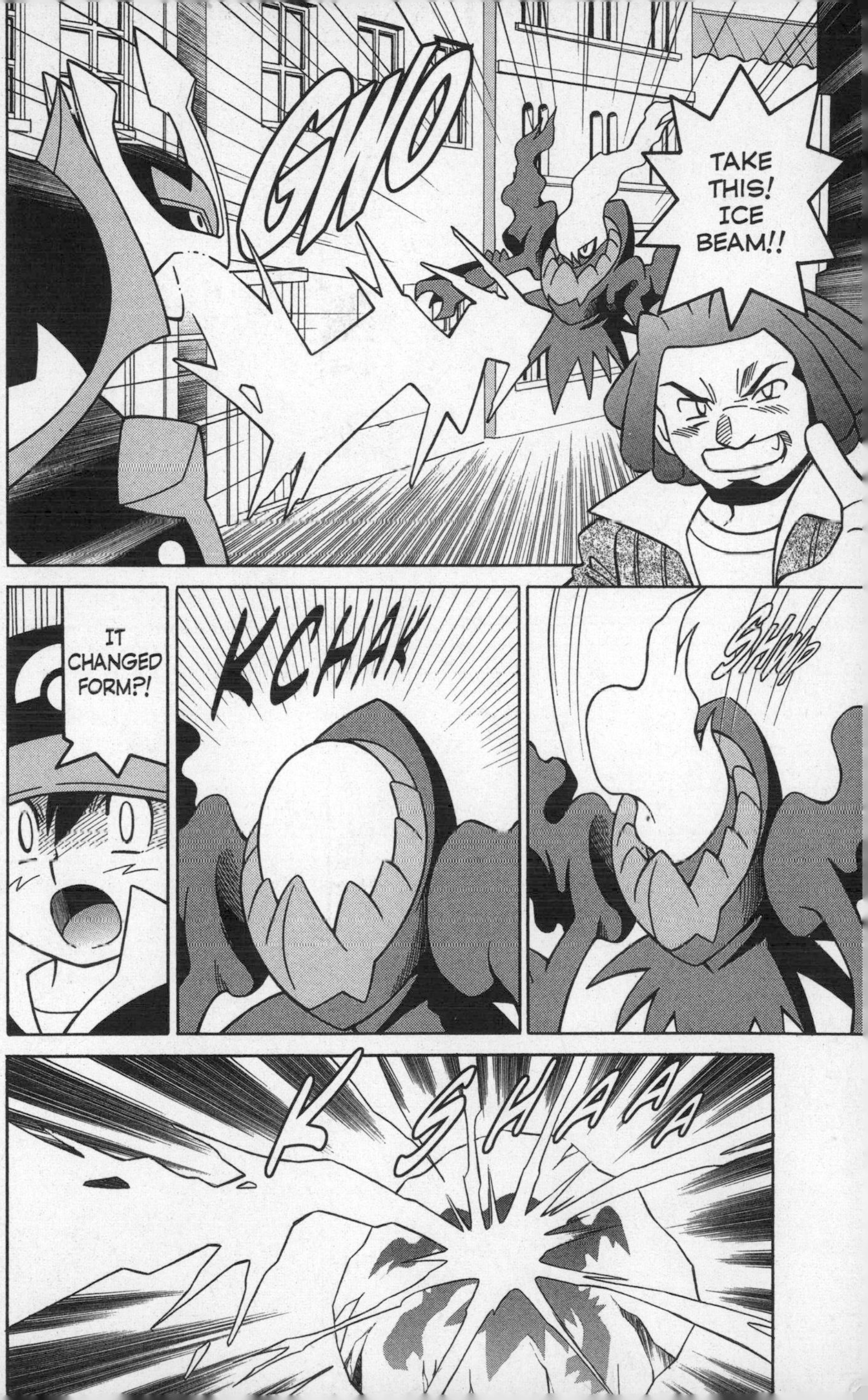
TAKE THIS! ICE BEAM!!
GNO
KCHAK
IT CHANGED FORM?!
KSHAAA

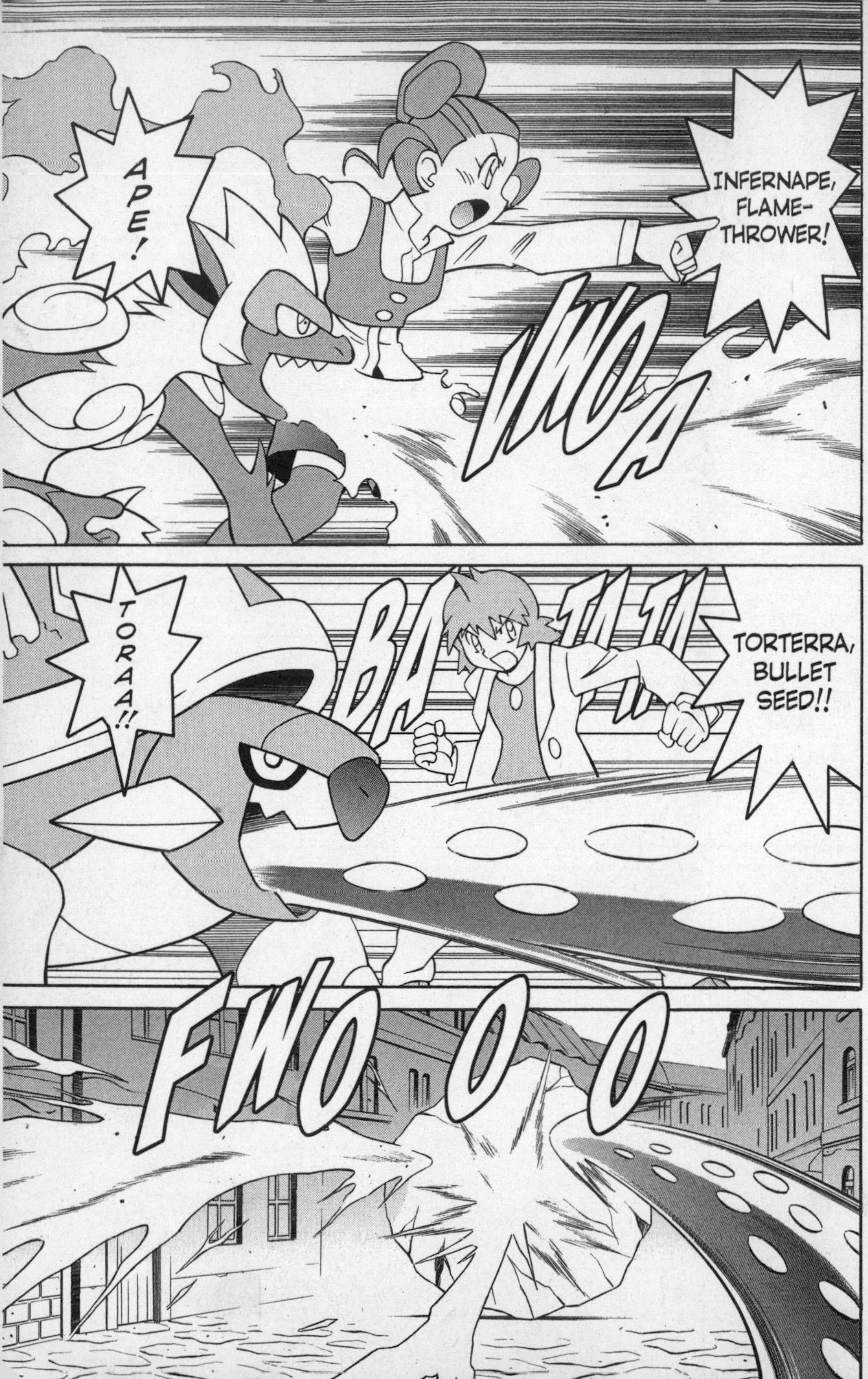
INFERNAPE, FLAME-THROWER!
VWOA
APE!
TORTERRA, BULLET SEED!!
BATATA
TORAA!!
FWOOO

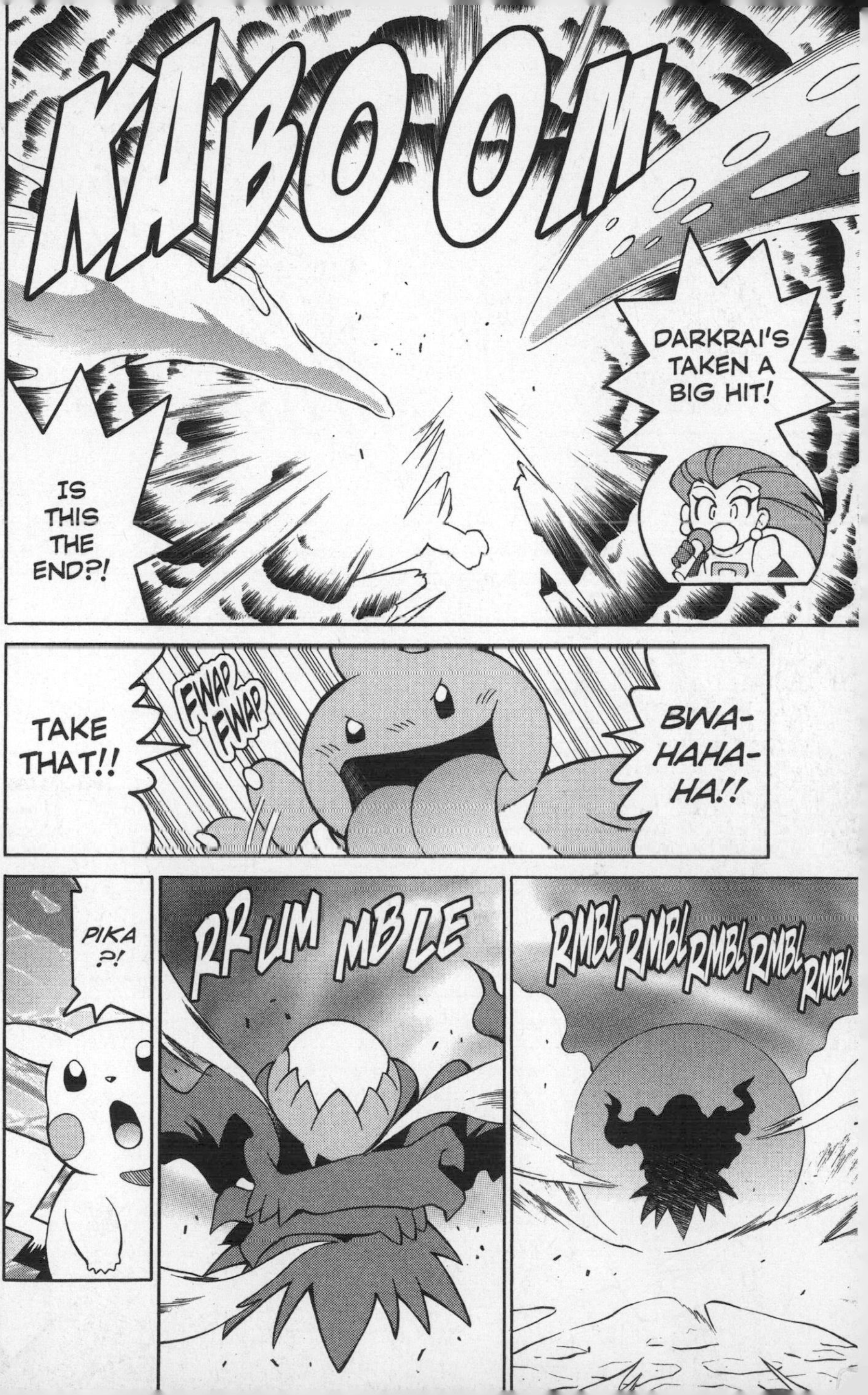
KABOOM
DARKRAI'S TAKEN A BIG HIT!
IS THIS THE END?!
BWA-HAHAHA!!
FWAP FWAP
TAKE THAT!!
RMBL RMBL RMBL RMBL RMBL
RRUMMBLE
PIKA ?!

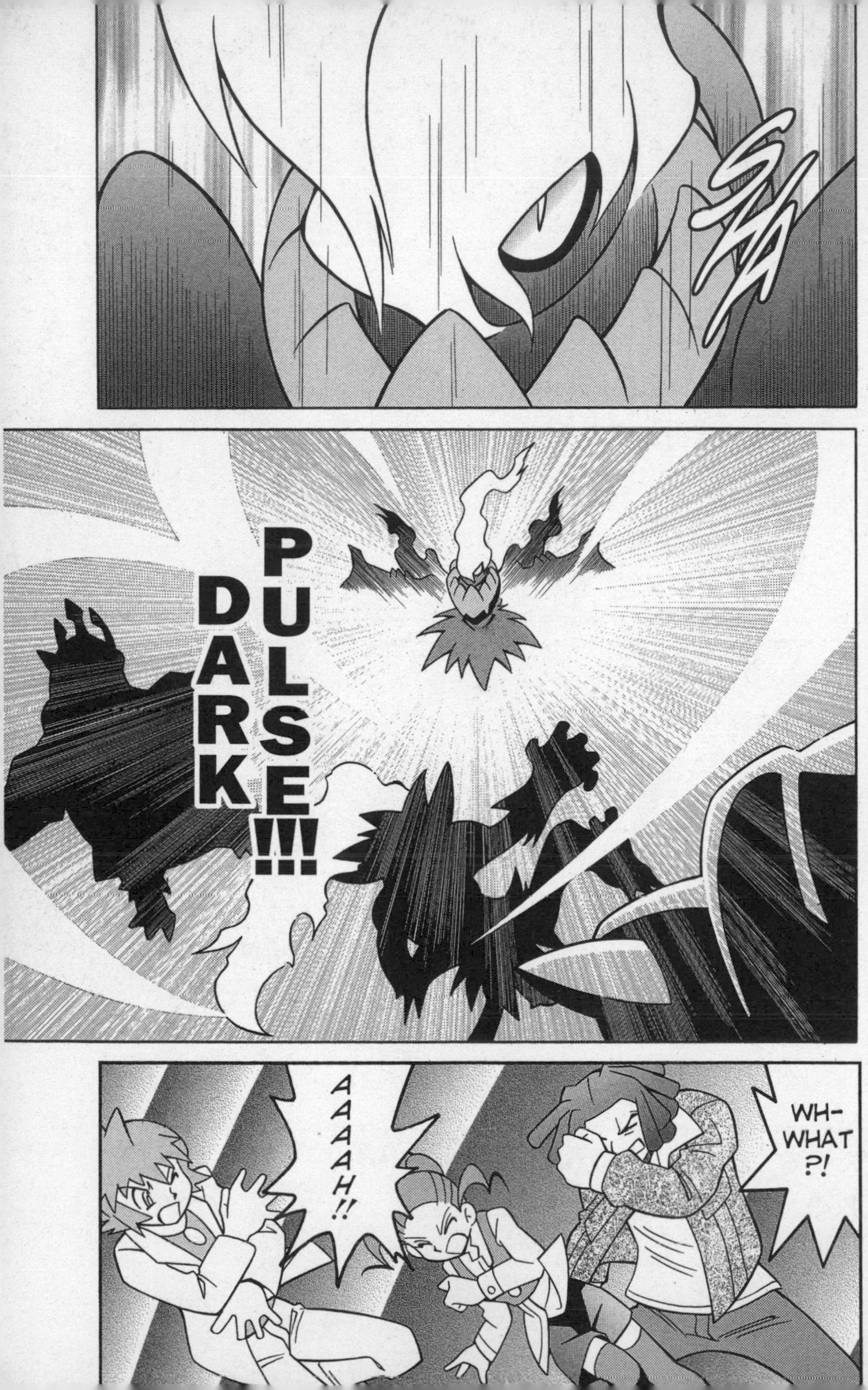
SHA
DARK PULSE!!!
WH-WHAT?!
AAAAAH!!

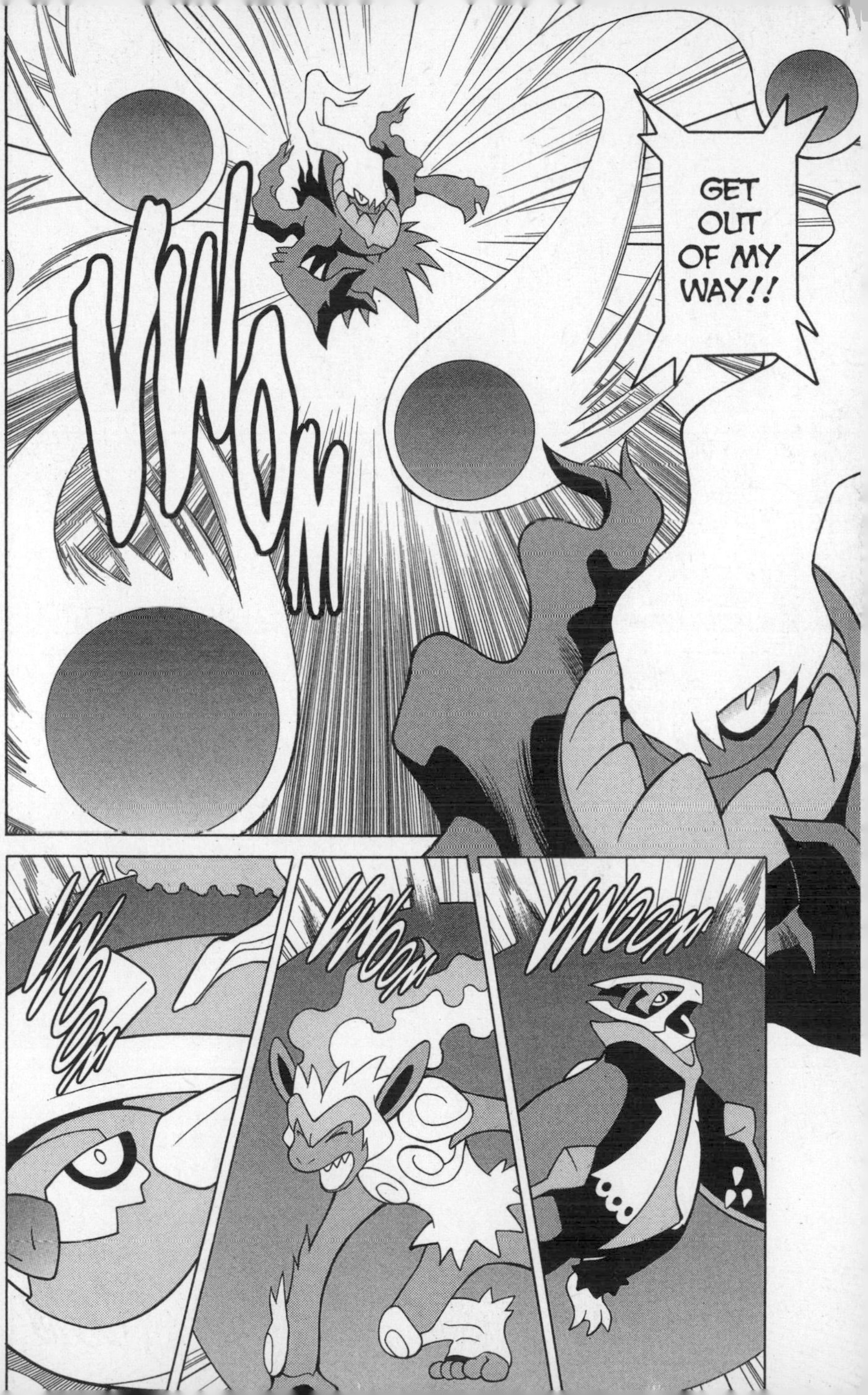
GET OUT OF MY WAY!!
VWOOM
VWOOM
VWOOM
VWOOM

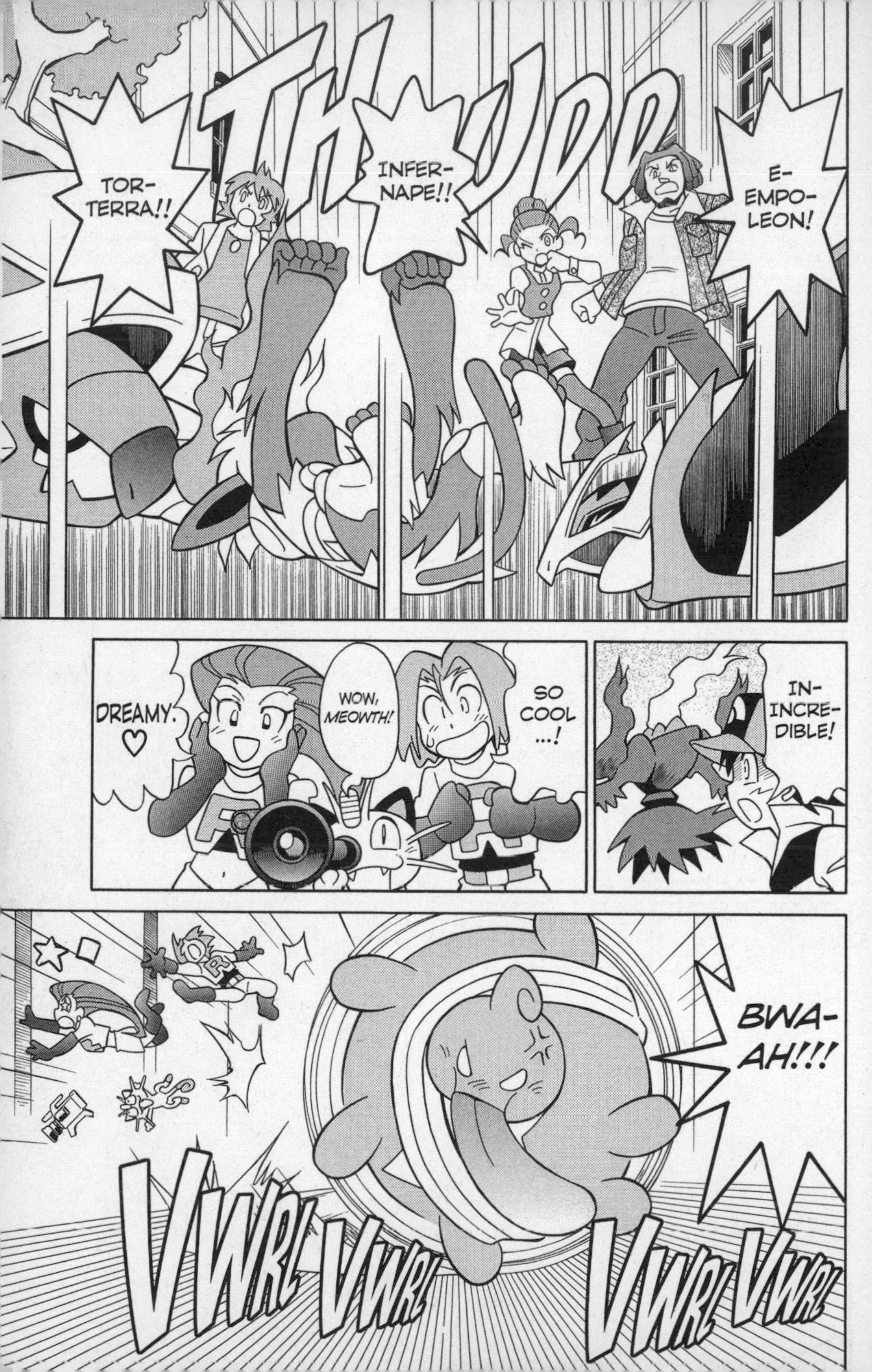
E-EMPOLEON!
INFERNAPE!!
TORTERRA!!
IN-INCREDIBLE!
SO COOL...!
WOW, MEOWTH!
DREAMY. ♡
BWA-AH!!!

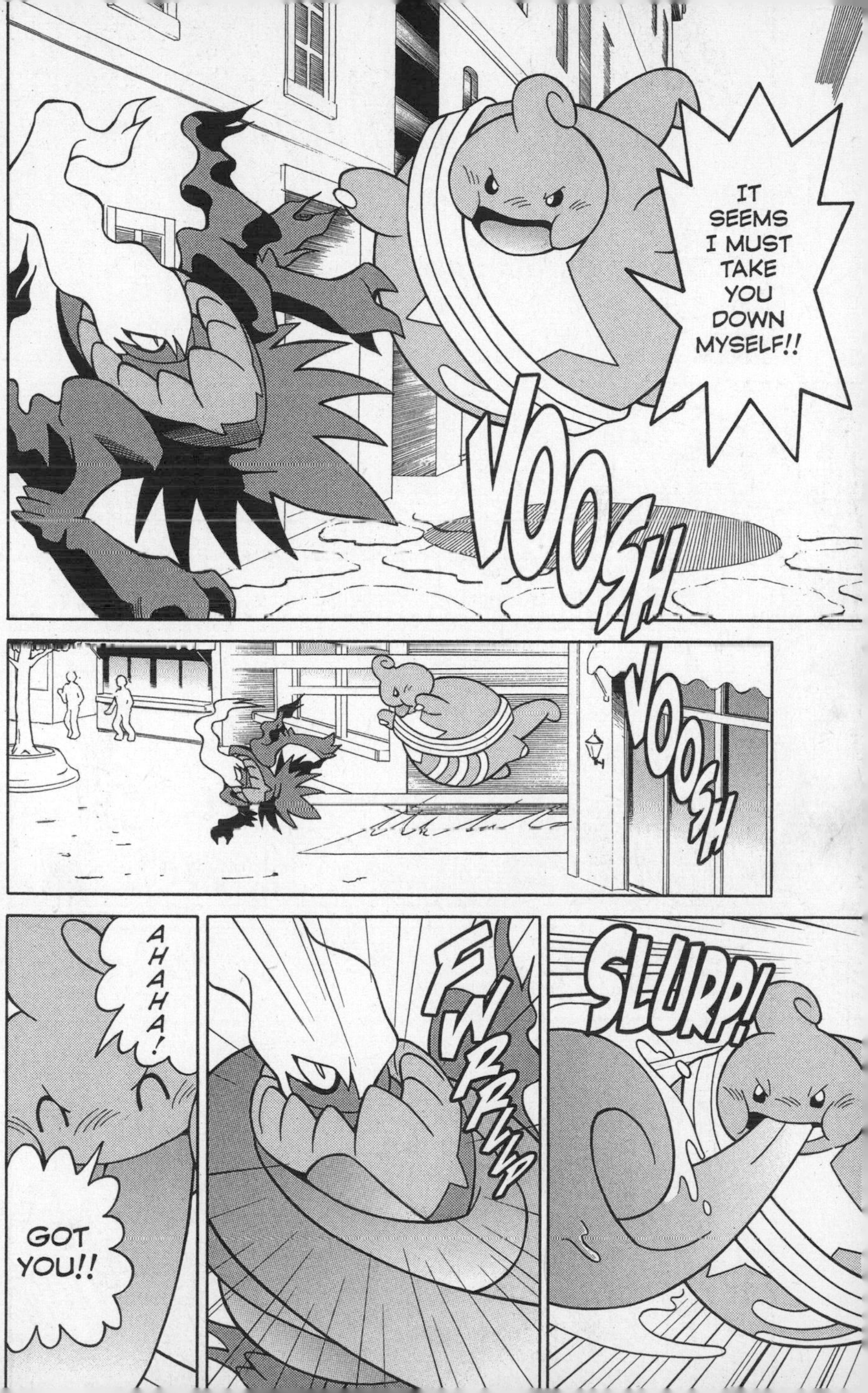
IT SEEMS I MUST TAKE YOU DOWN MYSELF!!
VOOSH
VOOSH
SLURP!
FWRRRR
AHAHA!
GOT YOU!!

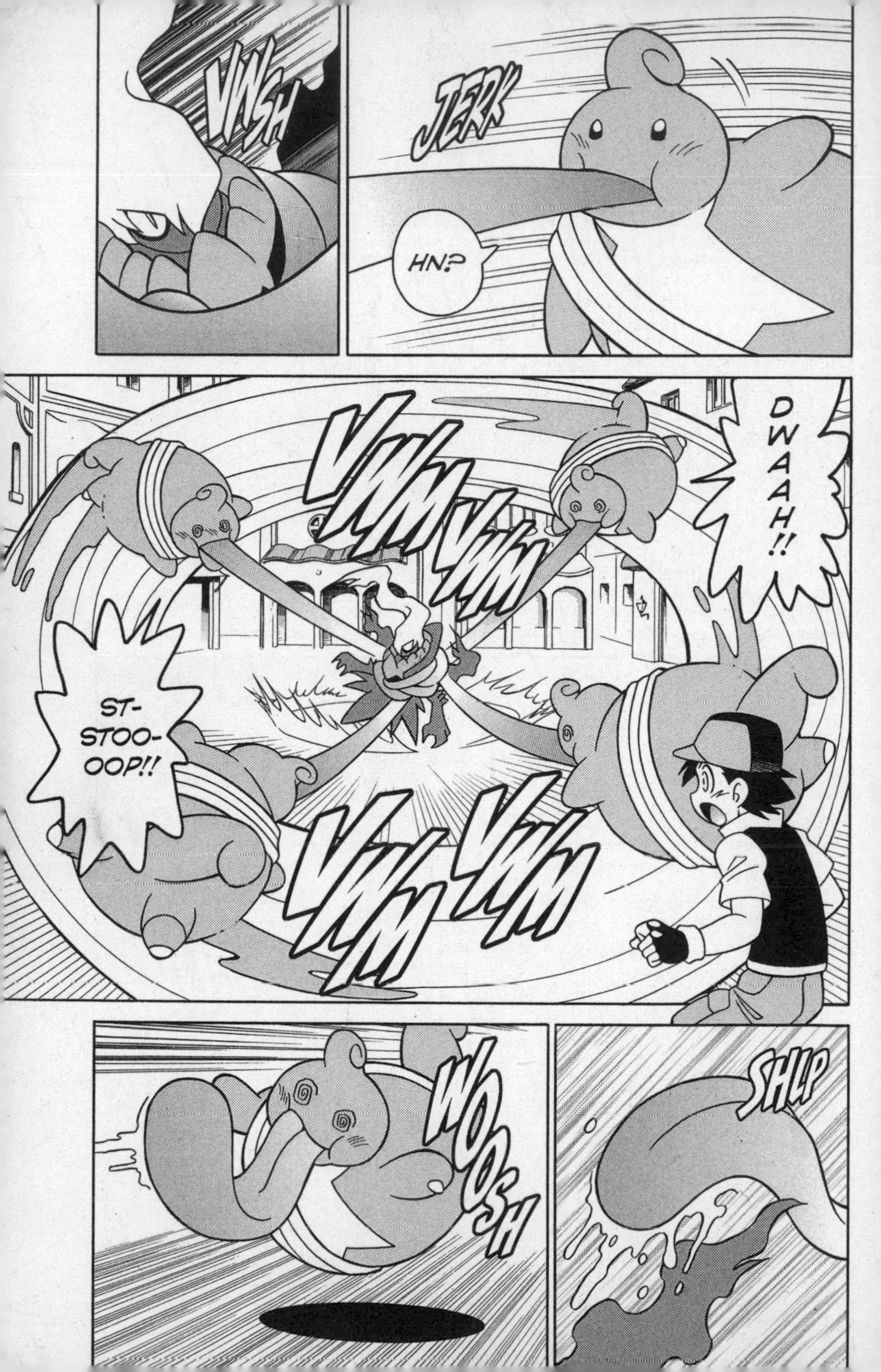
JERK
HN?
VWSH
DWAAH!!
VWM VWM
ST-STOOO-OOP!!
VWM VWM
SHLP
WOOSH

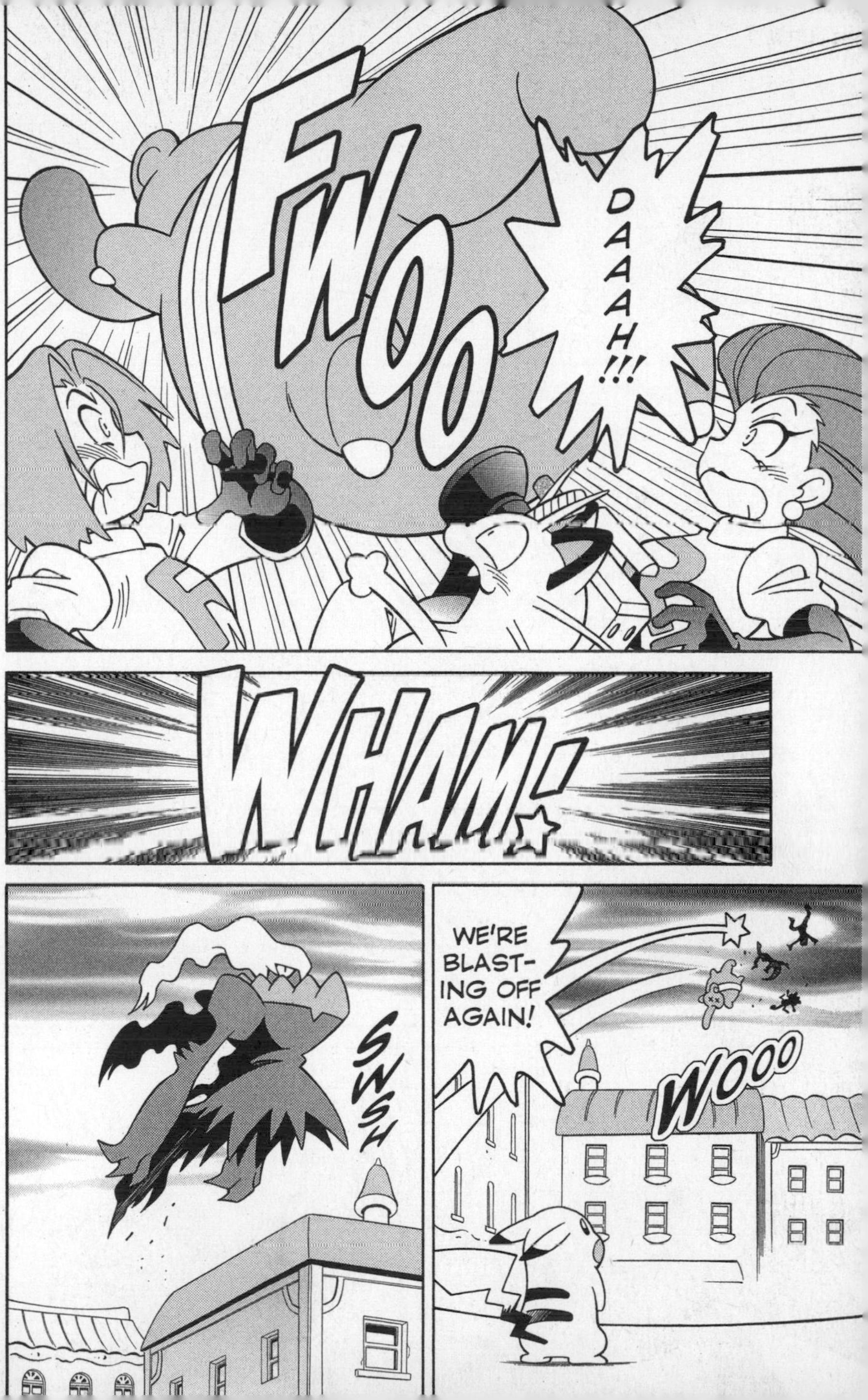
FWOOO
DAAAAH!!!
WHAM!
WE'RE BLASTING OFF AGAIN!
WOOO
SWSH

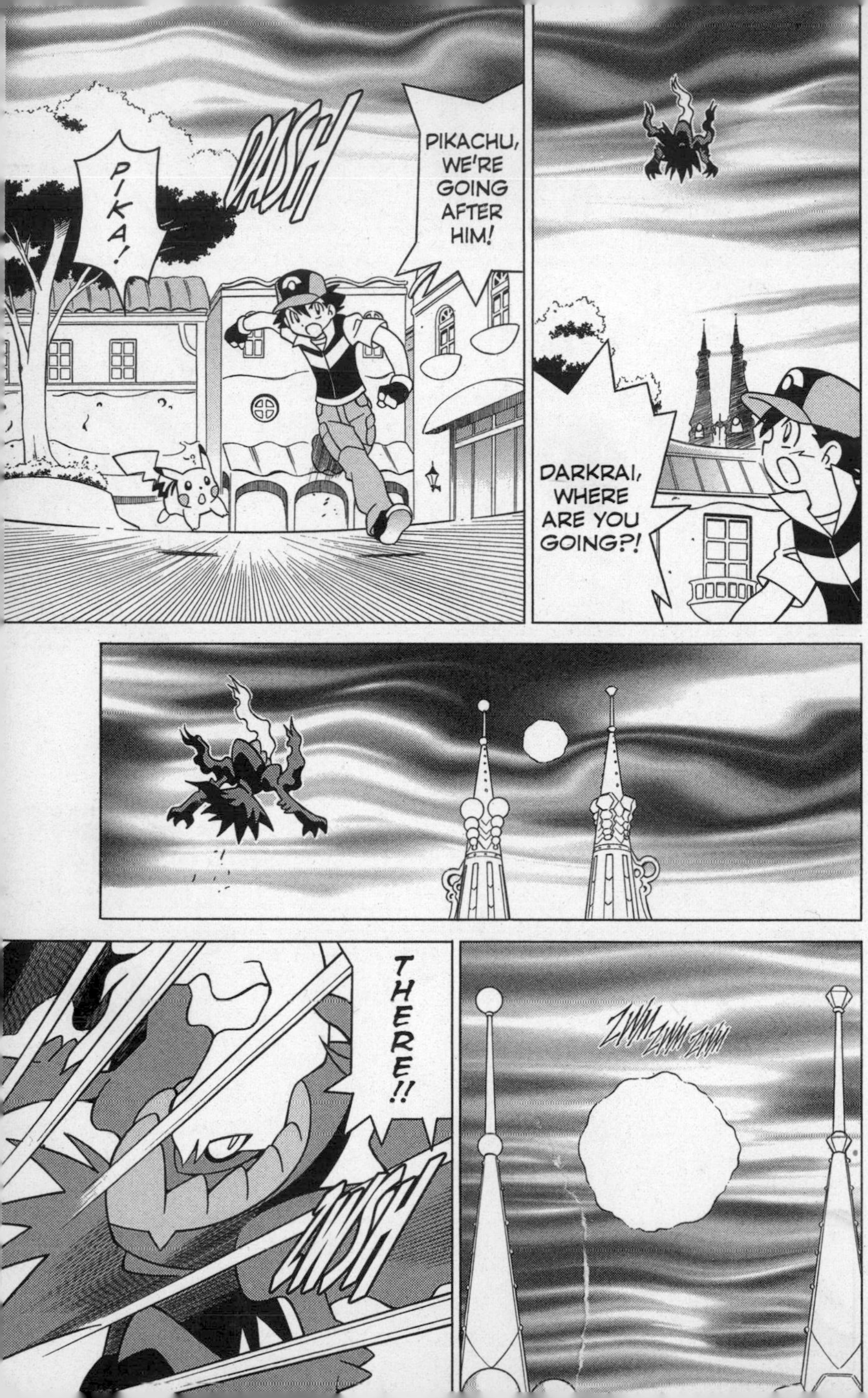
DARKRAI, WHERE ARE YOU GOING?!
PIKACHU, WE'RE GOING AFTER HIM!
DASH
PIKA!
ZWM ZWM ZWM
THERE!!

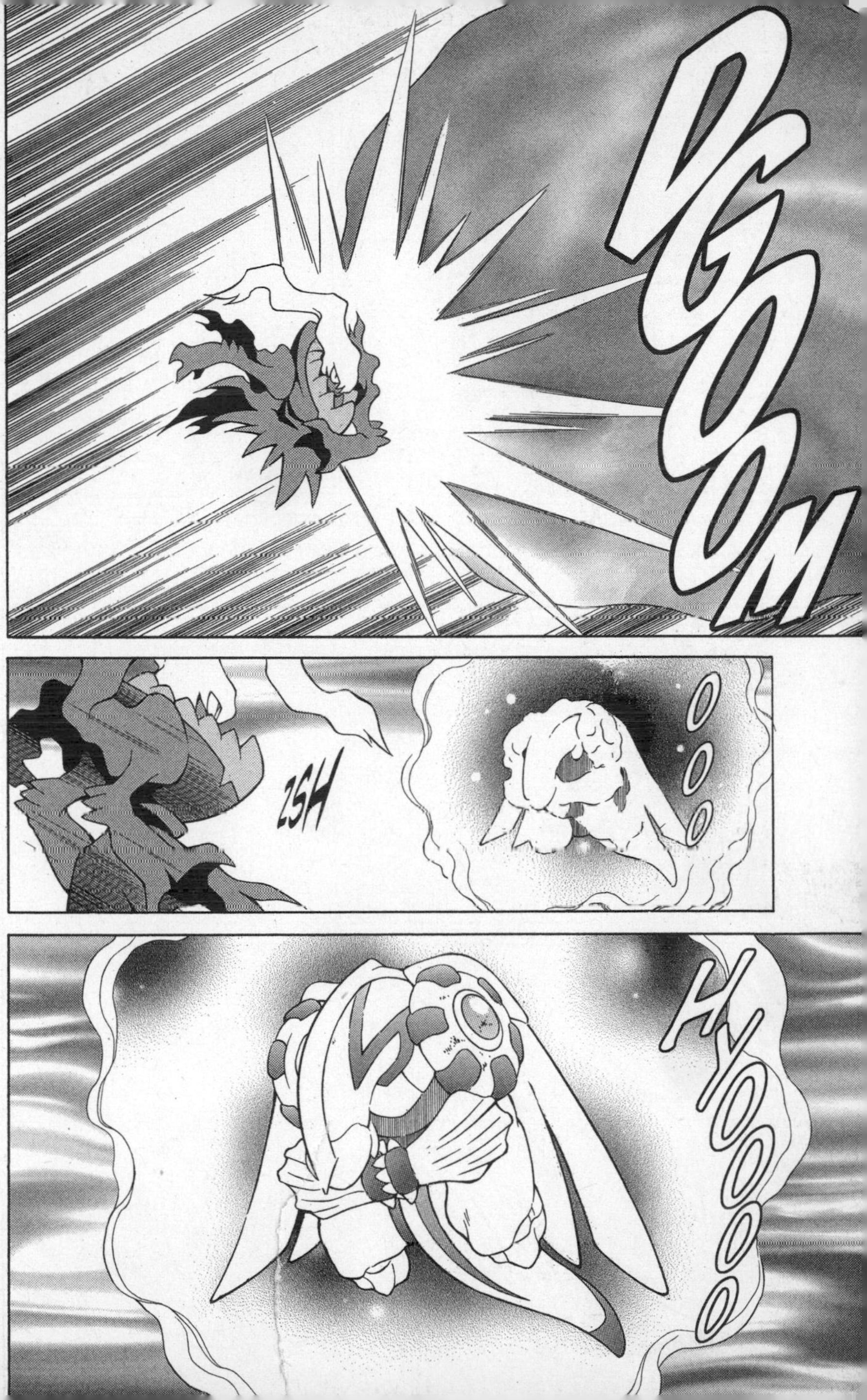
DGOOOM
OOO
ZSH
HYOOOO

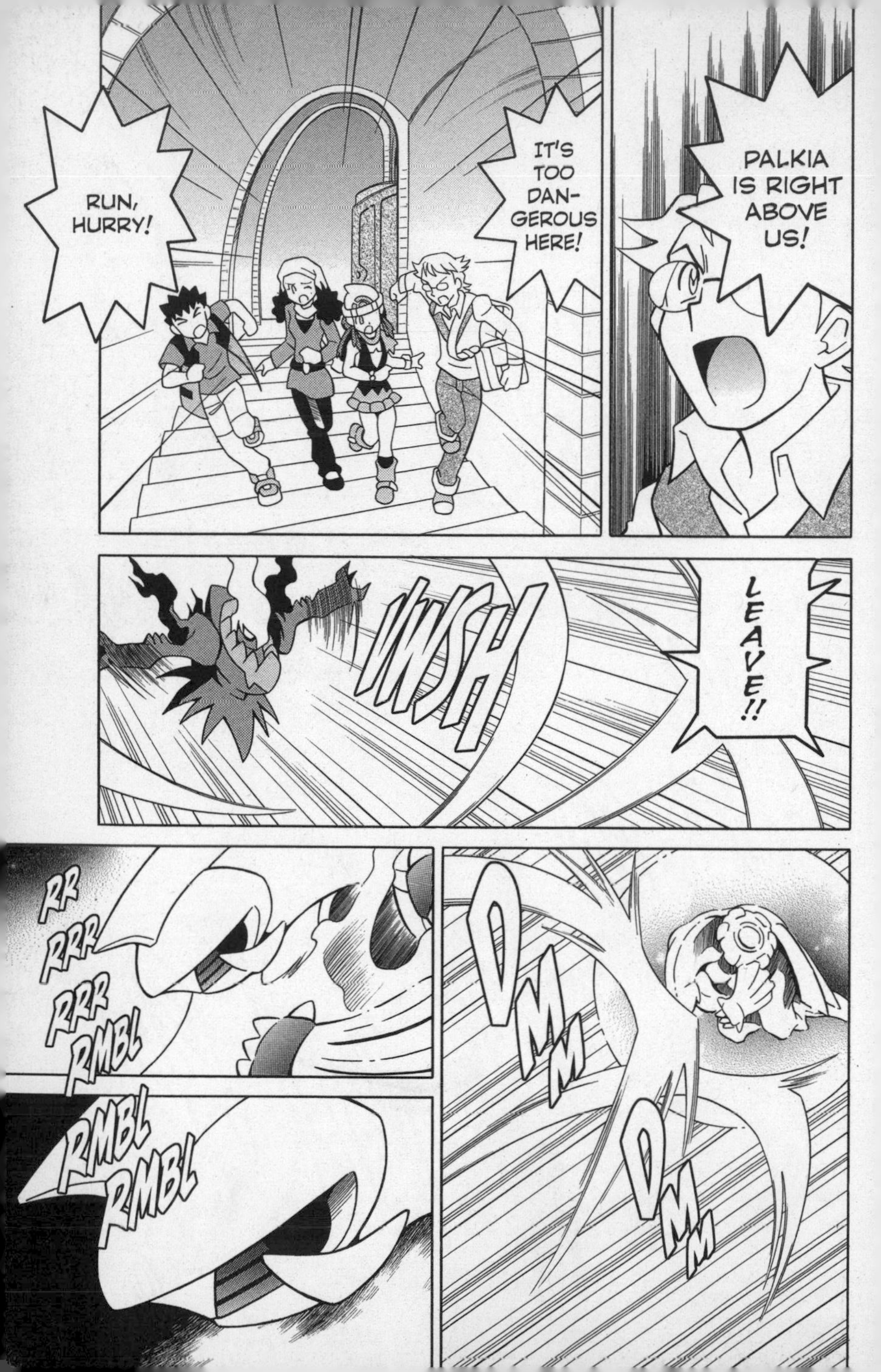
PALKIA IS RIGHT ABOVE US!
IT'S TOO DAN-GEROUS HERE!
RUN, HURRY!
LEAVE!!
VWSH
OMMM
OMMM
RR RRR RRR RMBL
RMBL RMBL

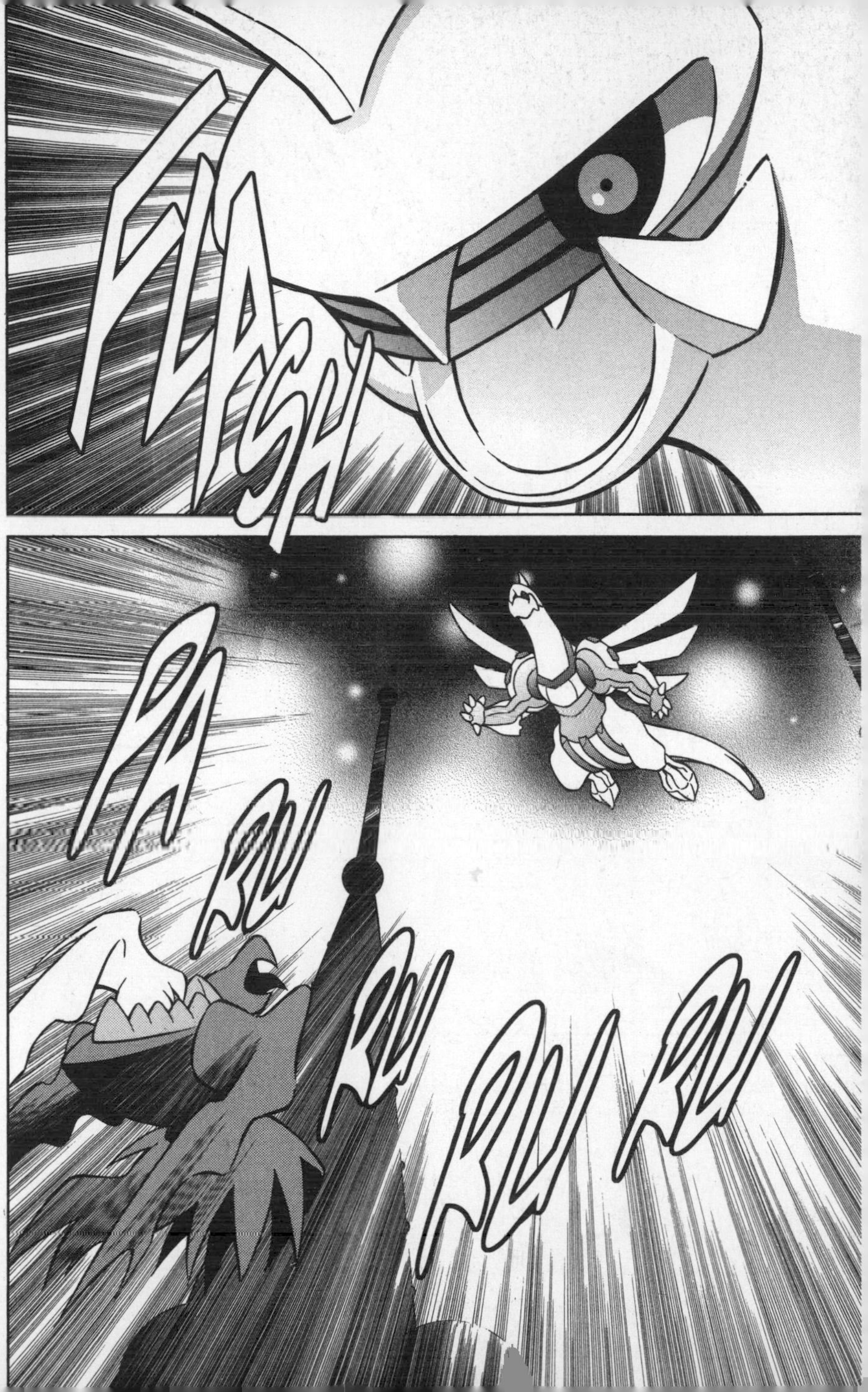
FLASH
PA RU RU RU RU

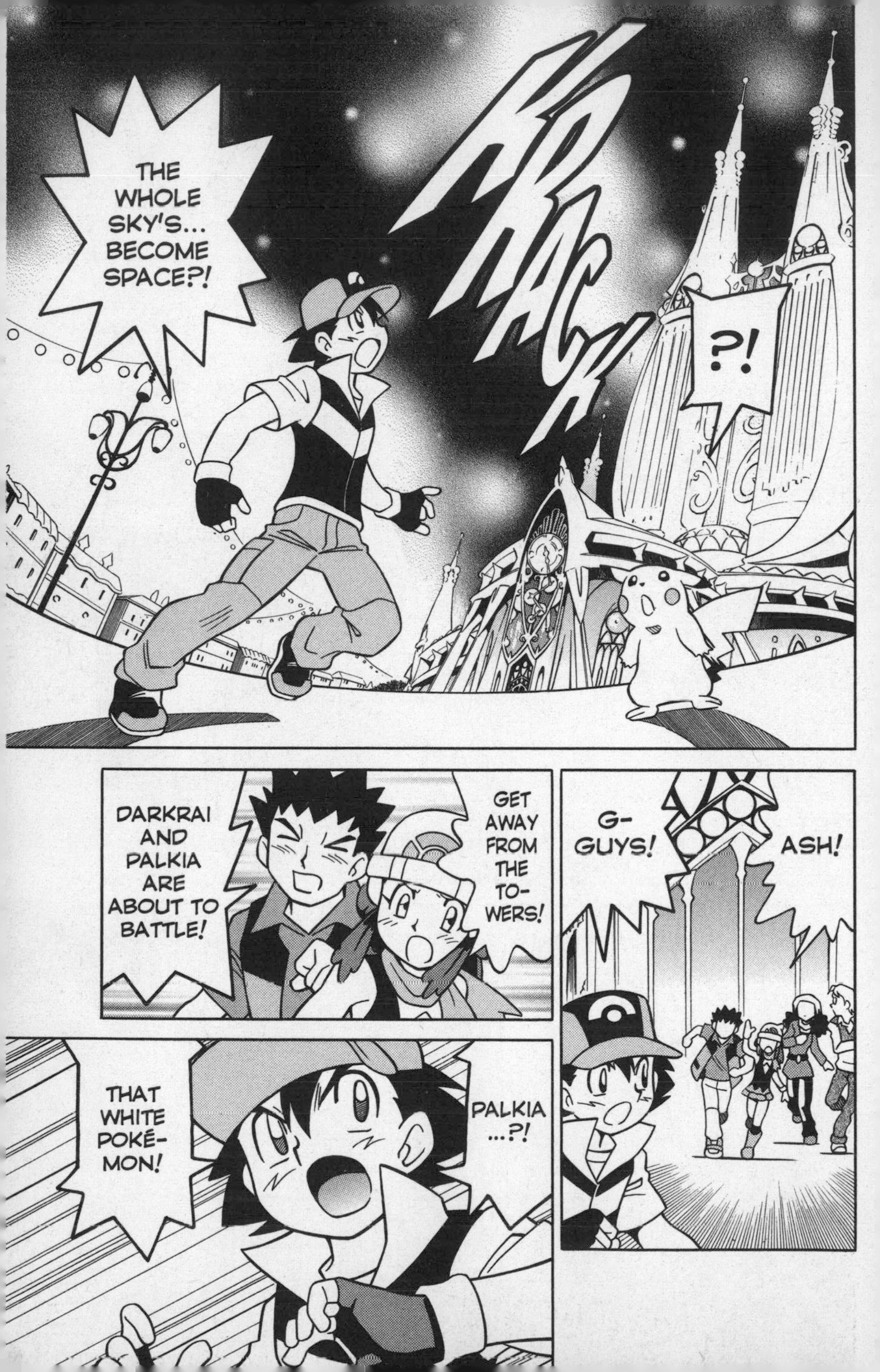
KRACK
?!
THE WHOLE SKY'S... BECOME SPACE?!
ASH!
G-GUYS!
GET AWAY FROM THE TO-WERS!
DARKRAI AND PALKIA ARE ABOUT TO BATTLE!
PALKIA ...?!
THAT WHITE POKÉ-MON!

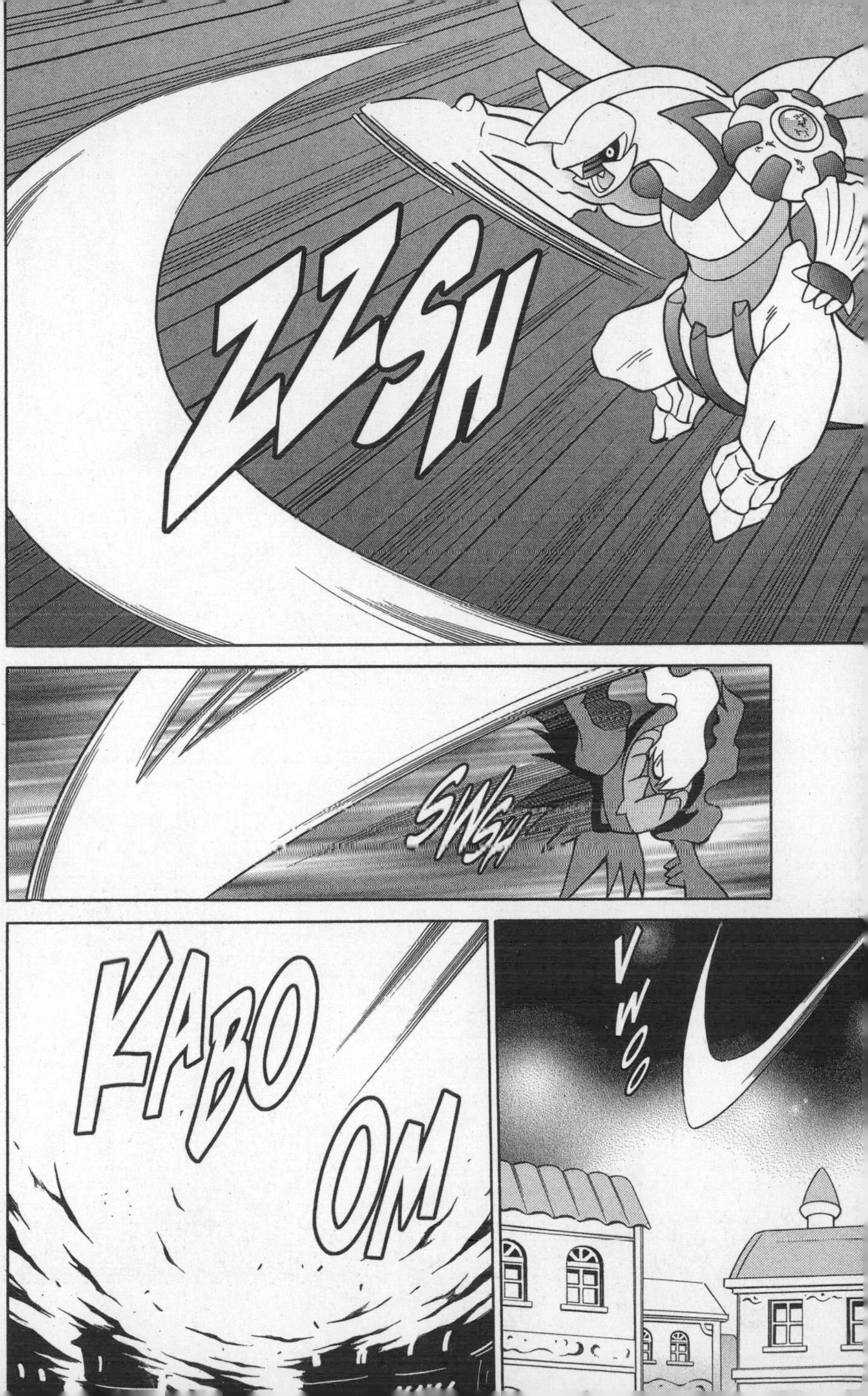
ZZSH
SWSH
VWOO
KABOOM

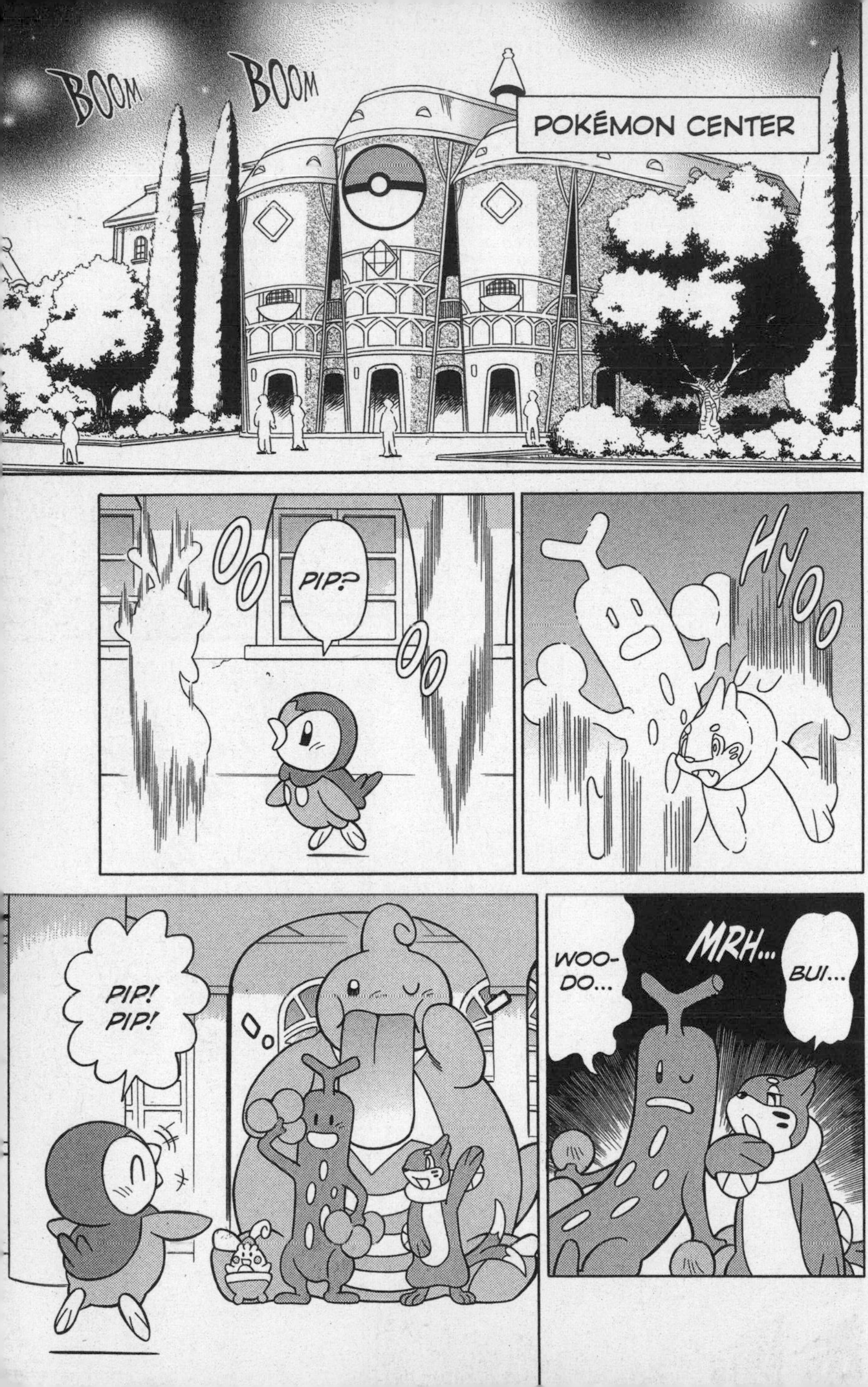
POKÉMON CENTER
BOOM
BOOM
HYOO
PIP?
BUI...
MRH...
WOO-DO...
PIP! PIP!

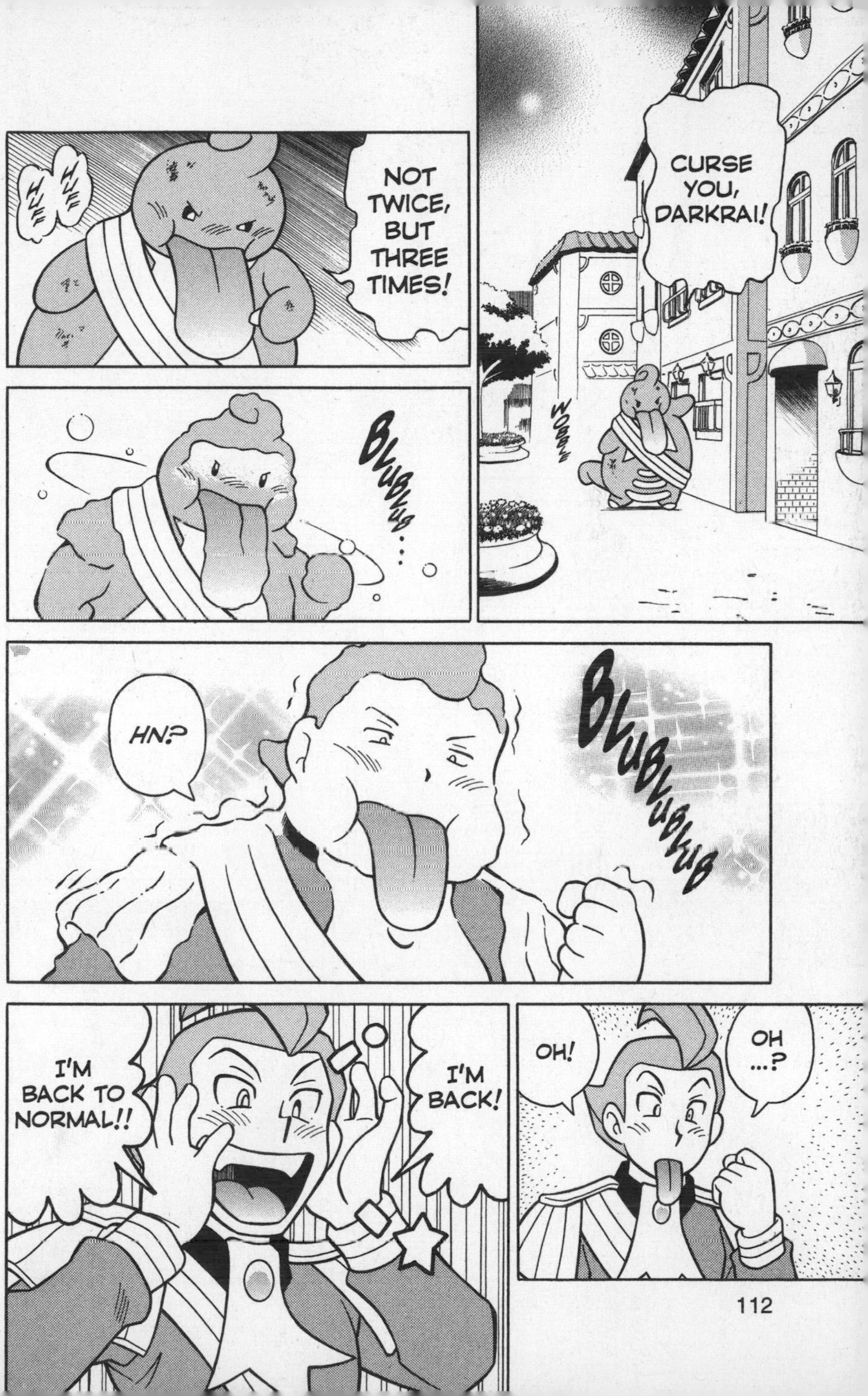
CURSE YOU, DARKRAI!
WOBBLE
NOT TWICE, BUT THREE TIMES!
BLUBLUB...
BLUBLUBLUBLUB
HN?
OH ...?
OH!
I'M BACK!
I'M BACK TO NORMAL!!

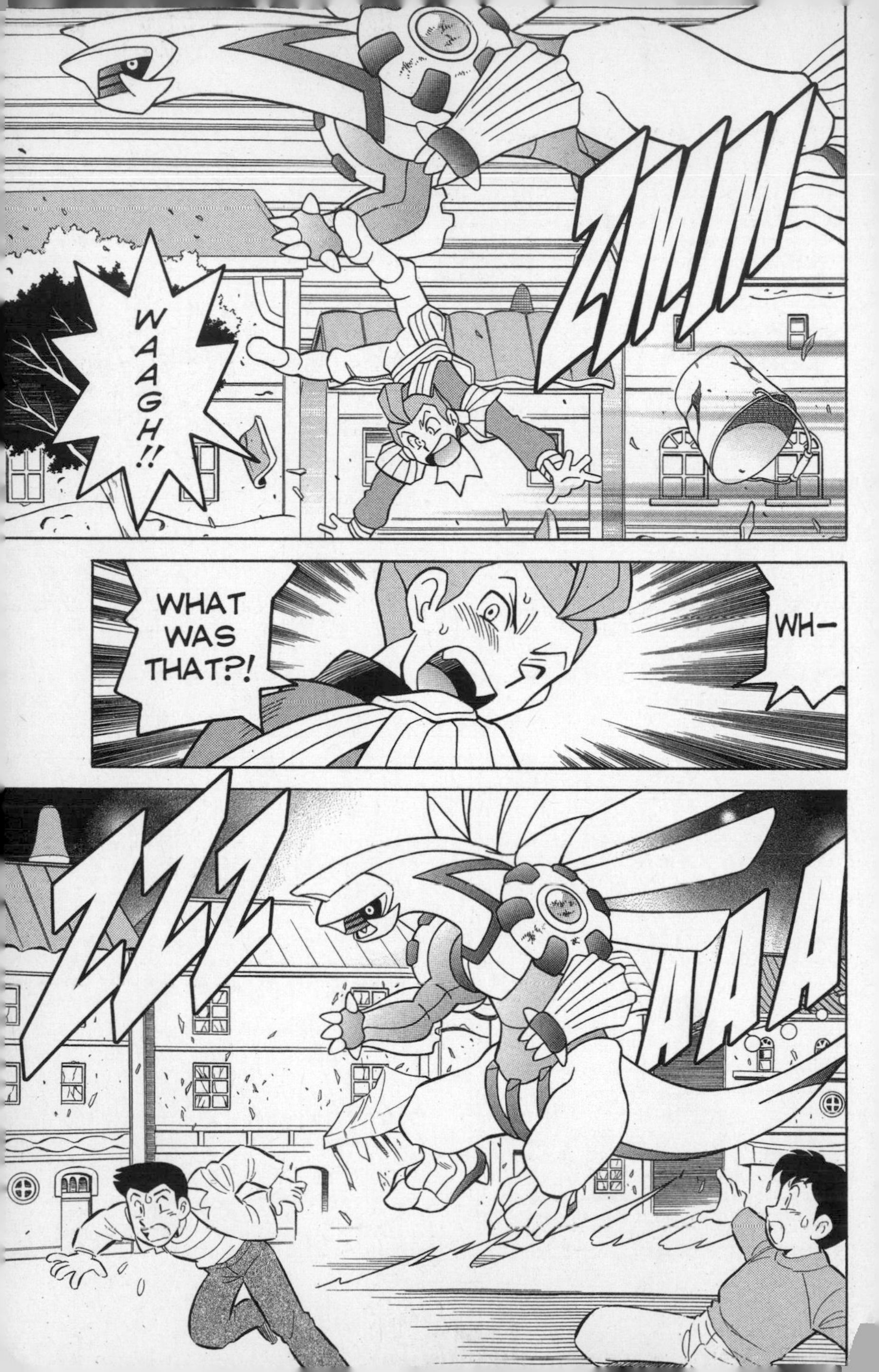
WAAGH!!
WH-
WHAT WAS THAT?!

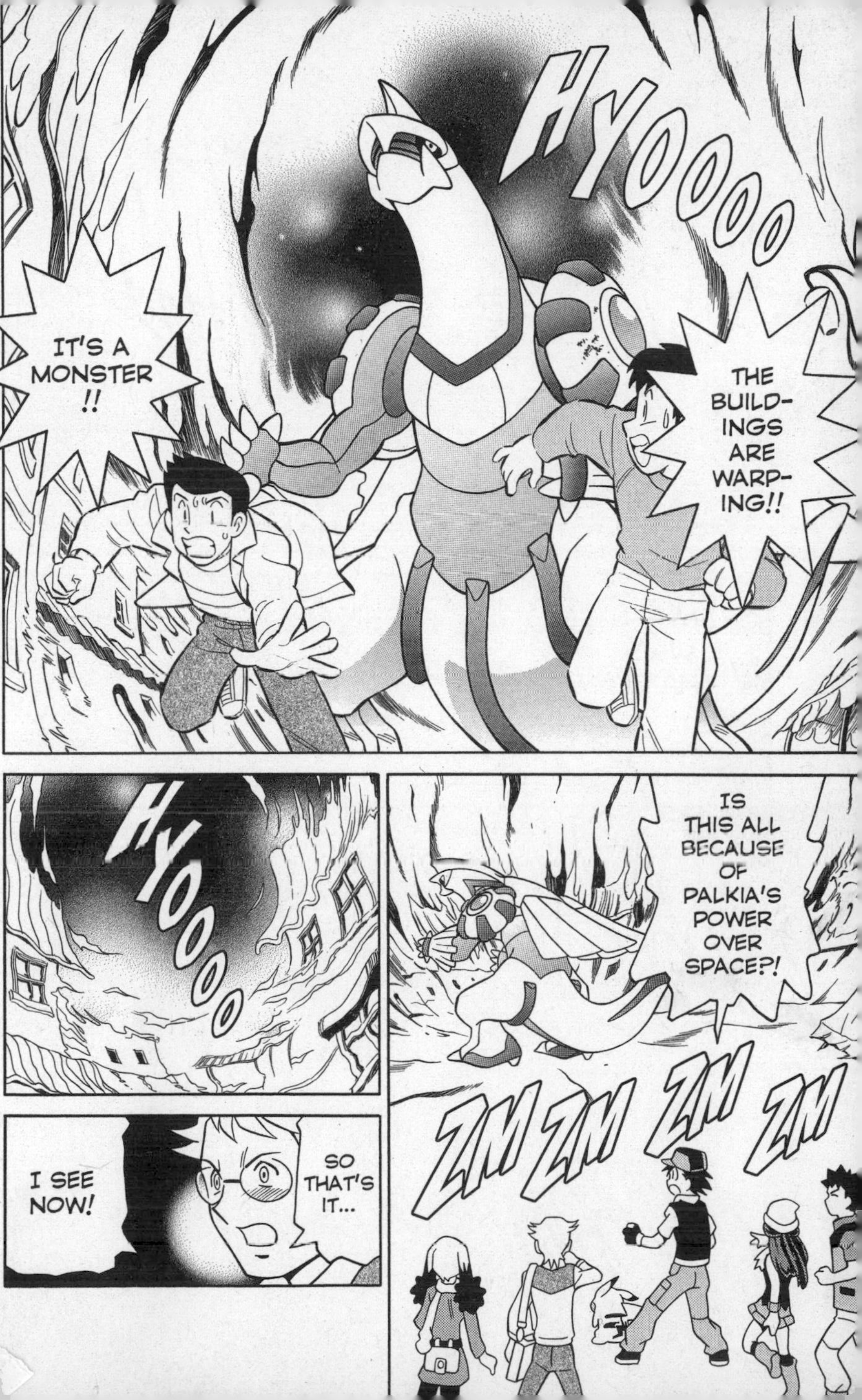
HYOOOO
THE BUILD-INGS ARE WARP-ING!!
IT'S A MONSTER!!
IS THIS ALL BECAUSE OF PALKIA'S POWER OVER SPACE?!
ZM ZM ZM ZM
HYOOOO
SO THAT'S IT...
I SEE NOW!

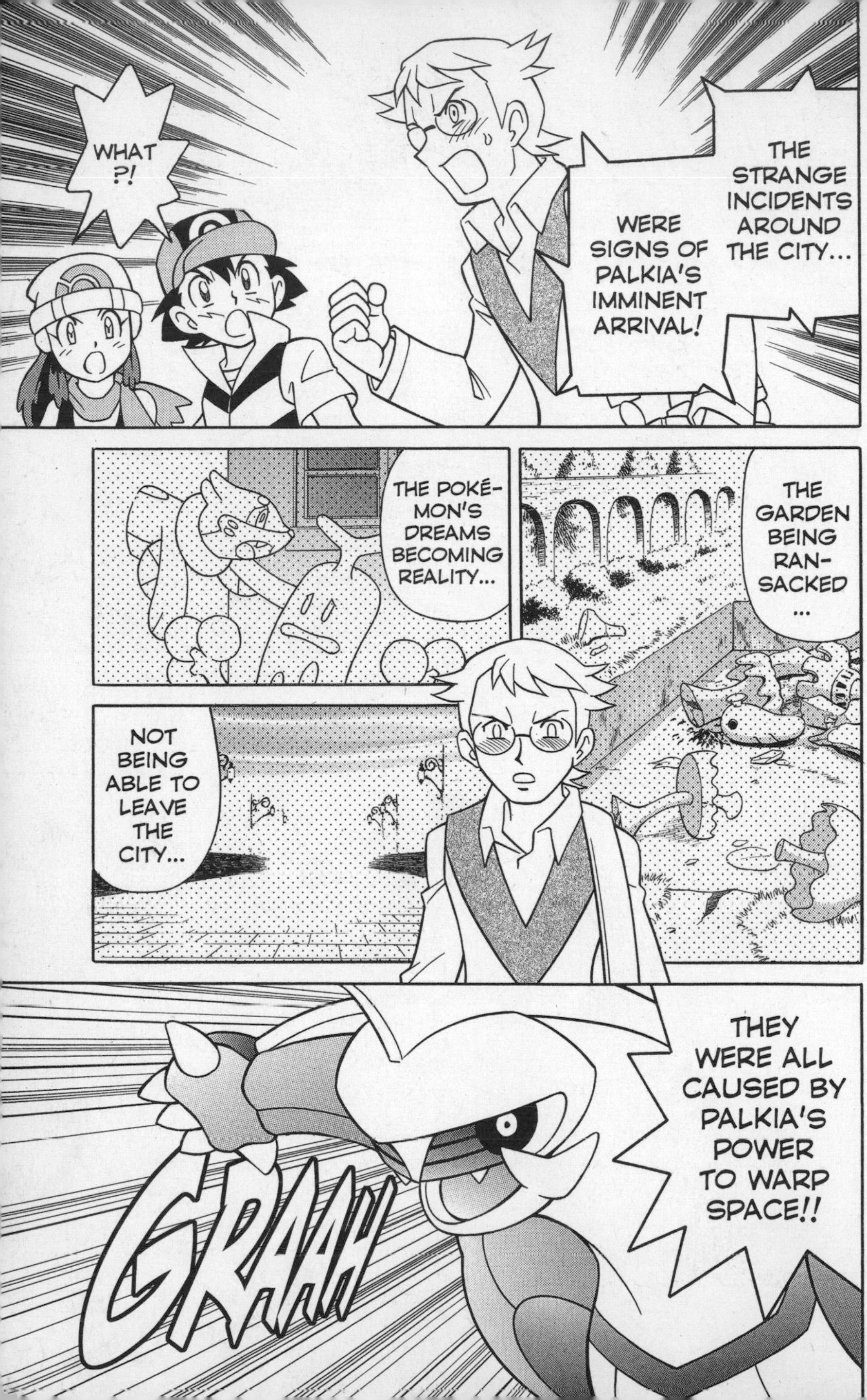
THE STRANGE INCIDENTS AROUND THE CITY...
WERE SIGNS OF PALKIA'S IMMINENT ARRIVAL!
WHAT?!
THE GARDEN BEING RAN-SACKED...
THE POKÉ-MON'S DREAMS BECOMING REALITY...
NOT BEING ABLE TO LEAVE THE CITY...
THEY WERE ALL CAUSED BY PALKIA'S POWER TO WARP SPACE!!
GRAAAH

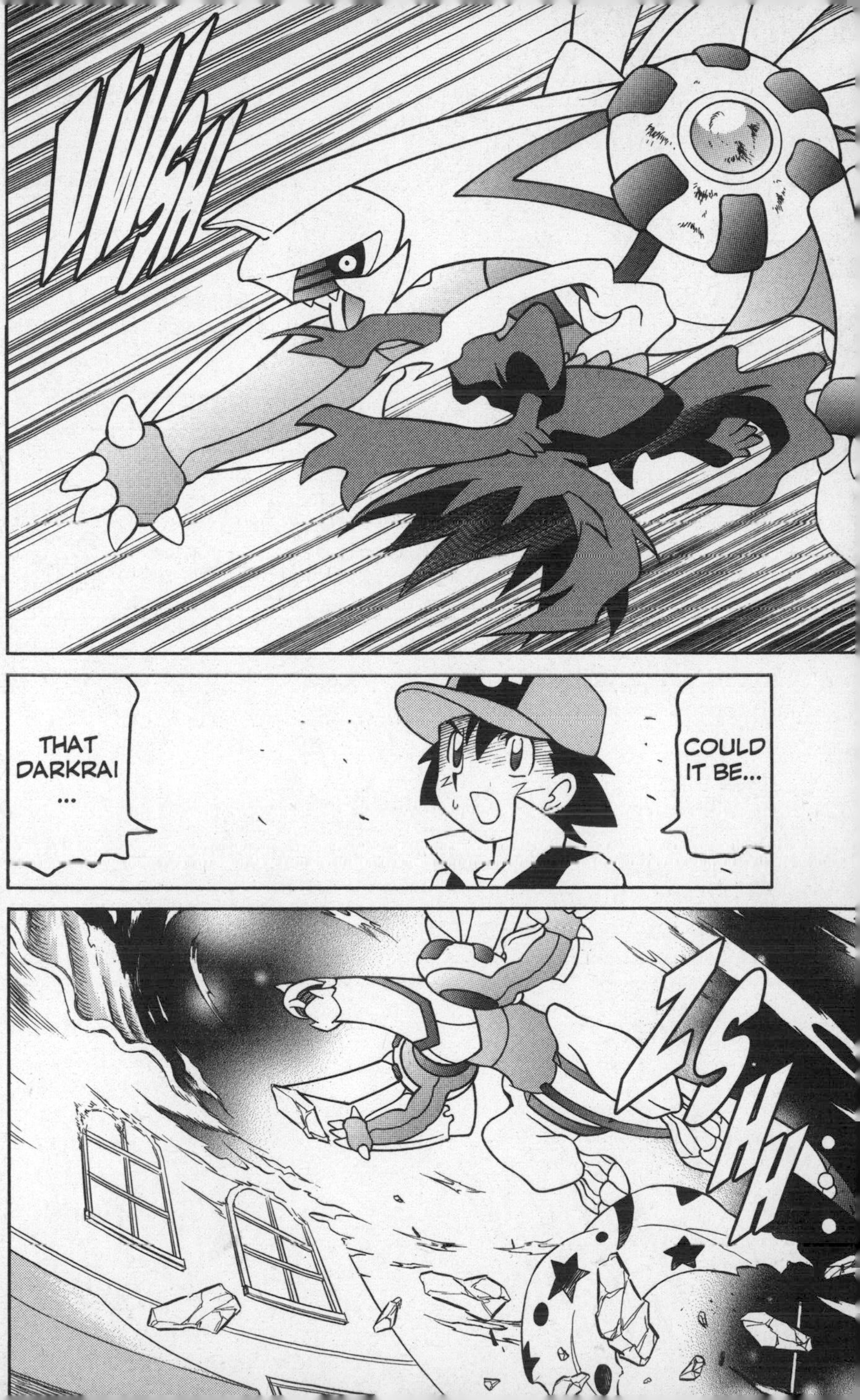
VWOSH
COULD IT BE...
THAT DARKRAI ...
ZSHH

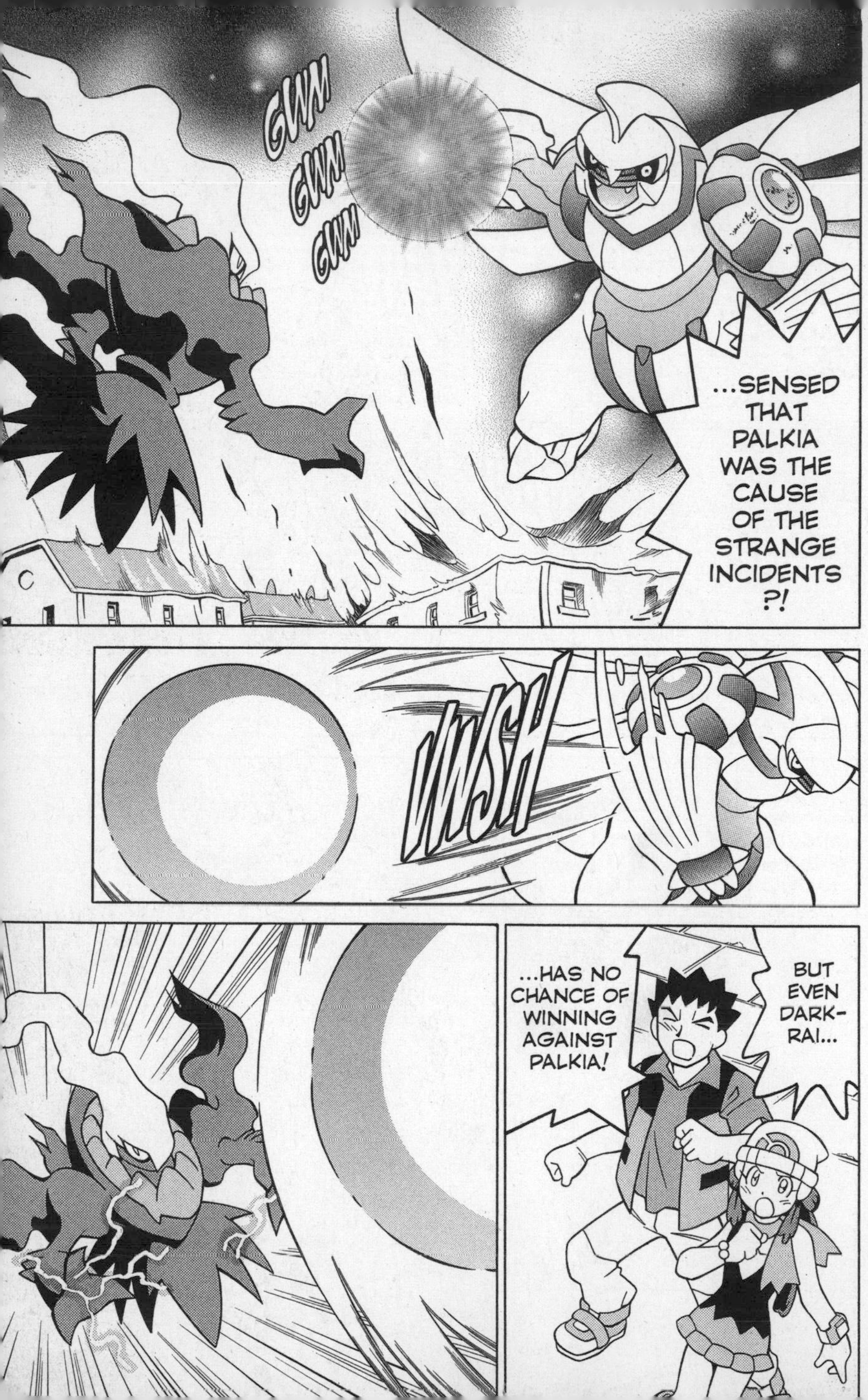
GWM GWM GWM
...SENSED THAT PALKIA WAS THE CAUSE OF THE STRANGE INCIDENTS?!
VWSH
BUT EVEN DARK-RAI...
...HAS NO CHANCE OF WINNING AGAINST PALKIA!

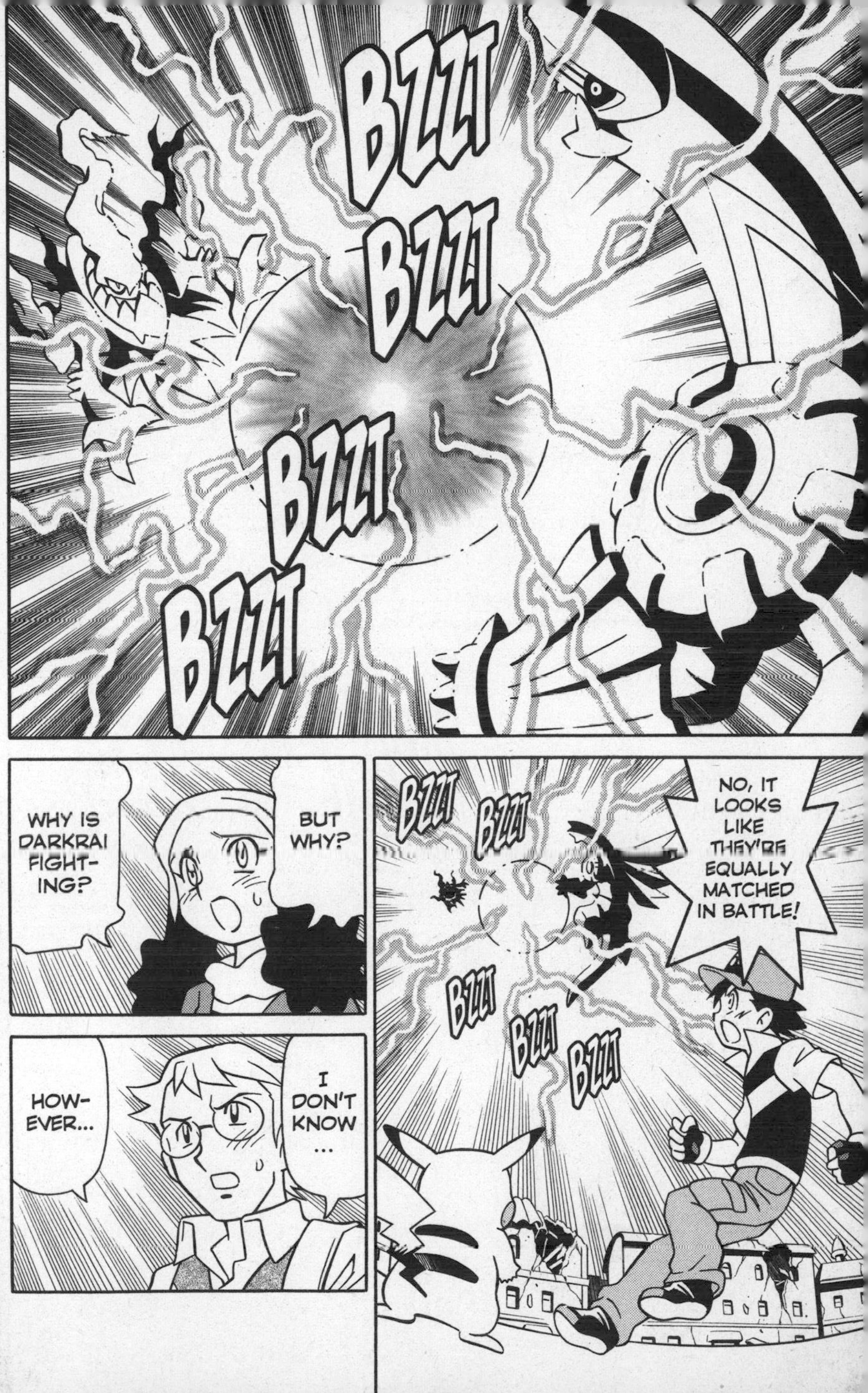
BZZZT
BZZZT
BZZZT
BZZZT
BZZZT
BZZZT
NO, IT LOOKS LIKE THEY'RE EQUALLY MATCHED IN BATTLE!
BZZZT
BZZZT
BZZZT
BUT WHY?
WHY IS DARKRAI FIGHTING?
I DON'T KNOW...
HOWEVER...

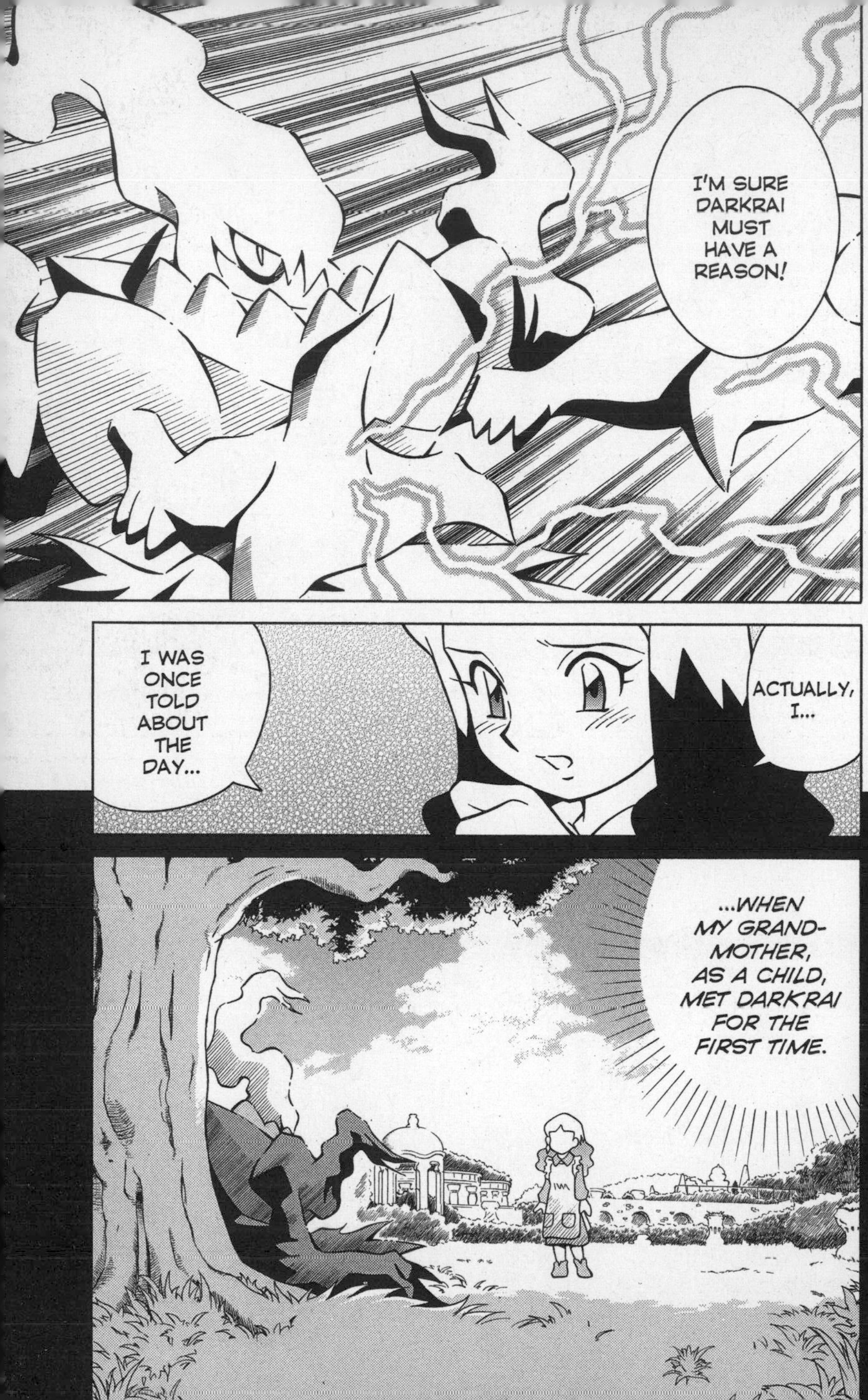
I'M SURE DARKRAI MUST HAVE A REASON!
ACTUALLY, I...
I WAS ONCE TOLD ABOUT THE DAY...
...WHEN MY GRAND-MOTHER, AS A CHILD, MET DARKRAI FOR THE FIRST TIME.

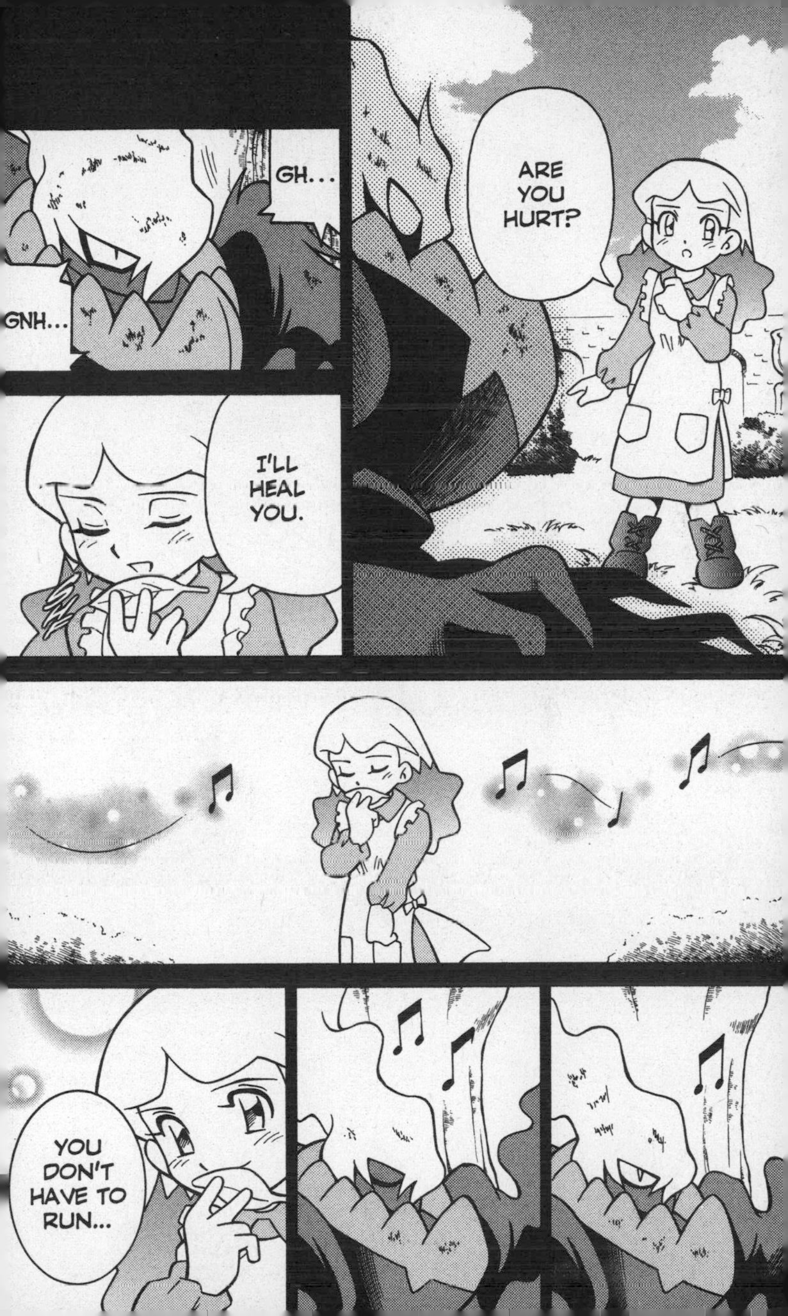
ARE YOU HURT?
GH...
GNH...
I'LL HEAL YOU.
YOU DON'T HAVE TO RUN...

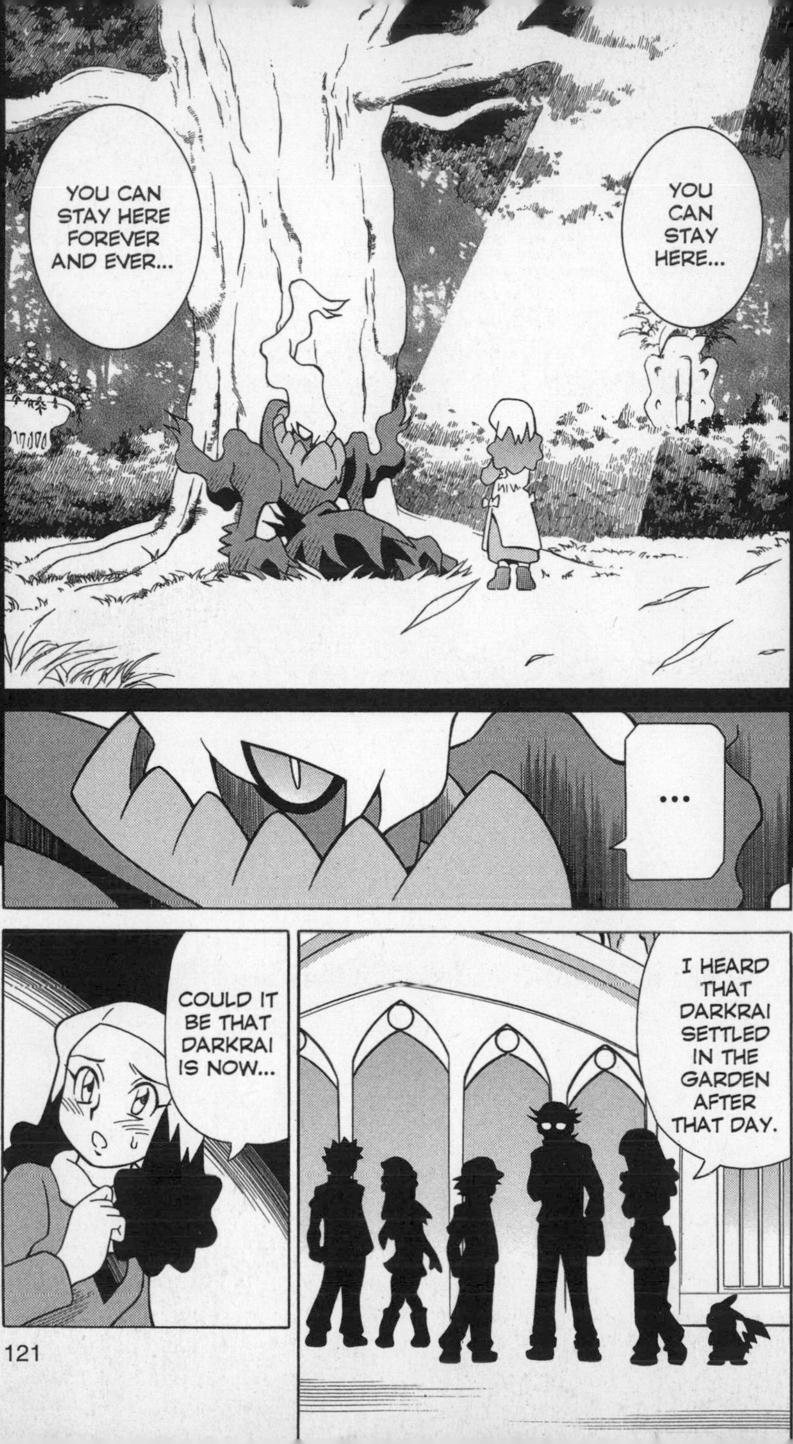
YOU CAN STAY HERE...
YOU CAN STAY HERE FOREVER AND EVER...
...
I HEARD THAT DARKRAI SETTLED IN THE GARDEN AFTER THAT DAY.
COULD IT BE THAT DARKRAI IS NOW...

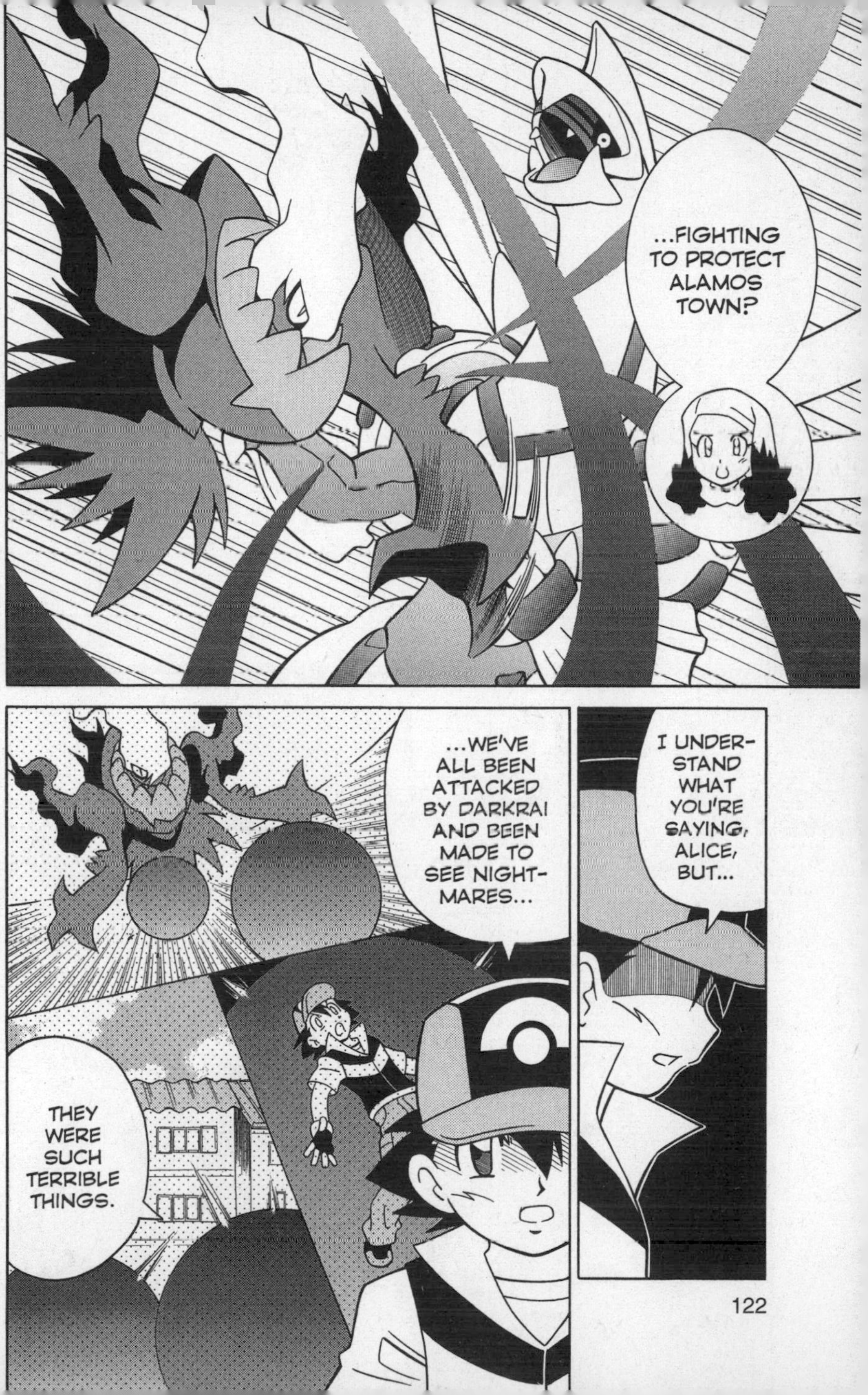
...FIGHTING TO PROTECT ALAMOS TOWN?
I UNDER-STAND WHAT YOU'RE SAYING, ALICE, BUT...
...WE'VE ALL BEEN ATTACKED BY DARKRAI AND BEEN MADE TO SEE NIGHT-MARES...
THEY WERE SUCH TERRIBLE THINGS.

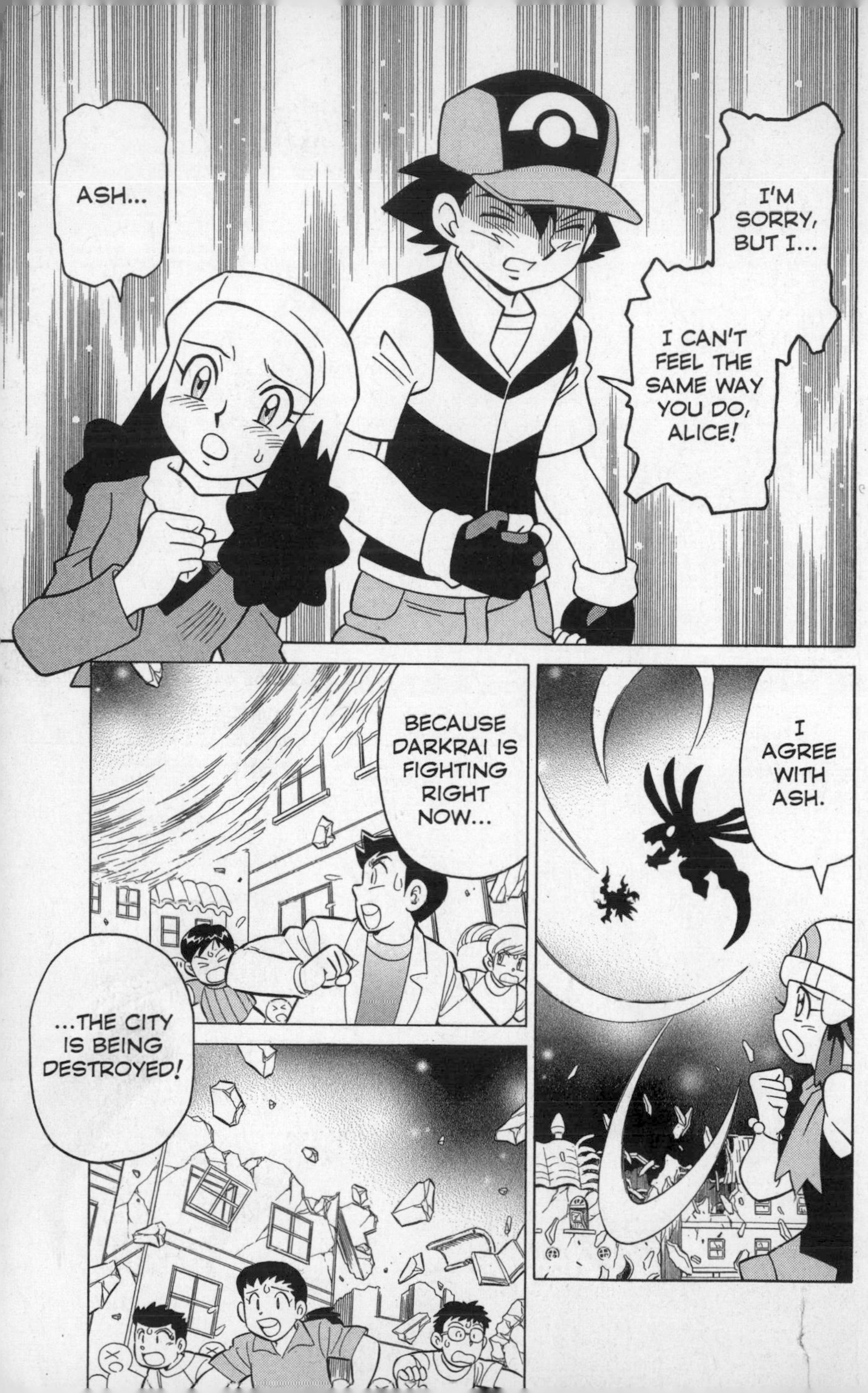
I'M SORRY, BUT I...
I CAN'T FEEL THE SAME WAY YOU DO, ALICE!
ASH...
I AGREE WITH ASH.
BECAUSE DARKRAI IS FIGHTING RIGHT NOW...
...THE CITY IS BEING DESTROYED!

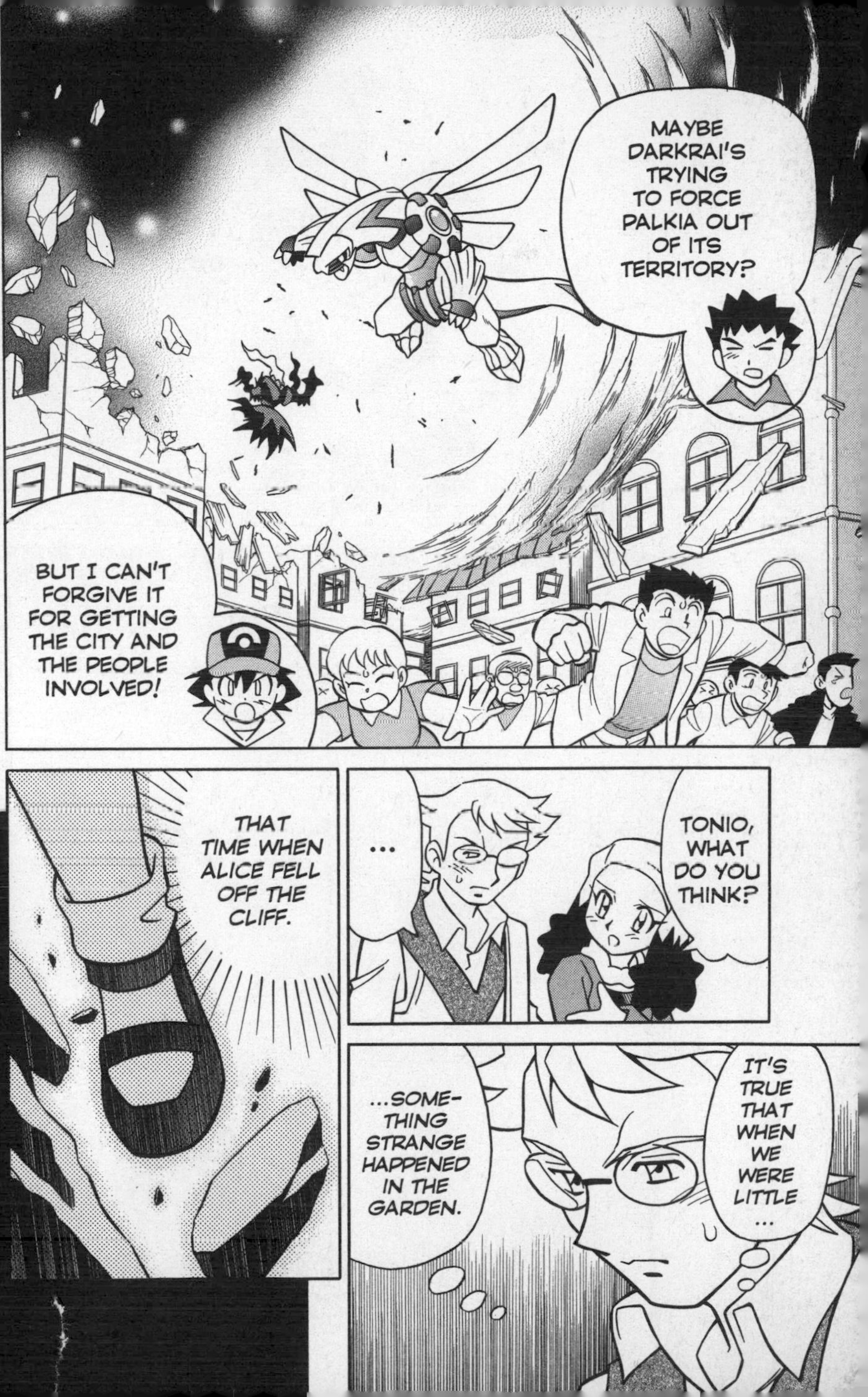
MAYBE DARKRAI'S TRYING TO FORCE PALKIA OUT OF ITS TERRITORY?
BUT I CAN'T FORGIVE IT FOR GETTING THE CITY AND THE PEOPLE INVOLVED!
TONIO, WHAT DO YOU THINK?
...
IT'S TRUE THAT WHEN WE WERE LITTLE ...
...SOME-THING STRANGE HAPPENED IN THE GARDEN.
THAT TIME WHEN ALICE FELL OFF THE CLIFF.

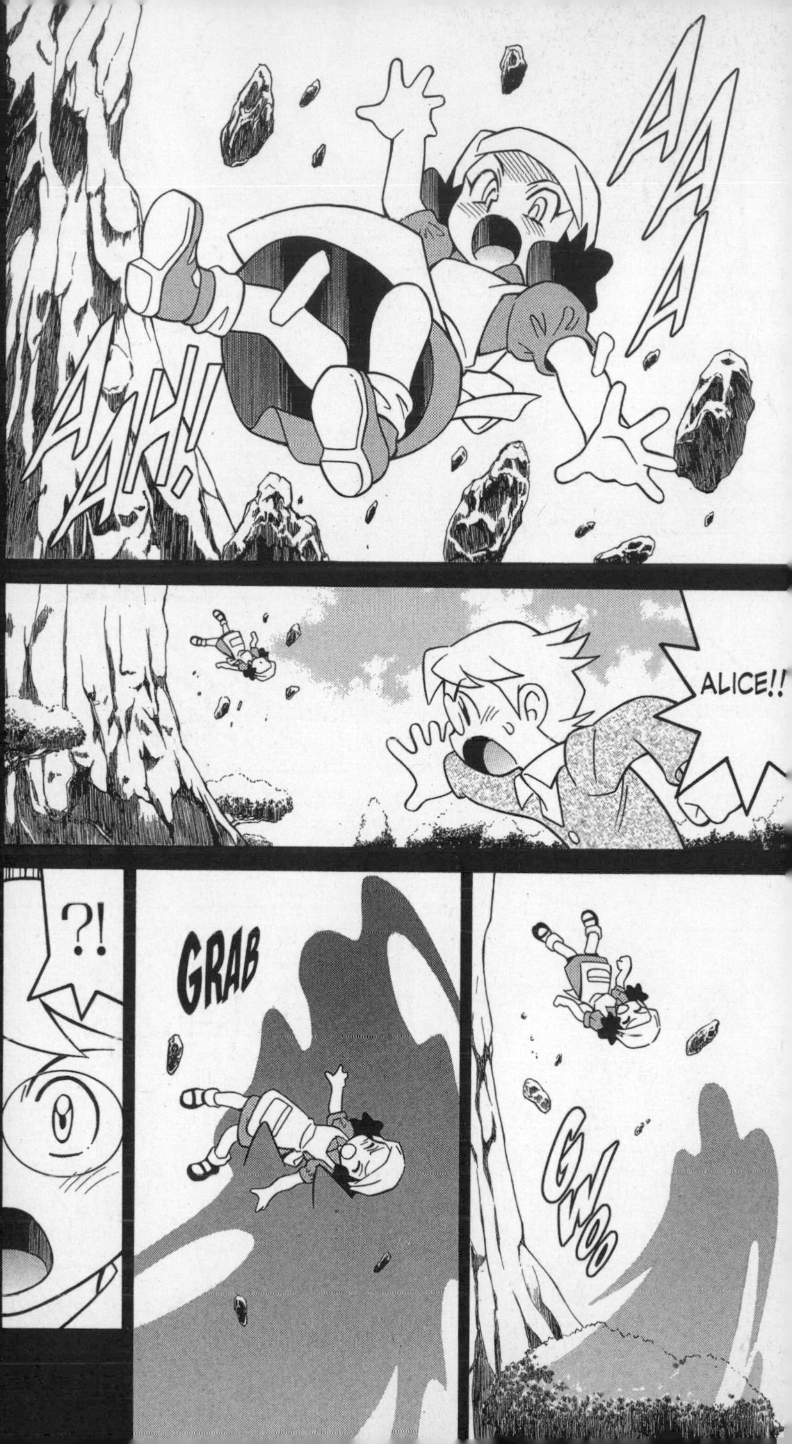
AAAA
AAH!
ALICE!!
GWOO
GRAB
?!

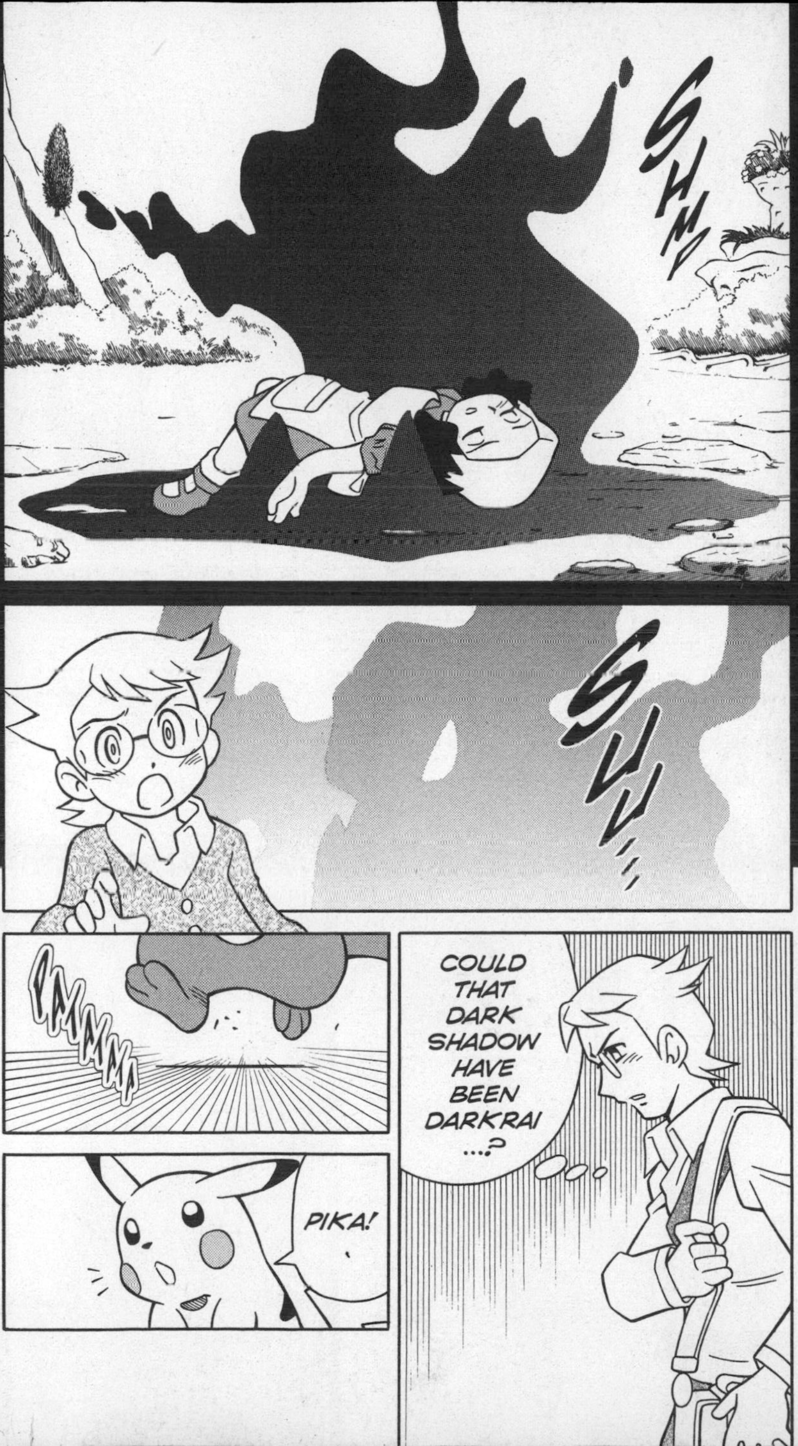
SHMP
SUU...
COULD THAT DARK SHADOW HAVE BEEN DARKRAI ...?
PIKA!

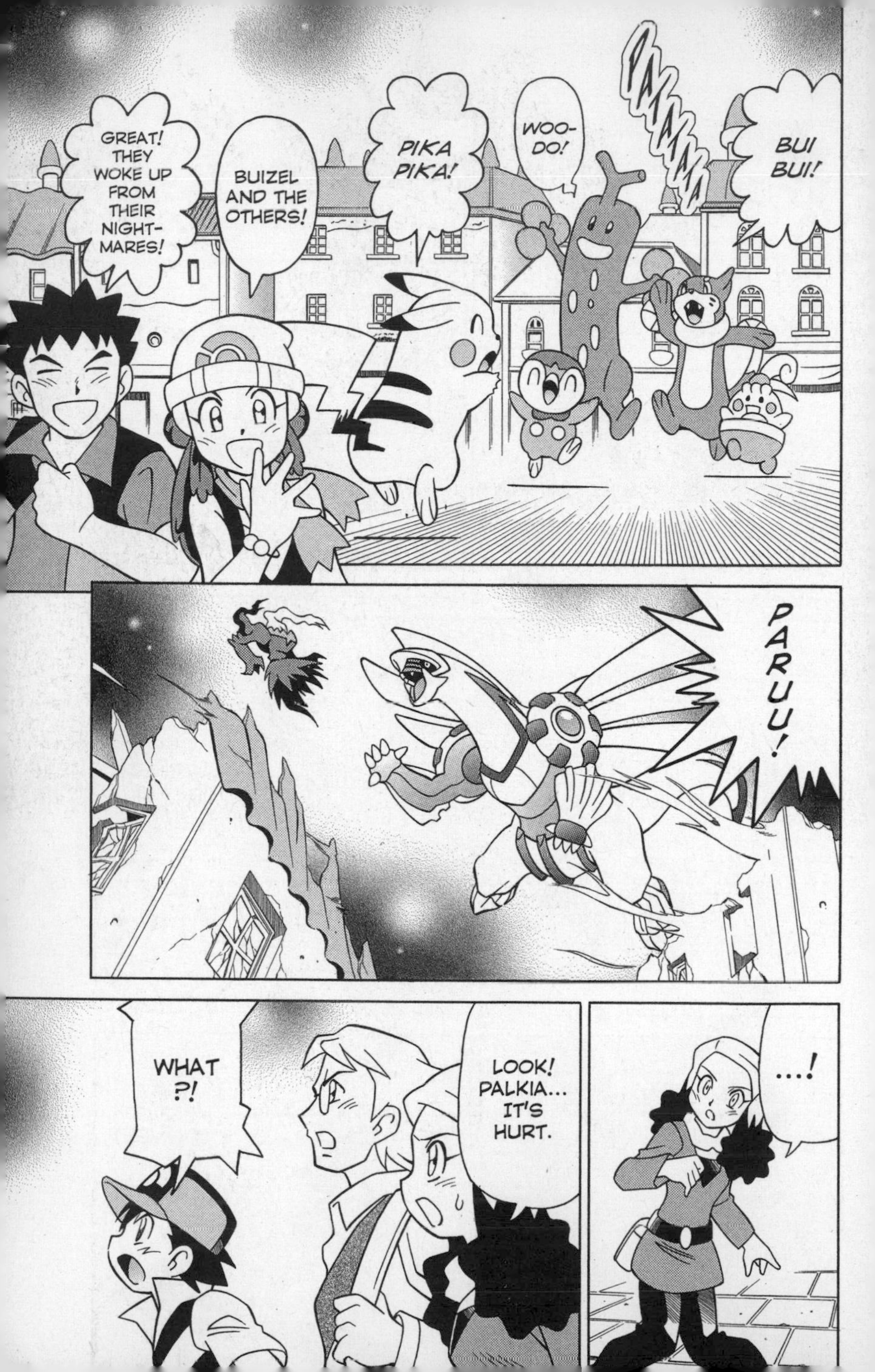
BUI BUI!
PAAAAAA
WOO-DO!
PIKA PIKA!
BUIZEL AND THE OTHERS!
GREAT! THEY WOKE UP FROM THEIR NIGHT-MARES!
PARUU!
...!
LOOK! PALKIA... IT'S HURT.
WHAT?!

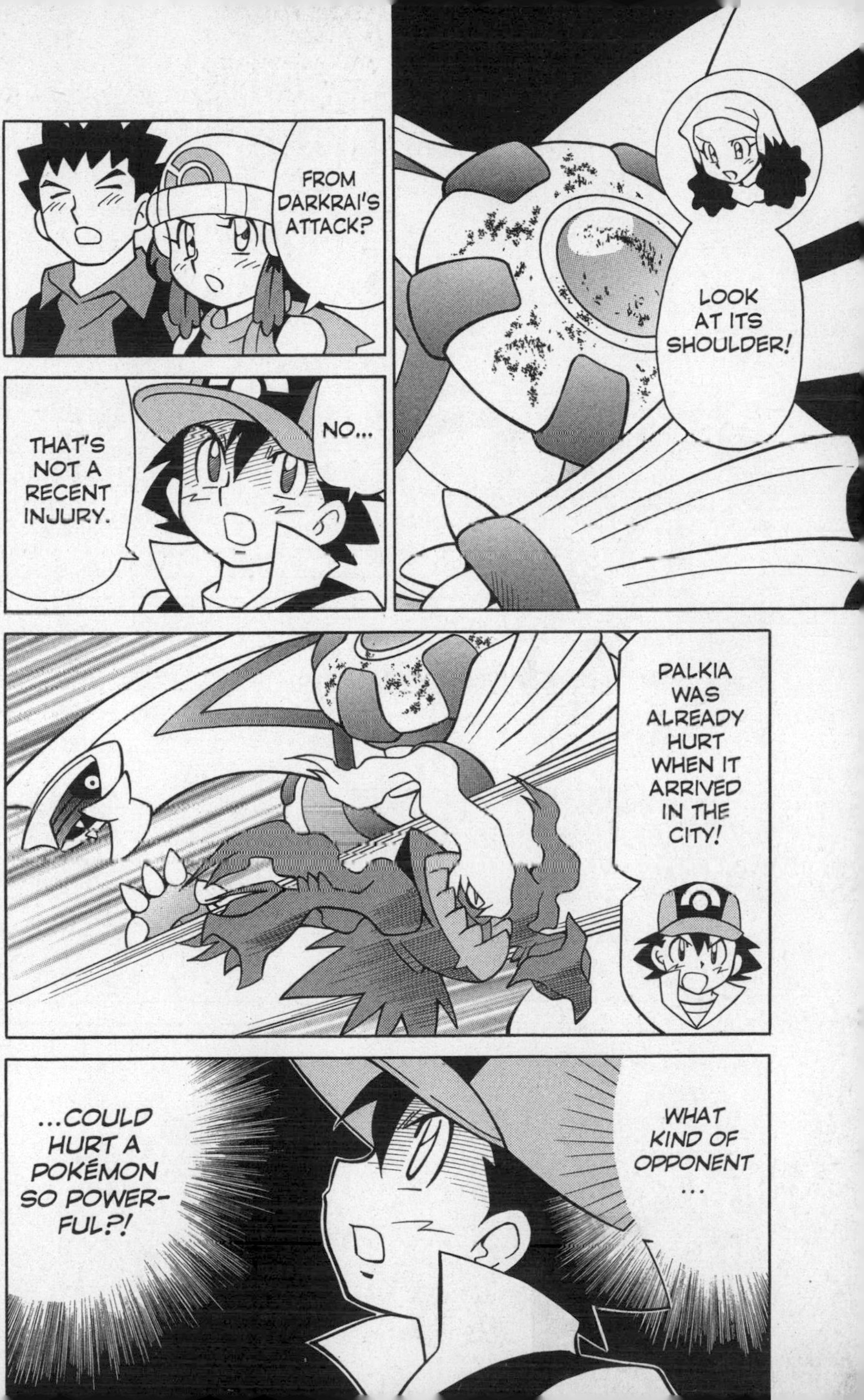
LOOK AT ITS SHOULDER!
FROM DARKRAI'S ATTACK?
NO...
THAT'S NOT A RECENT INJURY.
PALKIA WAS ALREADY HURT WHEN IT ARRIVED IN THE CITY!
WHAT KIND OF OPPONENT ...
...COULD HURT A POKÉMON SO POWERFUL?!

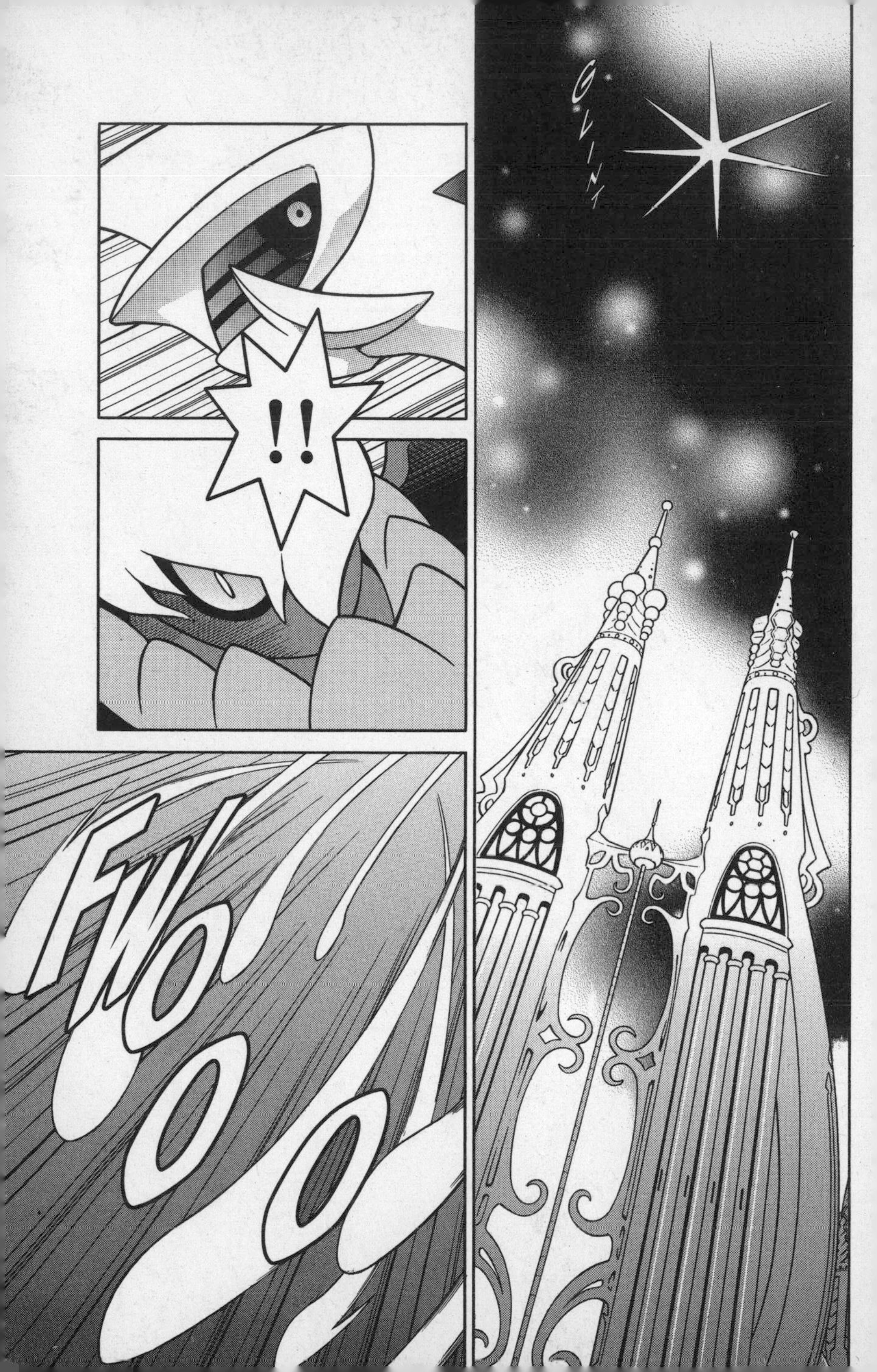
GLINT
!!
FWOOOO

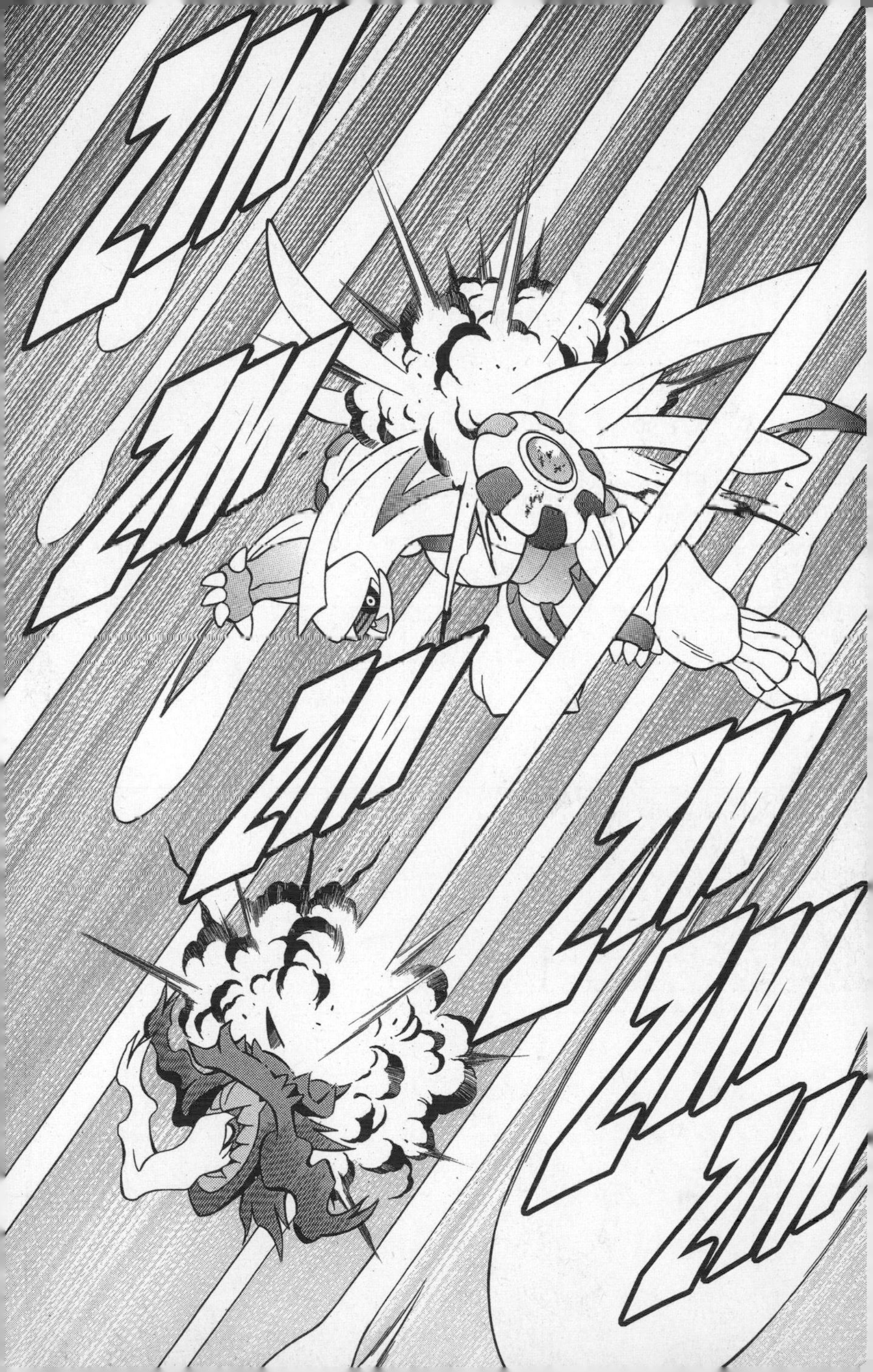

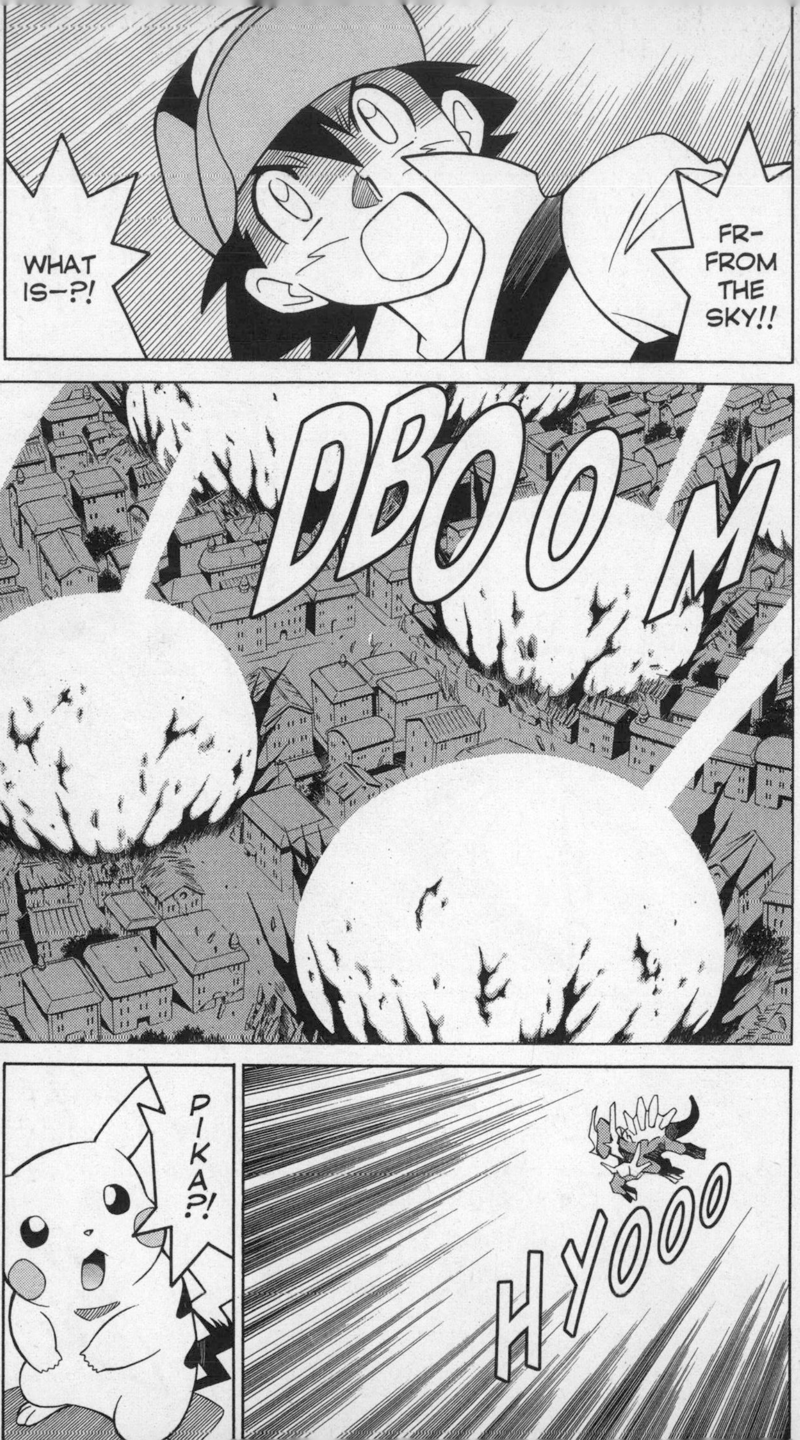
FR-
FROM
THE
SKY!!
WHAT
IS—?!
DBOOM
HYOOO
PIKA?!

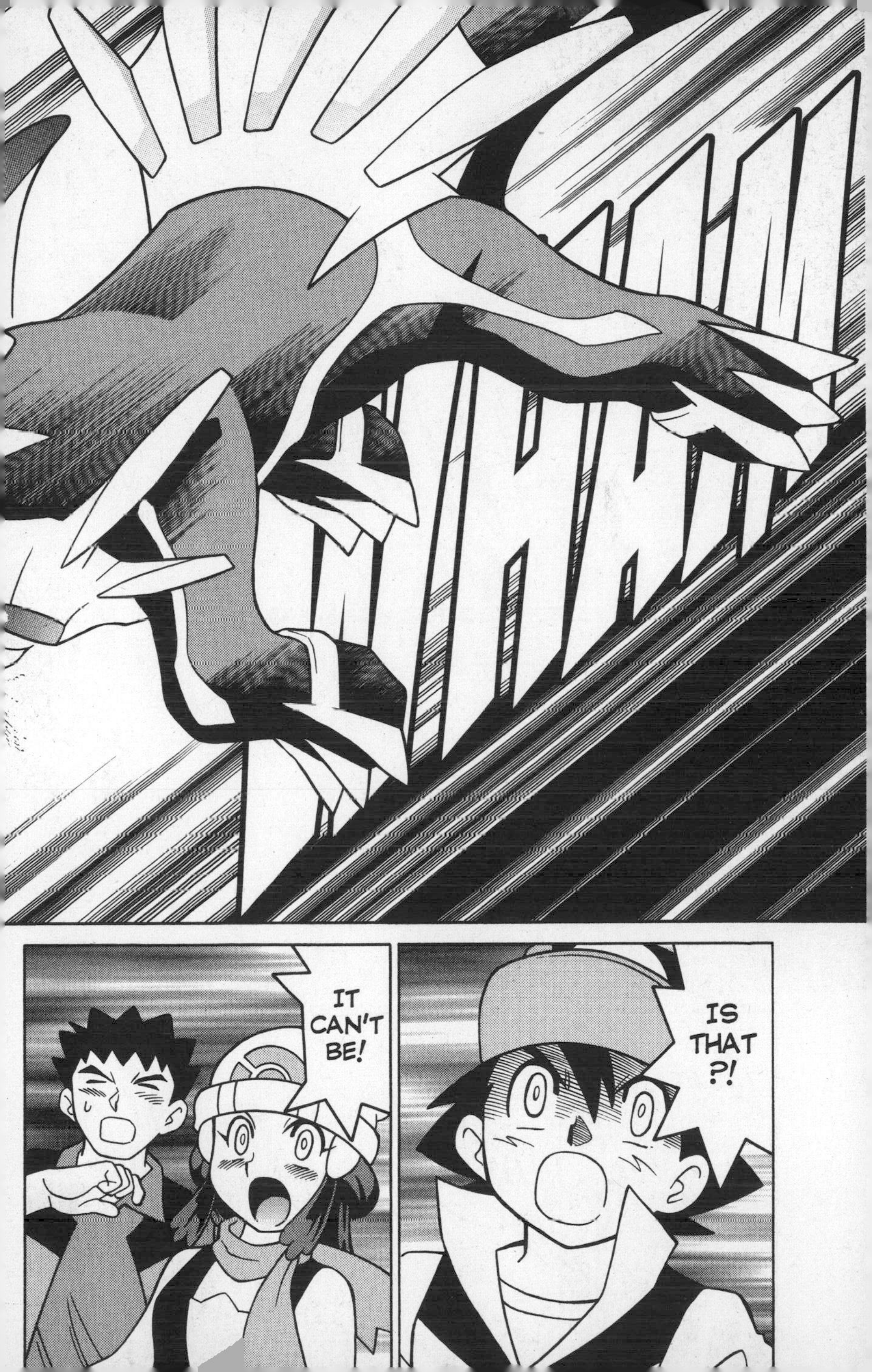
IS THAT ?!
IT CAN'T BE!

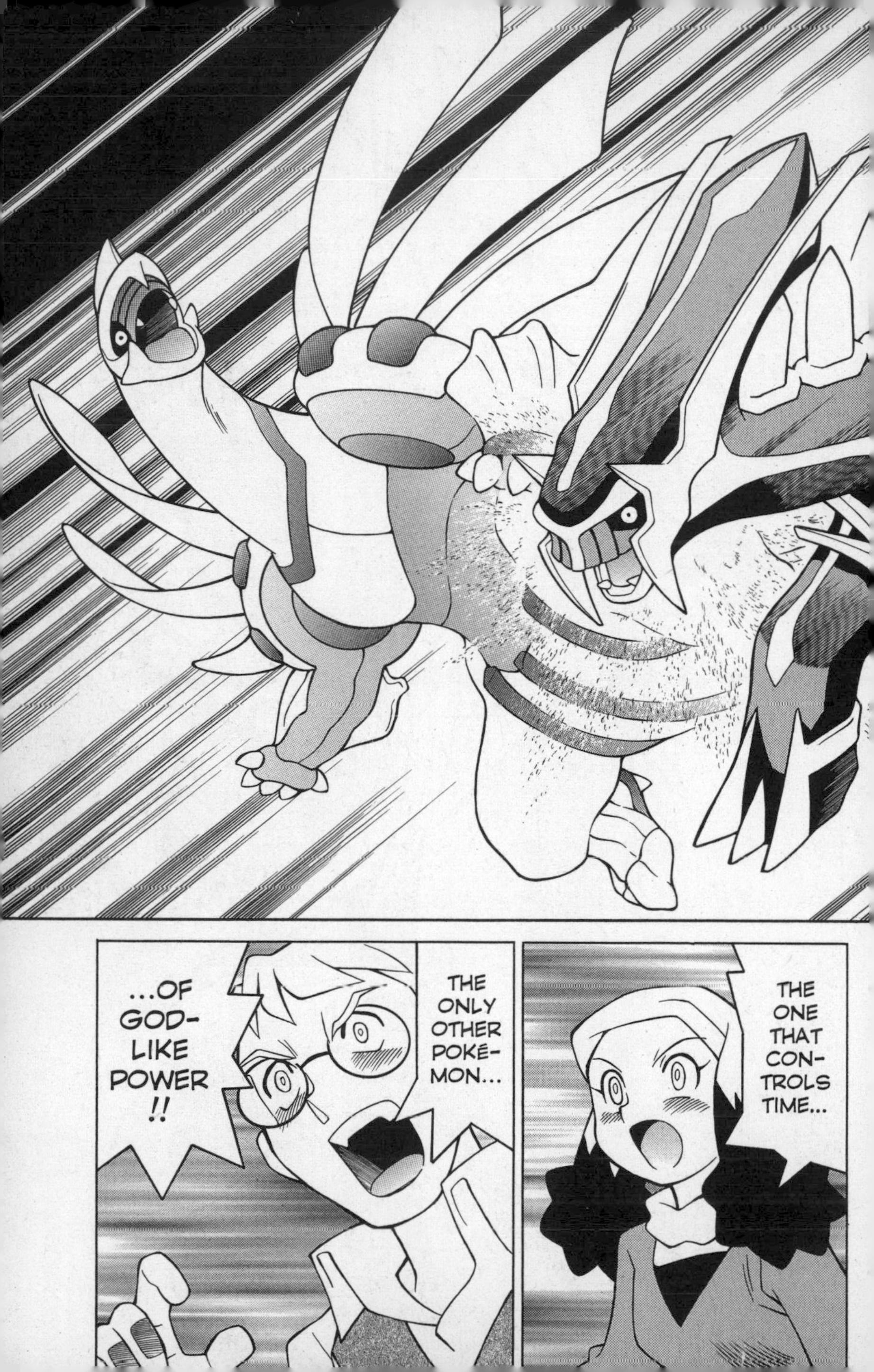
THE ONE THAT CON-TROLS TIME...
THE ONLY OTHER POKÉ-MON...
...OF GOD-LIKE POWER!!

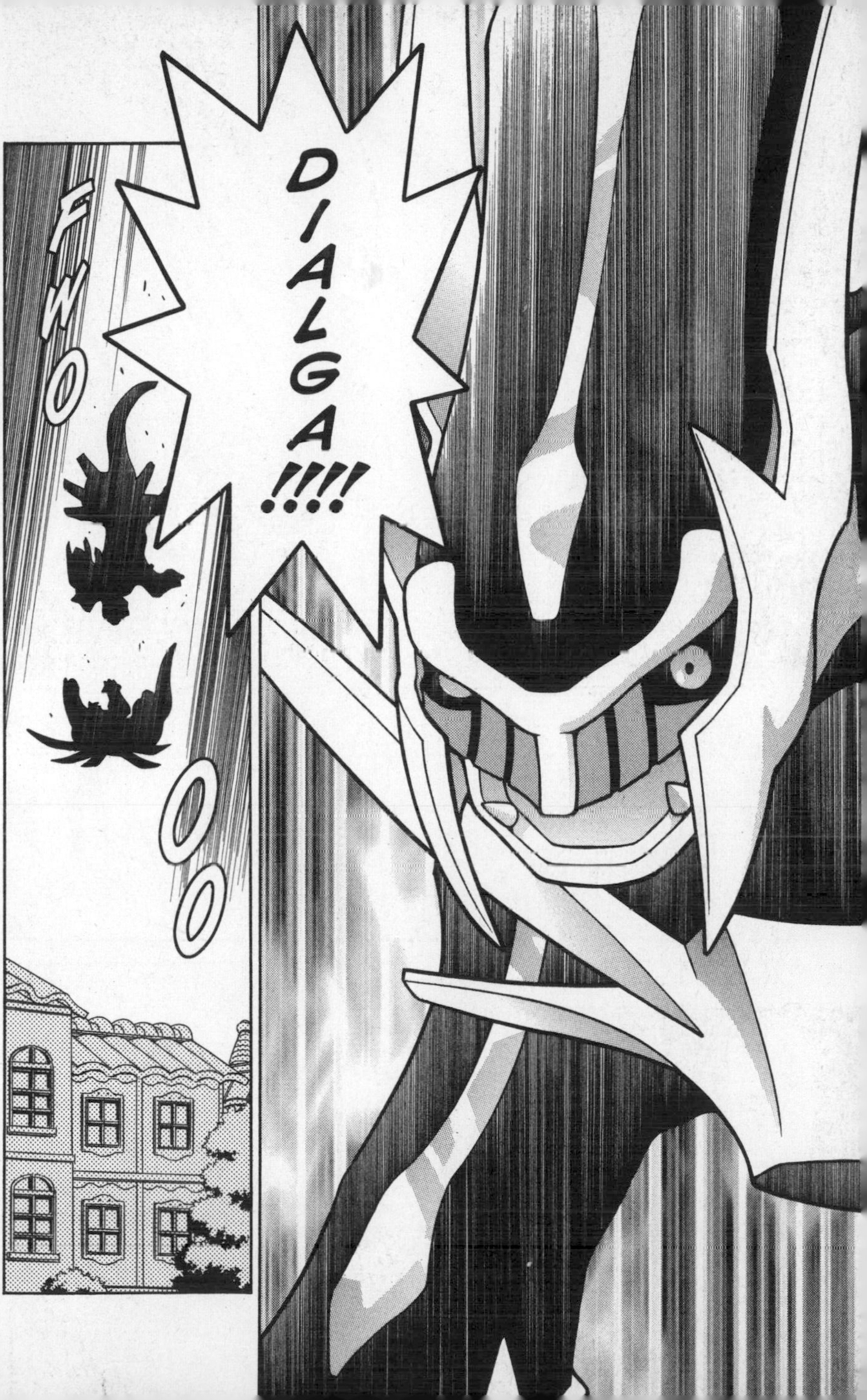
DIALGA!!!!
FWOOO

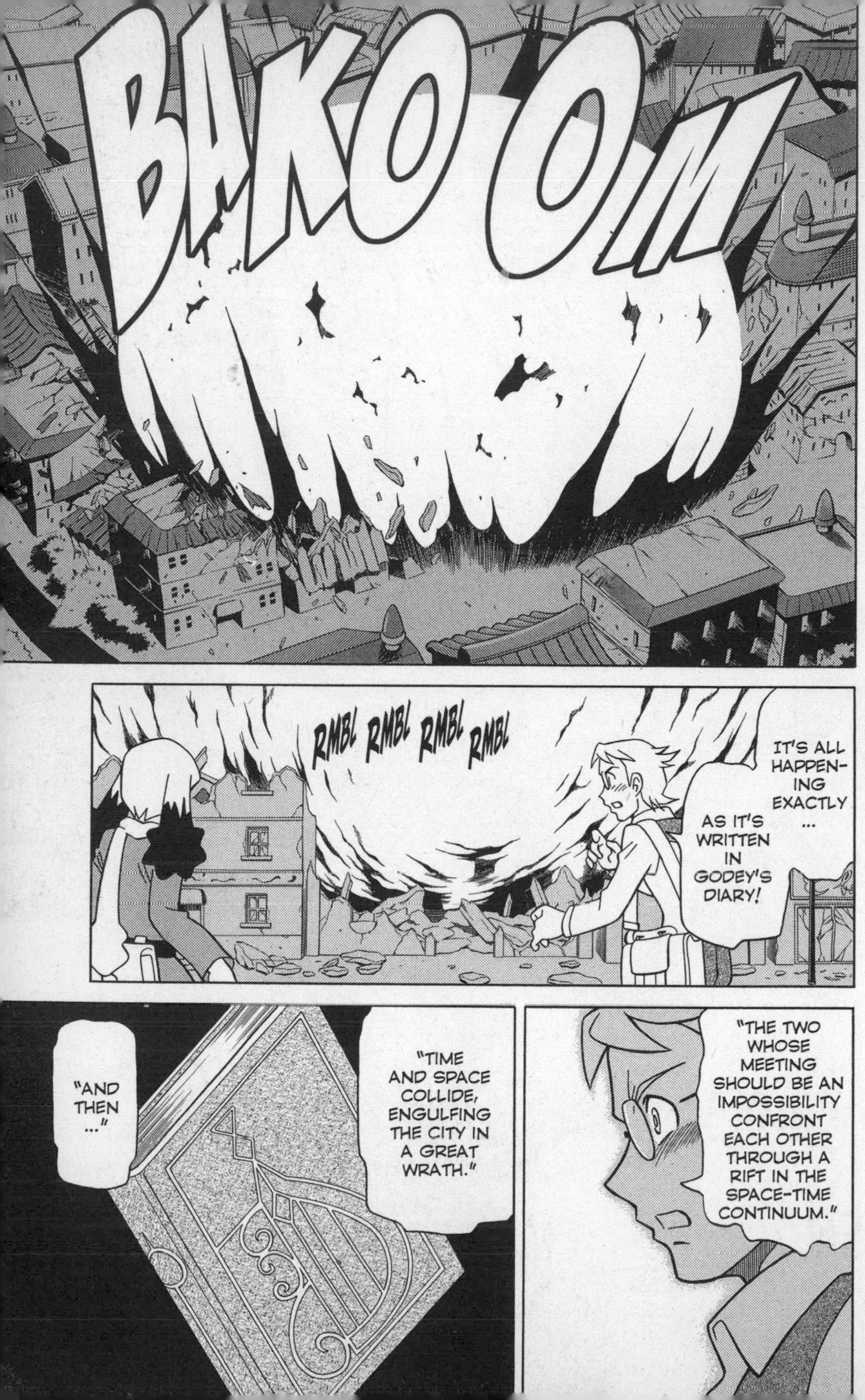
BAKOOM
RMBL RMBL RMBL RMBL
IT'S ALL HAPPENING EXACTLY ...
AS IT'S WRITTEN IN GODEY'S DIARY!
"THE TWO WHOSE MEETING SHOULD BE AN IMPOSSIBILITY CONFRONT EACH OTHER THROUGH A RIFT IN THE SPACE-TIME CONTINUUM."
"TIME AND SPACE COLLIDE, ENGULFING THE CITY IN A GREAT WRATH."
"AND THEN ..."

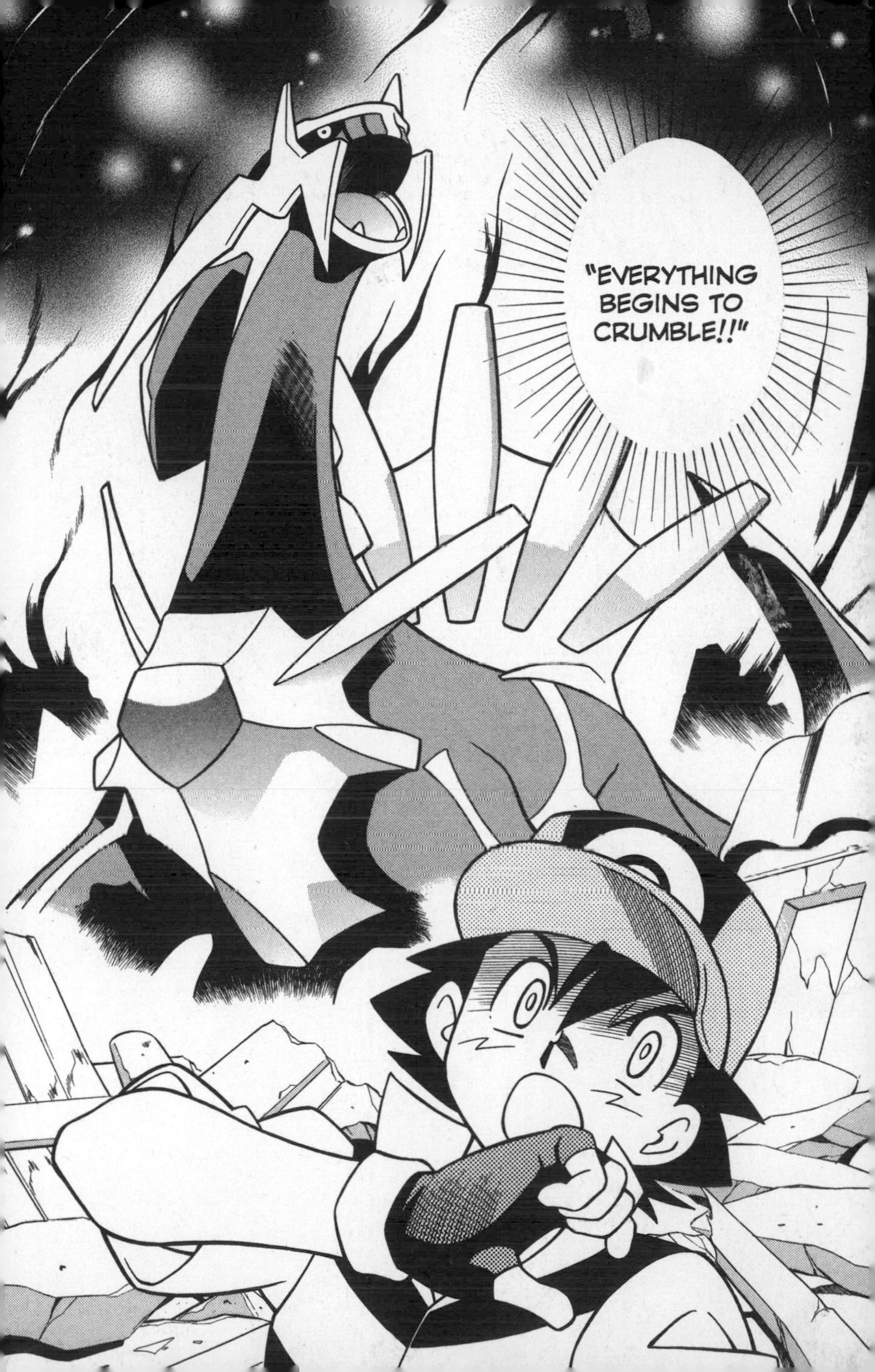
"EVERYTHING BEGINS TO CRUMBLE!!"

CLASH OF THE THREE TITANIC FORCES!!

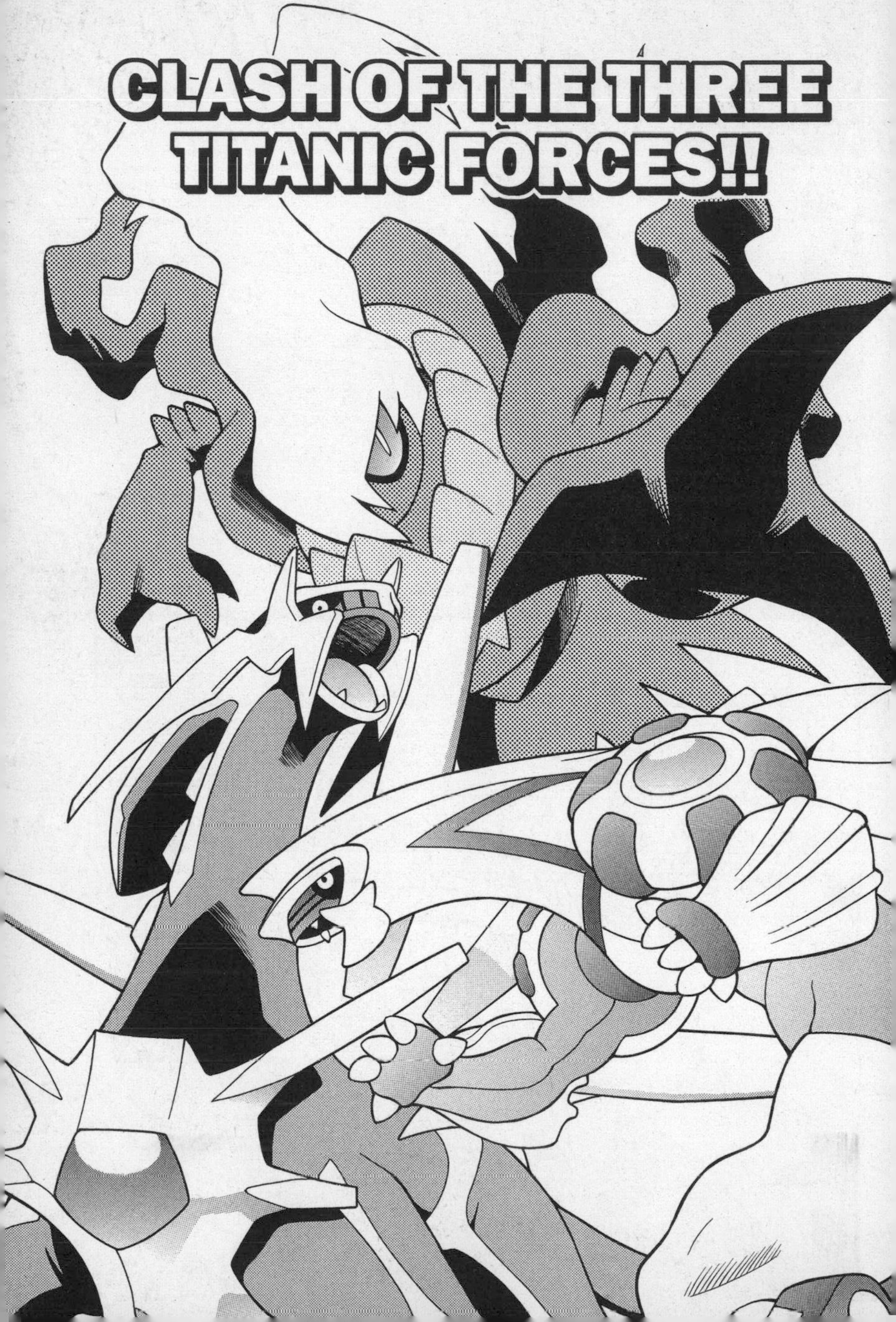

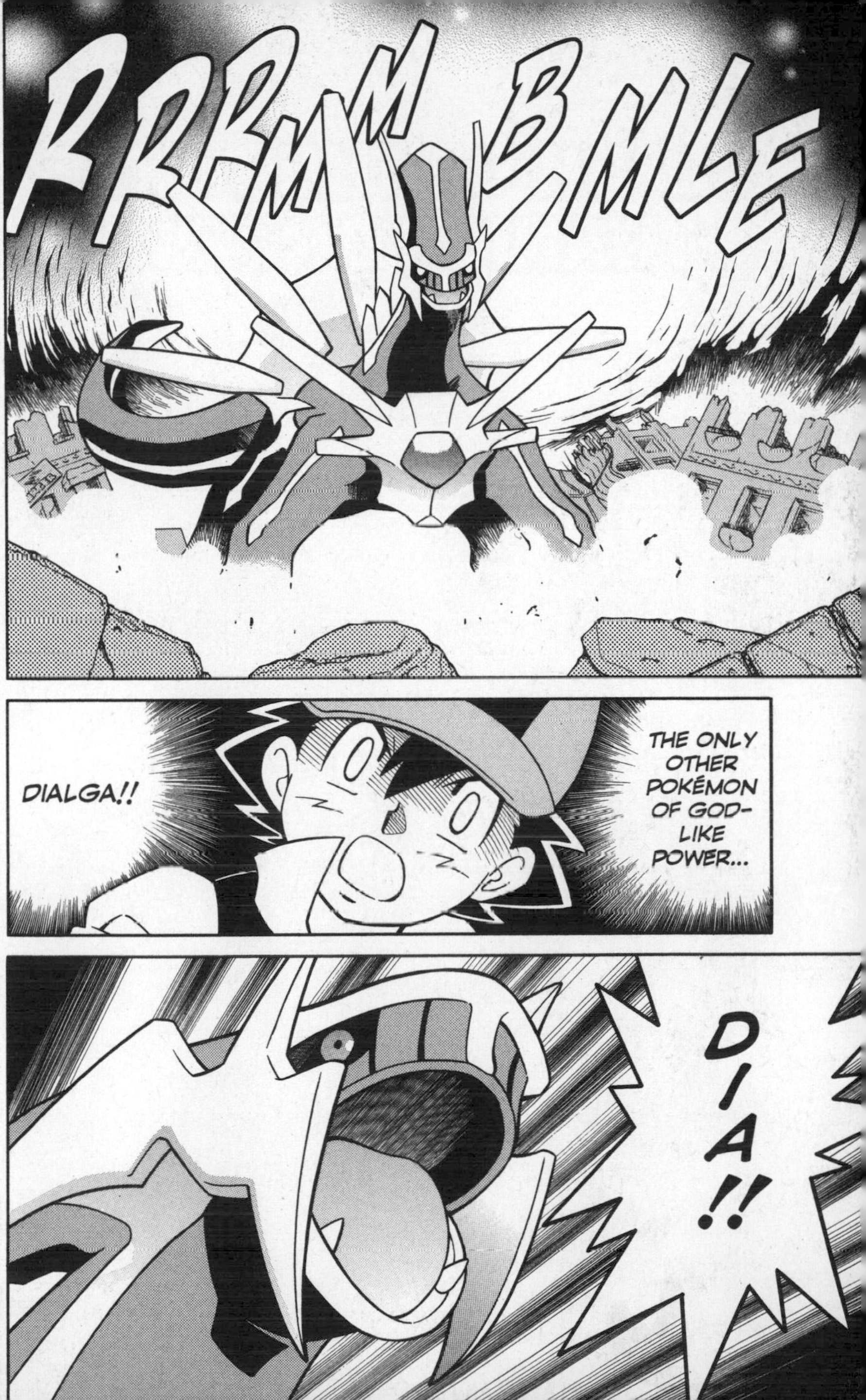
RRRMMMBMLE
THE ONLY OTHER POKÉMON OF GOD-LIKE POWER...
DIALGA!!
DIA!!

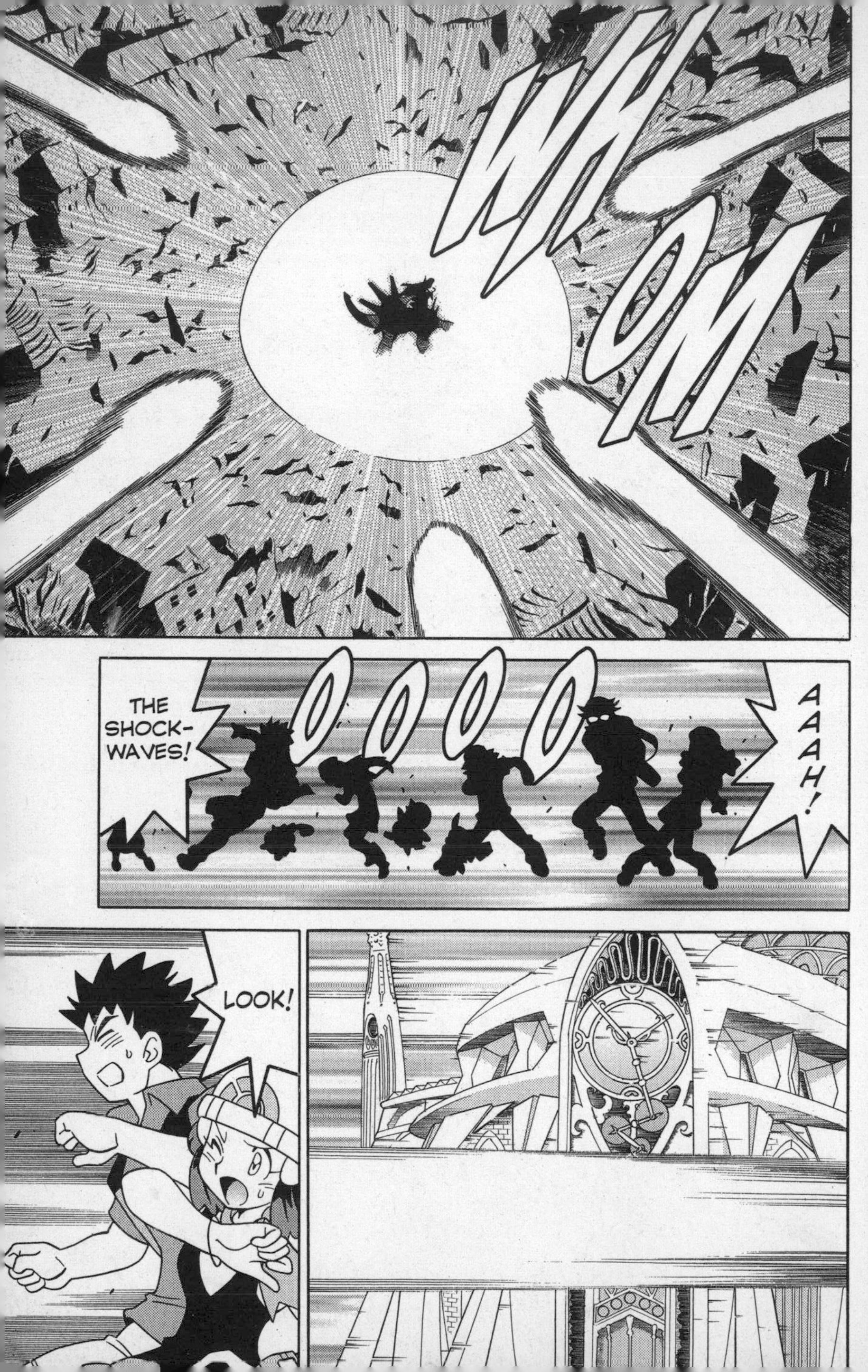
WHOOM
AAAH!
THE SHOCK-WAVES!
LOOK!

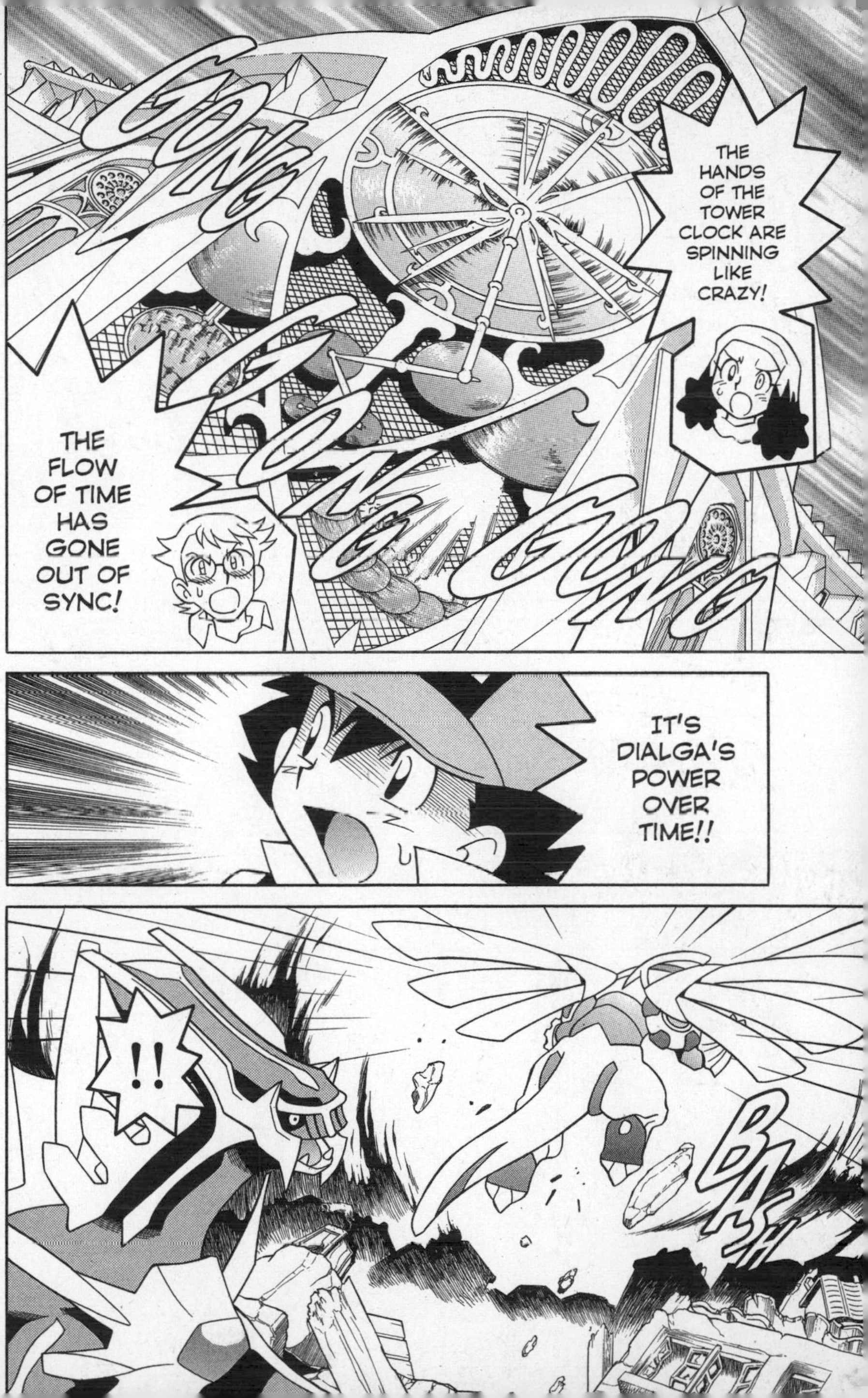
THE HANDS OF THE TOWER CLOCK ARE SPINNING LIKE CRAZY!
GONG
GONG
GONG
GONG
THE FLOW OF TIME HAS GONE OUT OF SYNC!
IT'S DIALGA'S POWER OVER TIME!!
BASH
!!

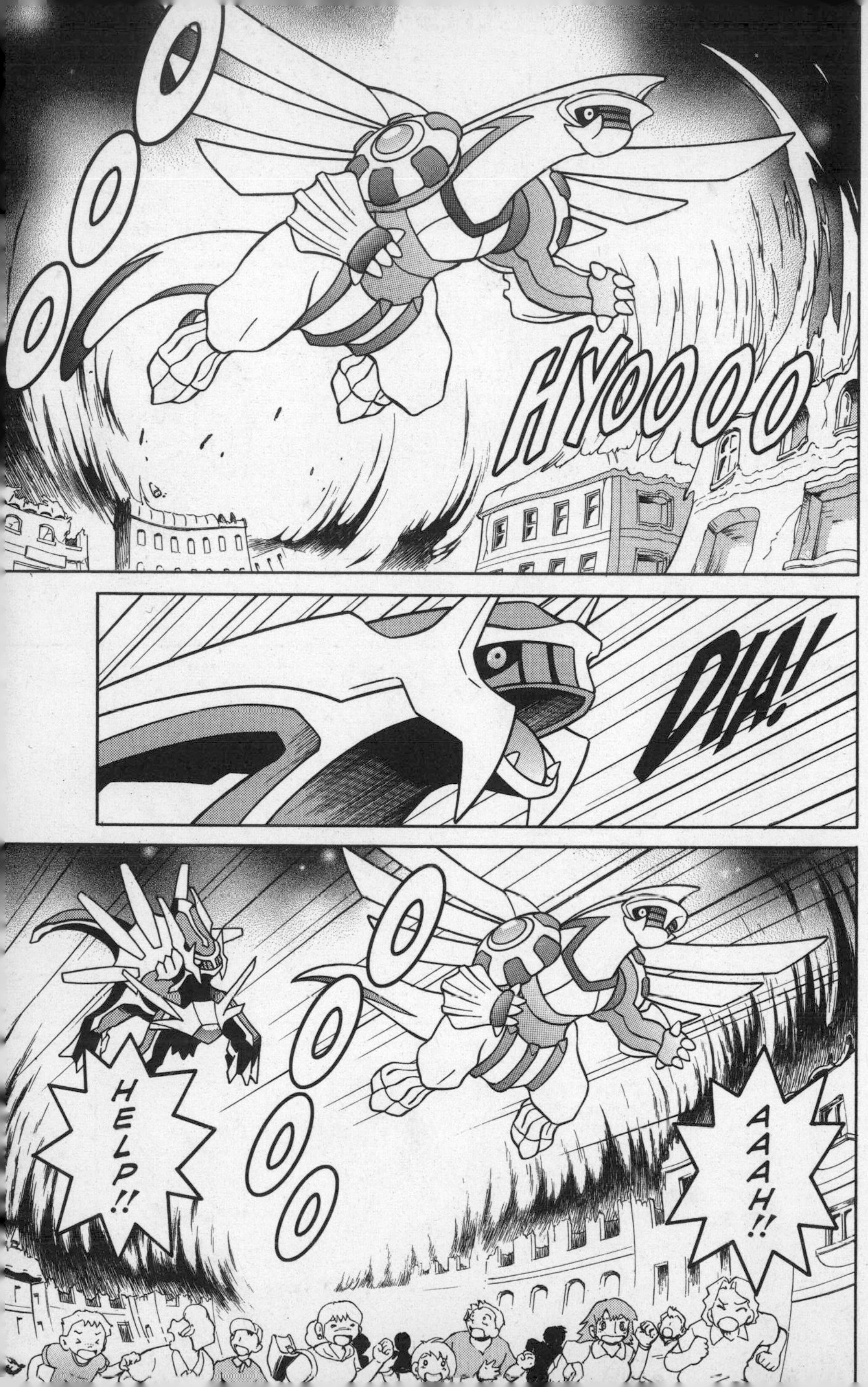
HYOOOOO
DIA!
AAAAH!!
HELP!!

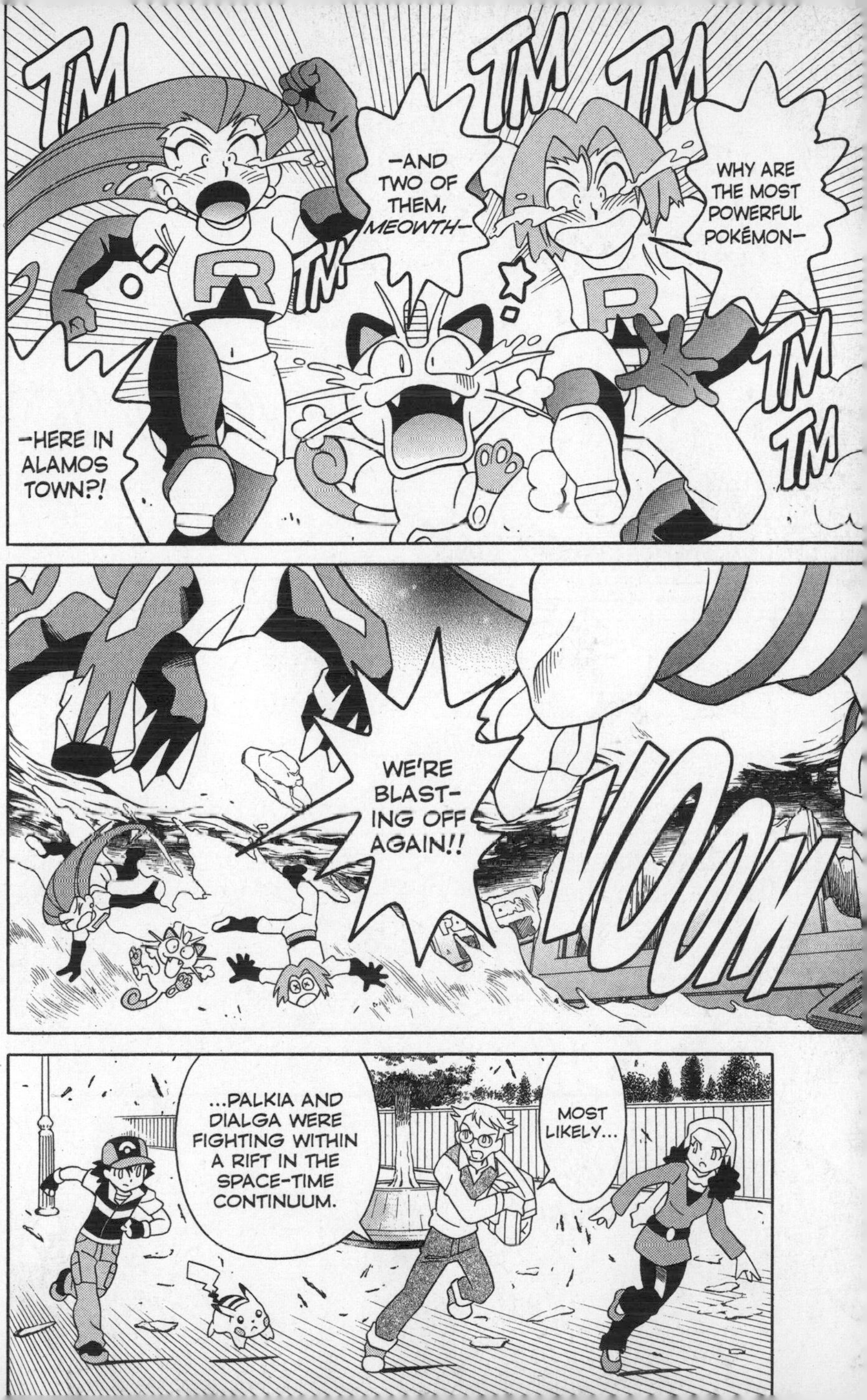
TM
TM
TM
WHY ARE THE MOST POWERFUL POKÉMON—
—AND TWO OF THEM, MEOWTH—
TM
TM
TM
TM
—HERE IN ALAMOS TOWN?!
VOOM
WE'RE BLAST-ING OFF AGAIN!!
MOST LIKELY...
...PALKIA AND DIALGA WERE FIGHTING WITHIN A RIFT IN THE SPACE-TIME CONTINUUM.

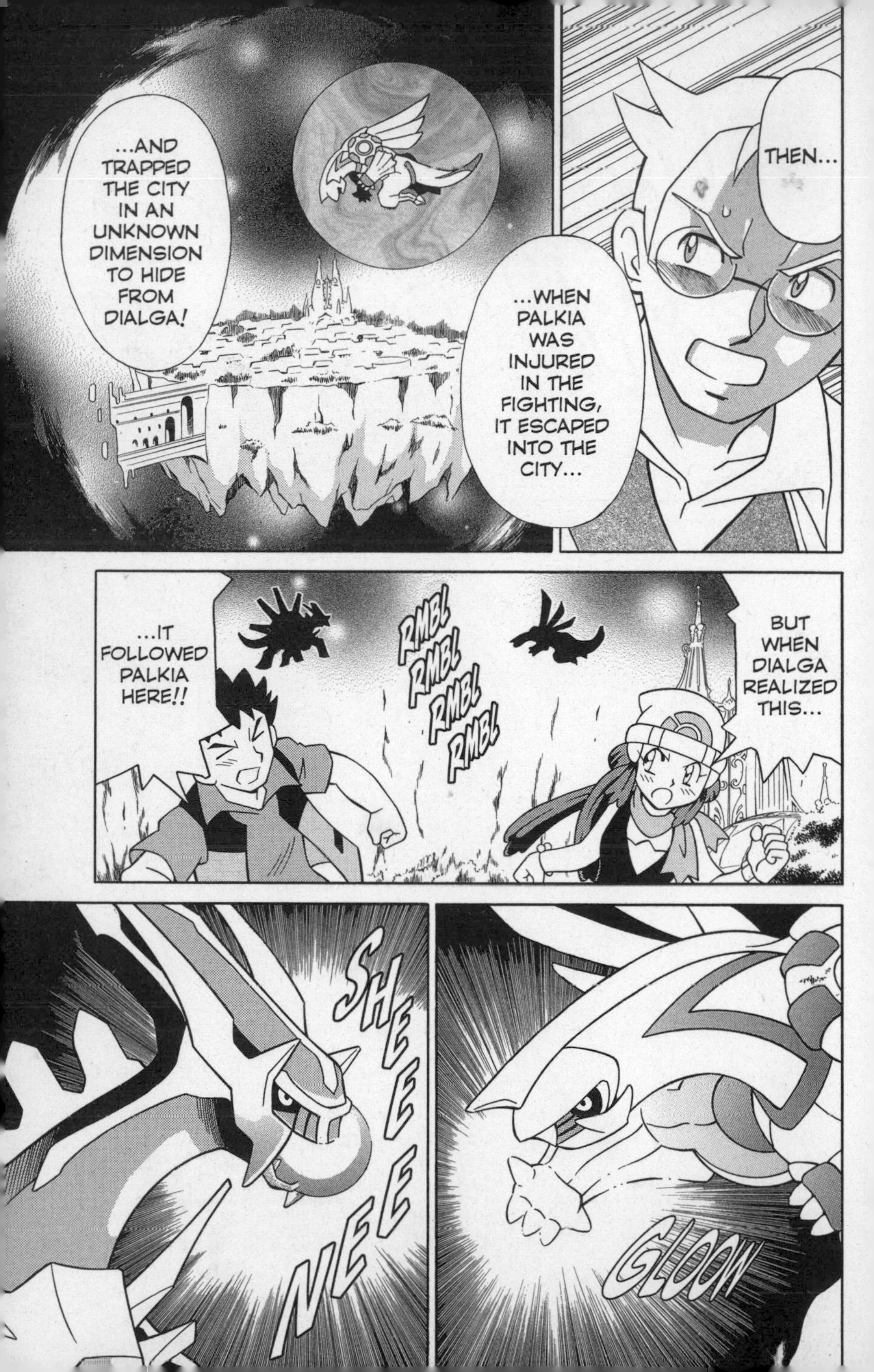
THEN...
...WHEN PALKIA WAS INJURED IN THE FIGHTING, IT ESCAPED INTO THE CITY...
...AND TRAPPED THE CITY IN AN UNKNOWN DIMENSION TO HIDE FROM DIALGA!
BUT WHEN DIALGA REALIZED THIS...
RMBL RMBL RMBL RMBL
...IT FOLLOWED PALKIA HERE!!
GLOOW
SHEEE
NEE

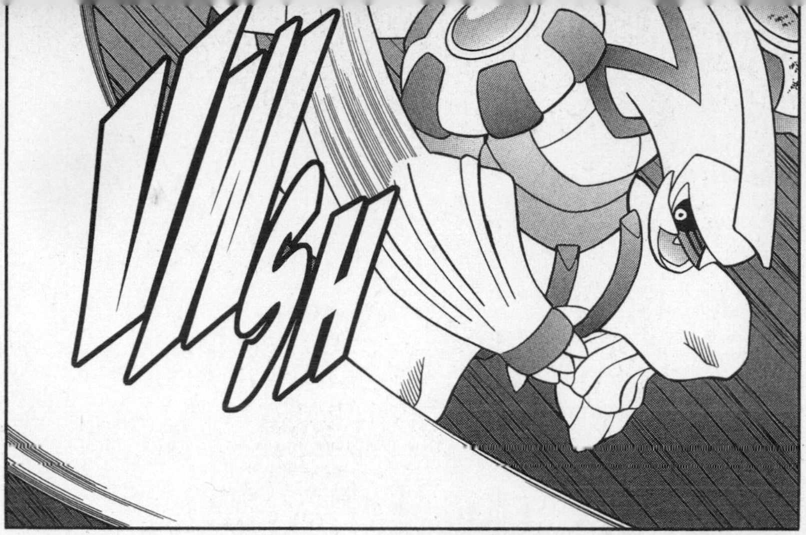

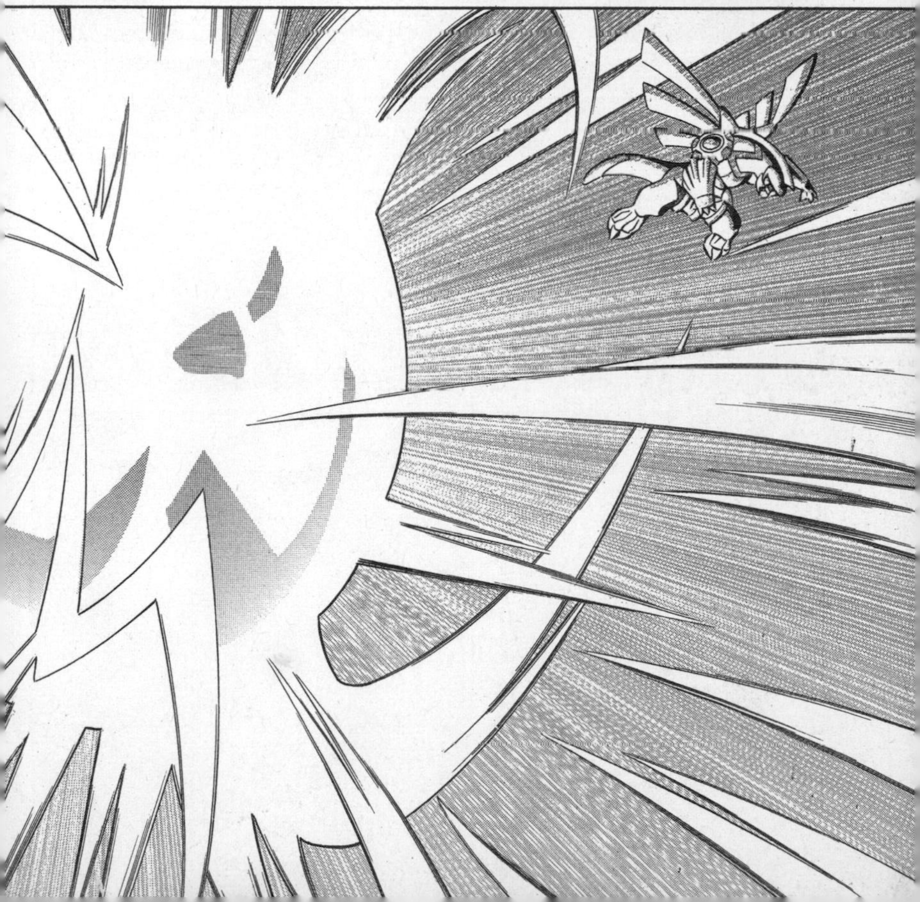

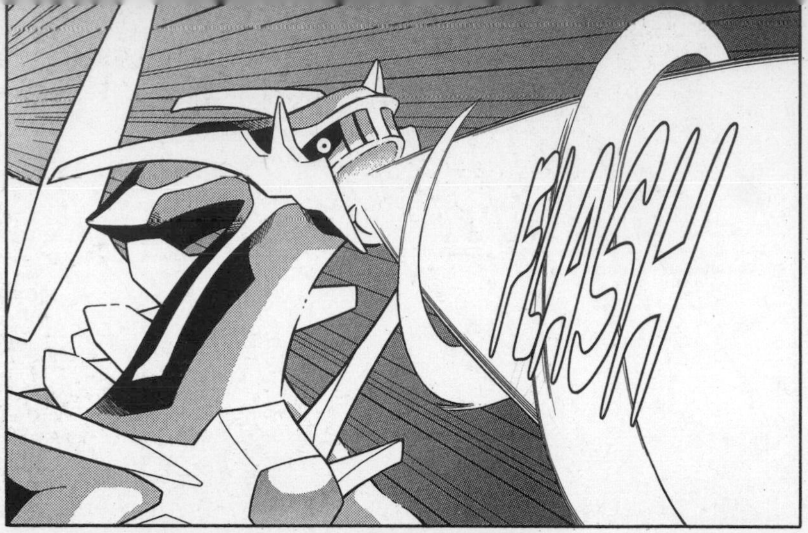
FLASH
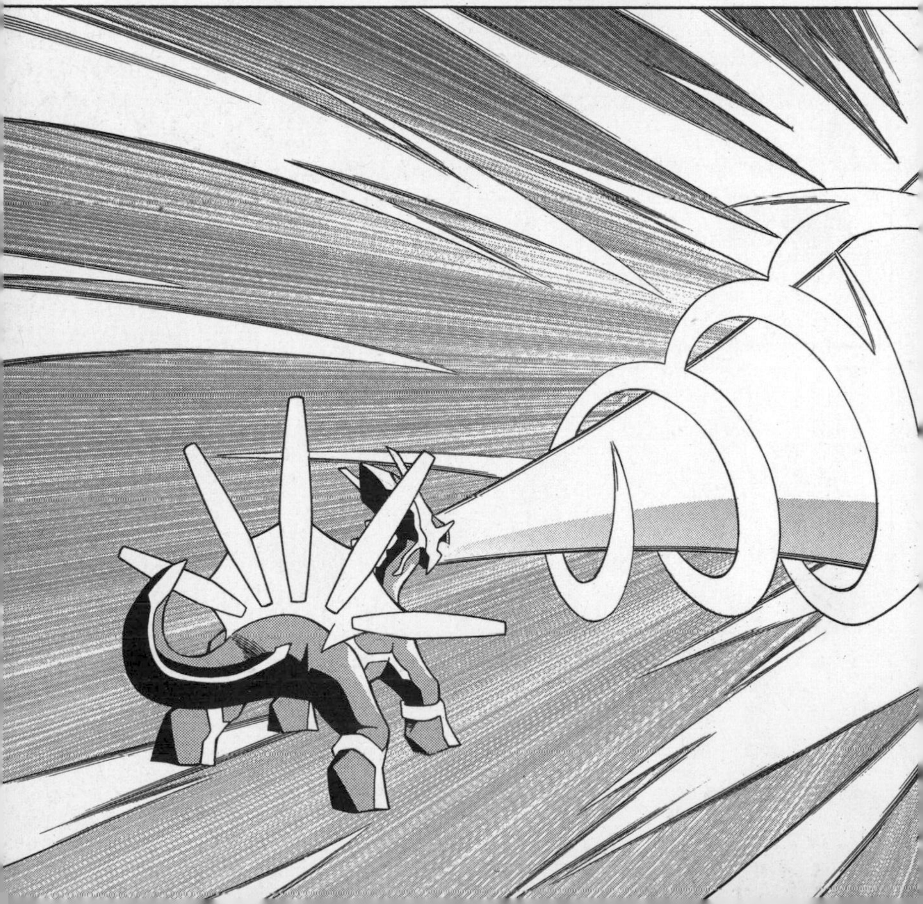

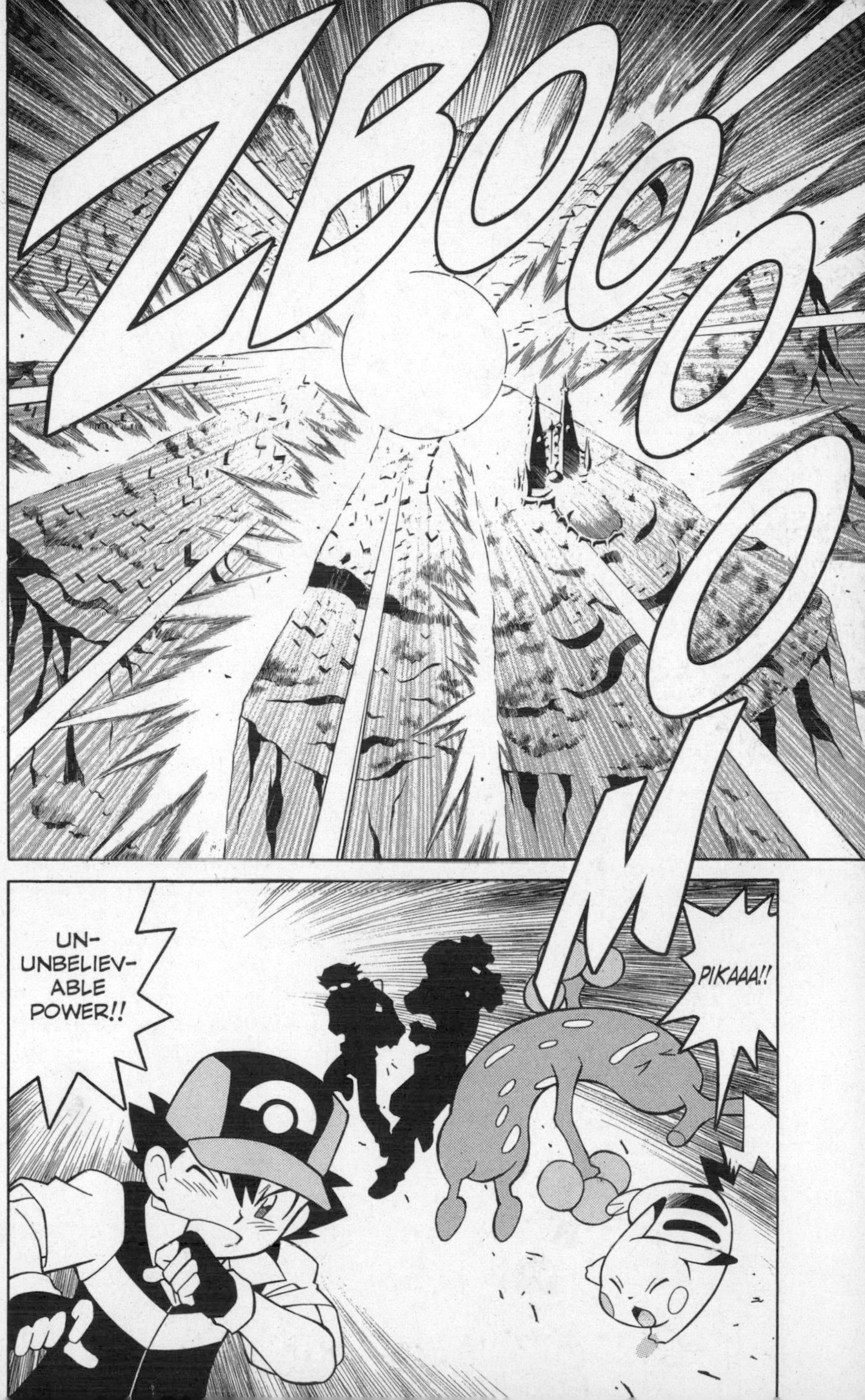
ZBOOOOOM
PIKAAA!!
UN-UNBELIEV-ABLE POWER!!

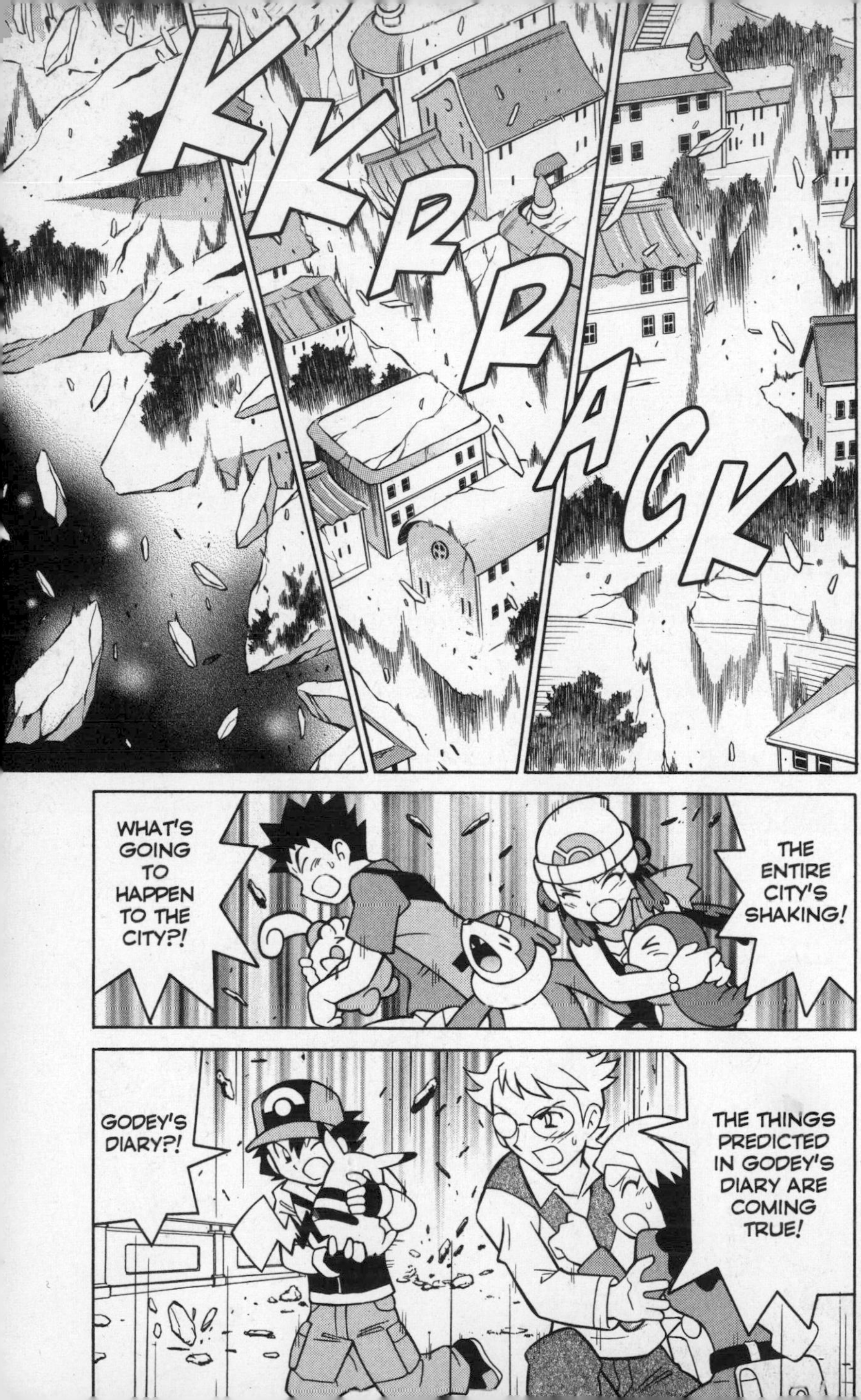
KKRRACK
THE ENTIRE CITY'S SHAKING!
WHAT'S GOING TO HAPPEN TO THE CITY?!
THE THINGS PREDICTED IN GODEY'S DIARY ARE COMING TRUE!
GODEY'S DIARY?!

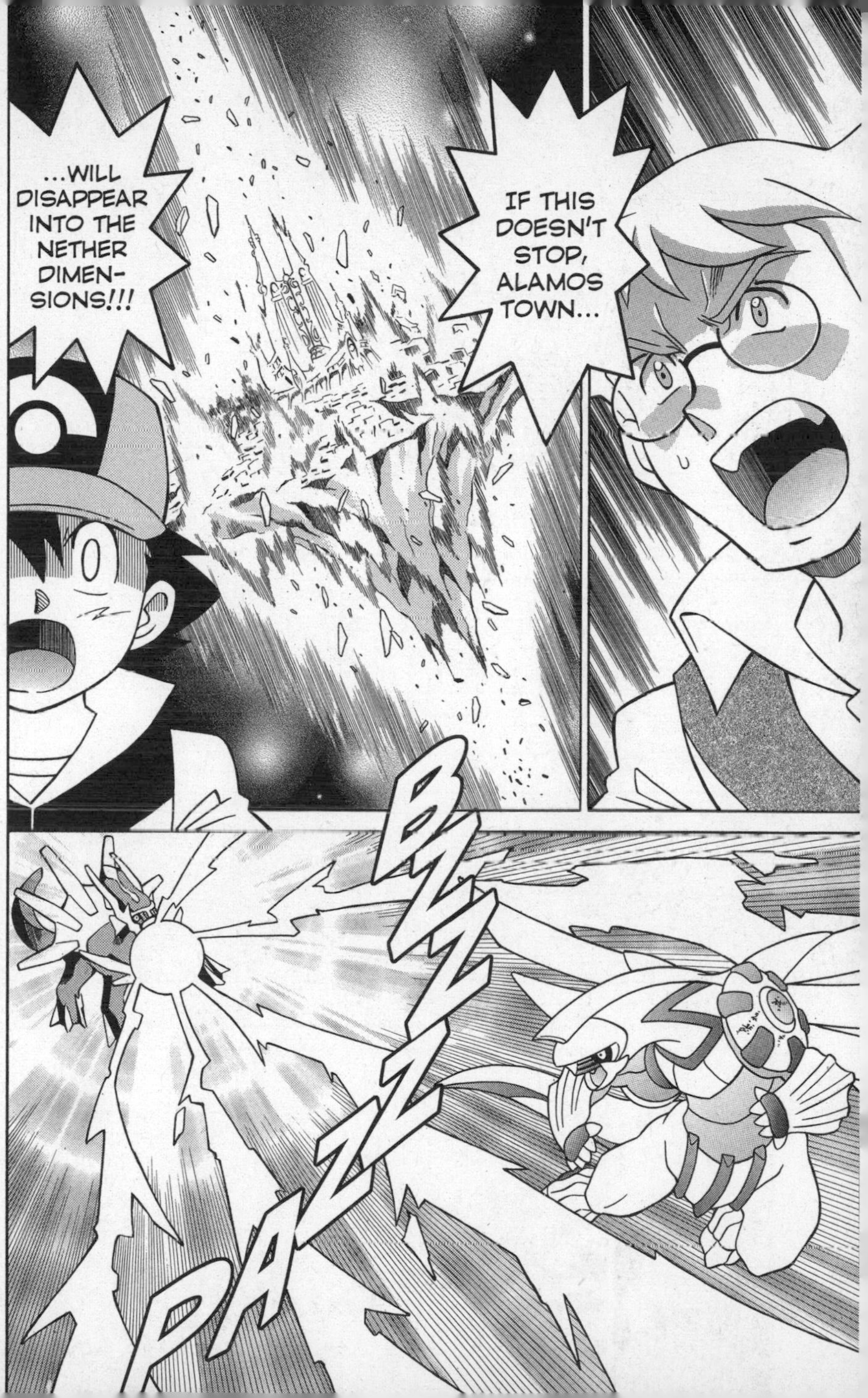
IF THIS DOESN'T STOP, ALAMOS TOWN...
...WILL DISAPPEAR INTO THE NETHER DIMENSIONS!!!
BZZZZAP

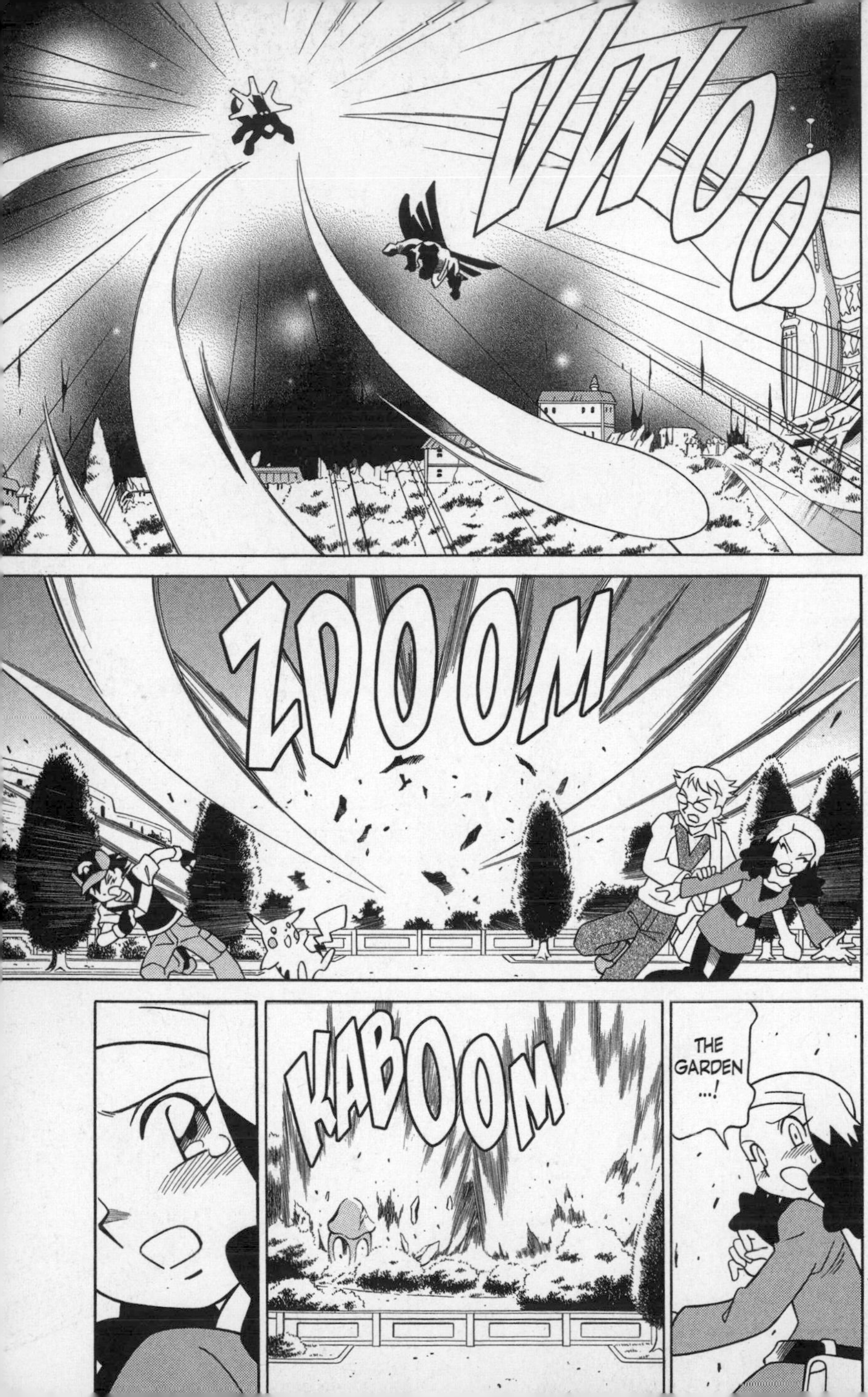
VWOO
ZOOOM
THE GARDEN ...!
KABOOM

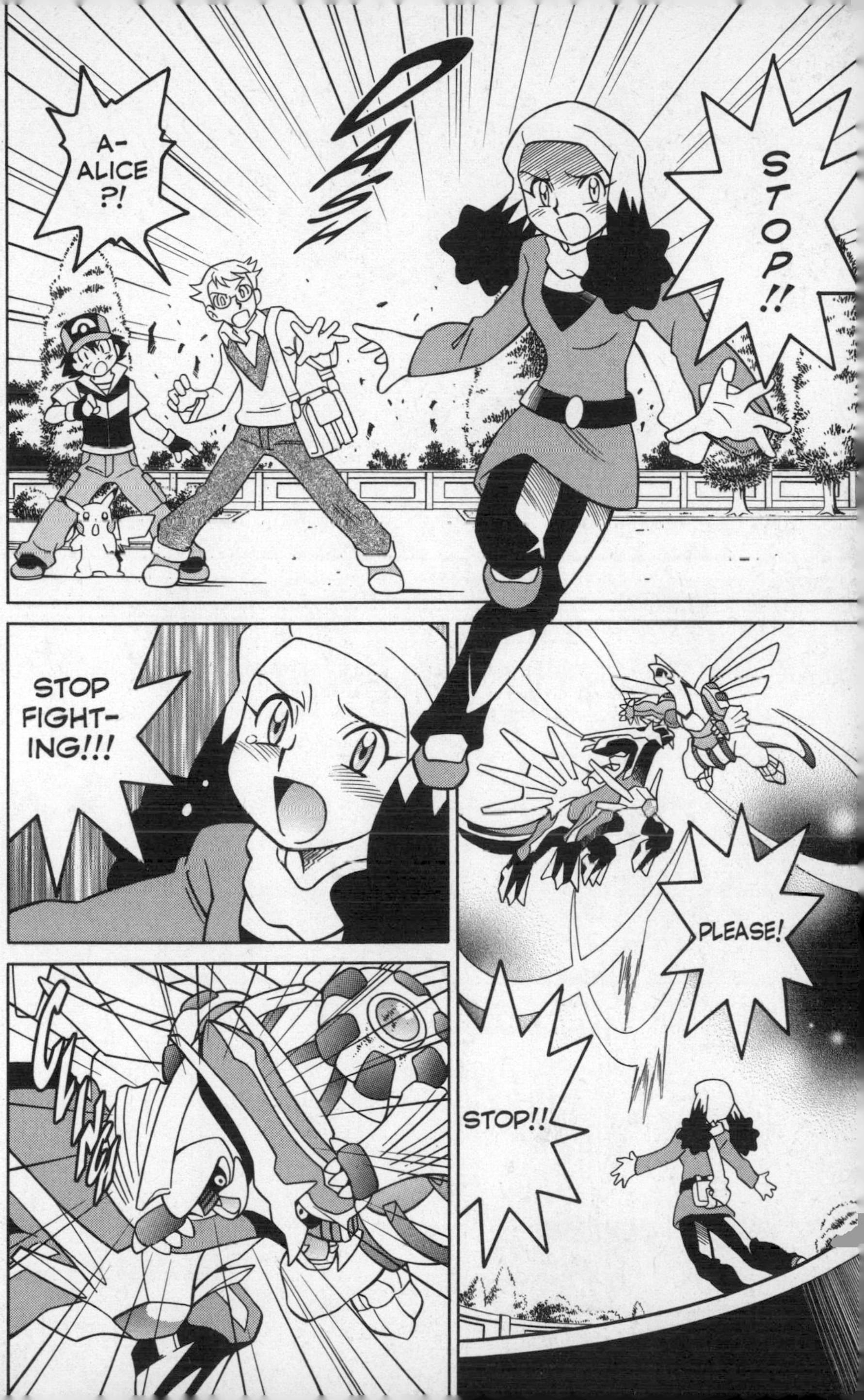
STOP!!
A-ALICE?!
PLEASE!
STOP!!
STOP FIGHTING!!!

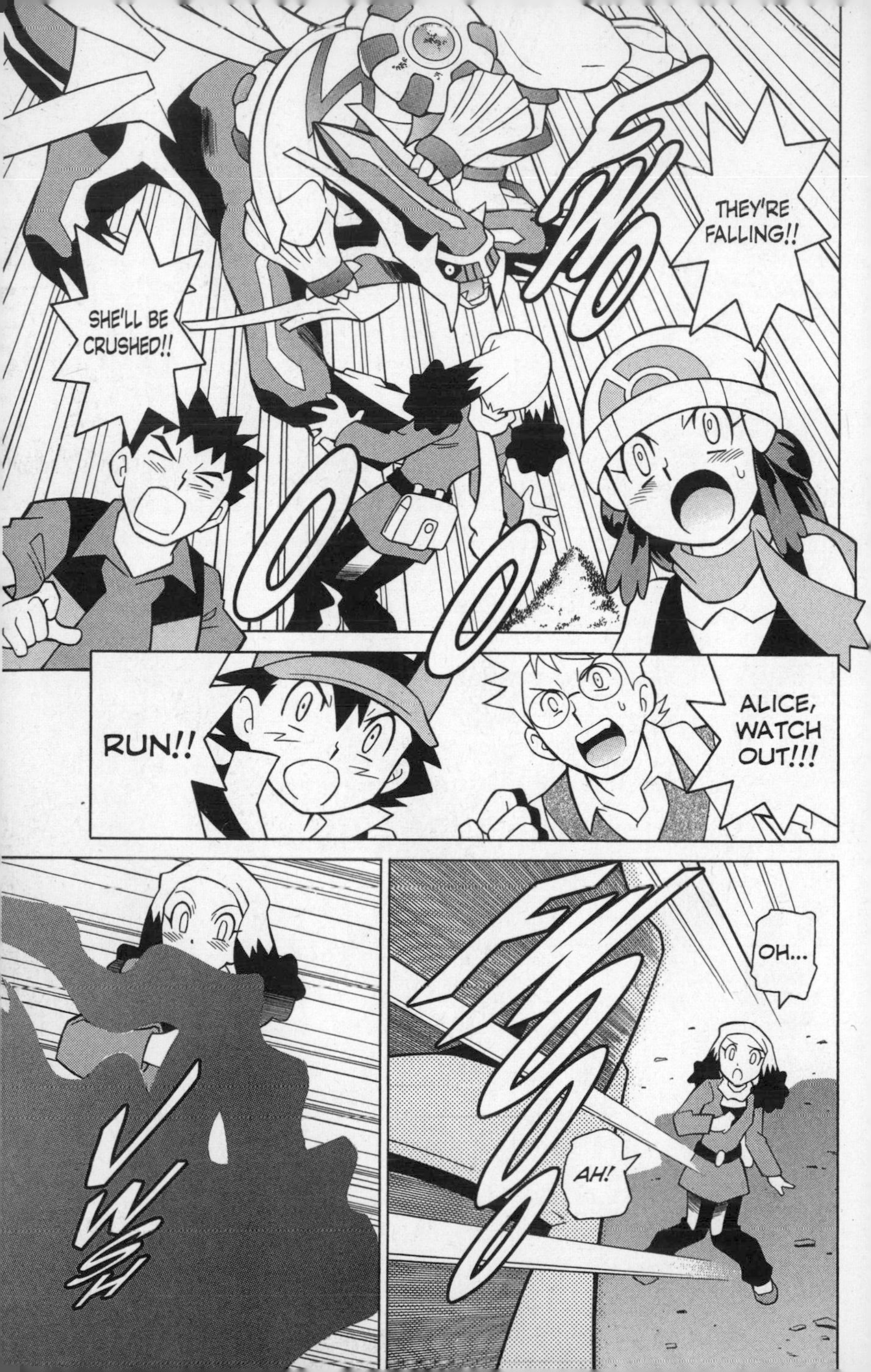
THEY'RE FALLING!!
SHE'LL BE CRUSHED!!
ALICE, WATCH OUT!!!
RUN!!
OH...
AH!

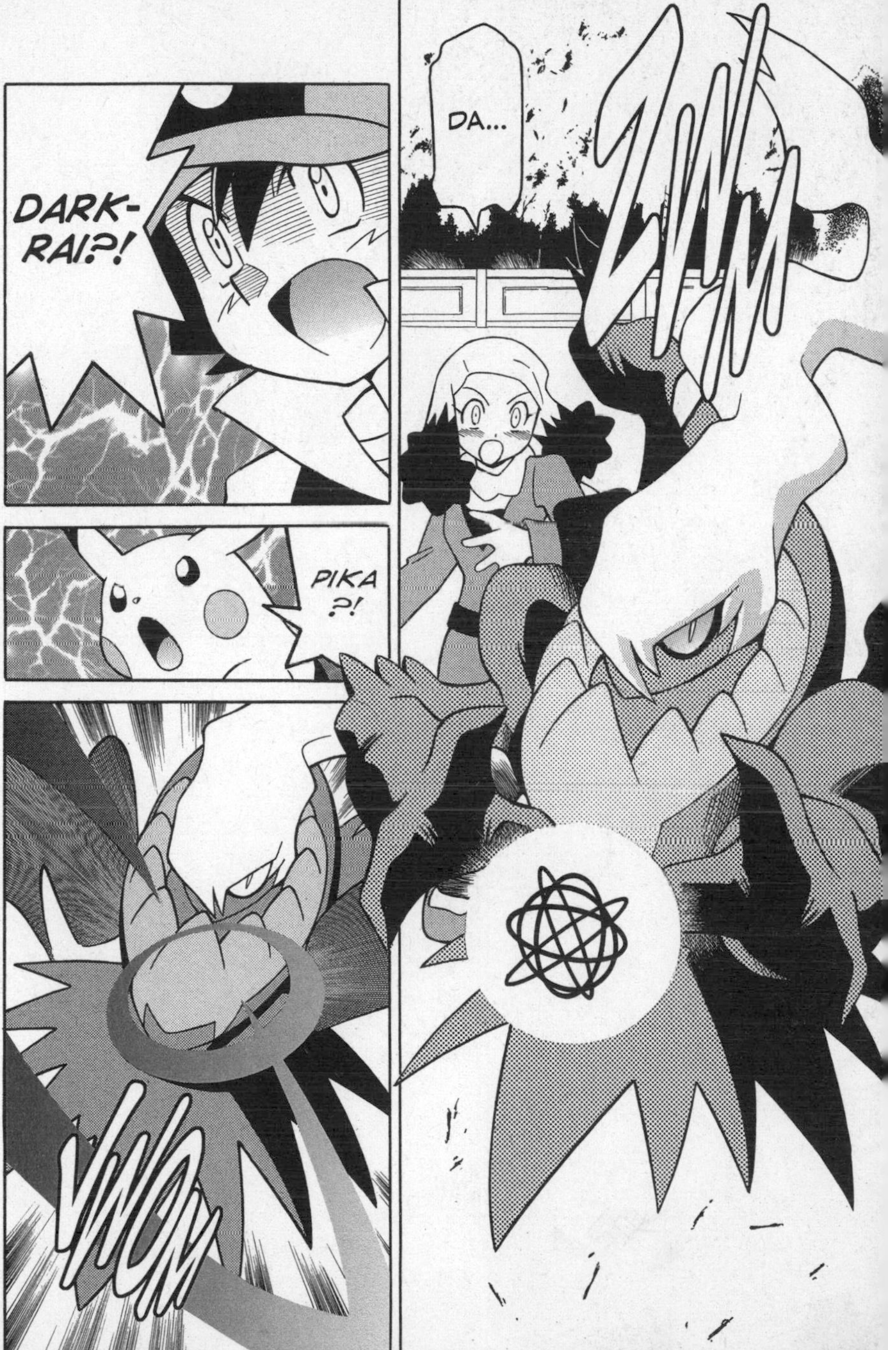
DA...
DARK-RAI?!
PIKA ?!

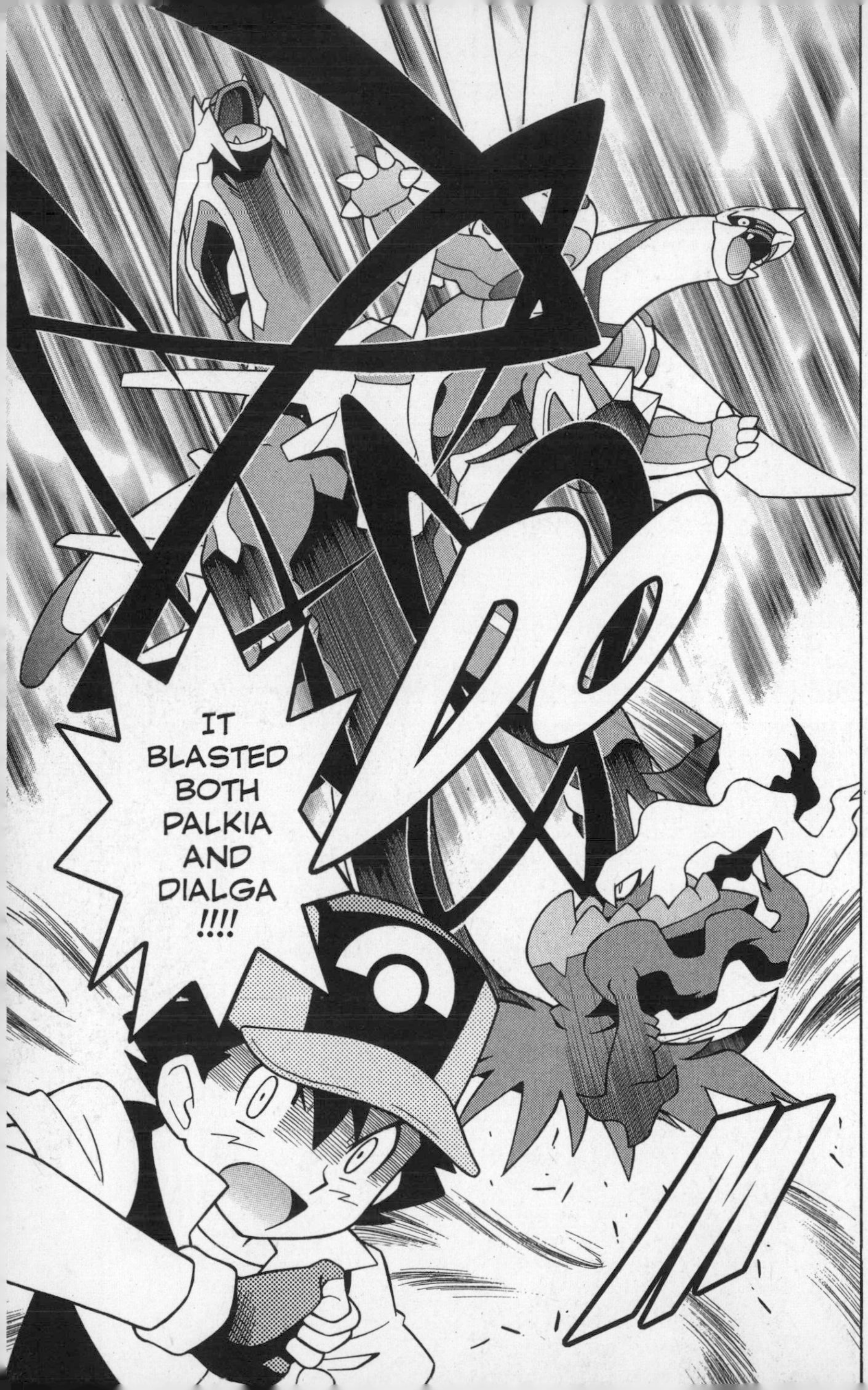
IT BLASTED BOTH PALKIA AND DIALGA !!!!

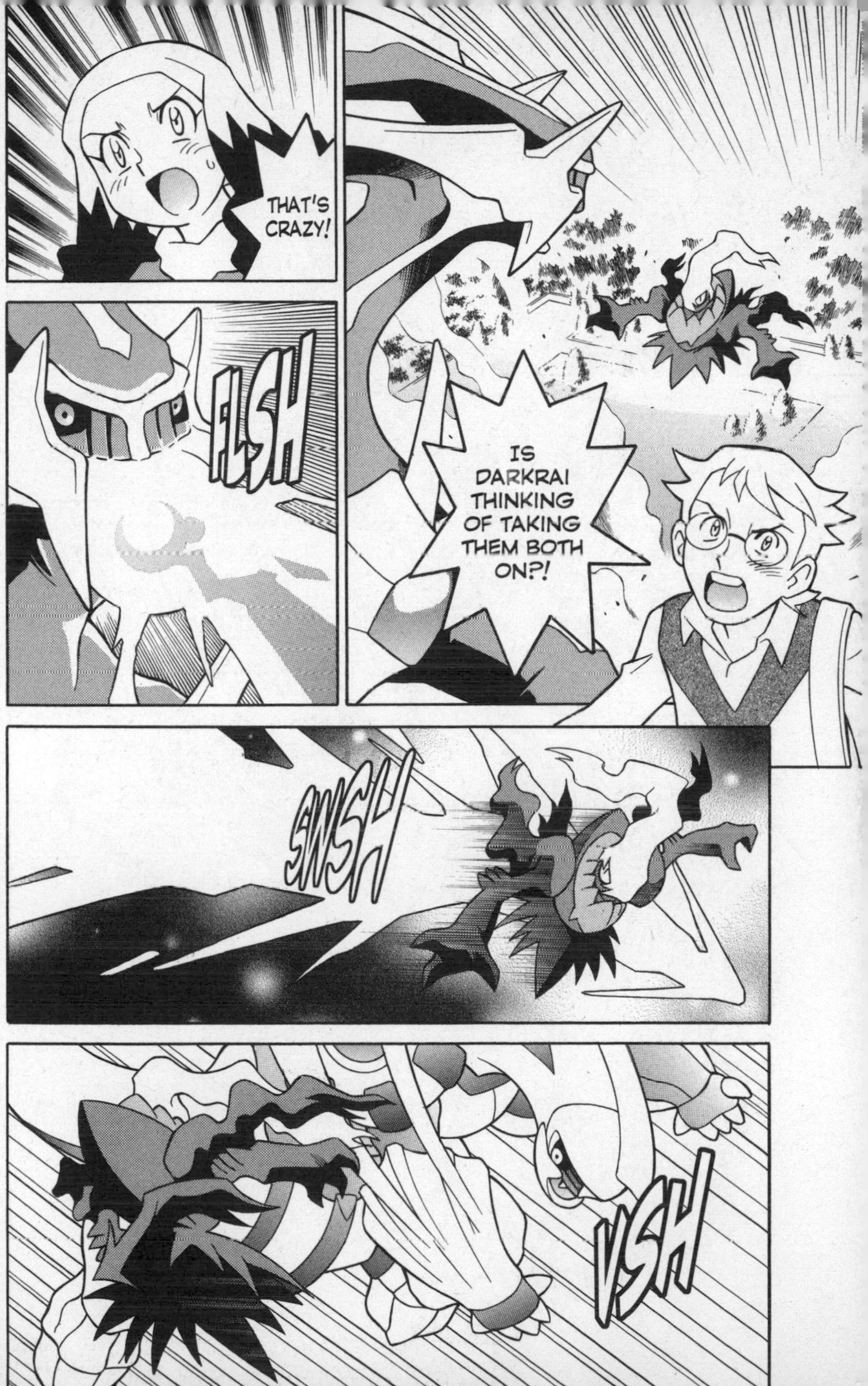
IS DARKRAI THINKING OF TAKING THEM BOTH ON?!
THAT'S CRAZY!
FLSH
SWSH
VSH

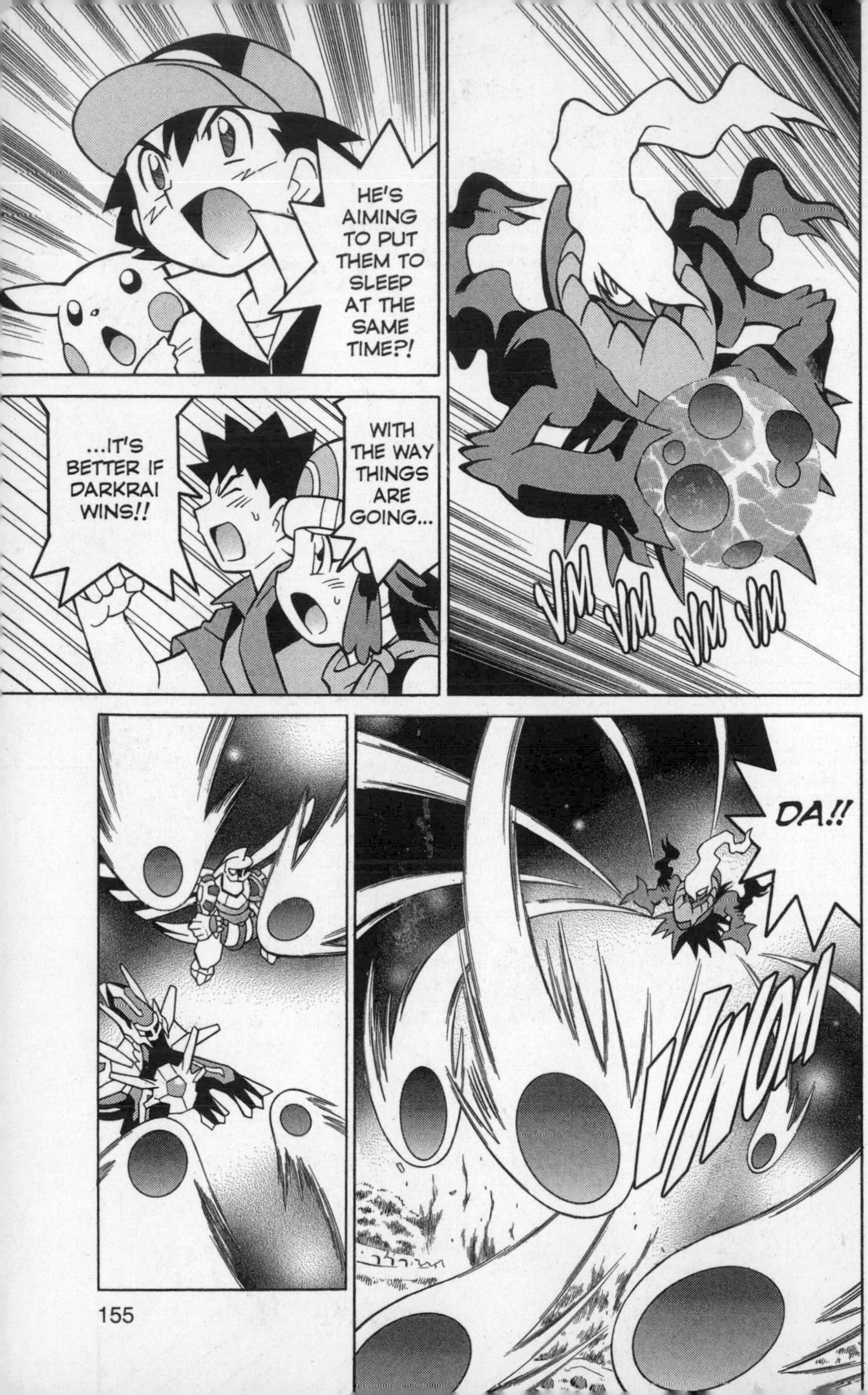
JM JM JM JM
HE'S AIMING TO PUT THEM TO SLEEP AT THE SAME TIME?!
WITH THE WAY THINGS ARE GOING...
...IT'S BETTER IF DARKRAI WINS!!
DA!!

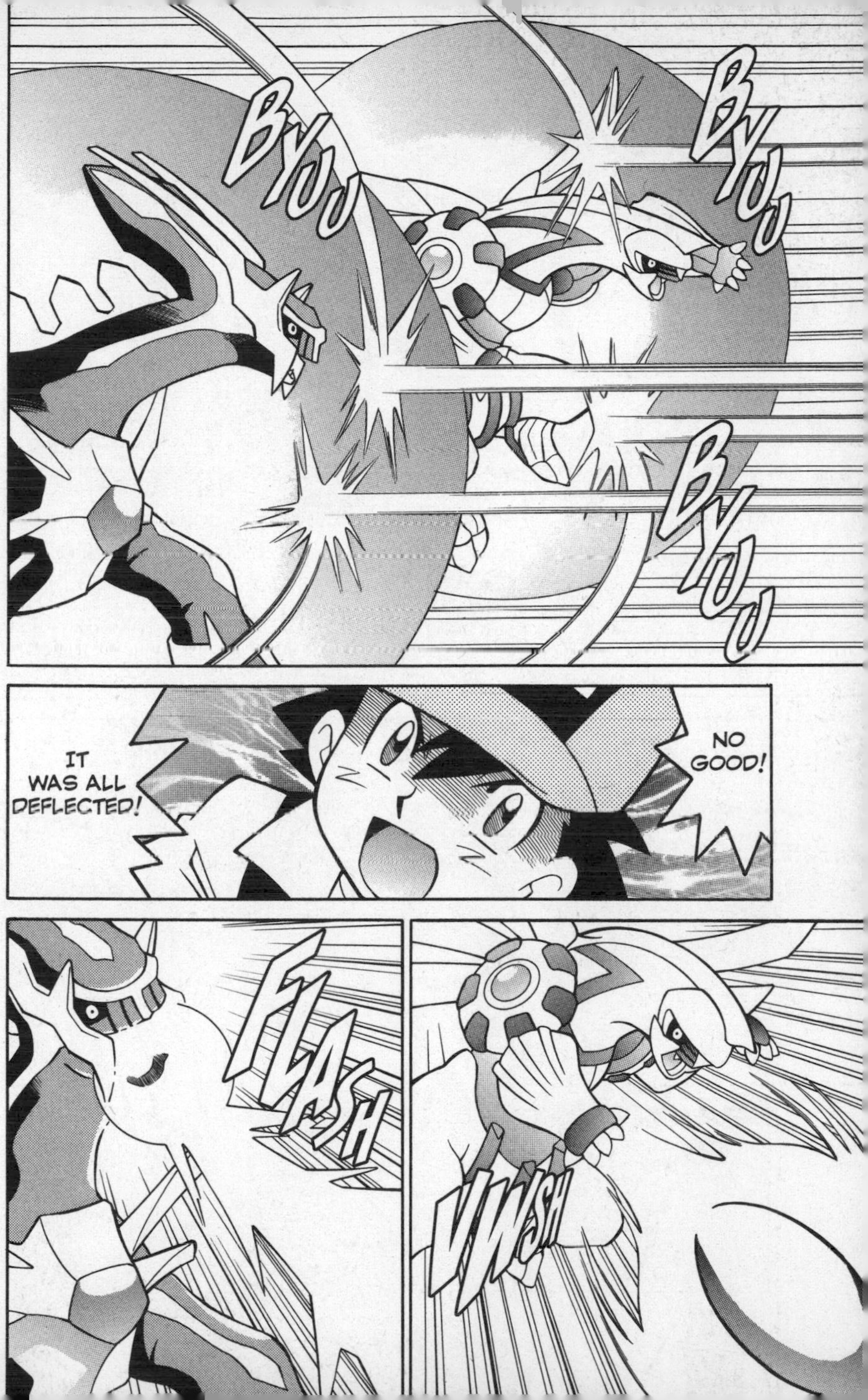
BYUU
BYUU
BYUU
NO GOOD!
IT WAS ALL DEFLECTED!
VWSH
FLASH

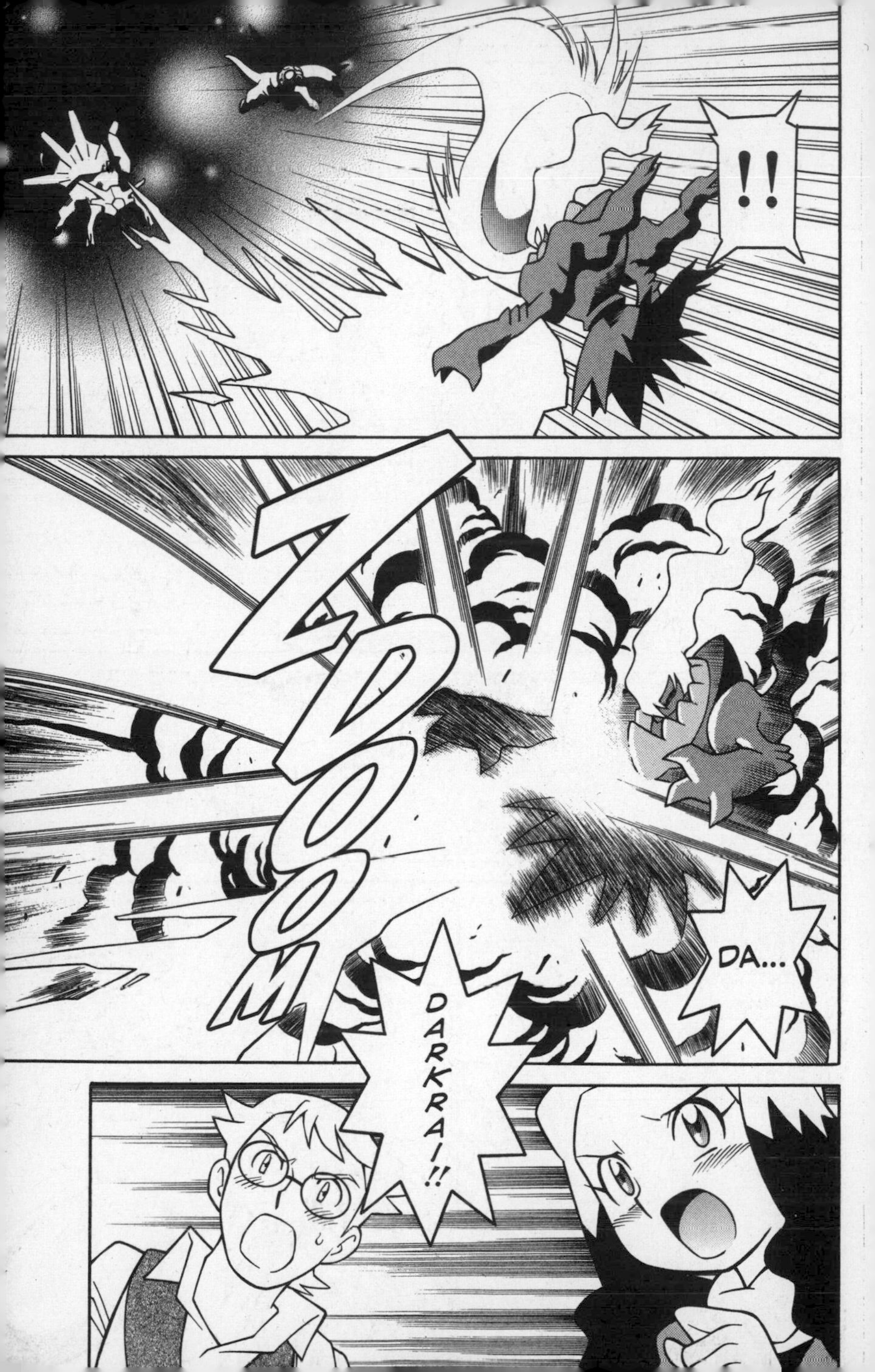
!!
ZOOOOM
DA...
DARKRAI!!

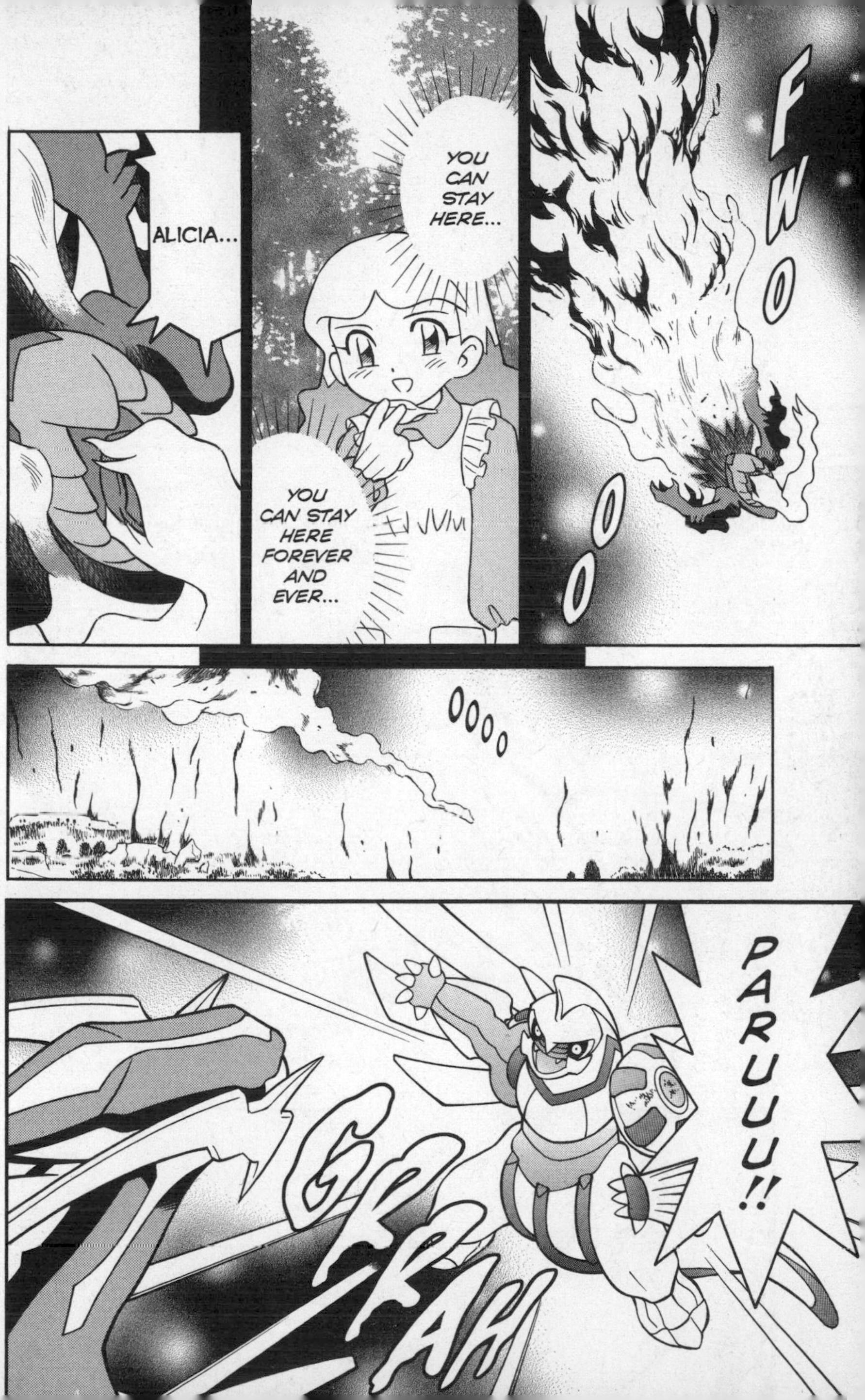
FWOOOO
YOU CAN STAY HERE...
YOU CAN STAY HERE FOREVER AND EVER...
ALICIA...
OOOO
PARUUUU!!
GRRAH

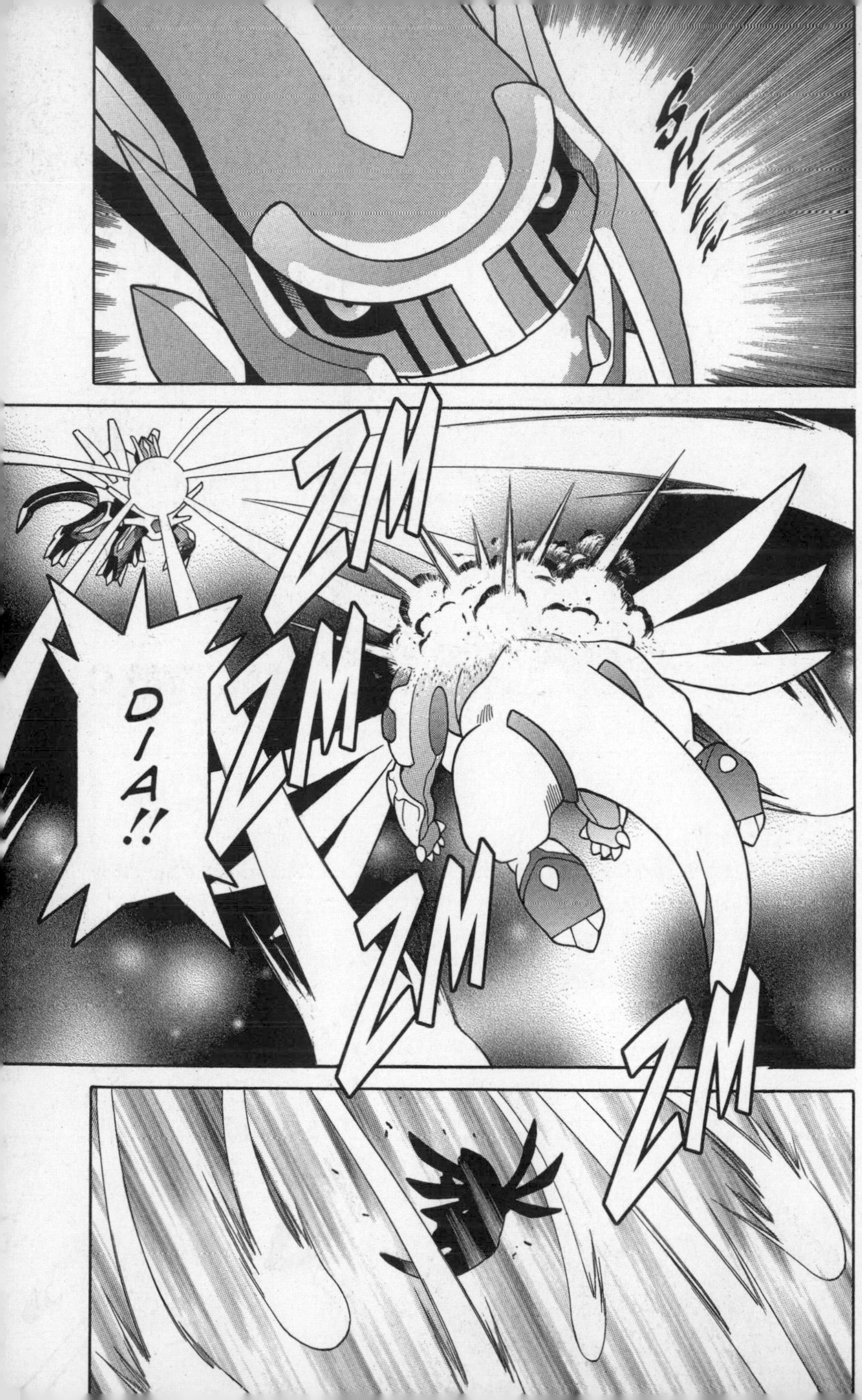
SHUNN
ZM
ZM
DIA!!
ZM
ZM

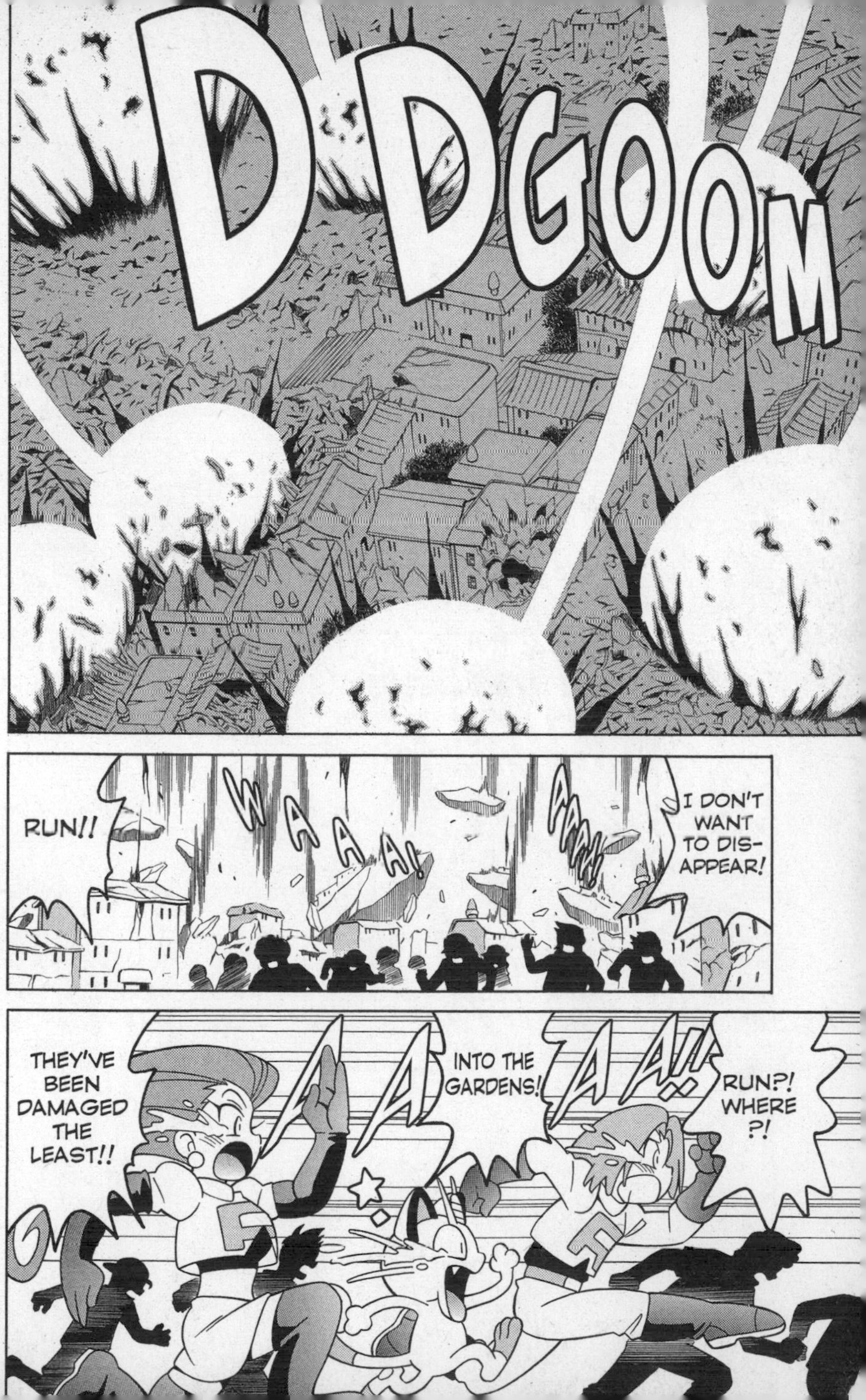
DDGOOOM
I DON'T WANT TO DIS-APPEAR!
AAAA!
WAAAA!
RUN!!
RUN?! WHERE ?!
AA!!
INTO THE GARDENS!
AA
THEY'VE BEEN DAMAGED THE LEAST!!

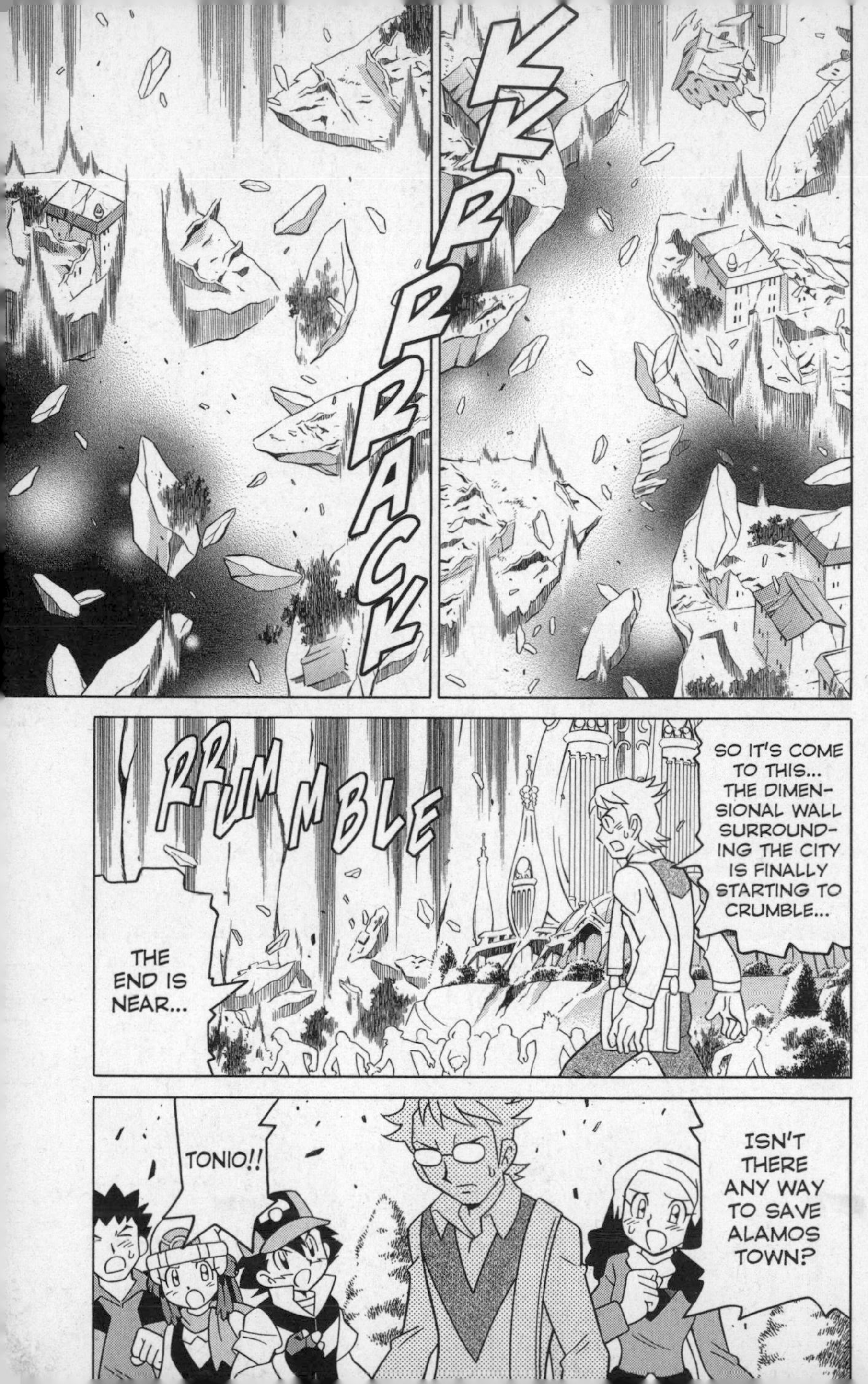
KKRRRAACK
SO IT'S COME TO THIS... THE DIMENSIONAL WALL SURROUNDING THE CITY IS FINALLY STARTING TO CRUMBLE...
RRUMMBLE
THE END IS NEAR...
ISN'T THERE ANY WAY TO SAVE ALAMOS TOWN?
TONIO!!

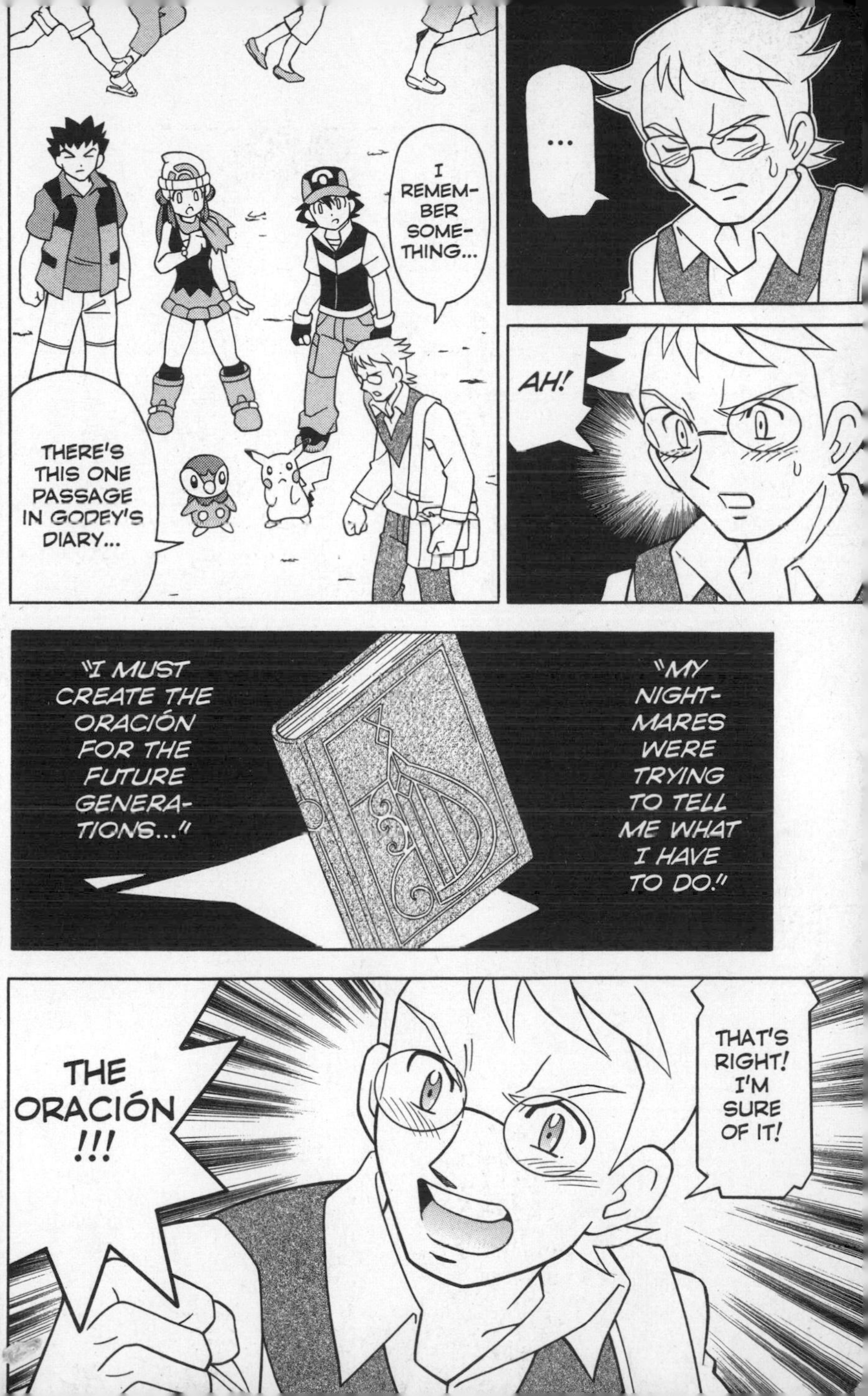
...
AH!
I REMEMBER SOMETHING...
THERE'S THIS ONE PASSAGE IN GODEY'S DIARY...
"MY NIGHTMARES WERE TRYING TO TELL ME WHAT I HAVE TO DO."
"I MUST CREATE THE ORACIÓN FOR THE FUTURE GENERATIONS..."
THAT'S RIGHT! I'M SURE OF IT!
THE ORACIÓN!!!

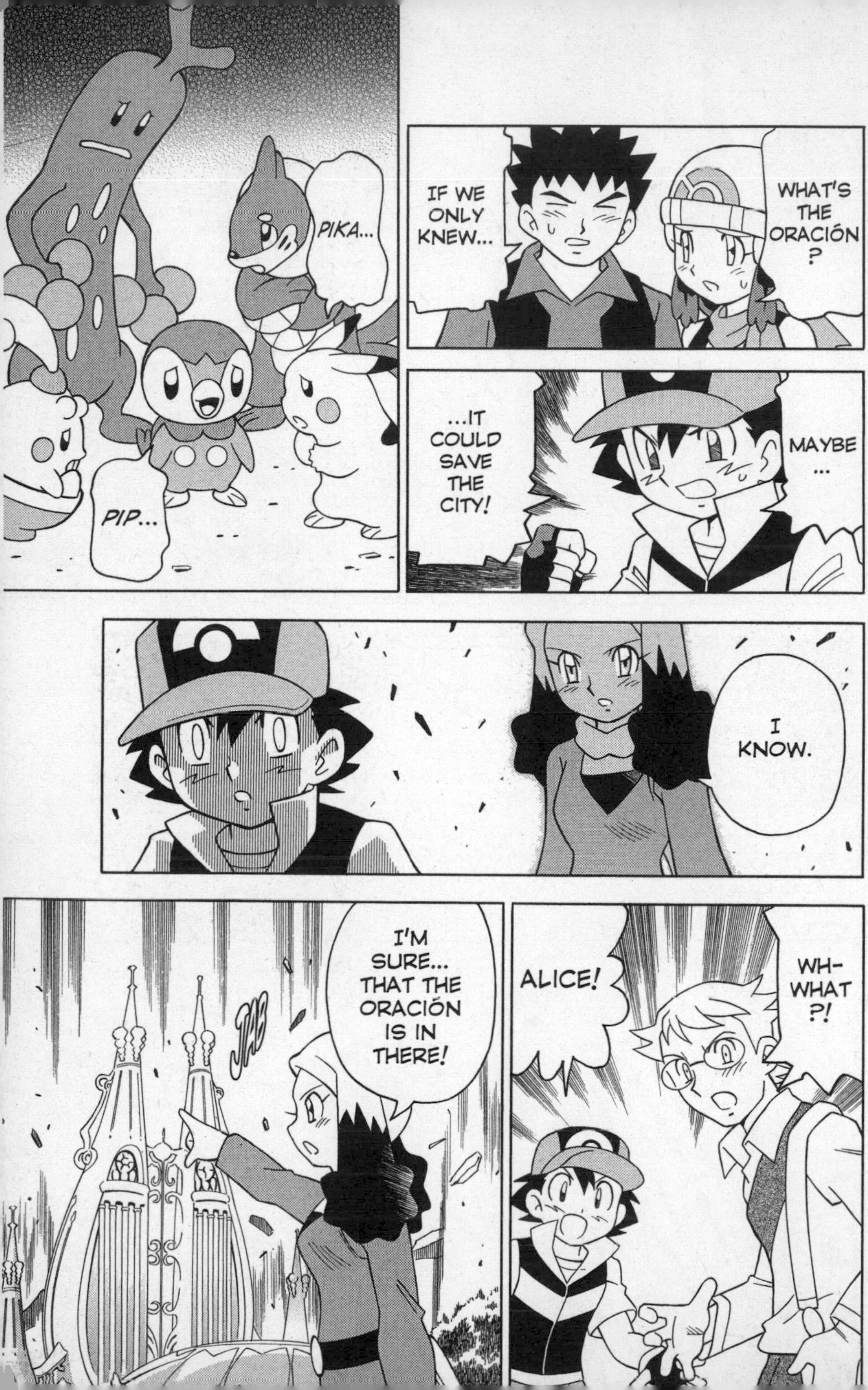
WHAT'S THE ORACIÓN ?
IF WE ONLY KNEW...
MAYBE ...
...IT COULD SAVE THE CITY!
PIKA...
PIP...
I KNOW.
WH-WHAT ?!
ALICE!
I'M SURE... THAT THE ORACIÓN IS IN THERE!

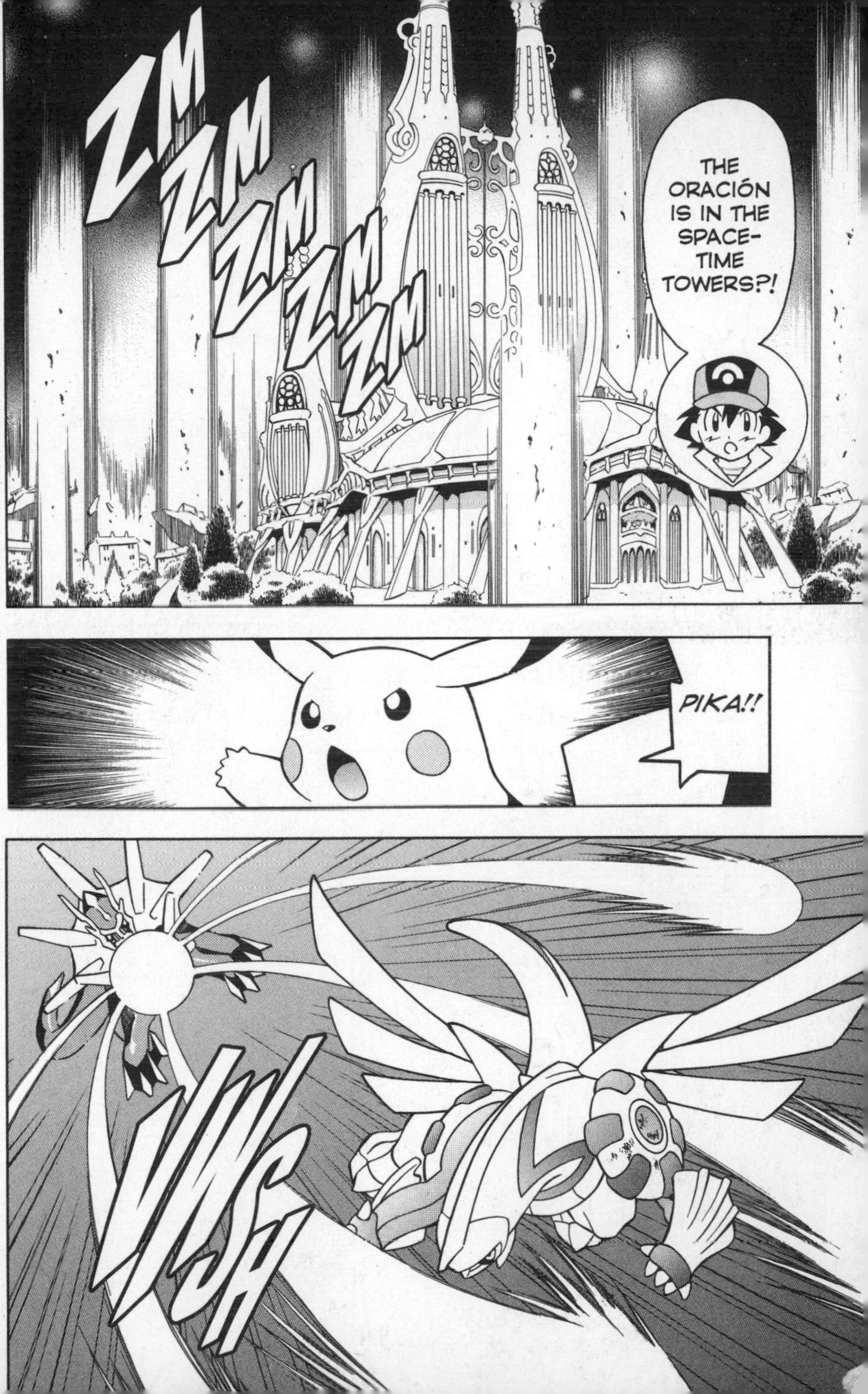
THE ORACIÓN IS IN THE SPACE-TIME TOWERS?!
ZM ZM ZM ZM ZM ZM
PIKA!!
VWSH

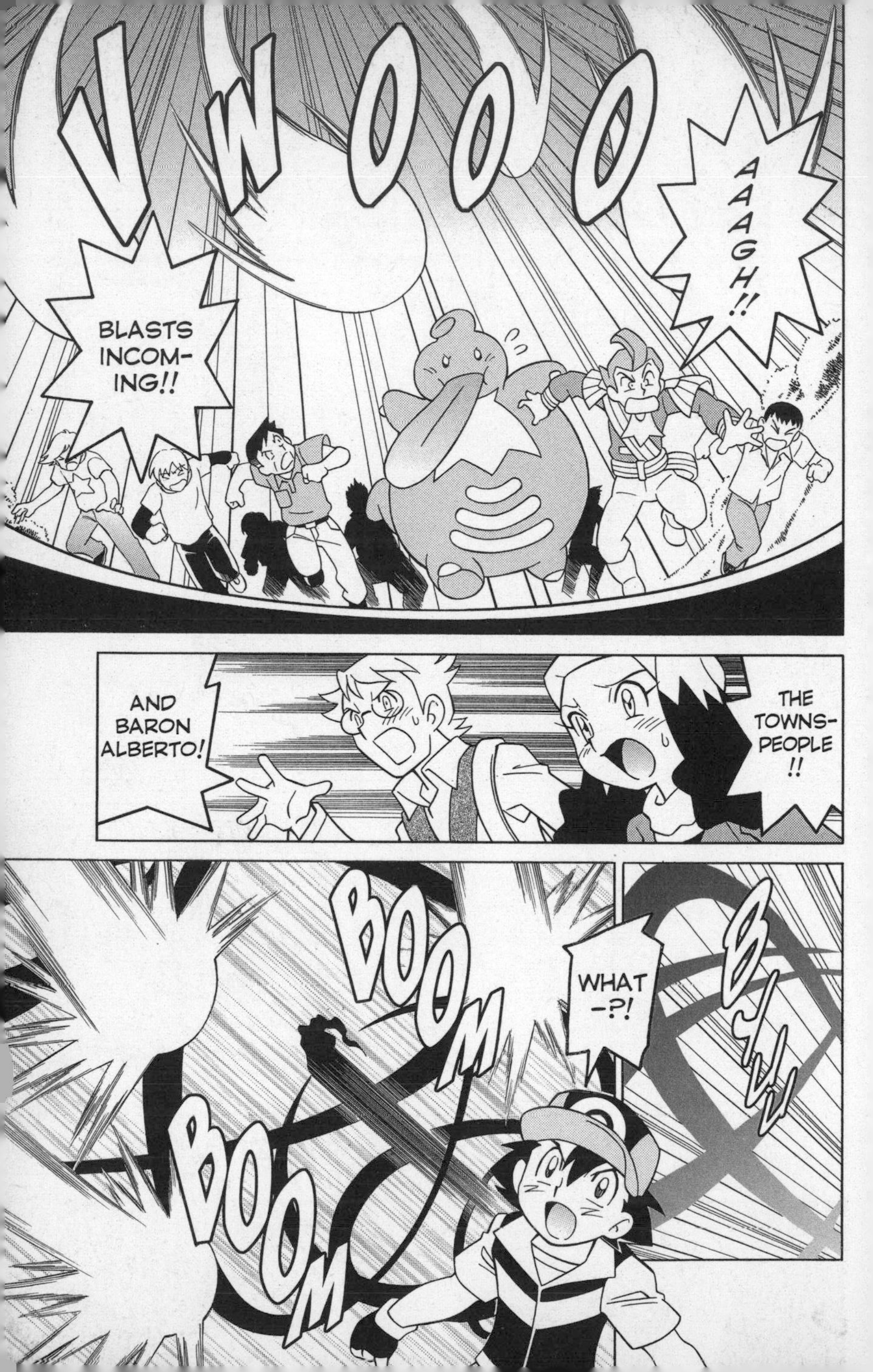
AAAGH!!
VWOOOO
BLASTS INCOMING!!
THE TOWNSPEOPLE!!
AND BARON ALBERTO!
WHAT-?!
BOOM
BOOM

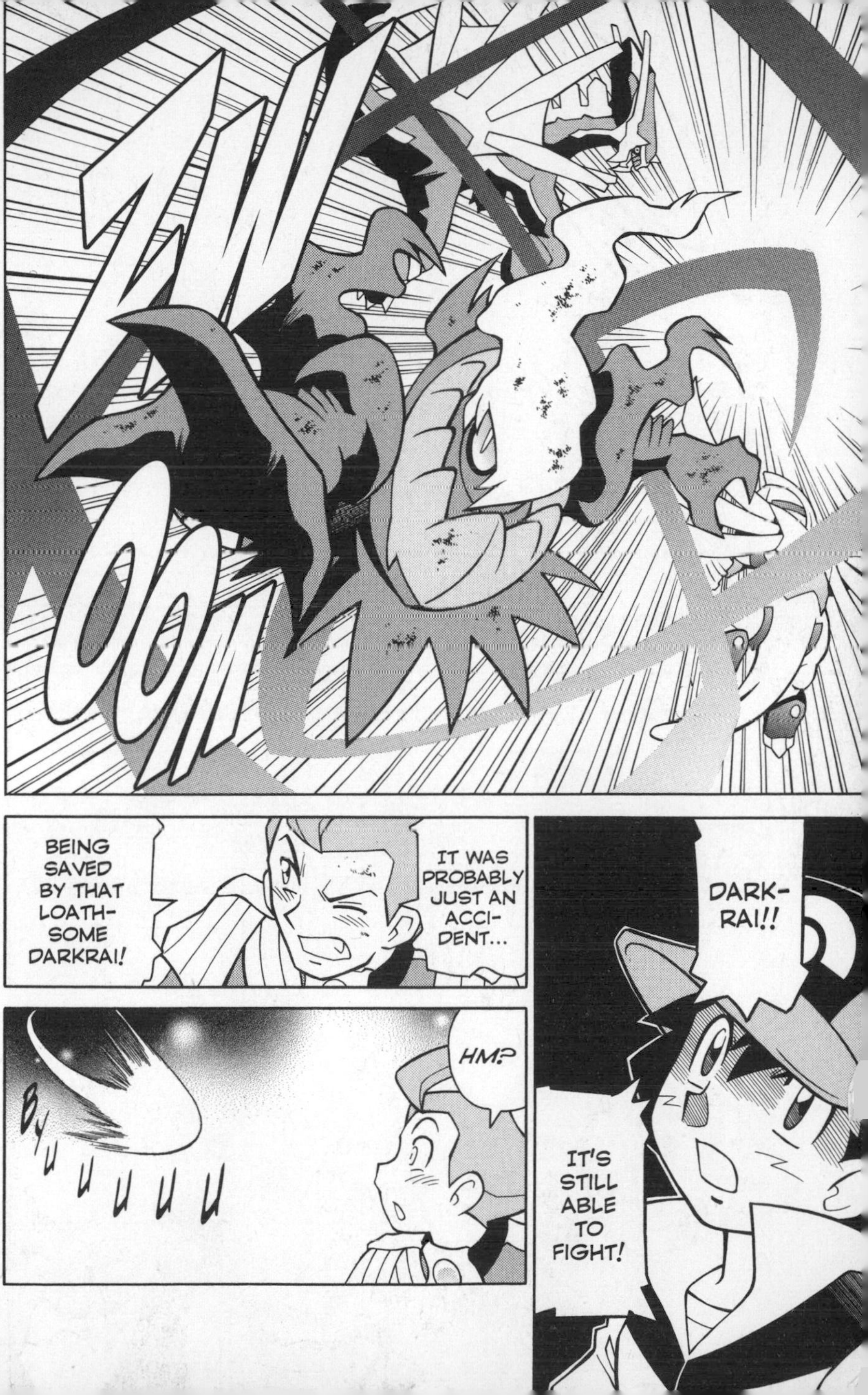
ZWOOM
DARK-RAI!!
IT'S STILL ABLE TO FIGHT!
IT WAS PROBABLY JUST AN ACCI-DENT...
BEING SAVED BY THAT LOATH-SOME DARKRAI!
HM?
BYUUUUUU

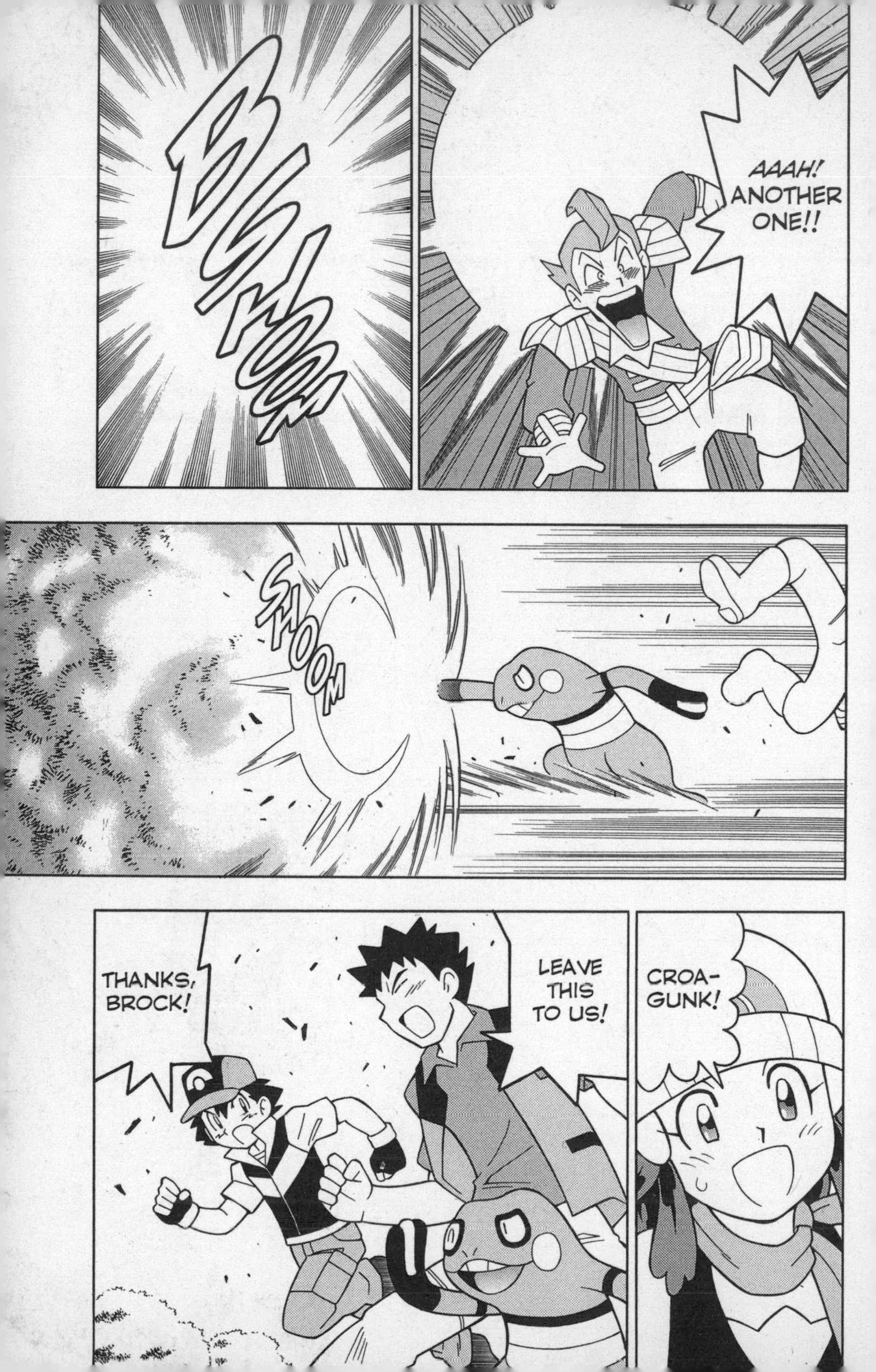
AAAH! ANOTHER ONE!!
BISHOOM
SHOOM
CROA-GUNK!
LEAVE THIS TO US!
THANKS, BROCK!

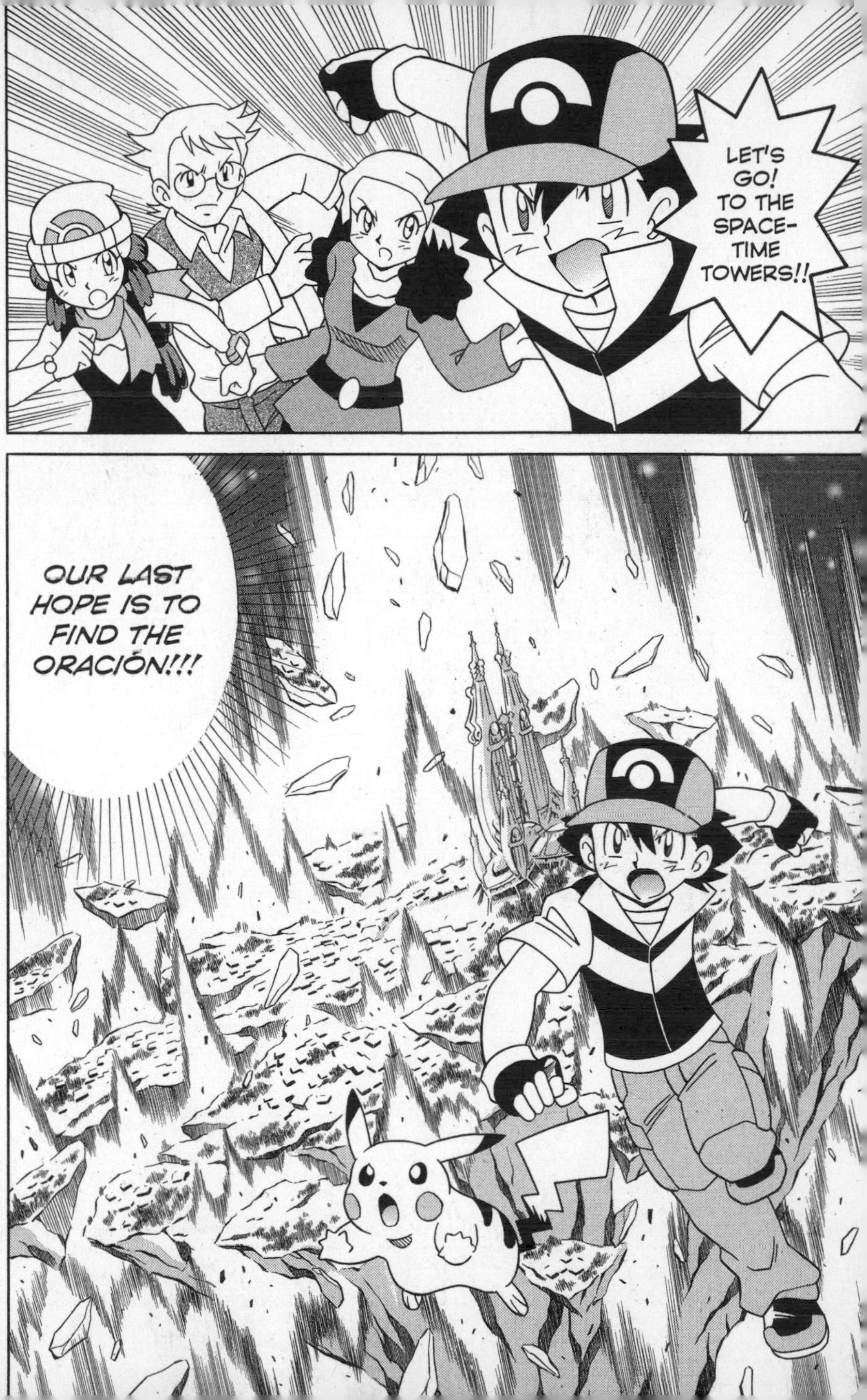
LET'S GO! TO THE SPACE-TIME TOWERS!!
OUR LAST HOPE IS TO FIND THE ORACIÓN!!!

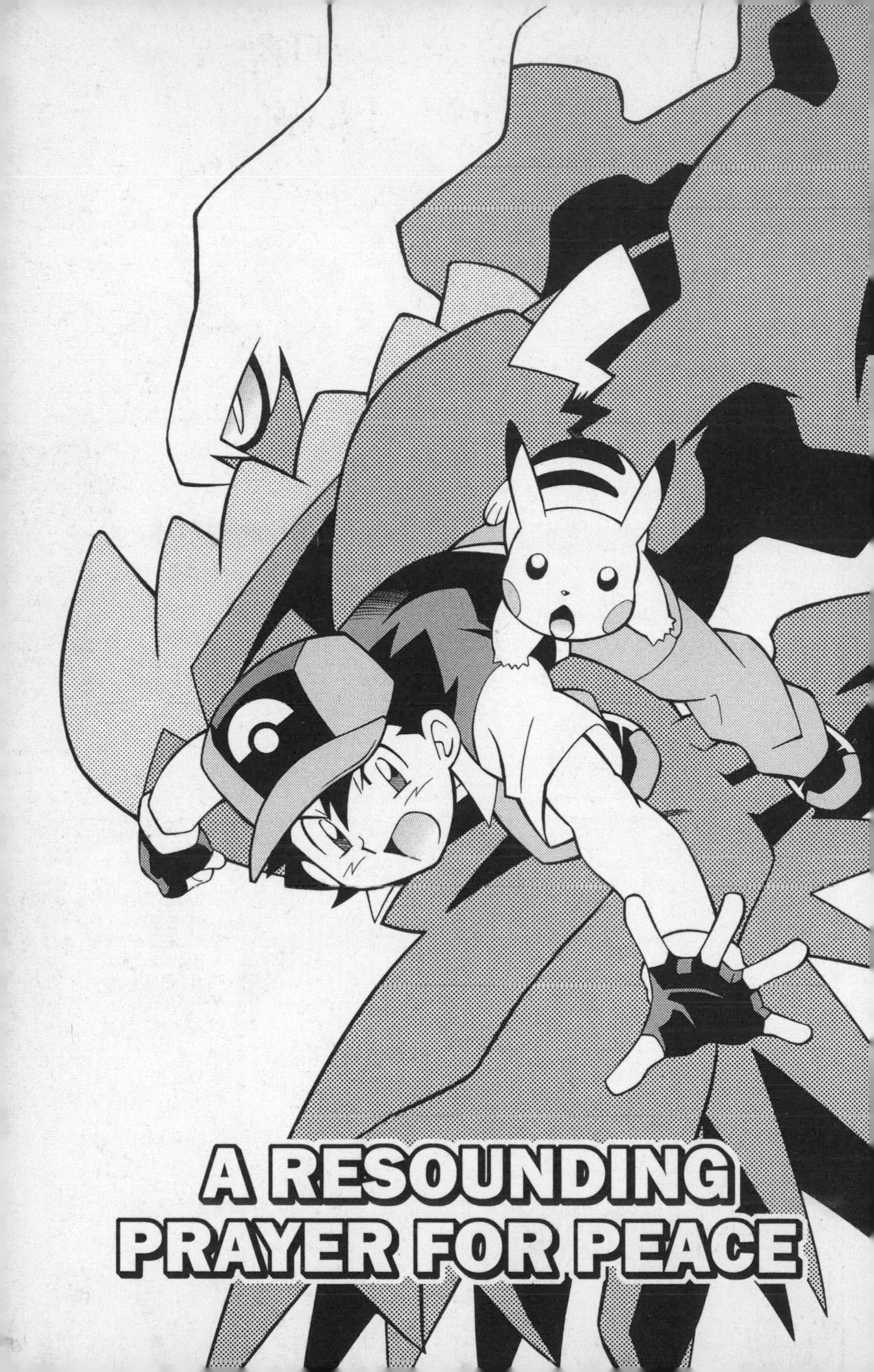

A RESOUNDING PRAYER FOR PEACE

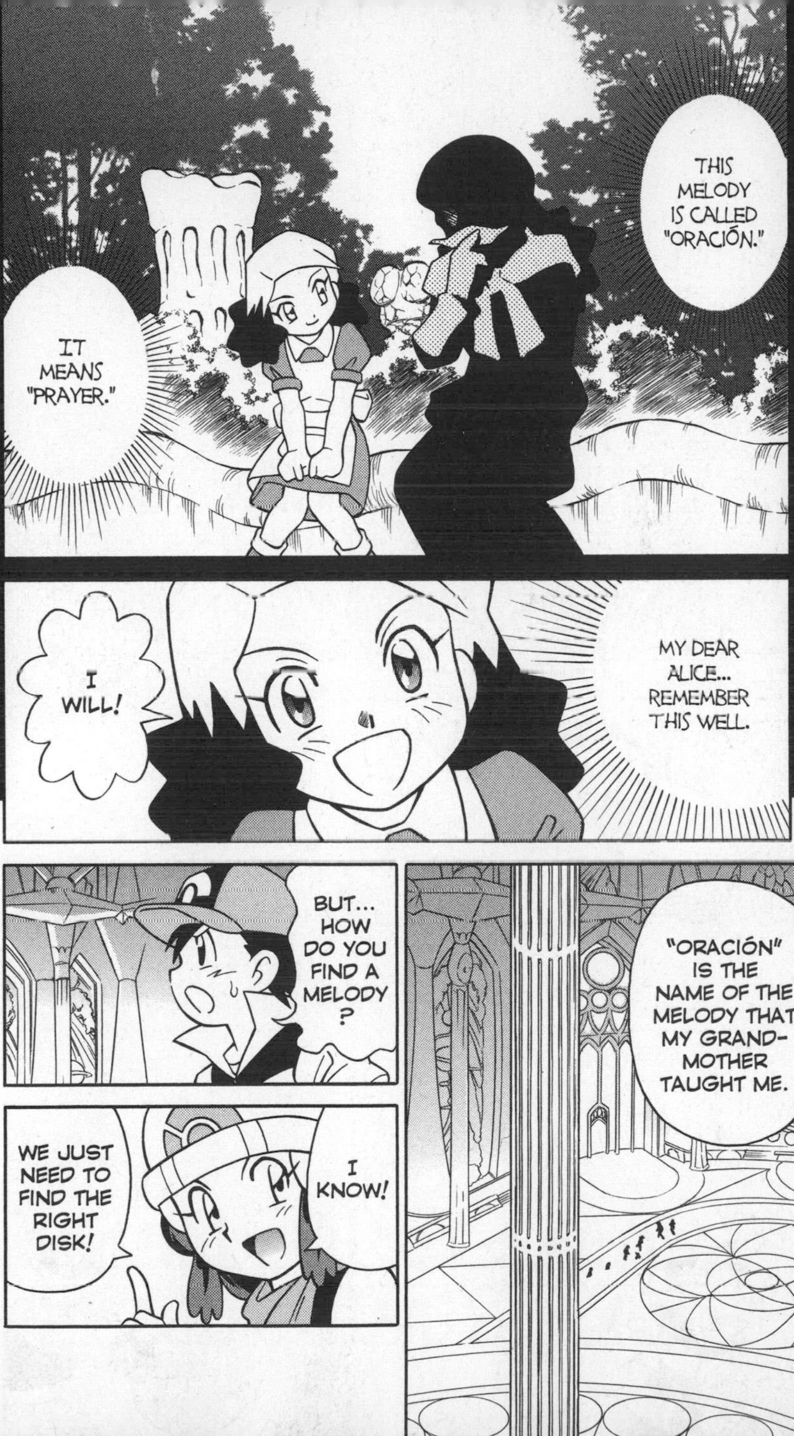
THIS MELODY IS CALLED "ORACIÓN."
IT MEANS "PRAYER."
MY DEAR ALICE... REMEMBER THIS WELL.
I WILL!
"ORACIÓN" IS THE NAME OF THE MELODY THAT MY GRAND-MOTHER TAUGHT ME.
BUT... HOW DO YOU FIND A MELODY?
I KNOW!
WE JUST NEED TO FIND THE RIGHT DISK!

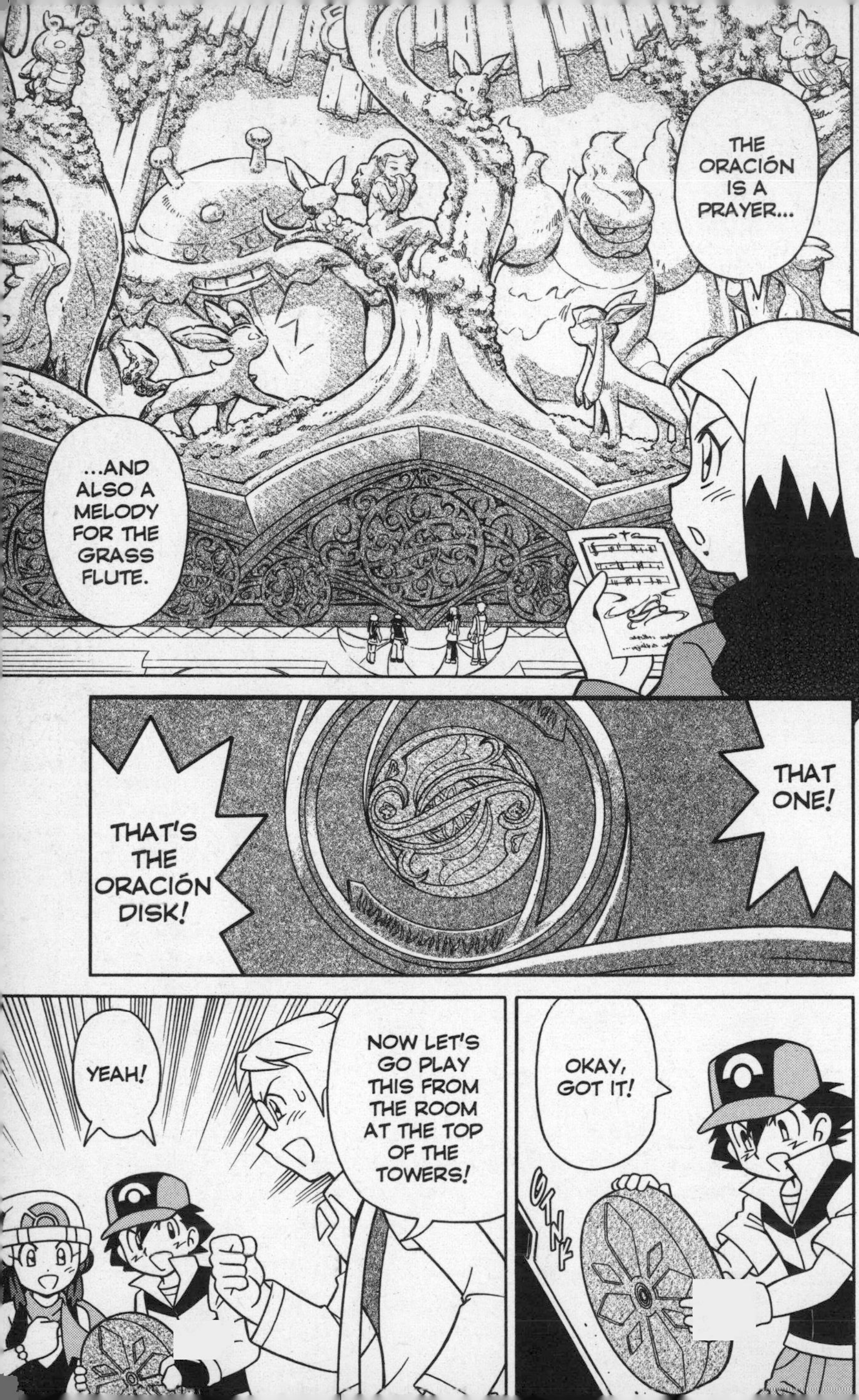
THE ORACIÓN IS A PRAYER...
...AND ALSO A MELODY FOR THE GRASS FLUTE.
THAT ONE!
THAT'S THE ORACIÓN DISK!
OKAY, GOT IT!
NOW LET'S GO PLAY THIS FROM THE ROOM AT THE TOP OF THE TOWERS!
YEAH!

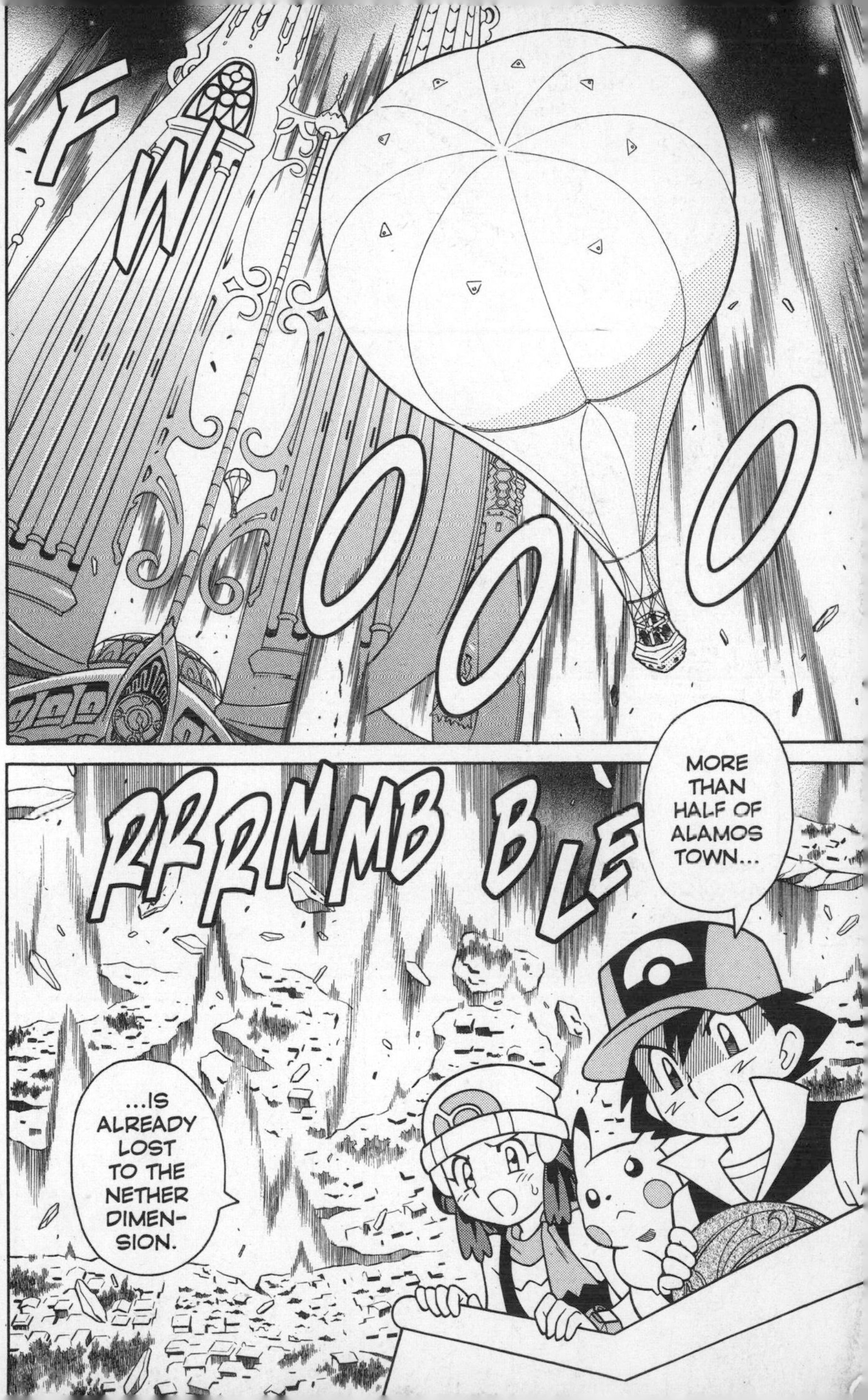
FWOOOO
RRRMMB BLE
MORE THAN HALF OF ALAMOS TOWN...
...IS ALREADY LOST TO THE NETHER DIMENSION.

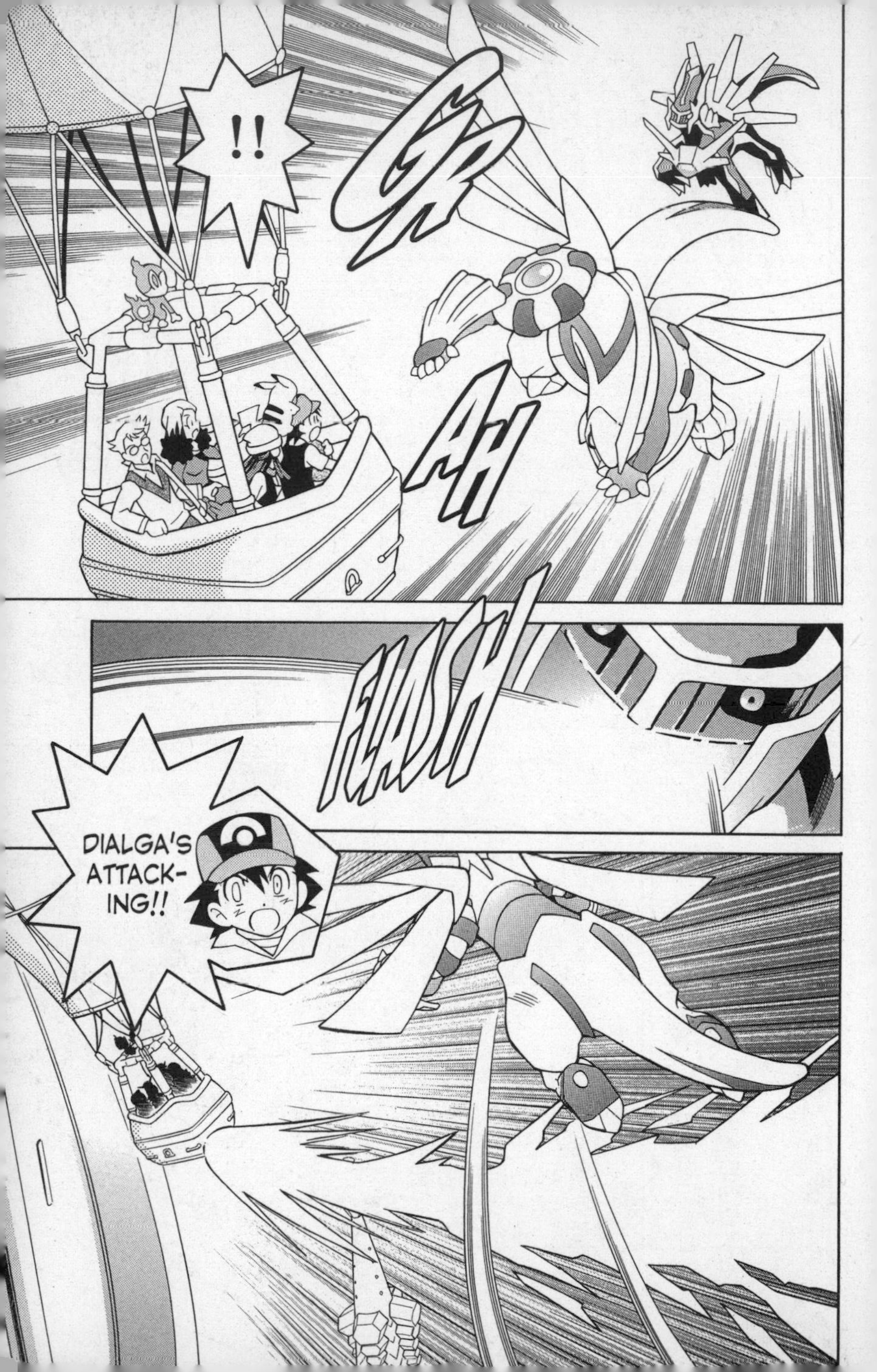
GRA
!!
AH
FLASH
DIALGA'S ATTACK-ING!!

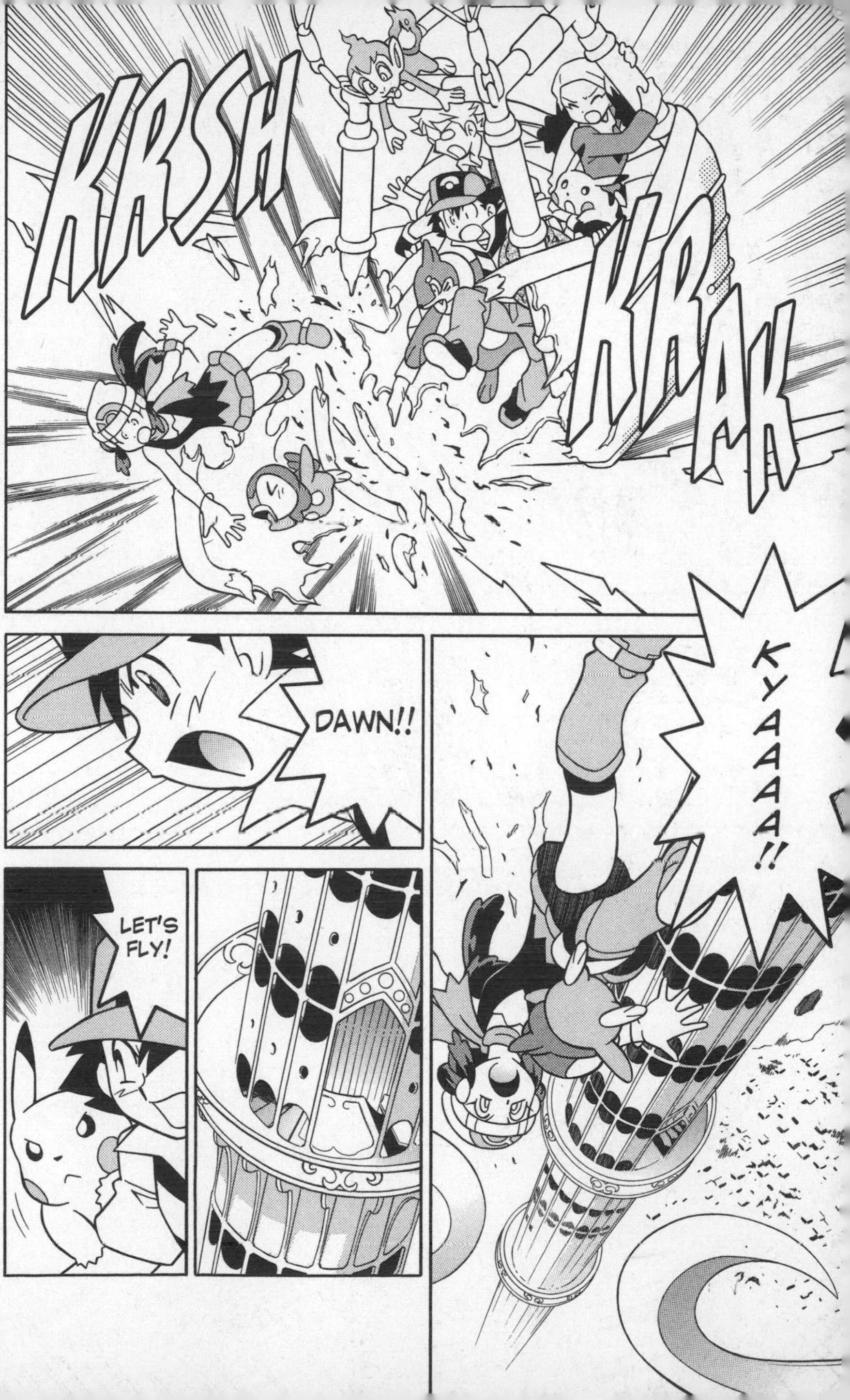
KRAK
KRSH
KYAAAAA!!
DAWN!!
LET'S FLY!

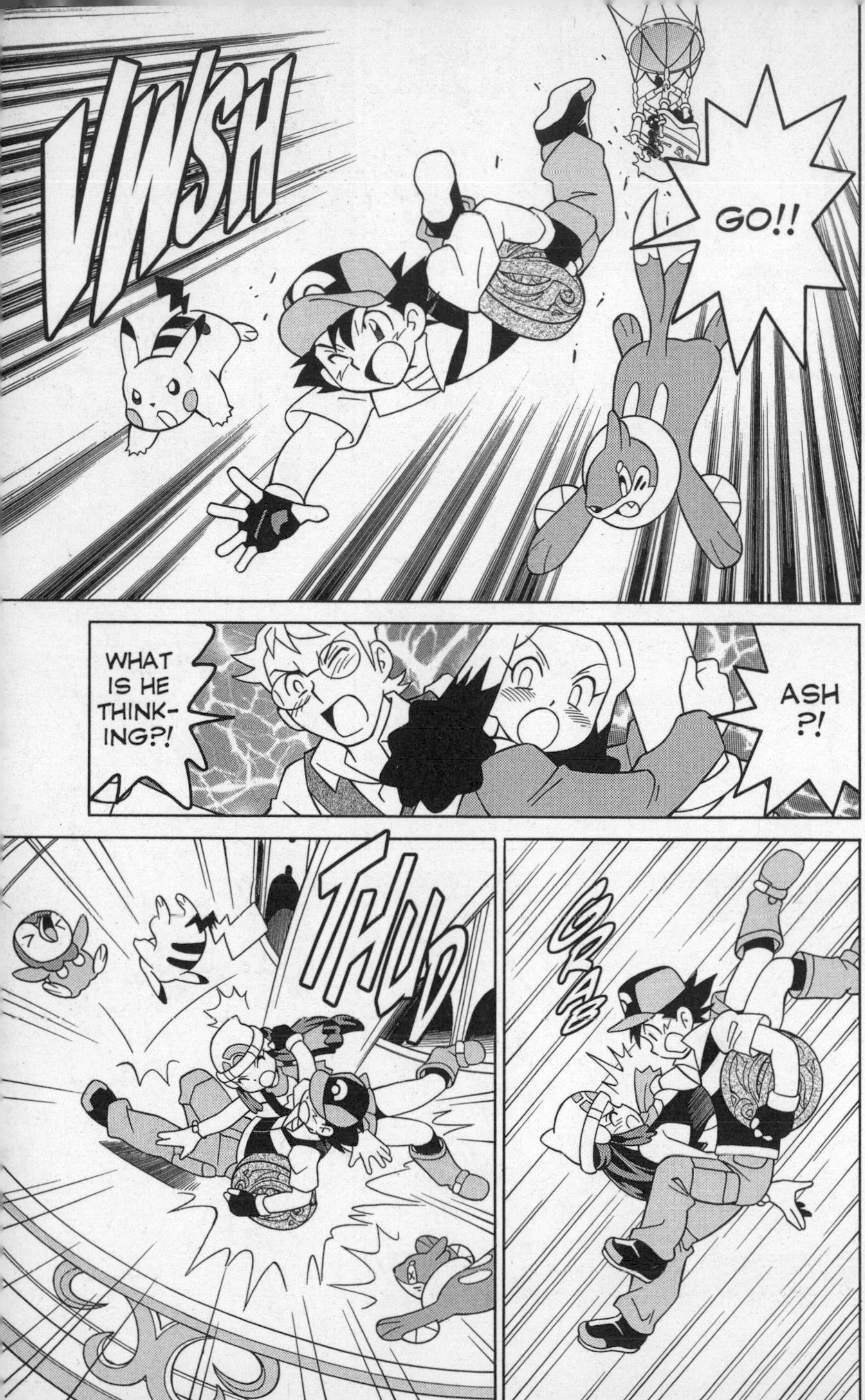
GO!!
VWSH
ASH ?!
WHAT IS HE THINKING?!
GRAB
THUD

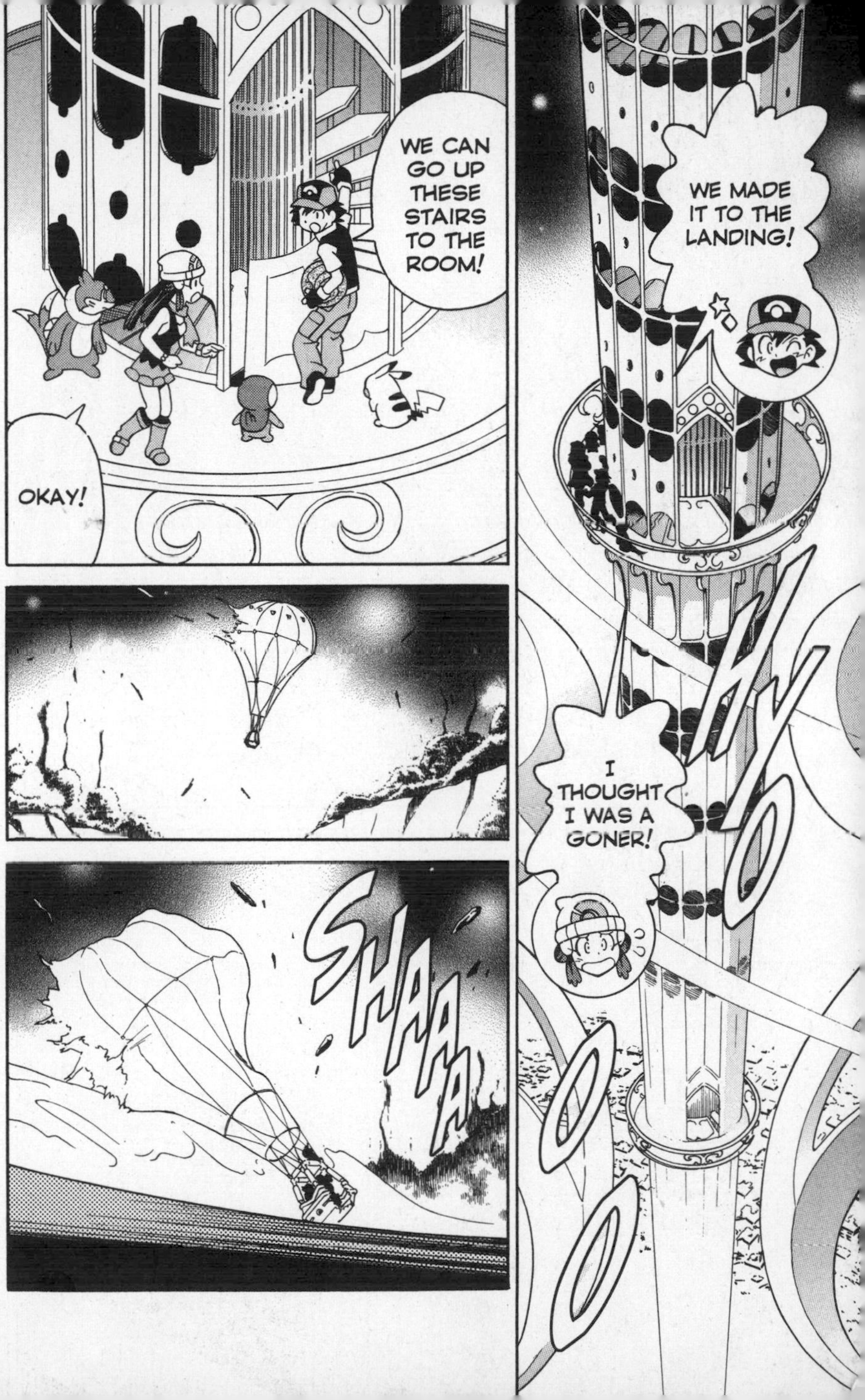
WE MADE IT TO THE LANDING!
I THOUGHT I WAS A GONER!
WE CAN GO UP THESE STAIRS TO THE ROOM!
OKAY!
SHAAAA

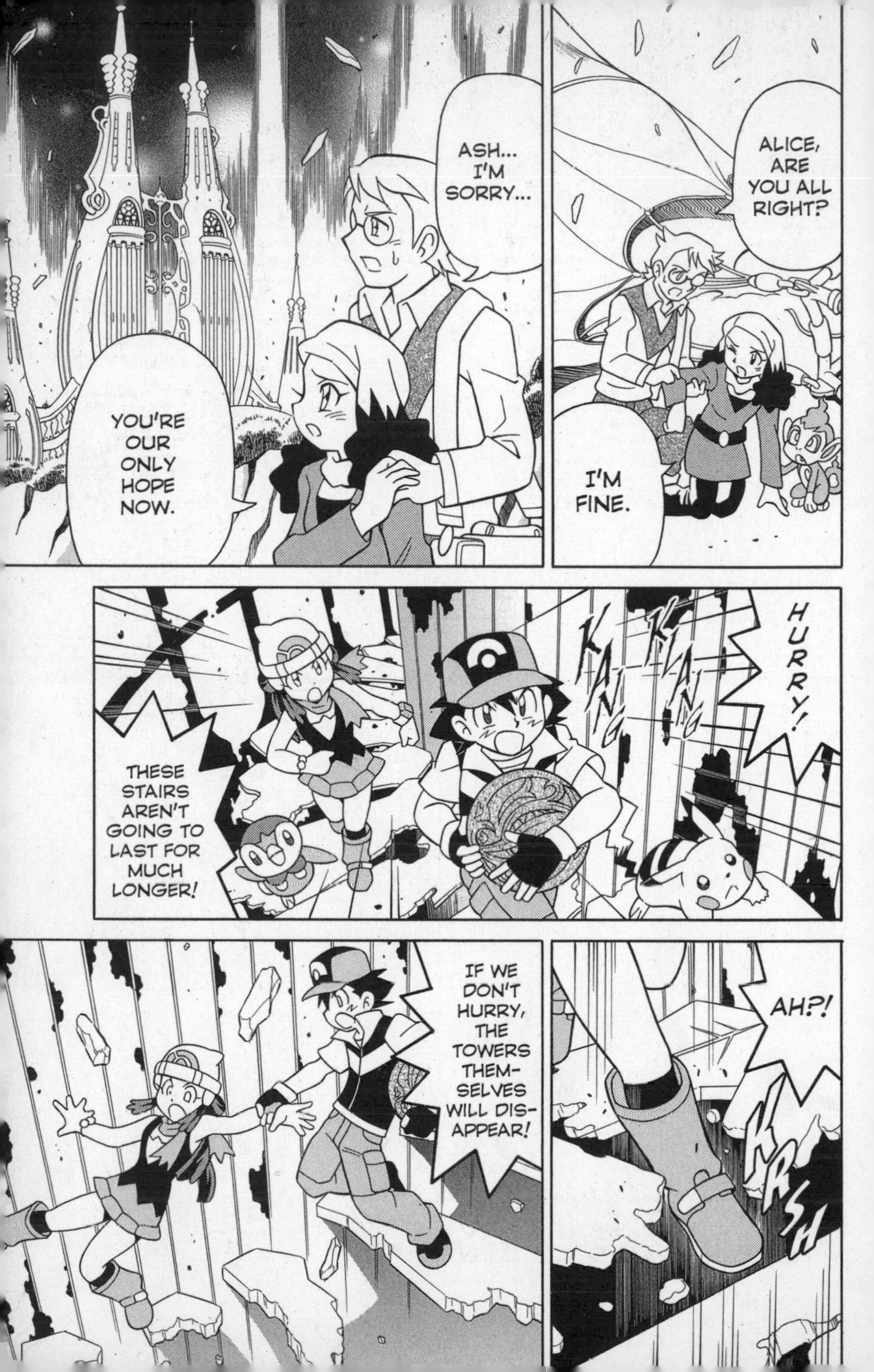
ALICE, ARE YOU ALL RIGHT?
I'M FINE.
ASH... I'M SORRY...
YOU'RE OUR ONLY HOPE NOW.
HURRY!
KLANG
KANG
THESE STAIRS AREN'T GOING TO LAST FOR MUCH LONGER!
AH?!
KRSH
IF WE DON'T HURRY, THE TOWERS THEM-SELVES WILL DIS-APPEAR!

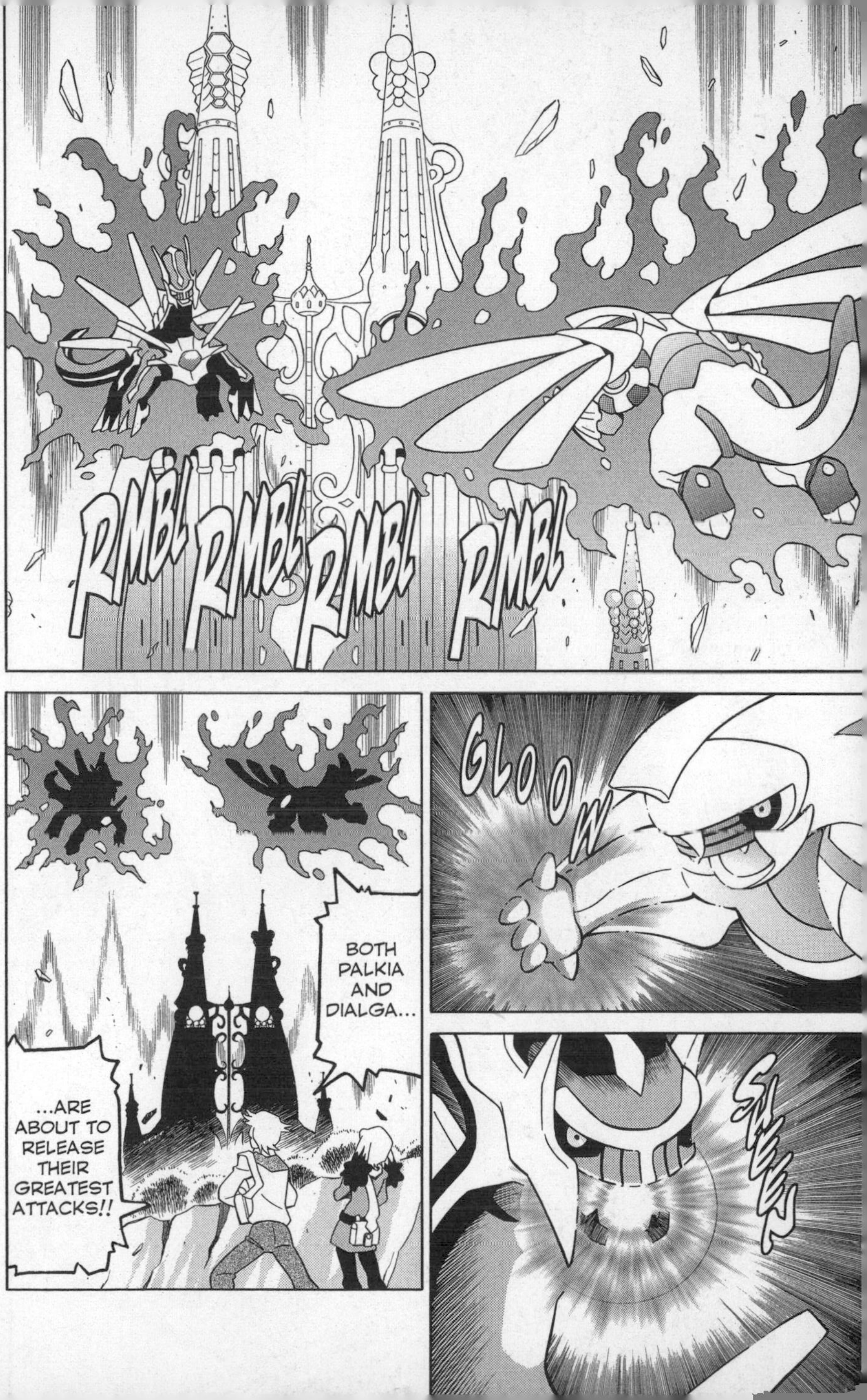
RMBL RMBL RMBL RMBL
GLOOOW
BOTH PALKIA AND DIALGA...
...ARE ABOUT TO RELEASE THEIR GREATEST ATTACKS!!

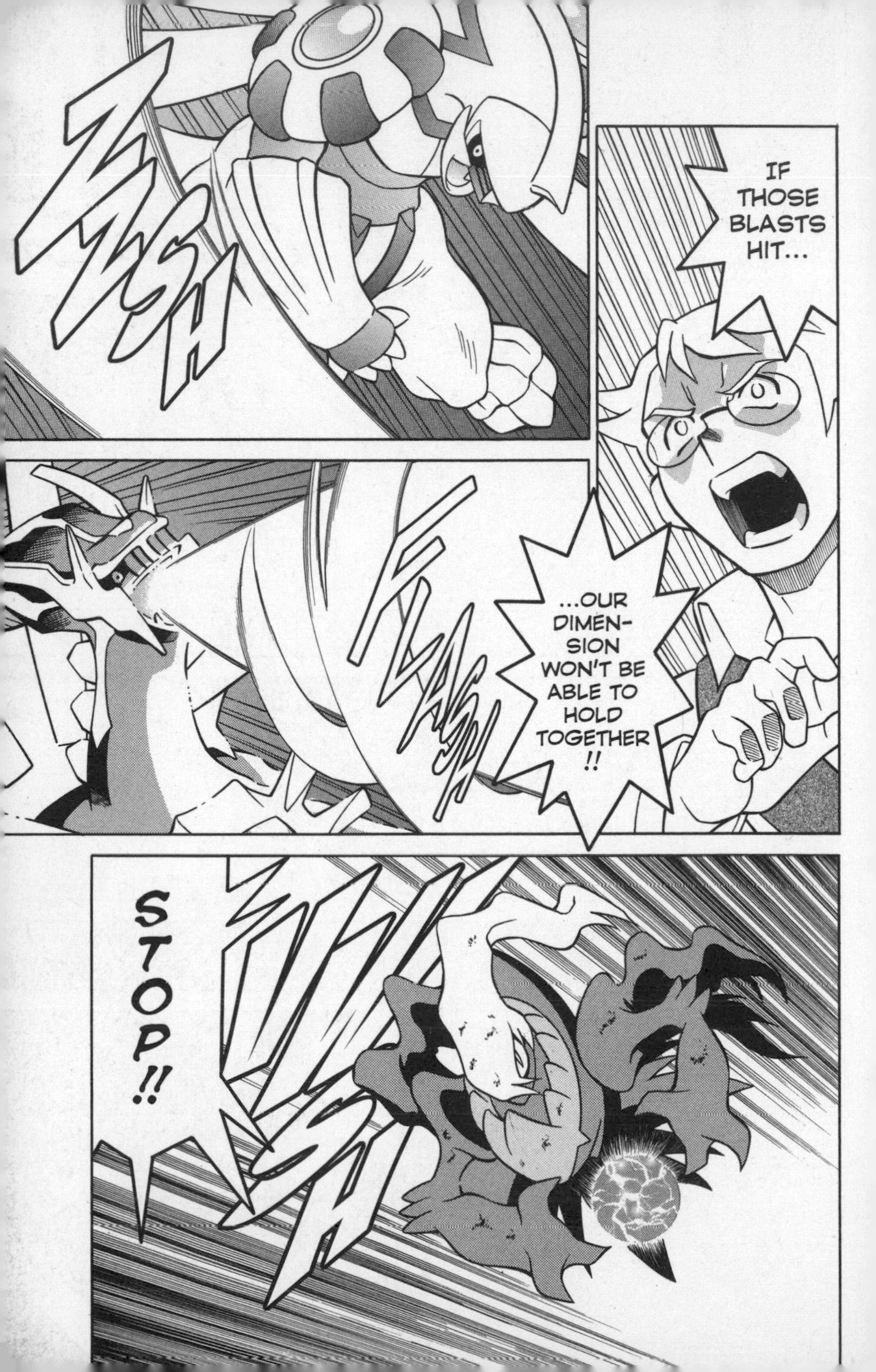
IF THOSE BLASTS HIT...
...OUR DIMENSION WON'T BE ABLE TO HOLD TOGETHER!!
WHSH
FLASH
STOP!!

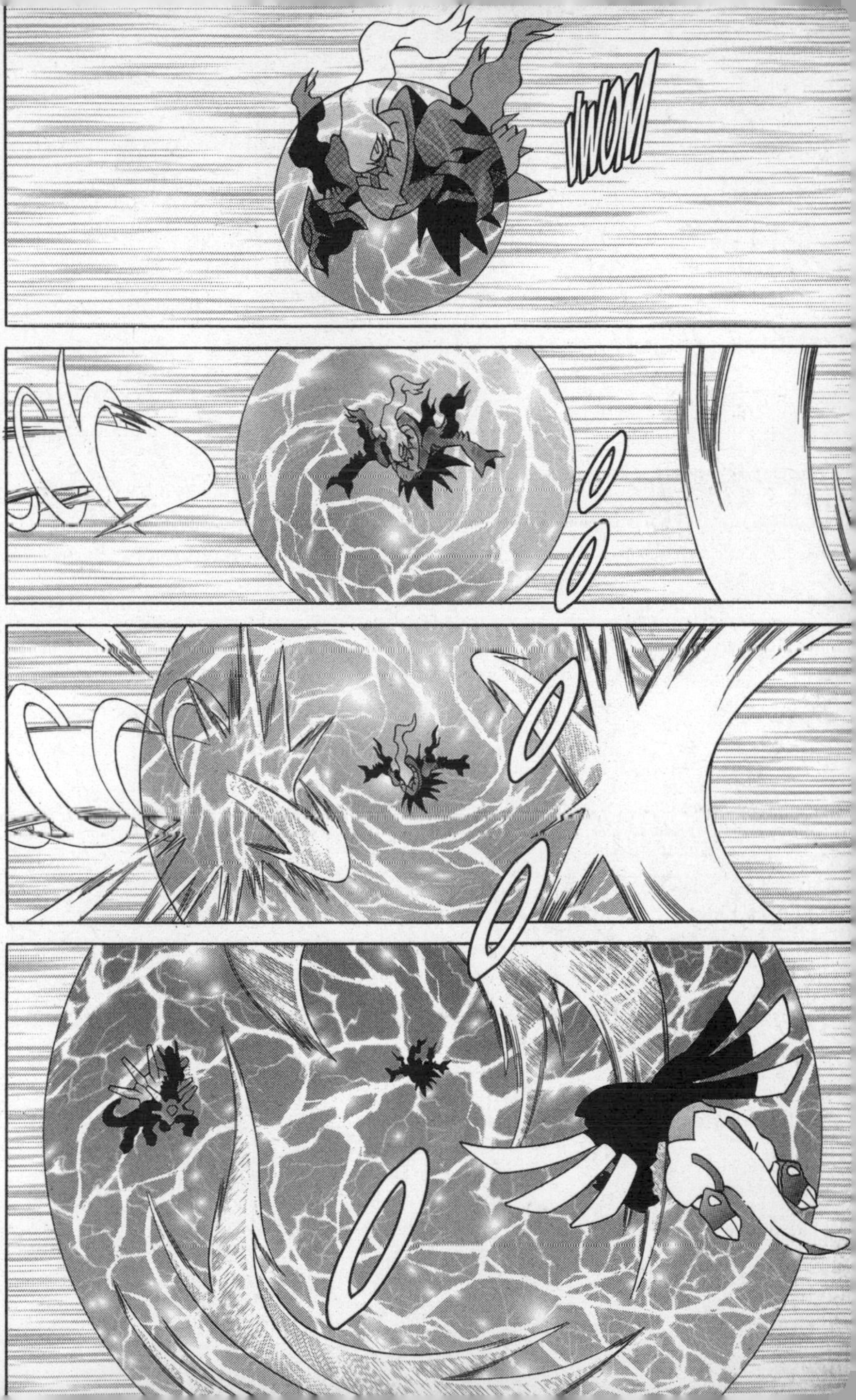
WOM

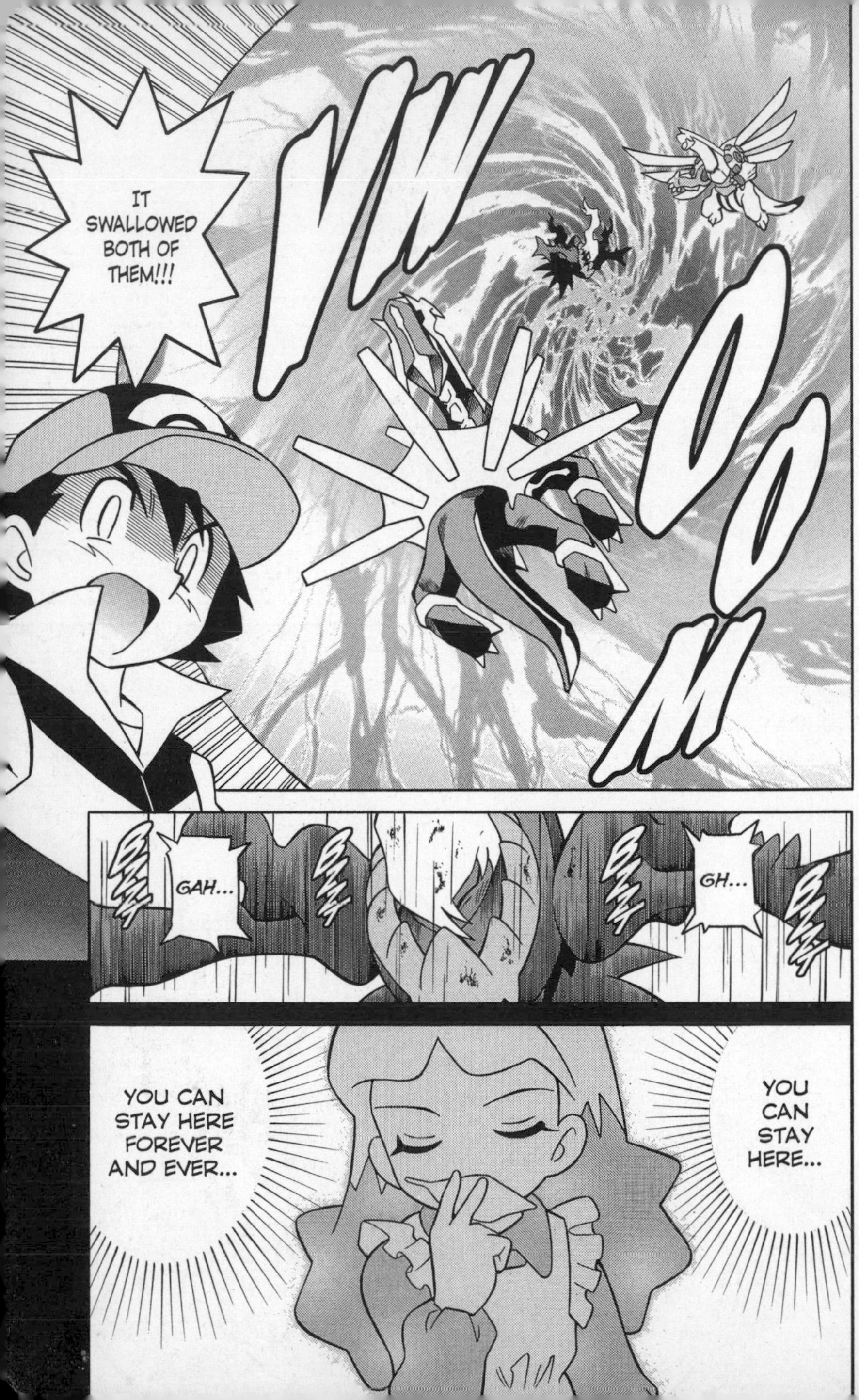
VWOOOM
IT SWALLOWED BOTH OF THEM!!!
GH...
GAH...
YOU CAN STAY HERE...
YOU CAN STAY HERE FOREVER AND EVER...

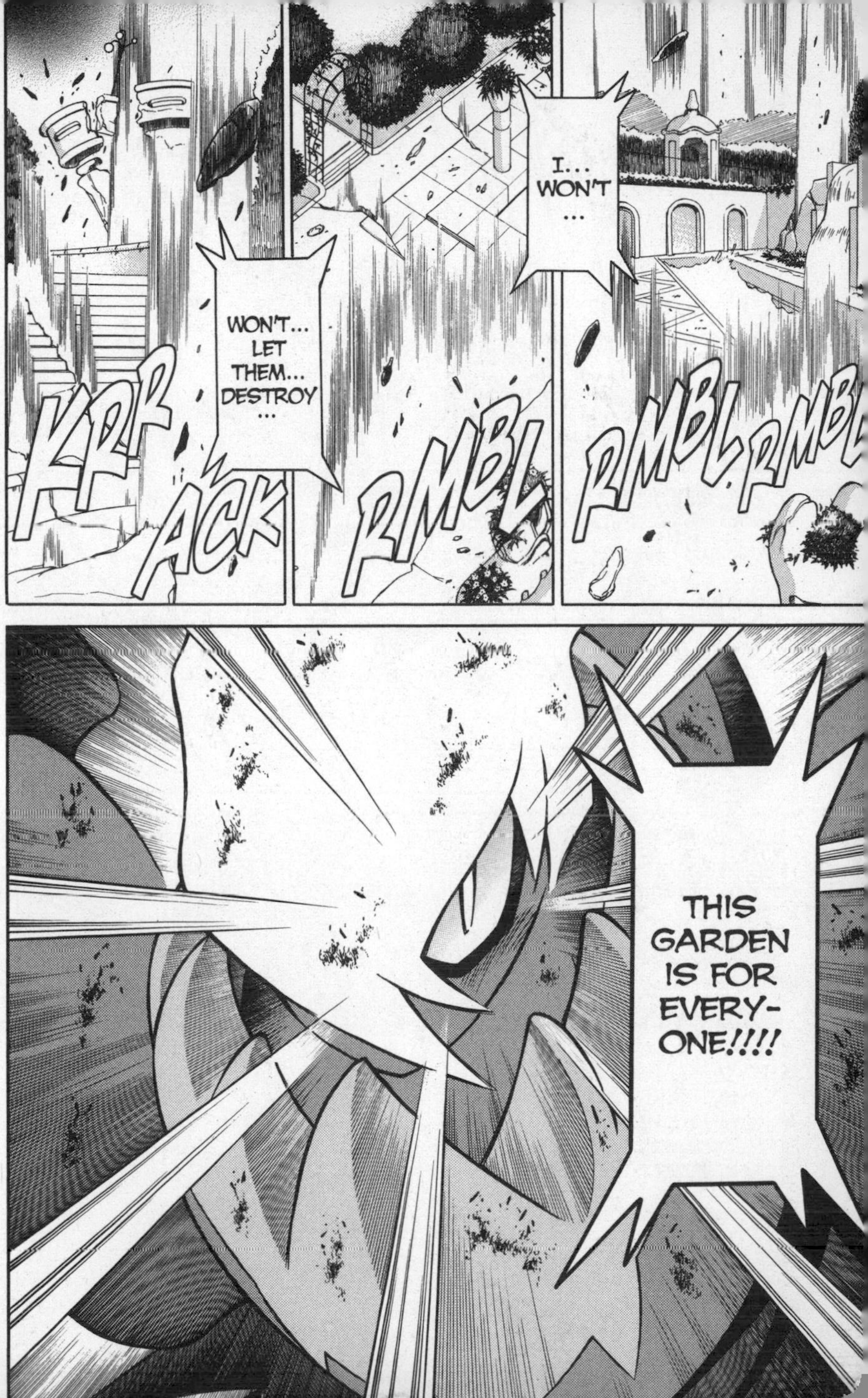
I... WON'T...
RMBL RMBL
RMBL
WON'T... LET THEM... DESTROY...
KRRACK
THIS GARDEN IS FOR EVERY-ONE!!!!

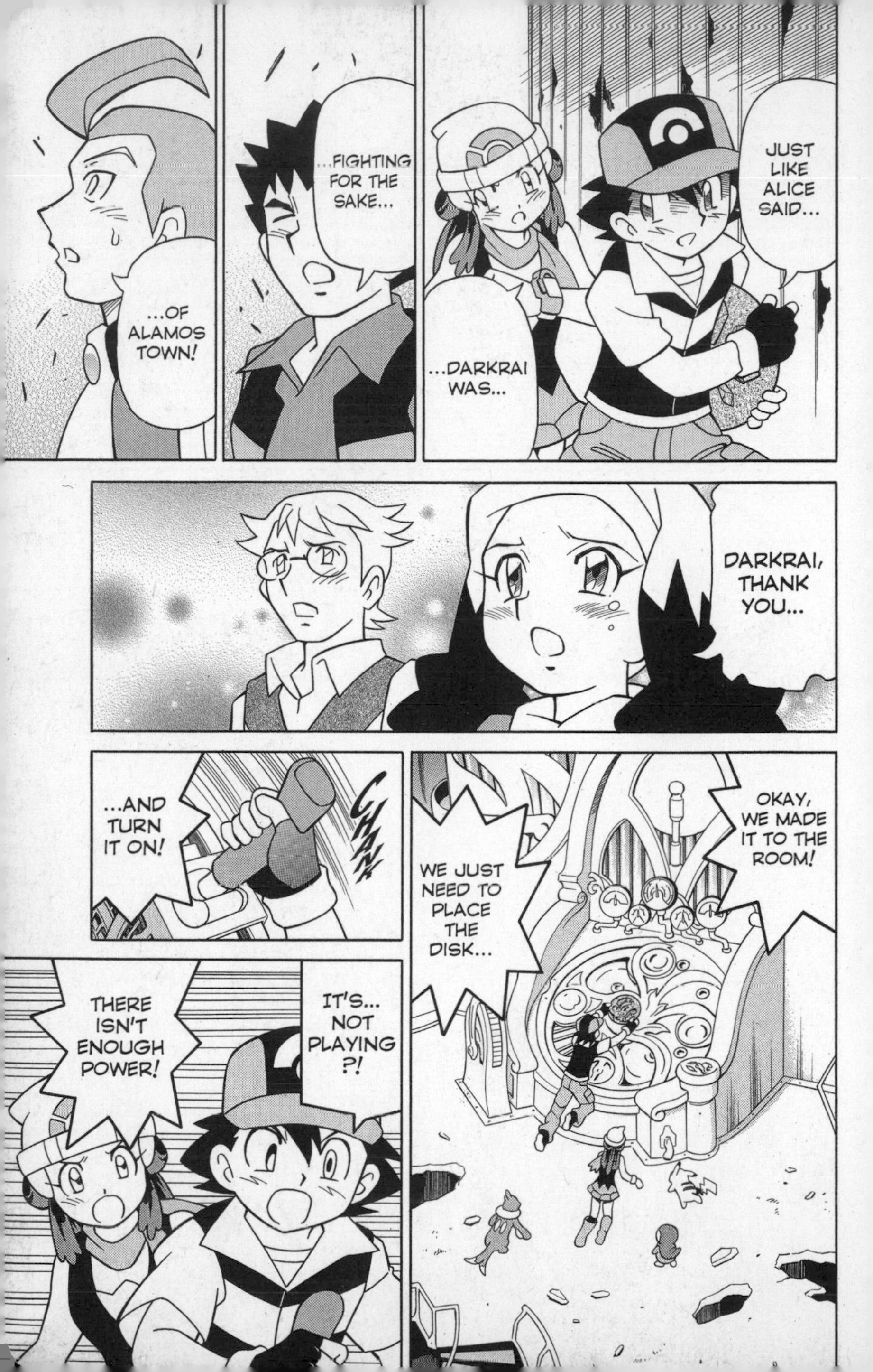
JUST LIKE ALICE SAID...
...DARKRAI WAS...
...FIGHTING FOR THE SAKE...
...OF ALAMOS TOWN!
DARKRAI, THANK YOU...
OKAY, WE MADE IT TO THE ROOM!
WE JUST NEED TO PLACE THE DISK...
...AND TURN IT ON!
CHAN!
IT'S... NOT PLAYING?!
THERE ISN'T ENOUGH POWER!

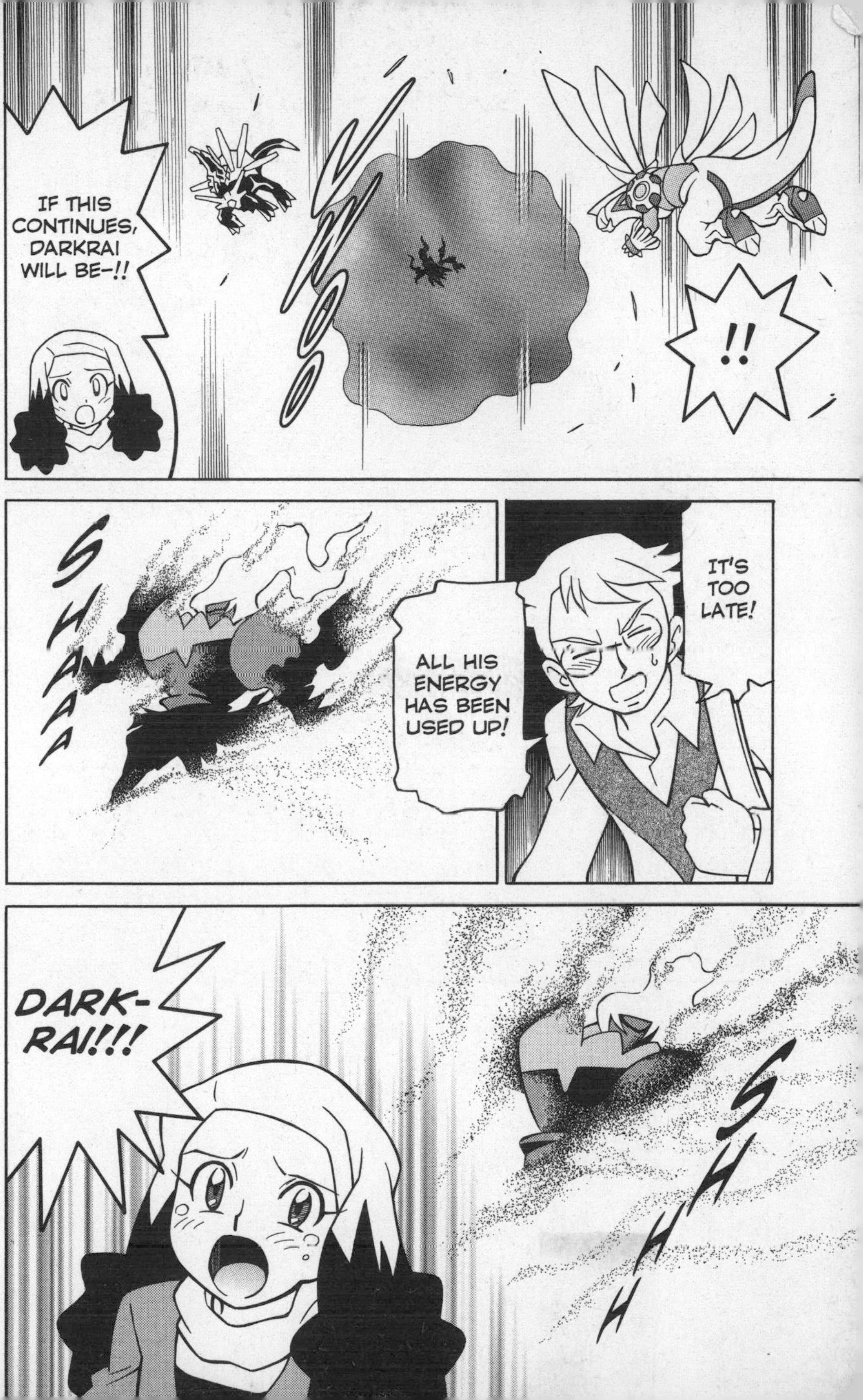
IF THIS CONTINUES, DARKRAI WILL BE-!!
!!
IT'S TOO LATE!
ALL HIS ENERGY HAS BEEN USED UP!
SHAAAA
SHHHH
DARK-RAI!!!

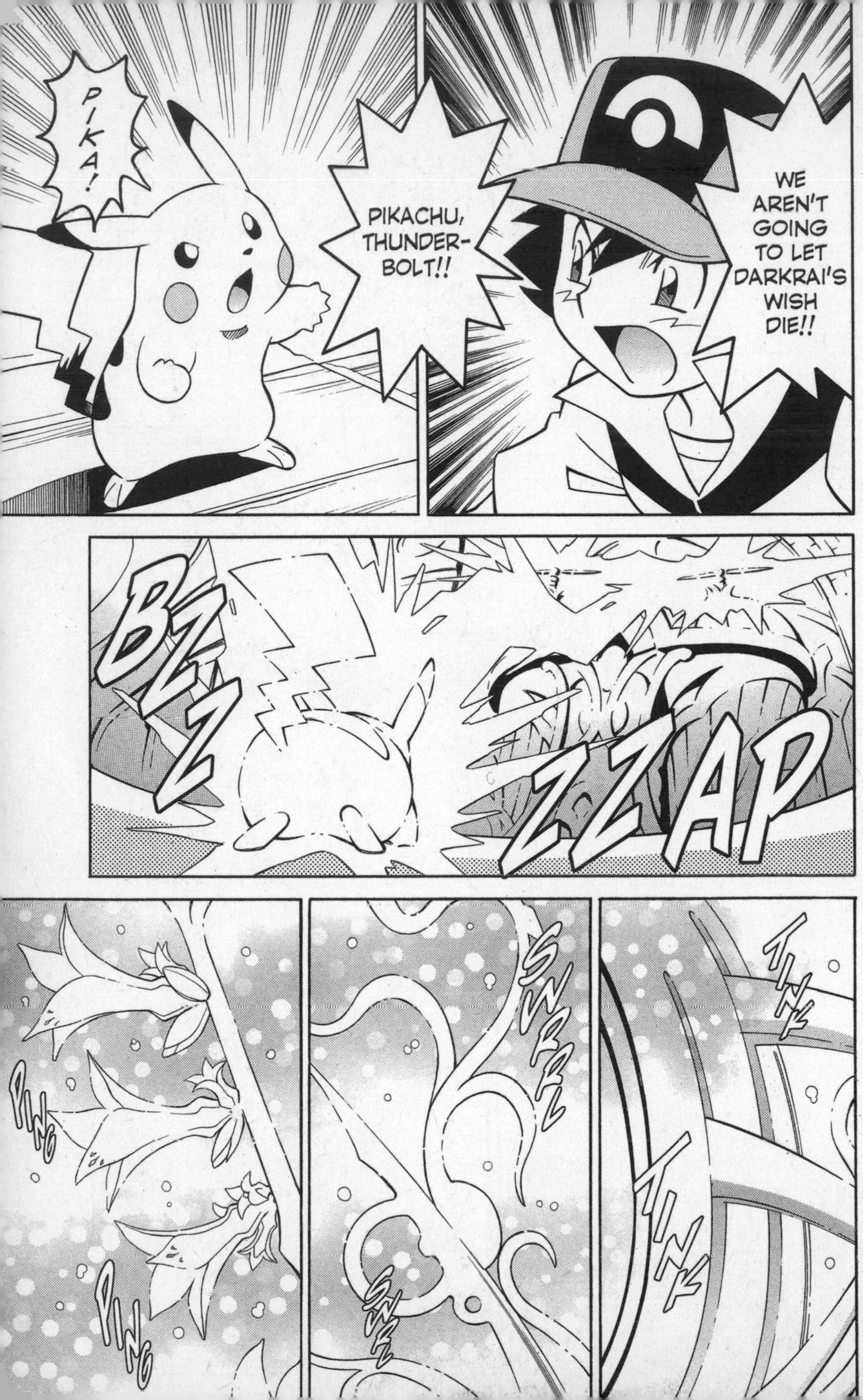
WE AREN'T GOING TO LET DARKRAI'S WISH DIE!!
PIKACHU, THUNDERBOLT!!
PIKA!
BZZ
ZZAP
TINK
TINK
SNRRL
PING
PING

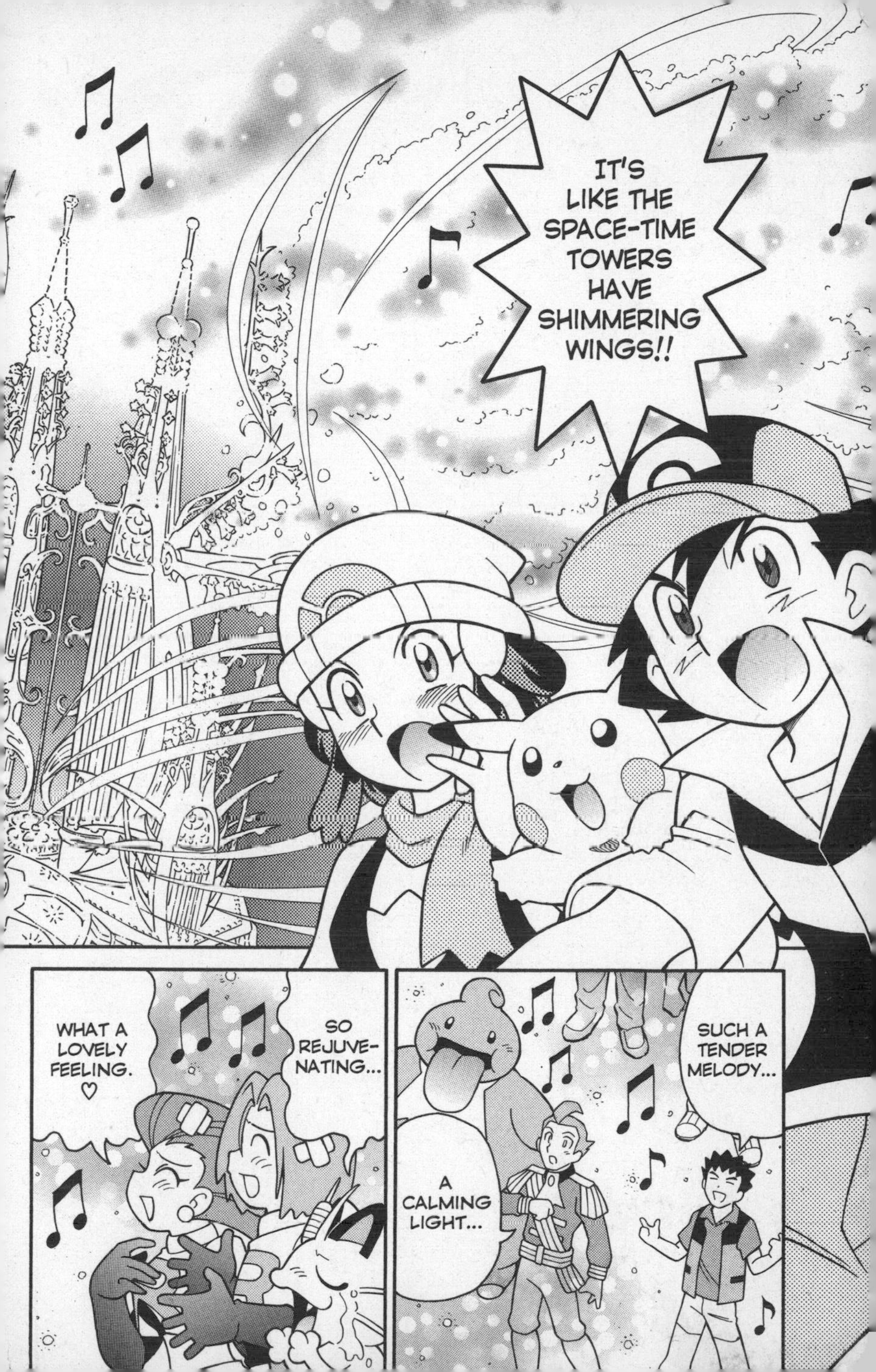
IT'S LIKE THE SPACE-TIME TOWERS HAVE SHIMMERING WINGS!!
SUCH A TENDER MELODY...
A CALMING LIGHT...
SO REJUVE-NATING...
WHAT A LOVELY FEELING. ♡

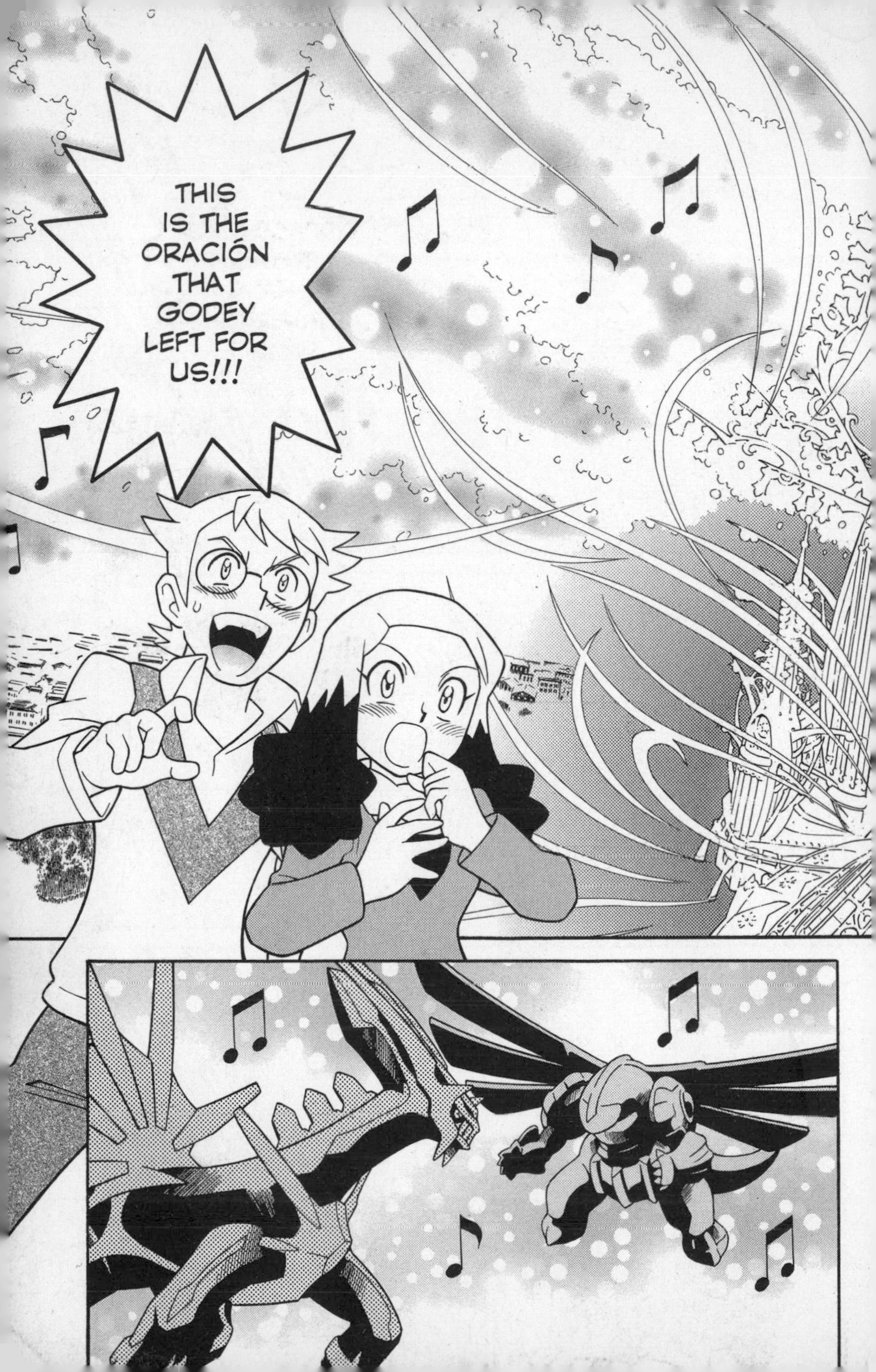
THIS IS THE ORACIÓN THAT GODEY LEFT FOR US!!!

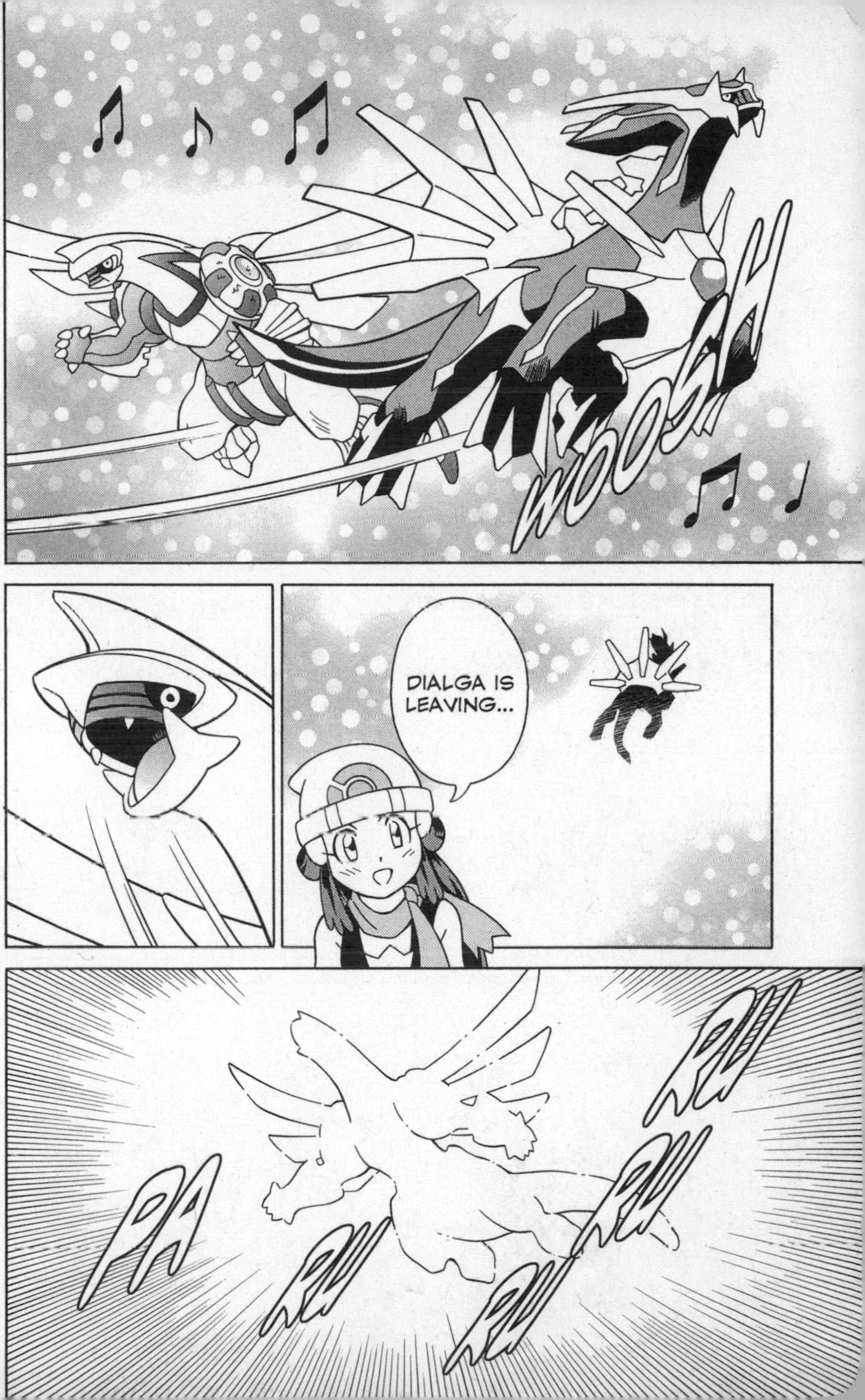
WOOSH
DIALGA IS LEAVING...

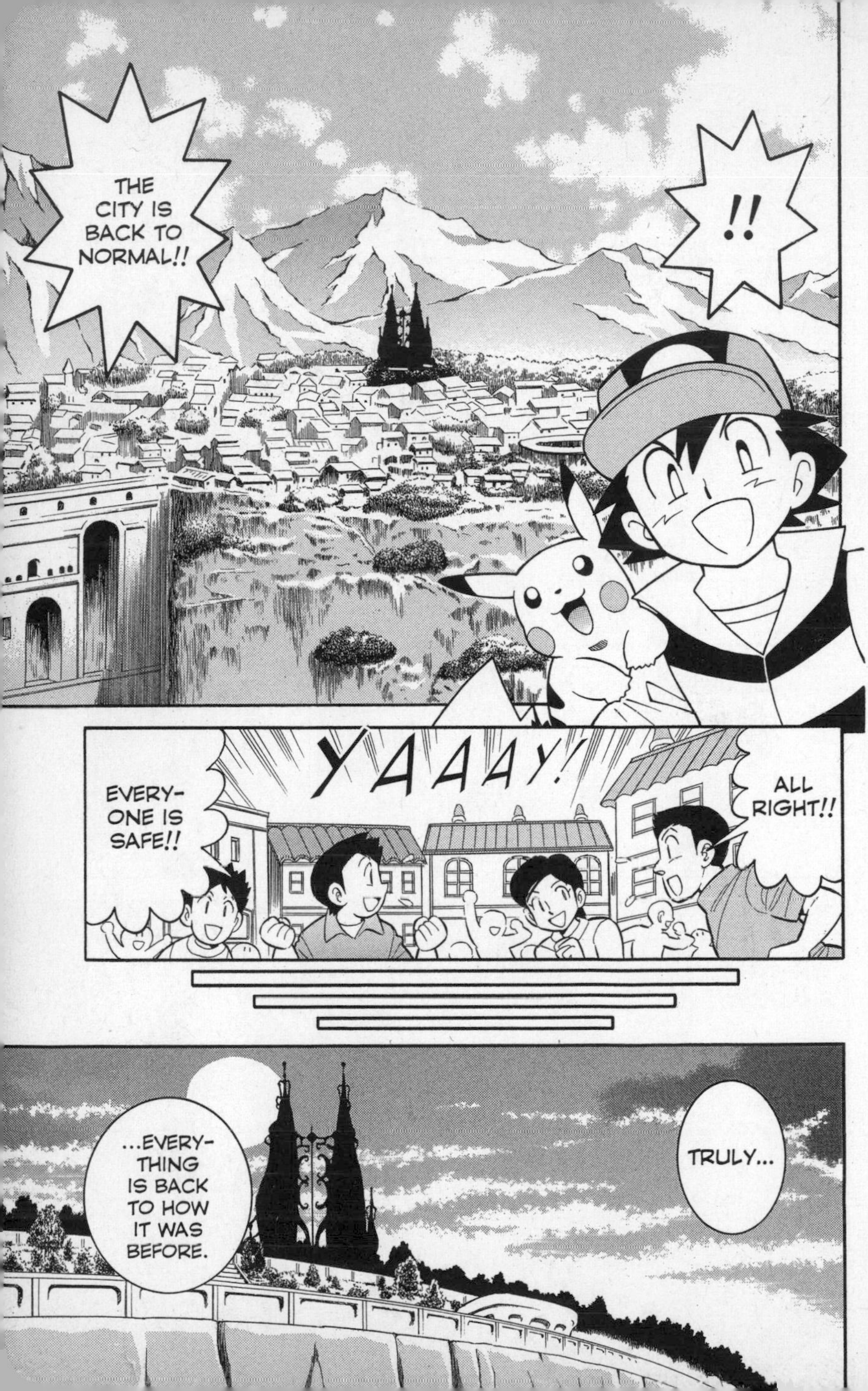
!!
THE CITY IS BACK TO NORMAL!!
ALL RIGHT!!
YAAAY!
EVERY-ONE IS SAFE!!
TRULY...
...EVERY-THING IS BACK TO HOW IT WAS BEFORE.

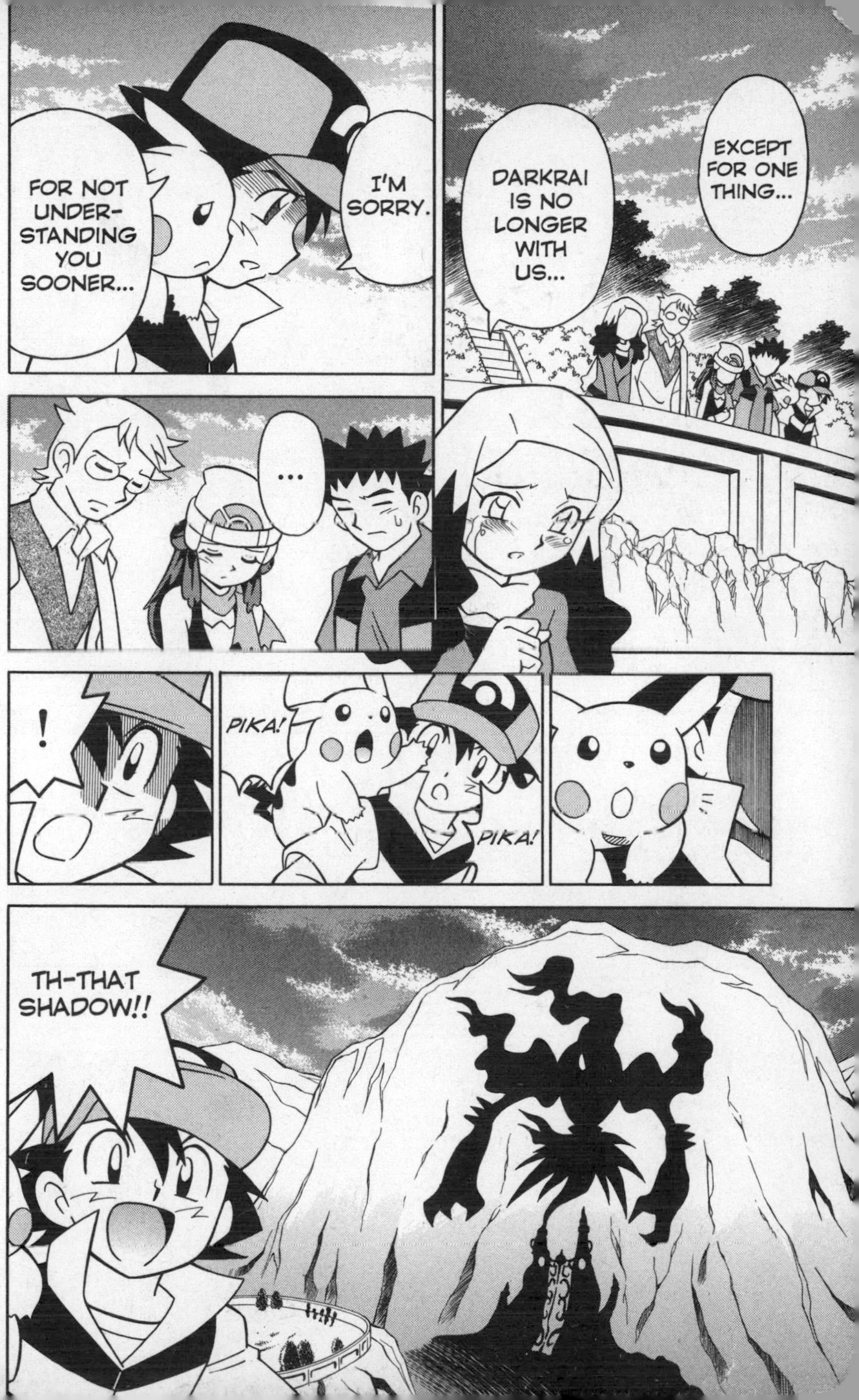
EXCEPT FOR ONE THING...
DARKRAI IS NO LONGER WITH US...
I'M SORRY.
FOR NOT UNDER-STANDING YOU SOONER...
...
PIKA!
PIKA!
!
TH-THAT SHADOW!!

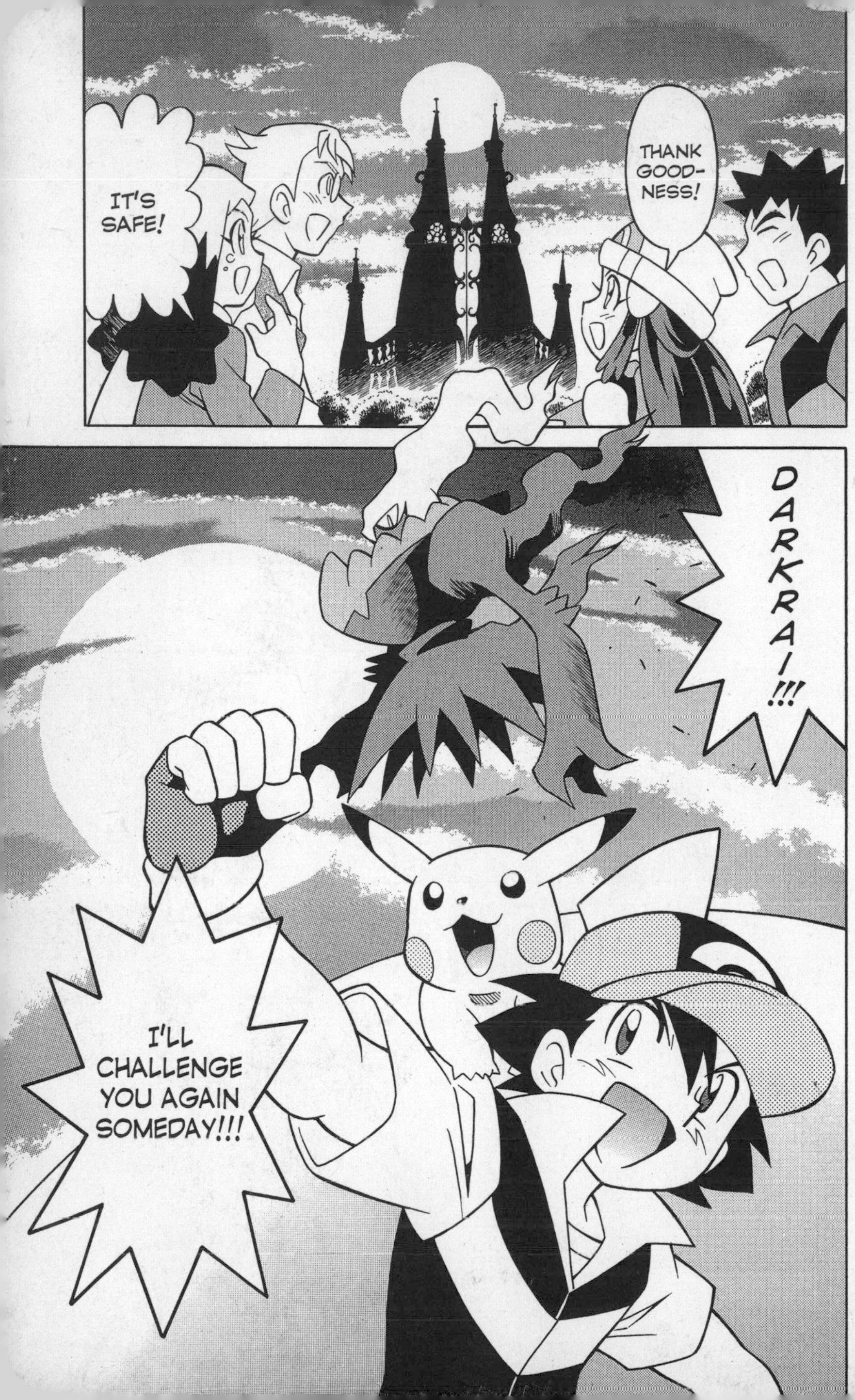
THANK GOOD-NESS!
IT'S SAFE!
DARKRAI!!!
I'LL CHALLENGE YOU AGAIN SOMEDAY!!!

Hey! You're Reading in the Wrong Direction!

This is the *end* of this graphic novel!

To properly enjoy this VIZ graphic novel, please turn it around and begin reading from *right to left.* Unlike English, Japanese is read right to left, so Japanese comics are read in reverse order from the way English comics are typically read.

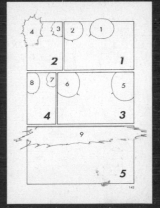

Follow the action this way

This book has been printed in the original Japanese format in order to preserve the orientation of the original artwork. Have fun with it!